AN
UNDISTURBED
PEACE

AN UNDISTURBED PEACE

A NOVEL

MARY GLICKMAN

OPEN ROAD

INTEGRATED MEDIA

NEW YORK

Copyright © 2016 by Mary Glickman

Cover illustration by Jesse Hayes

Cover design by Andrea Worthington

978-1-5040-1834-0

Published in 2016 by Open Road Integrated Media, Inc.
345 Hudson Street
New York, NY 10014
www.openroadmedia.com

For Peter, who gave me the idea
And for Stephen, who nurtured it

CONTENTS

CONTENTS

AN
UNDISTURBED
PEACE

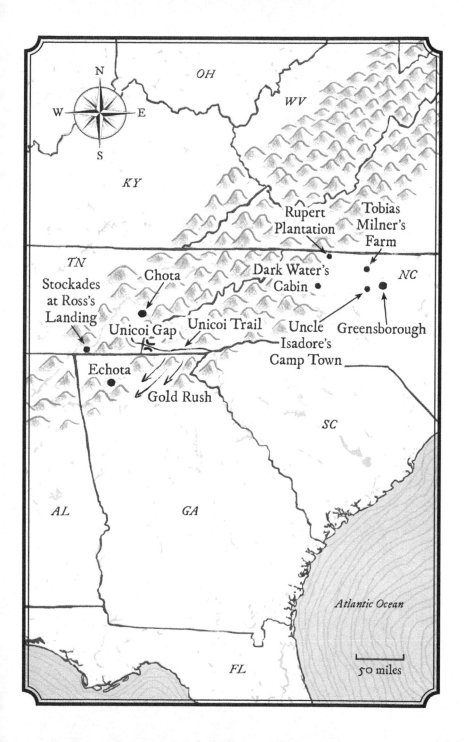

We, the great mass of the people think only of the love we have to our land for . . . we do love the land where we were brought up. We will never let our hold to this land go . . . to let it go will be like throwing away [our] mother that gave . . . [us] birth.

. . . Inclination to remove from this land has no abiding place in our hearts, and when we move we shall move by the course of nature to sleep under this ground which the Great Spirit gave to our ancestors and which now covers them in their undisturbed peace.

—*Cherokee Legislative Council at New Echota,*
July 1, 1830

GENESIS

THE PIEDMONT, NORTH CAROLINA, 1828

W ait."

He put out a hand to grab her wrist and pull her back to the bed with him but she easily eluded his grasp.

"Be patient," she said. "I'm not going far." She knelt by his side where he lay, sated and drowsy on a pile of animal skins. Tilting her head with its full, curled lips and raised eyebrows as if asking a question, she removed a small wooden box from the chest by the side of the bed. The box was studded with bits of river glass on its sides. A bird in flight was carved into its lid, the bird's long brass beak formed its latch. Sticking a stone pipe in her mouth, she opened the box, then waved it around the close room so that the air filled with the sweet scent of wild tobacco. She filled her pipe and lit it with a thin bundle of twined straw she stuck in and out of the oil lamp's center. She inhaled, exhaled, raised her big black merry eyes to the heavens while muttering some kind of incantation, then passed the pipe to her chosen lover of the moment, Abrahan Sassaporta, a peddler who had wandered by her cabin offering packets of seeds, scraps of lace, and tin utensils.

Abrahan puffed on the pipe in a fog of wonder. He could not believe his good luck. Four hours ago, they'd been strangers. Abrahan was a fresh immigrant on his virgin sales expedition for his uncle's business. After he left the mainstay of his wares at Micah's Trading Post, to which he'd return for resupply as needed, he'd traveled on foot, a pack on his back, to five of the farms on the list and map given him. He'd made a wrong turn at a fork along the beaten path.

The path he'd chosen narrowed until he found himself aimless, wandering between trees, unable to locate the way back. He'd begun to imagine himself forever lost, starving to death in the forest, facing down strange, wild beasts and savage men when out of a verdant chaos of trees and roots and vines, the clearing appeared, a grassy hillock crowned by a log cabin with an open door. A native woman leaned against the doorway with crossed arms and a determined expression. She was dressed in a red cotton shirt and deerskin britches.

As he approached, he saw that her face was a pleasing assembly of angles and light, her skin as dark as his own but lit with golden copper as if from the very blood beneath it. Her eyes were almond-shaped and heavy-lidded, which lent them a sly look. She'd a strong nose, a big gorgeous mouth. From beneath a blue bandana slung low over her brow, her black hair, straight and thick like the mane of a horse, hung well past her clavicle to brush the tips of her breasts. He marveled at how very strong she looked. He felt excited and a bit afraid. A thin, hot wire inside his chest vibrated from his toes to his scalp. Despite his anxiety, he managed to introduce himself and show her his wares.

"Seeds?" she'd said, mocking him. "Seeds? When I cannot

make my own seeds for growing, I'll drown myself and give my flesh to the Earth, who will surely make better use of it."

The lace she also discounted. But there was a large fork she could find use for, along with two sizes of spoons. He produced a pouch of gunpowder from his pack and her eyes danced. She grabbed his arm and pulled him into the cabin. "Here," she said, slapping four coins on the wooden table that stood in the center of the room. "I'll take as much of that powder as I can get."

Abrahan looked around, buying time. He saw the quiver of arrows near the door, the longbow as tall as he was beside it, the half-size hunting bow next to that. Opposite the door a variety of knives were mounted against the wall. The largest might have been a kind of broadsword, the shortest was narrow with a hooked tip. There were firearms also. A flintlock pistol, a rifle, and a shotgun hung by leather straps above the fireplace. There were no additional decorations on the walls. Weaponry alone graced the raw, unmilled timber as if the entire structure was built solely as a monument to defense. For a moment, Abrahan wondered if he'd stumbled upon some private armory. Flustered, he looked down at her coins.

"You won't get much with that," he said.

"Then take back your fork and spoons."

"I still can't give you more than half an ounce. I only have four to spare. The rest I carry to fill long-standing orders. And my rounds are not half done."

Her mouth twisted. The air between them went hot and humid, full of scent. They could hear each other breathe. He did not know why but something in him longed to please her. Maybe it was fate calling to him, with finger crooked and eyes sparkling. Whatever it was, it came from a place so deep in him he made a rash decision.

"But I could give you credit," he said. As soon as the words flew out of his mouth, he regretted them. He had no authority to back them up. But there they were, on the table, beside the two spoons, fork, and coin.

The great black eyes blinked with surprise. She leaned backward, tilting her head while she folded her arms across her chest and studied him. Now, here, her posture seemed to say, was a new creature under the sun. He blushed under her scrutiny.

"Well, that's settled then," he mumbled. He reached into his pack for the gunpowder and she was on him, her mouth hot on his neck. When she pulled back and saw the alarm on his face, saw the wide eyes, the open, dry mouth, she grinned.

Four hours later, the sun had begun its daily descent behind a distant ridge of smoky-blue mountains, and the air had grown cool. He puffed again on the pipe and drew one of the skins over his naked limbs.

She got up. Her bare backside was to him as she crouched at the hearth and placed the night's logs in the fireplace. He marveled that while he'd begun to feel numb at his toes from the deepening chill of twilight, she'd not raised so much as a goose bump. Then he fell to admiring the slope of her hip.

"Marian," he called out sweetly so that she'd turn in his direction. He used the name she'd given him, although he was certain she'd another meaningful one, a tribal name. He had more than one name himself. His full name was Abrahan Bento Sassaporta Naggar, but that was too much for the London gutter weeds with whom he'd grown up and from whom he'd escaped as soon as Uncle Isadore had been convinced to accept him as an apprentice in America. He'd stopped using his name in full when he was ten to avoid torment by the others, although when he needed to encourage or remonstrate himself, he'd still say in a voice remarkably like his mother's, *Abrahan Bento Sassaporta Naggar! You are a coward, a fool! Get up and do your job!* At the moment, all his emotion was directed outward, and with great warmth he said to the woman regarding him, "Marian, you are beautiful."

She laughed, then stood before him with her arms raised, her legs spread, unashamed.

"You think so, Mr. Peddler?" She laughed again and struck the pouty pose of some whorehouse vixen, the kind who advertised her goods from window frames in London's East End, where he'd grown up. It was a pose so unnatural to her as to be both witty and ridiculous, so he laughed also. She strutted the room and continued.

"You should have seen me twenty years ago! When I did not have this!"

She slapped her right flank, then grabbed a handful of extra flesh and shook it.

"When I had these!"

She cupped her breasts and held them up high.

"How proud they stood—like soldiers at attention!"

She fell back in the bed next to him. Her eyes no longer laughed.

"Twenty years ago, you would have killed another man, or yourself, out of love for me. I'm not lying when I say both things happened. Twenty years ago."

"Is that why you live alone here? Away from your people?"

Her eyes were guarded as he gathered her in, pulling her under the deerskin blanket with him. She put a hand through his tangle of black curls and tugged at the back of his head, then rode her hand slowly around his neck to the under part of his beard.

"Yes, my bear. It is exactly why."

"Tell me more."

"No."

Over the three and one half days he spent with her, she told him many stories about herself. She told him about her childhood in the house of her father, a great chief. He was proud and distant and mostly ordered people about, herself included. She'd been taught many skills by her mother, her aunts, and her mother's slaves—kitchen skills, gardening skills, both the spinning of cotton and the making of garments from skins and hats from various reeds. She told him of her first pony, who was called Bright Star for a mark on his forehead. Without seeming to brag, she told him she was also expert in the skills of warriors. She told him of her ability to launch arrows from Bright Star's back at full gallop, striking her mark often enough to win competitions ahead of any man. She was so skillful at this and also with knives that her father would not allow her on the hunt or his warriors would be consumed by jealousy and despair. She told him that at sixteen, her father sent her to London so that on her return she might attract his grandest hope for her—the son of a wealthy white man as her husband. He was convinced along with many others that adoption of settler ways and alliance through marriage was essential for his people to survive the wave of whites flooding the land. "Even a shopkeeper like you would do," Marian of the foothills told him, laughing at her inflation of Abrahan's humble profession, "any man who was of European blood and had a little property." But no one ever asked her what she wanted, and she had her own ideas.

It was at this point, the most interesting point, the point at which the story of who had killed another man, who had killed himself out of love for her young, magnificent self might have been revealed, that Marian stopped talking when he again questioned her on it. "No," she said. Abrahan, already in love for the first time in his life, pushed to convince her he was worthy of the tale. No. No. No. He continued to push. He wheedled a little. Suddenly her back was turned to him and her britches were laced. His appetite for her increased to the point of pain. He wooed her back to him by comparing derisive notes about the English. The ones he knew growing up were the filthy Jew-hating brutes of the street. Hers were privileged minor peers who felt that keeping a civilized Cherokee as houseguest was as droll as the antics of their little pugs and spaniels.

"Tell me about your people, these Jews of yours," she said. "In England I heard of them, but you are the first I've known well enough to ask."

He sighed, wondering how to explain such a long and complex subject to her.

"Once we were a great nation," he said, "blessed by our God, who gave us a land of milk and honey and also many laws."

She nodded solemnly.

"Giving laws. It's what gods do," she said. "I've noticed—how could I not?—you have your morning rituals, your forbidden foods. So do I. For every fringe on your undershirt, I have sacred feathers or beads of great meaning."

Moved by her desire to seek out similarities between them, he kissed the top of her head and continued.

"Conquerors expelled us from our land and we became wanderers. Everywhere we went, we were treated with suspicion and envy. We are citizens wherever we rest, until our overlords decide we are not wanted anymore."

"It was because you gave up the land."

"We had no choice."

She shrugged as if to say there is always a choice.

"My nation," she said, "was also given our land by the Great Beings. We would never abandon it. Although now we have to share it with you English."

At the word "English," she punched his side playfully, but there was a darker intent behind her smile. Abrahan opened his mouth to expound on what he knew about Old Hickory and his proposals to drive her people west of the Mississippi, but all he really knew was whatever gossip other peddlers traded on cold nights over a bottle of spirits. Politics does not a cozy bedfellow make, he decided. The wording pleased him. He made a mental note to remember it for use another time when he wanted to impress someone.

"I'm not English. Not really. My poor, exiled tribe was driven to England from Portugal, where we found haven for many years. But our cousin tribesmen who were English never accepted us, even after generations. It's they who sent our fathers here a hundred years ago, to get rid of us. Worthy paupers they called us, off to the New World for a better life. I'm the latest of that long chain." He paused, looking thoughtful. "I think what I am now is an American. At least until they remind me that no, I am a Jew."

She reached out and busied herself with his britches. "I see part of what I have heard is true. Mutilation is not unknown among my own people, but this . . . this shortening. Only the Creek do this. Our men say it is because they tried to lie with the Horned Snake and he bit them down to size. But they only say this to make sport of a rival. Maybe you can tell me. Truly, why there? Why that?" She gave his sex a warm tug and left her hand around it, caressing.

He winced. "I have no idea why the Creek do anything," he said. "As for Jews, we cut ourselves because our God told us to so we would not damage the ladies with our greatness." They both laughed. The pain of his desire was thereafter eased.

Before he left her, he learned from her his location, both in miles from Uncle Isadore's camp town, which was approximately fifty, and by the stars she pointed out to him in the night. He wrote in his book: *Marian of the foothills southwest of Tobias Milner's farm, northeast of Micah's Trading Post: one fork, two spoons, four ounces of gunpowder.* He drew a star to the left of her name, as he did for all new customers he felt worth passing by again, then he drew a second star, which was completely unnecessary. Marian of the foothills was not someone he would forget.

Uncle Isadore was choleric when Abrahan came home light of both coin and gunpowder. His face turned red and his hands shook as he demanded explanation. Abrahan lied and told him he'd slipped crossing a stream and the powder had gotten wet. He tried drying it out, but it was ruined. Isadore grumbled, took up his book of debts, and marked the price of the gunpowder next to Abrahan's name, adding it to a sum the young man despaired of clearing before he was dead.

Soon after, winter came. That year, it was hard and long in the foothills and the mountains beyond. Much of the route assigned to Abrahan was made impassable by snow and ice. If he could not sell, the rule was he must collect new stock before the thaw or make it if none was to be found. Sassaporta and Company provided only a handful of materials for his pack, things like gunpowder, cooking utensils of tin, and small tools made of iron. Each bondsman peddler of the Sassaporta brigade was expected to acquire what was needed to fill the rest of his pack, his saddle-bags too if he had achieved the rank of mounted salesman. The most desired items were ribbons, lace, serving pieces of silver, scented soaps, whatever small luxuries could be easily stored and carried in significant number. But without thinking it through, Abrahan lost himself in the company workshop trying to carve a series of wooden boxes with birds' beaks for clasps. They made him feel closer to Marian, although the first few were a mess. He took counsel from the company carpenters. His construction of boxes steadily improved. But when Uncle Isadore discovered a store of useless products taking up space on his drying shelves, he boxed his nephew's ears and booted him out into the snow to knock on doors and barter for things the hill people on his route might actually want. Those isolated farmers and loggers desired manufactured things, European things, things they could not make for themselves or find on the barter table of every back-woods trading post.

Abrahan stood, brushed himself off. "*Mamzer*," he muttered at his uncle's back. If his mother only knew, he thought. His mother idolized Isadore, her late husband's big brother, the brave one, the smart one, the one who'd ventured to America when he was twelve years old in service to an earlier generation of uncles and cousins. In those days, a smart young lad with a cultivated English accent could separate a country yokel from his coin in two heartbeats and a handshake. By his early twenties, Isadore had carved his own territory out of the Sassaporta Brothers empire headquartered in Savannah. He had all of North Carolina, a smidgen of Georgia, and parts of Tennessee under his sway. By the time he was forty, his work camp boasted more laborers and warehouse space than any two Sassaporta entrepreneurs put together. Now fifty, he planned to build the largest retail store in Greensborough, North Carolina, the big town ten miles away.

Back in the ghetto of London, Abrahan's mother had gone daily to Bevis Marks in Bethnal Green, where the men gathered for morning prayers. From her perch in the balcony, she davened with them in her ignorant manner without comprehension of the Hebrew she imitated, while in her pure heart she beseeched God that her son might find favor in the eyes of Isadore Sassaporta and win a future as brilliant and secure. God answered her prayers and at the age of eighteen, Abrahan Bento Sassaporta Naggar found himself on a ship of passage, a foul, hideous vessel overstuffed with warring, hopeful émigrés. He was not entirely sure how he'd got there, except that his mother had made decisions for him. When he'd objected, she reminded him of the life in store for a fatherless Jewish son of London, where anti-Semites lurked around every corner waiting to thrash him, and opportunities were scarcer than a gentile's welcome.

"You're very clever," she told him. "But you're idle. Your friends are rascals, every one. All you've learned in the East End is trickery and deceit, the poor man's games to a quick penny. Keep up with that lot and the docket and jailhouse will grab you before long. If I let that happen, your father of blessed memory will rise from the grave and berate me. Do not fear. The New World will liberate you, I promise."

Reluctantly, he took his leave of her and, sadly, also of sweet Ariella Levy, the neighbor girl whose hand he'd once dared to hold. There followed weeks of suffocating squalor, loneliness, and storm-tossed seas.

When the ship landed, he stepped on unsteady legs into the harbor at Beaufort, North Carolina, and rejoiced. The sun was shining, the sea at his back sparkled, the buildings all around were well spaced. None of them reeked of age. He filled his lungs with fresh, pristine air, his eyes with a vision of all that was open and new. The taste of liberation filled his mouth. "Oh, Mother, how wise you are!" he wrote in a letter composed that very day. "You were right. I was tumbling down the road to dissipation and ruin. But here, in this fair place, I will learn new ways and save myself. I will find favor in the eyes of Ha-Shem. He will help me prosper and I will send for you within the year!" Such were his hopes and simple ambitions. Instead, he was soon locked in vilest servitude to Uncle Isadore, a harsh and demanding taskmaster who took a lion's share of the profits Abrahan won out of hard labor and cunning, leaving him pennies to spend in the company store. "You owe me your passage," he'd tell his nephew when he complained, "and the roof over your head."

Some roof. Uncle Isadore's peddler barracks were even worse than the military ones on which they were modeled. Cold in winter, stifling in summer, they were dark, cramped, filthy longhouses with narrow barred windows. The men lodged there prayed for an early selling season if only to escape their confines. They were a motley crew with barely a common mother tongue among more than five of them at a time. They bunked in sections of the longhouses segregated by country of origin and insulted one another anonymously in the night. Most hated Jews but were afraid to voice their animosity within Abrahan's earshot, given it was widely known he was nephew to the boss. He knew their sentiments nonetheless. All in all, that first year of his servitude, Abrahan felt as if he'd never left the ship of passage. Many a time as he lay in his cot, a Babel of language swarming unwholesomely around him, he counted in his head the pittance of earnings that Uncle Isadore allowed him to keep. Abrahan dreamt of walking off his sales route to disappear, to find his own life without being beholden to anyone, especially that *mamzer*, Uncle Isadore, beloved of his poor deluded mother. There were stories of bonded peddlers attempting to quit the camp who were hunted down by men with dogs. Abrahan judged these to be tall tales meant to frighten Uncle Isadore's debtors into submission. If he could gather enough money, he would leave without a trace and never return. America was a big country and beyond her ever-expanding borders, there was frontier, a wild land overflowing with opportunity. Lately his dreams were colored by fantasies of a life with Marian of the foothills, of taking her with him wherever he decided to go. She would know every way there was to tame the wilderness, he figured, an invaluable asset to a tenderfoot like him, and he would be her grateful devoted love.

That winter, while amassing a stockpile of wares to sell in the spring, there was more than one item Abrahan tucked away for himself, things he might need for a new life with Marian. He remembered everything about her home, noting that she drew water from her backyard stream using a dried gourd, for example, and so he made sure he had an extra tin dipper and wooden pail among his wares. She kept goats for milk and cheese so he packed lengths of cheesecloth and a wide metal comb. When he assembled his wares, those he would sell and those he would give to Marian, there was, of course, far more than he could carry. He imagined himself tying the dipper and comb to his shoulders and wearing the pail on his head while clanking his way up and over hill and dale. He lobbied Uncle Isadore for a horse.

He managed to arrange a meeting with him in the barracks, during a rare pleasant day with the taste of an early spring in the air, a day no sane man would stay indoors. The barracks was a place Isadore Sassaporta rarely appeared, but Abrahan told him he'd amassed a store of treasure no other foot peddler had amassed before. It was something that must be seen to be believed.

Isadore Sassaporta entered the place with a scented handkerchief tied over his nose and mouth against the stench of men. His nephew had lit lanterns and placed them from end to end of the hallway so they could see through the dank dark. He closed the door behind them for privacy. Thanks to the lamplight, it was not difficult to find the place where Abrahan displayed his booty. Spread over and aside his cot, extending up and down the hallway, were the wares Abrahan had scavenged since being cuffed on the head and tossed in a snowbank. Aside from the pail, the dipper, and the comb, there was a bolt of velvet cloth, leather boots in both adult and child sizes, chain link, little boxes of spice seldom seen in that part of the world, wedding rings, and as many rare utilitarian items as there were luxuries. There was even a saddle and a whip. He failed to inform his uncle that much of it he'd gotten on consignment from peddlers too broken to travel, the old ones who lived in tents on the outskirts of town, desperate, hungry men. Let the old bugger think the profits will be whole, he reasoned.

"I've been with you a year now, Uncle," he said. "I'll never repay you for my passage by peddling scraps in these poor hills. Look at all this I've got to sell! I need your permission to increase my territory and also I need a horse."

From the glitter in his uncle's eyes above the scented cloth, he knew he had him. The old man clapped him on the back, celebrated their bond of blood, and agreed to give him a horse, although, he added, it would mean an additional fifty dollars of debt to his account. Abrahan rejoiced. With a horse, his expanded inventory, and tricks of the trade his newfound, tent-dwelling associates relayed to him over the course of their dealings, he could be out of debt within a season. His brilliant future in the frontier beckoned.

There was no doubt in his mind that Marian would accept his gifts and proposals. He was in a mad state of desire. When he thought of her, he compared her to the valiant heroines of his people, to Queen Esther, to Deborah and Jael. He murmured sadly to himself when he measured her against his mother, a simple, distracted woman who had foolishly sold him to Uncle Isadore, thinking it would make him rich. *Mother,* he said to her from across the great sea, *whenever we are settled and established, I'll work to send for you.* While he thought of that great occasion, of reuniting with his mother in the golden frontier, he imagined Marian at his side, as loving to his mother as Ruth to Naomi.

Four weeks before the traditional start of selling season—a season that varied according to patterns of weather, but one that usually began just after Purim—Uncle Isadore's stable master sent a boy to fetch Abrahan for the purpose of introducing him to his mount and providing whatever instruction in the care of equines and the art of riding was required. The winds were high that day and the sky was full of clouds. The trees about were winter bare. Their branches swung and dipped in the wind. In at least two, hundreds of crows mourned their dead. Their clamor was alarming. Men left their lodgings to stare at them and then the sky. Everything about the day announced fateful signs of things to come. Abrahan barely noticed. He trod through the muddy thoroughfares of Uncle Isadore's camp town of two hundred souls in a state of delirious anticipation imagining the noble steed that awaited him and the dashing sight the two of them would make galloping up to the cabin door of Marian of the foothills. He knew little of horses beyond the fantasies of a city-born youth. For Abrahan, horses meant wealth. Horses meant manly achievement. Horses meant the ability to flee. But the closest he'd been to an actual equine experience was when he'd ridden in the cab of a carriage on the occasion of his father's death. The burial society had seen fit to grant his family such a conveyance for the funeral due to the man's outstanding piety. At the time Abrahan was seven years old. What little he remembered was shrouded in his mother's grief and his own. He recalled the horse seemed to share in their loss. To this day, what he knew of the rules of horsemanship was limited to keep out of their way, pet them only if they're tied up, and keep your fingers away from their mouths. All other intimacies with horses belonged to a different class of men entirely, that of brawny, gentile men. But now, a miracle! Thanks to the motivation of his love, the reason of his uncle, and the rewards of his ingenuity, he was about to transcend class and attain the elevated status of horseman. In this dreamy state, he traversed the camp town oblivious to the crows, the beggars, whores, and hawkers who called out to him.

The stables were situated near the center of the camp town, which also accommodated a company store, a warehouse and workrooms, a bathhouse that doubled as infirmary, and an ill-used house of worship. It changed denomination three times on Sunday and served as synagogue—if a structure without Torah scrolls can be called such—on Friday night for those few members of Uncle Isadore's crew who had not yet abandoned their vows of spiritual fidelity to mothers in Germany, England, Ireland, and France. From Monday to Thursday, the worship house served as town hall, meeting place, and jail. All of the central buildings were two-storied and fashioned of whatever scraps of milled lumber were at hand when the decision to build them had been made. They stood on stilts against surrounding waterways swollen to flood by melted snow at the spring thaw and by thunderstorm in summer. They were better than shanties but not much and their haphazard construction lent them a cockeyed look. While Uncle Isadore kept a residence in the camp town for occasional use, he and his managers lived most of the time ten miles away in fine houses in Greensborough, conveniently located upwind from the new Mount Hecla textile mill. They had little interest in improving life for their peddlers as long as their stock kept dry.

By contrast, the stables were palatial, which made sense given the treasure that was horseflesh. The primary barn was raised from the ground by stone ramps and the walls were of stone also. Its aisles were paved with brick. There were airtight shutters on the stall windows. The doors were thick as the span of a man's hand. The water troughs were scrubbed and cleaned more often than the pool at the bathhouse. In the back were numerous paddocks and exercise rings, along with a separate stone building that housed the stable master, his crew, wagons, and tack. Approaching the compound with awe, Abrahan felt he had entered a world separate from the dreary grit of the camp town.

Such was his distraction on entering the barn that he walked straight into the burly chest of the stable master. "Ho, there!" the man barked in a graveled voice of infinite command. Abrahan stopped short, jumped back, then craned his neck to look up at the giant towering above him, a red-bearded man in a leather apron tied over the buckskins they all wore. A pair of dung-covered great boots covered his giant's feet. His gloved hands were on his hips and his dirty blue-eyed face was a mix of scowl and smirk.

He was an Irishman named O'Hanlon who ate and slept with the equines and stable boys under his care. Abrahan had never heard a word against him. On the contrary, the mounted peddlers all but worshipped him for his knowledge and devotion to their steeds. The stable boys were largely black slaves. The rest were O'Hanlon's handpicked indentured apprentices. Both slaves and apprentices respected him without rancor. Still, Abrahan was off to a clumsy start with the man. He quaked a bit in his own short, mud-spattered boots. O'Hanlon saw this and softened his voice without seeming to coddle him.

"You would be Abrahan?"

"Yes sir, I am."

"I'll be callin' you Abe, if you don't mind, lad. Now, what do you know of God's most noble creature, a beast far nobler than man?"

"Little, sir."

"I thank you for your honesty, Abe. Many of the fools who come in here expectin' me to hand 'em their reins and give 'em a leg up and out into the wide world have not such candor. But as it is, we have our work cut out for us, don't we. I think you'd best be stayin' here with me and the boys the next weeks or more. I'll work you hard and I'll work you day and night but you'll know a thing or two before you're off into the sunset with one of my dears for the fortune and glory of Isadore Sassaporta. It's the least I owe him."

Abrahan understood O'Hanlon meant the horse, not his uncle. He gathered his nerve, puffed out his chest, and nodded in agreement with all the man's conditions. Next thing he knew, they were marching off to a dirt paddock where a fearsome equine was engaged in a vigorous effort at liberation, pulling against the rope that tied him to a fencepost. His eyes showed their whites. His teeth were bared. His thick mane rose and fell with each mighty toss of his head, and to Abrahan's eyes, he looked huge, although he was barely a horse at all, just 14.2 hand with his shoes on. He was a dark bay with a full tail, a mark in the shape of a crescent moon on his forehead, and two rear socks. He'd been chosen based on Isadore's description of his nephew. "Be on the lookout for him in days to come," Sassaporta had written O'Hanlon in a note of introduction. "From the neck up, a handsome boy, dark with a trim beard and a salesman's flashing eyes. From the neck down, on the runty side, short with a strong trunk and thick thighs." The horse may have been small for his kind, but nonetheless at a scant nine hundred pounds, he looked formidable while struggling against his restraints.

O'Hanlon gestured that Abrahan should enter the paddock. "Go right up to him, lad, and make his acquaintance. His proper name is King of Harts. We call him Hart."

Like many a man before him, Abrahan summoned images of his darling's soft breast and warm, enveloping thighs to give him courage for the task at hand. For Marian, he swore to himself as he bent to step through the fence rails and enter the arena, where—for all he knew—a hoof might soon plow through his skull and end his dreams forever. For Marian.

Watching him approach, the horse twisted and strained toward him. He planted his hooves firmly on the ground and locked his knees, a pose that made his powerful outstretched neck look monstrously long. The rope keeping him attached to the fencepost looked pulled to the point at which it might suddenly snap. He made a deep, rolling hum Abrahan could not translate. It sounded menacing, like the low chortle of a pirate about to send a man off the plank with the point of a dagger at his back. He broke into a sweat. The sky above went darker yet and from the distant hills a roll of thunder echoed the beast's sound. The young man marshaled his courage and put one foot in front of the other until he was inches from the horse's muzzle. He followed O'Hanlon's instructions. "Mr. Hart," he said, clearly although not without a tremor, "I am Abrahan Bento Sassaporta Naggar, known as Abe. I am to be your master."

The horse bobbed his head up and down, emitted that rolling hum again, but at least did not seem ready to kill him. Behind him, Abrahan heard the shuffle of feet and the murmur of men. He glanced over his shoulder to see O'Hanlon and three of his slaves hanging off one another, weak with muffled laughter. Found out, they erupted into guffaws.

"He's playin' with you! He's only beggin' a bite to eat!" said O'Hanlon. "We took him off his hay to meet you!"

Abrahan turned full about to face down those who'd ridiculed him. His cheeks burned. He set his lips to a grim line as he tried to imagine what he could possibly say to regain his dignity. Before he had a chance, Hart moved forward, which slackened the rope, giving him lead enough to head-butt poor Abrahan against the fence and push him into it with long, hard strokes of his enormous head against the greenhorn's back.

"Oh, forgive me, Abe, me bucko, me lad," O'Hanlon roared. "I'm forgettin' to tell you the first rule of horsemanship. . . ."

Hart pushed him into the fence rails so hard, Abrahan feared his ribs would break.

"Never turn your back on a horse!" finished O'Hanlon. His men near collapsed onto the ground with mirth.

Over the next weeks, Abrahan began to think of himself as Abe. It was difficult not to. The name rang through the air constantly. Abe! Bring water! Abe! Polish that harness! Abe! Clean these stalls! Abe! Brush that horse! Abe! Pick his feet while you're at it too! Every day, he began work just before dawn and slept only when the horses were fed and watered, the barn aisles swept, the tack polished, the buckets scrubbed, and the horses watered again. For three hours a day, he did nothing but ride.

He loved that part. Despite the pain of a beginner's bottom full of saddle sores, the joy of sitting there, galloping in circles around the exercise ring, made him feel a lord of the earth and sky. He fell many times, but eventually by dint of sheer will and desire for Marian of the foothills, he managed to learn how to point a horse right and left, how to speed him up and slow him down, at least in principle. At first the horse Hart and he found themselves at war, then they came to truce, and finally, to a kind of partnership of which Abe was the junior member. Abe learned to trust the animal's good sense and worked to win his loyalty. After a month, he felt his true master. Yes, he thought in the end, difficult and arduous as these weeks have been, they've made a horseman of me and I believe a good one. Which is why on that fine spring day he left the stables with Hart under saddle, both of them packed with all the merchandise man and beast can comfortably carry at one heroic go, O'Hanlon's parting words to them seemed not jocular but queer, wildly queer. Perhaps it was his tone.

"You've got a good, honest horse, there, Abe," he said, normally enough, with just a hint of manly sentiment. "List to what he tells you. And you, you bugger," he said to Hart, and this is where his voice changed, becoming dark, full of foreboding. "No funny business. Give the lad a break now and again. Alright, be off with you."

O'Hanlon slapped Hart's rump. Hart trotted off into the woods, absently chewing his bit with a puzzled Abe astride. He wondered at the boss's words for a few minutes before remembering to shorten his reins and pay attention to his mount, who had begun to go willy-nilly, grabbing whatever tender leaves he found at nose level. Leaning forward to rip the branches out of Hart's teeth while straightening him out took all the young man's concentration. O'Hanlon faded from his mind.

THE PIEDMONT, NORTH CAROLINA, 1829

They started out soundly enough. It took a little time for man and beast to settle down but for their first venture out alone together, it went well. Hart took the downhill paths faster than Abe would have liked considering the load they carried. A lot of weight bounced against their backs and the hills just below the Blue Ridge Mountains were rocky. But that was Abe's only complaint of him. They came to a clearing the second morning, a beautiful hollow with tall grass and wildflowers in every color imaginable. It looked an oasis of some kind, an expanse of lovely dirt after the punishing, stony route they'd taken so far. Hart wouldn't cross it. He clung to the inside of the tree line, happy to walk the long way around, but when Abe asked him to advance into the open, he refused. Abe asked again. Again, he refused. Abe was frustrated. He made to force him. He kicked Hart's sides as hard as he could. He slapped his rump and his neck with the flat of his hand and when that didn't work, he used the whip. Hart snorted. He sped up but shortened his step. He pulled against the reins 'til Abe thought his arms would leave their sockets.

He should have listened to the horse as O'Hanlon instructed

him. Instead, he kept up the struggle. The inevitable moment came when he lost the battle. Just inside the edge of the woods, Hart broke into a gallop. Abe lost control completely. Hart raised his head, nostrils flared. He had a mad look in his eye. He was entirely to himself and the peddler an annoyance he ignored. Abe flopped about on his back as bothersome to the horse as a cloud of gnats.

Abe was terrified. If he fell off at that pace, he might die. He lost his reins and clung for dear life to the front edge of the saddle. Hart galloped on without concern for him. The two knocked against branch and brush. Some of the wares they carried came loose and flew through the air. Tin cups and pans banged into tree trunks, china plates smashed against rocks.

Oh, they made a terrible racket. All of nature tried to get out of their way. Birds flew from the trees. Rabbits leapt through the grass. Abe heard larger things, he knew not what, bound off, throwing clods of dirt into the air, making odd thuds. Then, suddenly, without warning, Hart stopped short. Abe shot from his saddle like a cannonball, landing at the foot of a grandfather oak. He lay on the ground, breathing heavily, thanking God he hadn't crashed into it. The trunk would have cracked his spine. After checking his limbs—it was a miracle nothing broke—he got up, bleeding from his arms, his thighs, and the back of his head. Hart, meanwhile, had slunk under the cover of a stand of trees just behind him. His ears were splayed out at the sides, listening, waiting, and then Abe heard what kept Hart from the clearing all that time, what stopped him short, the thing he knew that Abe did not.

Screams. Horrid, bloodcurdling screams. The screams of women, and, he judged, children. Many of them. Out of nowhere, a stiff breeze came up and then he could smell what Hart smelled earlier. The iron scent of blood, rivers of it, he was sure, because the scent was strong and whatever its source, whatever mayhem was happening, it was too far away for him to witness with his eyes. He had only his ears and his nose, which next caught the scent of smoke, the burning of grass and wood and he didn't dare think what else, but it was something stinging and sour. All he knew for certain was that hell lay ahead and so he did what was reasonable.

He fled. He mounted, dug his heels into Hart's side, and loosed his reins. The horse didn't need a second prod. He bolted deep into the wilderness. Once they stopped, miles later, Abe took out his map and realized that again, he was impossibly lost. He hadn't a clue where they were or how far off the map's route they'd got. All he knew was that they'd run a long time until they were well free of the screaming, the blood, and the smoke.

It was night, but he was afraid to sleep. He tried to determine from the stars where Marian was and headed in what he prayed was the right direction. Sometime in the night, he rested Hart by a place where he could drink. Later, he fed him what grain he had left. He would have rested longer but the horse pulled his head up again. His ears twitched. He started to prance. Abe understood he had to mount him straightaway and ride wherever the horse judged best because again the beast heard danger that he did not.

After a time, clouds covered the moon and the stars. The sky went dark and he could not see much before them. A low-hanging branch jostled him. His seat went wrong, which tottered the horse. They tumbled down a steep slope of rocks, ripping their flesh 'til both bled freely, but then once more they heard horsemen and wagon wheels and weeping. They were pursued by demons no matter what direction they chose. There was nothing to do but rise and flee from where they had fallen. Abe struggled up and hoisted himself onto Hart. They rode through what was left of the night and all the next day until by some holy accident they arrived at the blessed clearing that was home to Marian of the foothills.

Marian stood halfway between her cabin and the goat pen. Through half-closed eyes slit by pain and exhaustion, Abe watched her shield her face with one hand and look into the brilliant yellow red of the setting sun behind them, which doubtless blinded her. He hoped she could make out that a compromised horse and rider approached, that the horse moved in a halting way, listing to one side every other step, and that the rider was bent over its neck. Her neck straightened, her pose suddenly full of urgency, as if there were no reason she could imagine a man would continue to ride a horse that perilously lame unless he was dead. They came closer. The sun set a little more. Her hand dropped. "Oh, Great Father of the Trees and Sky!" she cried out. "It's my little peddler!"

She broke into a run toward them.

When she reached them, she checked Abe first, saw that he was breathing. He was barely conscious and moaned out of great pain from several wounds to his limbs that had already closed and dried. She pulled him from his mount, quickly assessed his condition, and let him slide to the ground. Through barely open eyes, Abe watched her tend to the horse as she stripped him quickly of saddle and gear, ripping her shirt to bind his right foreleg where a long gash dripped blood. He tried to speak to tell her the flesh around the wound was swollen and hot, which indicated infection, but his voice failed him. "Come, horse," she said, "come with me to where you can rest." She herded the goats out of their pen and put her mare in it, then led Hart to the three-sided shed where her own horse usually sheltered and bedded its floor with fresh straw. Twice she slapped Abe's horse hard on his belly with both hands to keep him on his feet. She washed his leg, applied an herbal paste, and wrapped him again, winding long strips of cloth from his ankle to his knee. She washed other less serious injuries. She gave him water, holding a bucket under his nose for his ease. She fed him a warm mash. Abe stretched out a trembling hand to her, supplicating for like treatment, but she did not come to him. He closed his eyes and slipped into unconsciousness.

Early the next morning, Abe came to on the grass in front of the cabin. He was surrounded by munching goats, one of whom had woken him by biting at his hair. He limped to her door. She was not inside. He found her in the shed, sleeping next to his horse, who was reclining. Her head lay against his back. With difficulty, considering the pain of his own disabilities, Abe got inside the fence and then kicked at her foot. She opened her eyes and looked at him without expression. "You left me there to die," he said. She blinked. "You look alright to me." He blushed. "Well, I am now, but I could have died out there. I could have." The woman shrugged. "You were not in danger. This one was in greater peril." Hart's ears twitched at the sound of Abe's voice. In one sweeping move, the horse shifted his weight, got his feet under him, stood and rubbed his head once over Abe's trunk. The greeting looked to cost him significant effort. Abe took his head in his hands and kissed him above the eyes. Marian got to her feet as well. "Come," she said. "We'll change his wrap and feed him. Then we'll have a good look at you."

When they removed the bandage from Hart's leg, the wound looked much improved. Marian offered a prayer of thanksgiving in her sacred language. Abe did the same in his. By the time they finished ministering to his mount, he felt as close to her as he had after three and one-half days of lovemaking at the end of last summer. As if answering his unspoken prayer, she put an arm around his waist and helped him into her home, where she stripped him, washed his wounds with all the care she'd given the horse, applying the same paste to those she reopened. Abe summoned every ounce of stoicism he possessed not to wince or groan while she worked on him and he was successful, although once or twice he sucked air through his teeth. "Now, tell me what happened that brought you to my door in this state," she said once she put him to bed, naked under the animal skins. He sipped one of her healing soups from a clay bowl and felt oddly at home. He wanted to gather her in his arms but she was at the wood stove stirring more soup so he reported every detail he could remember instead.

Marian took in all he told her in silence. She left to tend her animals and his. When she returned, she sat on the bed. He was nearly asleep by then, but through his fog of pain and longing, he heard her say, "I know who it was, torturing women and children, carting them away."

"Who?"

"It was the hirelings of my beautiful white neighbors who want my people gone from these hills. That's who."

"What do you mean?"

"It's as regular as the seasons. The whites raid our villages. We raid theirs. This happens usually at the borders of our territories, but lately, they hire the most vicious warriors to advance deeper and deeper into our forests. First it was the low country, now the foothills. They think to ride over us into the mountains."

"Then you're in danger, Marian. You must come back to my uncle's town with me."

Marian laughed. "I've been in danger ever since I left my clan. I've been in more danger ever since I took over this cabin when the daughter of old Turkey Foot went to live with her new man in Tennessee. I will not go with you. I've fought white men off before. I will not leave the land."

"Come with me. I owe you this much." She looked at him with her eyebrows raised and shrugged. *Why?* the shrug asked. *Why do you owe me?* He said, "For everything you've done for me today and for my horse." Her expression went from questioning to something with a touch of exasperation in it. "Why would I not help two injured creatures at my door? Consider my debt for the gunpowder paid."

He reached for her and took up her hands, kissed them. He fixed his gaze to hers.

"Marian. I fear you are underestimating the troubles around you. I heard those people. I heard the screams. I smelled the burning, perhaps of their very flesh. I want you to come with me. I am in love with you. I will take care of you forever."

"Peddler," she said, because she could not remember his name, "I will not go with you. I do not love you. I do not even know you. Except now, I am beginning to see you are a fool."

The young lover was dumbstruck. His jaw flapped uselessly, as he had not words for her nor could he pull any out of his heart or mind or the thin mountain air. The sight of him, wide-eyed and robbed of speech, jaw flapping away, his lower lip dropping to expose pink gums, proved the point of her assessment. She shrugged, told him the soup had something in it that would make him sleep, as sleep would heal him, and prepared to leave the cabin for her daily chores of milking goats, working her fields, and hunting game. When finally he managed to shout, "Marian, wait!" she was gone.

He tried to get up, but the drug in the soup made his limbs too stiff and there was nothing to do but close his heavy eyes and drift away.

He slept like the dead. Had a fire, earthquake, or hurricane occurred, he'd have entered paradise yawning and confused. When he did wake, it was near noon the following day. The streaming sun opened his eyes. He was alone. His limbs were still stiff but less so. His clothes were at the foot of the bed, clean and folded. His boots were next to them. He washed his hands in a pot of standing water and dressed before muttering a short, hasty version of his morning prayers, adding at their end an entreaty to the Divine that what he foggily remembered as insult and rejection from Marian was in fact a drug-addled phantasm, a dream. In the unlikely event he was wrong and it had really happened, he added yet another prayer for the cleverness required to change her mind, which was surely inevitable, for what woman could resist the power of a grand, pure, and eternal passion?

A wooden bowl with a spoon sticking out of it lay on the stone mantel. Inside was a breakfast of boiled wild grains, chopped nuts, and fresh red berries. There was a jug of goat's milk nearby. He poured milk into the bowl and walked out the door, spooning away. It was a pleasant afternoon, the air warm, the sky blue. A gentle breeze caressed his skin and hair. Hart grazed peaceably with the goats. Marian and her mare were gone.

Abe lingered a bit with a preoccupied Hart and his goat

friends in case she'd just left for a short time, but he soon grew bored with waiting. He found his wares in her storage shed and went through them to see what he had lost and what remained. The result was not half as bad as he feared. When he investigated his store of gunpowder, a warm pride in his beloved enveloped him. It was all there. Marian had not taken a grain of it. So much for the lying, thieving Indian he'd been warned about constantly from the first day he arrived on the golden American shore!

The day wore on. He poked about the cabin. There wasn't much to explore. Most of the items in the cabin were practical. Each tool was kept in a logical place in prime condition. Such methodical order quickened the beating heart in Abe's chest. He admired a woman so unlike his mother who was self-effacing, provincial, ever fearful of doing something of which her neighbors would not approve. But this one. Everything about her home signaled that Marian was in charge, that she kept her house and her mind under command. He imagined what it would be like to submit to her authority, to linger in a warm bath of submission under the eye of a benign mistress, and then he blushed there in her one-room home, ashamed of his fantasies, regarding them a perversion of his mission to care for her, to save her from the hostile forces around them. He loved her infinitely, he decided at last. He'd never loved before. He had no way to measure the swelling of his heart, the obsession of his mind on her account, against a lesser love so this, he figured, was pretty much all that love could be. The way he'd met her a year earlier by accident, the way he'd found the route back to her while injured, disoriented, barely conscious—it all felt like destiny. He knew that she'd inspired him to the greatest acts of industry and bravery in all his life and if being near her meant he must subject himself, even to the point of subjecting his very manhood, he'd do it.

Such was the fullness of his emotion when the toe of his left boot happened to strike the side of a plain pine box that was either hidden or stored beneath her bed. It felt a fateful discovery and so he knelt down and took it out. The box looked to him to be about two cubits squared but, on lifting it, he thought it very light for its size. He rattled it first, gently against his ear. It made little noise. When he opened it, he discovered a bundle of letters, most from a lover whom it appeared she had also rejected in some way. The letters were signed variously as "The Abandoned," "He Without Hope," and "He Who Adores You" but with no corresponding name as if secrecy, anonymity, was paramount to their author. They were full of regrets and pleadings on mysterious propositions that Abe found typically English—that is, masked in double or even triple meanings. "I choke on the fruit I gathered for you. Why, my beloved, have you returned it to me?" he read before rolling his eyes and putting the letters aside. Beneath the letters were a collection of feathers—he assumed these were of ritual importance for their being wrapped in sheaths of deerskin—and a few bones from small animals. On the dried skin of a creature he could not identify, there was a document written in strange symbols, ornate *o*'s and *t*'s with queer slashes, squiggles, and tails. There were two corked miniature amphora, one filled with a red powder and the other with white, and also, at the very bottom of the box, underneath a protective sheet of muslin, what appeared to be a family portrait, an oil on canvas stretched over a square wooden frame. What a surprise, he thought, to find a portrait, a formal one, in a Cherokee treasure box, even the treasure box of one educated in England and living a more or less civilized life in the foothills. His own mother did not possess a single one. Abe examined the portrait's family carefully. The men were dressed in cotton shirts, turbans, and buckskins. They wore long gold earrings. The women also wore cotton shirts but with tiered skirts of many colors cinched by beaded belts. There was a much younger Marian, a mature man wearing a stovepipe hat whom Abe assumed to be her father, and a small woman next to him who was likely Marian's mother. There were also two Cherokee boys, and by his stance, a warrior male several years older than Marian. In addition, there were two blacks—family slaves, Abe deduced—a male and female of indeterminate age in European dress, standing with inscrutable expressions behind the primary group. There was a smudge over the face of the black man nearly erasing his features. The father, the mother, and the warrior in the foreground looked stern, not only unsmiling but angry.

Proof of her boasts when they first met, the painted Marian was magnificently beautiful. Abe judged her no older when it was painted than he was at present. The artist was either in love with her, a remarkable genius, or both. He portrayed a young beauty with a gleaming freshness to her skin, a firm fullness to her shape, and a softness to her eyes and jaw line, none of which were present anymore. She wasn't merely lovely, she was a creature born to be worshipped. He looked at the portrait a very long time before carefully packing everything away in the box exactly as he'd found it. He lay back on the bed to daydream of the Marian of long ago. Who was the warrior? he wondered. A brother? A lover? Alive or dead? And the painter. Who was he? Most of all, why would she hide the portrait? Why didn't she display it proudly?

She returned at dusk, riding bareback on her horse, her short bow and quiver on her back, a brace of wild turkey draped over the mare's withers. He stood at the open doorway to greet her. She rode to him, nodded without expression, then with a speed and grace that tortured him, she swung a long shapely leg over the mare's neck, slid to the ground, and handed him the fowl. "Do you know how to dress them?" she asked. "I think so," he said. He'd watched his mother prepare fowl many a time. "Go to it then," she said. "I have animals to feed."

Determined to please her, Abe sat on a stool outside the cabin and plucked with his head down, deeply concentrating on his task. Soon, the tops of his boots were buried in feathers. Each time he inhaled, feathers flew to his mouth and stuck there 'til he ripped them off. It was wretched work. Wretched women's work, he thought, and cursed softly so she would not hear him although she was far off in the shed doing he knew not what. He plucked on. He bit his feathered lips and wiped sweat from his brow with the back of his arm when he thought he heard her approach. He kept his head down, furiously plucking, hoping to be done with at least one of the birds by the time she came up to him. Then he saw another man's boots, rapidly becoming buried in feathers as well, facing his own at a distance less than the span of his right hand. He looked up.

Standing in front of him was not one but three men, Cherokee all, got up in European style, in dusty suits and soft-collared shirts with dirty ruffled cuffs. Each wore a wide silk tie knotted in a bow with ends that draped down to the first button of his jacket. None wore a hat. Their long black hair was tied back with ribbons, then braided. Strung through the braids were clusters of long, tapered feathers.

"Where is the woman who lives here?" asked the tallest and hardest of them.

"She is here," Marian said, at least that's what Abe assumed she said since she said it in Cherokee. The peddler knew but five words in that language and Marian had not employed these. He'd been so mesmerized by the men, he'd not seen her come up to the cabin as well. But there she was, positioning herself to stand between Abe and the Indian men, forcing them to back up a few paces. Abe wondered if she did this to protect him and decided yes, it must be so. Abrahan Bento Sassaporta Naggar felt a jolt of elation. Marian of the foothills cared for him. He no longer suffered doubts, he was certain of it, despite his clouded memory of rejection. He sat on his stool basking in the shield of her shadow with a tiny, irrepressible smile playing about his lips while Marian and the men discussed in their language a matter that appeared to be one of some gravity. Covered in feathers, sitting on his stool, he knew he must appear to her tribesmen a slavish idiot boy. He didn't care.

The end of the conversation came quickly. Marian said something that was maybe angry, maybe simply final. The men acquiesced. They turned and left. A covered wagon emerged from concealment inside the tree line to meet them, no doubt the very conveyance that had taken them to Marian's door. How had they got it through the woods? There were roads nearby, but not many. Why had they hidden it? One of the men ascended to sit next to the driver's seat, while the others climbed in the back, and then they were gone but not before Abe had a glimpse of the wagon's cargo.

People. Cherokee people. Women and children mostly, but also old men. They were dressed, like Marian's visitors, in

Western clothes. The women wore bonnets. The old men, shirts and vests. They were quiet. They were very quiet. Even the children. He could not see their faces well enough to determine why.

"What was all that about?" he asked.

She stared off in the direction of the wagon's egress, although it was already out of sight. When finally she looked at him, her brow was knit with worry. The corners of her mouth turned downward. Her eyes were round and blinked back tears. This was the first time he'd seen her anything but in control, either placid, lustful, or merry. The change in her touched his tender heart. His own eyes welled. He rose, took her by the shoulders, squared her to him, then put one hand to the side of her face as a gesture of comfort.

"What is it? What has troubled you?" he asked. "Who were they? What did they say?"

Slowly, she seemed to come back to herself. She sighed, then smiled at him, brushing a few stray feathers from his beard and hair, which elated him once again. Still, her eyes remained solemn, mournful.

"I'll finish the birds," she said. "You can split wood for me."

He knew her well enough by now not to press her on the matter. He would only irritate her. Instead, he rushed to the woodpile, whistling, happy to serve, especially in a manner that was profoundly masculine. He chopped and split a huge stack of logs until it grew dark and she appeared at the cabin door and called to him. He washed up. They sat together and ate a meal of roasted turkey and corn. He praised her food profusely, talking nonstop about its flavor and texture. When he ran out of reasonable compliments, he became ludicrous, then stuttered under the weight of his own flattery. She left her chair and lay on the bed.

After staring at him silently for a few minutes, she opened her arms to him. He went to her and worked to banish her sadness with the urgency of his love.

At the dawn, Abe opened his eyes to find Marian propped up on one elbow and studying him. She reached over and ruffled his hair affectionately as if she were his mother rather than his lover. He stretched and put his arms around her, drawing her close.

"How are you today?" he asked.

She smiled. "Well. I'm doing very well. Ready to face the day my Father the Sun has given me." She leaned forward and kissed his lips. "I'm getting used to you," she declared with the confidence of a queen. "You may stay a little longer."

"I will stay with you the rest of my life."

"No. You will stay until I tell you to leave, Peddler. Have you not work to do? Sales to make? Will you not be missed and your customers make inquiries?"

She had him there. He envisioned Isadore's trackers coming with their dogs to find him out. He feared what those brutal men might do to her should they arrive to drag him back to camp, and if she thought to object. Hiding his fears, he dissembled to affect a courtliness he imagined she'd experienced in her days abroad.

"Whatever you allow me will be the greatest gift," he said.

"Hmph," she muttered. She got up, put on her buckskins and shirt, and left to feed her animals before she fed herself. She gestured toward the potbellied stove on her way out the door. "Make us something to eat. I won't be long."

He opened the stove. It was full of kindling, which he lit. Marian had eggs in her larder and a kind of bread he'd never seen before. He broke it open and tasted its dark yellow dough. Potato, he decided, a very strange potato. There were also onions and mushrooms. Other foodstuffs she kept he did not recognize. He left the latter alone and mixed the identifiable together, breaking the bread into pieces, chopping the vegetables, mixing the eggs, then stirring the lot in a pan over the stove's hot burner. When she returned, they sat and ate. Although she finished every bite, she did not compliment him, an omission that stung until she said, "This will be your job while you're with me. To make the food in the morning while I tend the livestock." He thought this meant he had not exactly failed her and was pleased.

After breakfast, she taught him how to grind corn and grain, pointing out huge heaps of unhusked corn and fresh-cut grain that needed attention. Then she sent him to clean the horse shed and goat pen, and to re-bed them. Once finished with that, he was to empty, then scrub the water troughs and refill them, bucket by bucket, from the living stream behind her house. There was wash to be done also, if he had time to manage that. In the meantime, she would ride out and inspect her fields, which were in a valley in a place the white men did not know. Afterward, perhaps, she would hunt. Abe was so in awe of her by now he did not grumble but set to his work on the stable as soon as she and her horse were out of sight.

An hour or two later, he hauled water with worthy resolve until he heard the approach of strangers. He picked his head up. White men in long oilcloth coats and broad-brimmed hats, armed to the teeth with both shotguns and pistols, rode toward him on mounts as disheveled and mud-caked as the brutes astride them. He walked into the cabin as swiftly as he could without seeming to run or rush, so as not to betray his fear. He grabbed a rifle from the wall and went to face the visitors outside by raising his weapon and pointing it at them. Blood pounded through his ears. "Gentlemen, you can stop right there," he said, although the men had halted the moment he'd raised arms against them. Their caution gave him courage. He summoned up the best voice of command he had in him. "Who are you and what do you want?"

The biggest and roughest-looking of them sheathed his shotgun in a holster strapped to his saddle. He held up gloved hands in a gesture of peace. The others did not holster anything. They glared at him. He glared back.

"We're lookin' for a woman what lives here. An Injun woman."

"There is no woman here."

"Where the hell is she then?"

"Certainly not here. I don't know who you're talking about. This is my place since winter last. As you can see, I am alone."

They could not see any such thing, not with Abe standing in the doorway, rifle raised and pointing. The leader tilted his head to the man on his left without taking his eyes off Abe and told him to dismount and look around inside. "That alright with you, son?" he asked, giving Abe a smile that was half sneer. Enough of the man's teeth were missing to make his mouth look a dark, gaping hole. Abe once more marshaled his courage and said, "It's alright as long as he remembers who my gun is pointing at." He stepped aside to a position where he could keep his eyes on the man inside the cabin and the two on horseback both. Never was he so grateful that Marian rejected the feminine trappings of white women.

The man left the house with his weapon lowered and his shoulders raised as if to say *No sign of a female here.* He remounted his horse. The leader tipped his grimy hat. They left. Abe began a tense vigil, waiting for his beloved to return.

Marian appeared again at dusk. This time a large fish dangled from the quiver on her back. She held a spear of potatoes, both sweet and white, balancing it against one leg in the same way the men seeking her balanced their shotguns. Abe felt a great rush of relief, which he struggled to conceal, failing utterly. He stood red-faced and wide-eyed at her door, tongue-tied when she came to him, gave him her bounty, and left to put up her horse. Once she was done and in the cabin, washing up with the water he fetched for her and the soap he'd given her as a gift, he could contain himself no longer. "You sure have a lot of visitors," he said. She looked at him quizzically. He told him everything in a great spill of words. When he was done, he held his breath anticipating a response worthy of his intense concern but she said only, "Thank you." He asked what she was thanking him for. "You did well," she said. "You've bought me time." She dried her hands on a towel. "Were those men what you called once the hirelings of your neighbors?" he asked. She shrugged. "Likely so," she said.

Over the next week, they worked side by side to create a series of traps at the edge of the woods around her cabin, traps that would make significant noise when they did their work and so function as a warning system as well as restrain the unwanted. They were ingenious, Abe found, requiring the weight of a man or a horse, or a bear, to set themselves off, leaving the area safe for whatever lighter creatures might approach. When they were done, Marian created a ring of warning around all, using rocks and feathers in designs that looked random enough to Abe but that, she told him, would sound a loud and eloquent alarm to any of her people who came across them. "If," she said, "they have not forgotten everything their ancestors taught them."

It was not five days later that she gave him the boot. "Leave," she said. "You must make your route or you will bring attention to me." He wanted to argue, but he couldn't. He managed to wrest a promise from her that he could return when his rounds were complete and he'd reported back to Uncle Isadore. It would have to do. The next morning, he packed up his wares, gave her a parting gift of all the gunpowder he could spare, and rode Hart off to the farms on his list with a heart heavier than any load of staples and trifles any peddler anywhere could possibly carry.

TOBIAS MILNER'S FARM, TWO DAYS LATER

Abe and Hart rode all day to the northeast and slept that night on a bed of pine needles beside a waterfall. It was a hard bed for both after the comforts of their stay at Marian's, but a safe one. Abe was disturbed by fitful thoughts of Marian's failure to recognize that he was the ultimate love of her life, but that was the worst of his discomforts. No marauding mercenaries or vengeful Indians molested them. They rose at dawn. Abe offered thanksgiving that he'd got up in one piece, then washed in a chill cascade of mountain water while Hart munched at a breakfast of Marian's grains. He dressed in the best shirt and trousers he carried, broke camp, and tacked up his horse, packs and all. They set off at a pace that would guarantee they'd arrive at their destination near the northernmost corner of North Carolina, close to the border of Virginia, by afternoon; that is, at the farm of Tobias Milner, one of his best customers the previous year.

Sales volume and his devotion to Marian aside, Abe looked forward to visiting the Milner farm on account of the Milner daughters, three blossoming, buxom beauties near his own age. If their father didn't buy a nail, he'd still look forward to stopping there. Last year, they'd welcomed him into their home as if he were a wandering prince in disguise. They were all fluttering eyes and blushing cheeks. They hung on every word of his sales pitch and invented sly excuses to cozy up to him while examining his products. The oldest, Bekka, asked him to tie a ribbon on the end of the long, tawny braid that fell halfway down her back so she could see how it looked in the parlor mirror before she purchased it when her sisters were right there able to help. Their mother had gone out of her way to make a pointed remark that single young men were scarce in these hills and single young men with a secure future were scarcer still. She'd announced that the son, or even nephew perhaps, of one of the county's most successful industrialists was the answer to a mother's prayer. She was unconcerned whether prospective grooms for her girls were Lutheran or not. She dismissed lineage as something the family could work around. Abe knew well that in the old country, in Alsace, the Milners' forebears might have whipped a young Jew who even glanced at her daughters. But this was America, the New World. Here, in the lonely hinterland that was the Milners' little corner of the foothills, coerced at a great cost of blood and sweat into domestication, he got the clear message that a mother would take what she could get.

This year, his heart was heavy at leaving Marian. After only two days, he missed her dreadfully and worried that she'd cool to the idea of him before he managed to return. He knew he would love her forever, he nursed hopes that she would come to love him over time but for now, at least, he could do with a little feminine attention from someone who made him feel desirable—a catch, even. A harmless afternoon with the Milner girls fit the bill.

It was their father who rushed from the house to greet him as he rode up to their front gate. Calling for his stable boy to relieve Mr. Sassaporta of his mount, Milner took up the packs Abe unloaded and carried them himself into the house, chatting excitedly all the way.

"We've been waiting for your visit for so long, lad!" he said. "The women of the house have been on the lookout for you day and night. I confess, it approached annoyance." The man paused before the front door for a wink and a nod. "I'm not certain they need so many trinkets and notions!" His voice dropped to a near whisper as if the women in question were huddled on the other side of the door, listening. "Just two days ago, they moaned and moaned at dinner yet again. 'Where is that handsome young peddler,' they said, 'and why has he not yet come on his spring call?' Tired of it all, I muttered that a coyote or a bobcat must have eaten you and suggested they hunt for your remains. What a tumult erupted! My wife knocked on the table three times and threw salt over her shoulder while denouncing me for making dire predictions sure to attract evil to our own hearth and home. At the same time, the girls covered their eyes and wailed as if they'd just discovered the indigestible bits of your body in the herb garden." Milner stopped to puff up his chest to underscore how firmly he'd been required to react. "I pounded the table, first with my fist and then with my hobnailed boot, to quiet them. The next night none would speak to me at dinner. My meat was burnt and dry and two nights in a row, my wife failed to warm the sheets on my side of the bed. The girls would not so much as bid me good night. Had I not spied your fat pony riding up the road this morning, I would have thrown myself at their mercies. Anything to end that silence! I'm telling you, lad, there are few conditions that can unman a fellow faster than a houseful of disappointed women!"

Abe was not sure anymore if he was excited or afraid to enter the house, a well-kept structure of milled lumber with paned glass windows, evidence of Milner's modest success. He half expected to be devoured by ravenous harpies. But as they entered the foyer, all he saw of the girls was the backs of their skirts as their mother, Esther, shooed them into the kitchen, presumably to allow the men to conduct their business and so clear the way for the more important social congress that lay ahead. When the former was accomplished, Tobias Milner raised his voice loud enough for the entire household to hear, saying, "Let's shake on it then." Within seconds, his daughters appeared and swept into the chairs awaiting them while their mother offered tea. The charm of their flowery scents and the soft rustle of their skirts filled Abe with bittersweet sentiment. All this trouble for me, he thought, while Marian treats me as if I could be replaced in a heartbeat and in the next, forgotten. He rose from his chair briefly to greet the women with respect.

"You will, of course, spend the night with us?" Tobias Milner asked. "You could give all the news from Greensborough."

"Thank you for your kind offer," Abe said "But I must be off before dark, Mr. Milner. I lost a week or two coming here for various reasons. I need to make up for time lost."

The three Milner daughters were sitting across from him in a row of precisely equidistant straight-backed chairs. Colored ribbons threaded through the braids of their hair, their cheeks were pinched pink, and their hands were folded demurely in their laps. Despite their studied similitude, each delivered protest to his leave-taking in her own manner. Bekka, the plump pretty one, tapped her little feet lightly against the floor and whispered, "No!" Judith, the serious one, furrowed her brow and shot him a wounded look from her great blue eyes, fluttering a delicate hand over her breast and going so far as to feign the blinking back of tears. Hannah, the youngest, grabbed a lock of her auburn hair and stuck it in her mouth to stifle an anguished cry.

"I never would have marked you as a cruel lad, Abrahan," their father said, knocking his pipe out against the fireplace. "My daughters have such little company. You cannot deny them the pleasure of yours for a mere evening."

From out the corner of his eye, Abe spied their mother at the doorway of her kitchen. He pretended not to notice as she mimed instructions to her daughters with a desperation explained only by the fact that no matter how fresh, how dewy their cheeks, neither Bekka, Judith, nor Hannah were getting any younger. In the old country, it would have been scandalous to have them unmarried so long. Scowling, she communicated to the plump pretty one she must sit straight without fidgeting her feet, to the serious one she should turn up the corners of her mouth posthaste, and to the youngest to get her hair out of her mouth. Her hand then rested over her chest as if her mother's heart twisted there on their behalf.

The room turned still while Abe took his time to formulate a polite response to the farmer's insistence. Breath was held all around. He opened his mouth to speak but no sound emerged. Tobias Milner pouted pleadingly, nodding encouragement. "Yes? Yes?" he said, softly, sweetly, as kittenish as his daughters. A multitude of considerations swarmed through Abe's mind. On the one hand, if he delayed his rounds to stay overnight, that was one more night before he could return to Marian in the end and how

he ached for her! On the other hand, if he stayed, Tobias Milner
would be pleased and perhaps increase his invoice. These were
Hart's first days back on the road. Surely a horse coming back
from injuries might welcome a solid night's rest in cozy shelter.
Cooking smells from the kitchen also enticed. It had been an
American era since he'd eaten anything that resembled an old-
fashioned family meal. He could ride harder and longer the following day, perhaps knock more than two farms off his list, if
both he and his mount were better fed and slept well overnight.
The three doting, squirming young women who leaned toward
him in unison in a melting mass of feminine anticipation, waiting for an answer, pulled at him. How often had he the chance to
immerse himself in not just womanly, but gentile attentions? He
had to admit there was a dose of exotic spice added to the proposed dinner. Such an invitation would never have been extended
back in London.

He capitulated.

"Indeed," Abe said, nodding to the women with as much
grace as if he had a plumed hat to doff and sweep in their direction, "if my poor company can brighten the spirits of three stars
of the firmament which . . ."

The ladies' shoulders rose in expectant unison. Encouraged,
Abe colored his many-hued phrase with a splash more purple.

". . . already glimmer so impossibly as to near blind me. Yes,
I shall stay on the single night, though I must be gone before the
dawn or risk eternal bedazzlement!"

Parental eyes widened, filial sighs sang. Abe congratulated
himself on his sophistication.

After the sisters occupied him by selecting various items out
of his wares—a small brass candlestick for one, a paperweight of

pressed daisies under glass for another, and a brush with a tor-
toiseshell handle for the last—dinner was served. The meal was
as fine as he'd hoped. It was difficult to believe the family had
not spent days preparing for him. The table sparkled with their
treasures in crockery and cutlery. Esther troubled herself with a
holiday roast although it was only a Wednesday in the middle of
an unremarkable week. Besides the beef, she served mushroom
soup and airy biscuits for sopping it up. There were carrots, tur-
nips, and a tangy fruit stewed in the juice of the meat. When
Abe complimented Esther on her expertise, she shared credit
with her youngest. "Hannah's the baker in this house," she said.
"She made the biscuits, and the honey cake that's coming too."
Abe rephrased his compliments for the daughter in question,
who grinned from ear to ear, then dropped her head in belated
modesty.

After dinner, the older girls got to shine. Bekka played a fiddle
reasonably well, and Judith recited of a psalm of David, delivered with dramatic gestures and facial expressions. Despite the
delights of being an object of desire, Abe found himself struggling to stay awake until Tobias Milner brought up the legend
of an Indian woman who, it was rumored, lived in the woods
thereabouts though few had seen her.

"You could run into Dark Water out there, if you happen to
meander off established tracks," the farmer said. "And if you do,
pray to the Lord for deliverance is my advice. She's more than
fearsome to look at. The sight of her can freeze the blood of the
bravest man. To hear her war cries is to hear the howls of hell-
hounds. It's a sound that'll ring in your ears the rest of your life."

It took Abe time to catch on. At first he thought Tobias Milner was surely speaking of a child's nightmare, an old crone, a

barbarian witch, no doubt a harmless creature made shibboleth to frighten children into good behavior. Why his host would juggle fairy tales in the air was inexplicable. He affected a bemused interest.

"Might she steal my soul?" he asked, the joke playing visibly about his lips.

"She'll steal your life without thinking twice," Tobias Milner said. "Just ask Teddy Rupert. Are you headed his way?" Rupert was the owner of a vast plantation half a day's ride west at the very boundary of the Cherokee Nation. Abe nodded. Milner harrumphed and continued. "He lost a son to her flaming arrows. Now, Billy was a selfish boy and fairly impolite. I've no doubt he likely insulted her, as the story goes. But she cut him down for it, didn't she, and for a Cherokee woman to murder a white man in peacetime and in such a cruel manner. Well, there's no excuse. No excuse at all."

"Flaming arrows, sir?" Abe asked in disbelief.

"Oh, yes. Ones soaked in Injun pitch. They're thicker than the usual, you know. More like pegs or stakes. And once they pierce the flesh, the poor devil pinned by them cannot move while the flame devours his flesh. I'm telling you, these natives are savages. You can cover their nakedness and teach them English, stick a plow in their hands too, but they remain as malicious as Amalekites and as godless as the people of Sodom whom the Lord saw fit to destroy."

"Husband, please!" With two words, Esther put an end to the conversation. The two older girls had gone pale and trembling in the hearing of it while the youngest seemed eager for more details.

While the talk drifted into safer realms, Abe wondered if his

Marian knew this Dark Water. It hardly seemed likely the wilderness round about teemed with Indian women living on their own. In the previous year he'd come across only the one.

Before he retired that night to a cozy makeshift bed of pillows and comforters set up in the kitchen on a wide shelf usually reserved for the larger pots, Abe went to the stable to check on Hart. On entering, he stepped over the sleeping stable boy, a youth worked hard enough from dawn to dark caring for three cows, four goats, and two horses; the structure that housed them; as well as the chickens and geese kept separately that he did not stir from his slumber, not even when Abe stumbled over a bale of hay in that odorous dark and banged into a stall door, rousing every animal the Milners possessed. They lowed, bleated, and neighed alarmingly, although at his insistence, they quieted soon enough. Hart was calm throughout, nodding his great head from over a stall door at the end of the aisle. He nickered softly at Abe's approach. "How are you, my friend?" he asked the horse, petting his neck in long strokes once he'd entered the stall. Hart poked his nose along the length of Abe's trunk, sniffing in his pockets for a treat. The peddler could not help but laugh and hug the beast's head uselessly in an effort to make him stop.

"That horse surely loves you," a feminine voice said from a place in the aisle where a circle of light splintered the dark.

Abe started, mortified to be caught in such an unguarded moment. "Who's there?" he called out to the figure hidden by the glare of a lantern. It was disconcerting to be observed by an unknown entity. A vague unease replaced his embarrassment. "Who's there?" he repeated, this time in a more insistent tone.

"Only me. Hannah."

The youngest Milner girl stepped out from behind her lantern and approached Hart's stall so he could see her. She wore a plain muslin nightgown and a blue robe over it that she'd failed to close. On her head was a ruffled nightcap, which her thick auburn hair escaped to tumble down past her shoulders. Seeing her apart from her elder sisters, Abe realized that she was not quite as young as he'd thought. Her fair skin had gone a lovely pink, a thin line of moisture glistened above her upper lip, and another graced the shallow scoop of the gown's neckline. Her intentions were perfectly clear. She'd sought him out alone in the night where neither her parents nor her siblings could monitor what might next transpire.

Abe was terrified.

"What are you doing here?" he asked. She shrugged and lifted her gaze to the rafters as if to say, *It's my family's stable not yours, isn't it?* Hanging the lantern on a post in the middle of the aisle, she boldly stepped into the stall with him, standing close. She pet Hart along his topline and asked, without looking at Abe but also without shame, "Do you like me, Abrahan?" What was a young man to say to such a question from the ripe daughter of a valued customer? "Of course I like you, Hannah," he said, straightening his back and filling his chest with air in the hope that he might seem bigger, more powerful to her, and so inspire a shyness the girl plainly lacked. "You're quite charming." He coughed and lowered his voice to lend it authority. "But now we must leave Hart to his rest. Come along, child."

With the stamp of a slippered foot against straw and a raised hand, Hannah stopped him in his tracks. "I am not a child!" she said. Anger heightened her color further, her chest heaved with hot air. Petulance became her, Abe observed, and a place at the root of him ignited ignobly. "Yes, yes, you are not a child. I beg your indulgence, lady, but we must get from here," he said as rapidly and forcefully as possible.

Once the pair stepped over the stable boy and into the open, Abe was hopeful of escape. Only forty paces more and he would be back in the kitchen, where surely this bold girl could not linger without fear of discovery. Besides, now that she'd had what she wanted from him—a simple admission that he liked her, which was not half as much as he feared—she'd calmed, took his hand in an innocent way, and looked up at the stars. Heaven's lights stretched across the skies like a wedding canopy with not a cloud to dim them. "It's a beautiful night," she said. "Hard to believe there are creatures as awful as Dark Water creeping about, isn't it?"

Abe sighed heavily. It dismayed him that from the moment he'd arrived on America's shores he'd heard fanciful stories about the Cherokee. Though some had taken up European ways, it did not stop people from calling them primitive pagans, stubbornly resistant to both Bible and sword. He'd heard they were brutal, capable of the most grotesque tortures, and generally lived lives steeped in bestial habits. But having come to know Marian, who had only been helpful and generous to him, he was certain the worst of what he heard about this Dark Water was calumny, similar to the calumnies leveled against the Jews. According to most Europeans, he should have horns and drink the blood of Christian babies. Could the Cherokee dream up worse tortures than those his ancestors had suffered at the hands of the Inquisition? Why should he believe the worst of what Tobias Milner told him of Dark Water?

"Surely she cannot be as dreadful as your father claims, Hannah," he told the young girl, considering his instruction a kindness.

"Oh, yes, she is. I saw her once."

"Tell me."

"My sisters and I went berrying. I was only four at the time and they liked to ignore me, as I annoyed them. They found it a horrid chore whenever Mother said to look out for me or take me with them anywhere. Naturally, I wandered apart, going off our usual paths and into the woods. I was following a rabbit, I think, or it might have been a bird. Anyway, I don't know how long it was, but sooner or later, I came to a huge clearing and it was full of corn and squash and other cultivated plants. In the middle of these fields without farmhouse or shed was a savage Indian woman, tall it seemed to my child's eyes and dressed like a man. She was in a crying fit. Her hair stood up. It was full of twigs. Her face was streaked with dirt. She wailed and danced a terrible dance. Her body keened. Her feet stomped about in a circle. She ripped ears of unripe corn from their stalks and threw them down, wailing louder and louder as she did so. I'm telling you, the sight of her would make you, a grown man, frozen in fear. Just then my sisters called out for me. 'Hannah! Hannah!' they called, and the madwoman's head snapped up and, I swear, turned all around like a pumpkin twirled upon a stick. Her eyes met mine for an instant, an instant only, but I shall never forget them 'til my dying day. They sent ice through my veins. I took off, running toward my sisters' voices. I ran and I ran, and by the grace of Jesus, I found them. They beat me for wandering off and asked no questions about where I'd been or what I'd seen. I told them nothing because they beat me. Ah! Here we are," she announced, her tone taking a sudden lighthearted turn when they reached the house. "I'll say good night to you now, Abrahan, and cherish your fondness until we

61

meet again. Godspeed on your journeys, especially the one that brings you back to us."

The girl stood on her toes and kissed his cheek, then slipped swiftly and silently into the house through the kitchen. Abe followed and happily found himself at the hearth alone. He lay on his shelf, a row of birds on a wire drying above his head, and considered Hannah's story. Summoning his reason, he discounted it as the fevered imaginings of a small child lost in the woods, much colored over time. It made sense to him that this Dark Water was no nightmare creature as both the girl and her father had described but rather a flesh-and-blood woman who'd fallen on tragic times. He pictured a woman much like Marian in a demented misery. Imagining the whys of it agitated his sleep.

He headed west through midafternoon the next day until he was just below the highest mountain peaks, deep in a fertile valley where the ground plateaued and farms far richer than the Milners' dotted the landscape. As he neared Teddy Rupert's plantation, the full ramifications of the Milners' stories sunk through to the core of Abrahan Sassaporta's brain. He wondered with reluctance if the fair object of his most passionate affections might herself be the fearsome Dark Water. Twice now he'd covered the territory of the foothills where Dark Water was said to live and not come across even the slightest sign of any Indian woman on her own except Marian. If they were the same, his beloved one had a most violent history, an infamous one. Farfetched as it seemed, the possibility tormented him. It would explain much about her that he did not yet understand. If her native name was notorious, it would explain why she never told him what it was. If she were a pariah, it would explain the isolation in which she lived, which, he had to acknowledge, might be part and parcel of why she'd embraced the company of a stray peddler who'd happened by her sanctuary. Disturbingly, it would also explain why three rough customers had been searching for her that day. Perhaps, he considered, there was a bounty on her head? He decided he would have no peace until he investigated the matter.

Teddy Rupert and his wife did not receive him. They were elevated types too rarefied to bother with a peddler's errands. Mrs. Rupert's maid, a middle-aged black with an accent from the West Indies who seemed to have learned her airs and gestures from her mistress, stood on a high step at the back of the big house to look down at the wares Abe spread on a cloth over the grass below. She waved a dismissive hand above most of his display, selecting nothing for her mistress and only an ivory comb for herself, which she promptly stuck in her hair without pausing to look in the glass Abe held up for that purpose. She dropped two pennies in his hand while looking off at the row of field hands lining up at the edge of the vegetable garden. Abe studied his palm, incredulous at the meager amount she'd thrown him—and for ivory, ivory! He opened his mouth to protest. "Well, now, they're waiting for you, aren't they," she said in her singsong voice. She turned to enter the big house, patting the comb in her hair as she did so. "You'll thank me for every copper you get from that crew," she said with her back to him. "But not for me you'd never get near 'em. I could send them away like that." She snapped her fingers and closed the door behind her but not before she tossed him a snippet of noblesse oblige. "You may have them come up, rather than move your wares."

Abe waved those waiting forward and they came, approaching slowly, with some shyness but with eyes steady on the goods spread out before them. Both men and women wore the same yellow cotton shirts, loosely yoked at the neck. The women wore flour-sack skirts and the men pants of the same material. Everyone's feet were bare, everyone's clothes were patched. A year earlier, Abe questioned where they came by the coin to purchase goods from him, and was told that in the hours after their workday ended, Teddy Rupert permitted his slaves to hire themselves out to farmers around, taking a commission from them, of course, but allowing them to keep a percentage of their earnings. If they'd a craftsman's skill in woodcarving or shaping iron, they could make a tidy enough sum, all they'd need to pay for a few luxuries. If they did not, there was always some service they could trade among one another, and so, an economy took hold in the slaves' quarters that was a kind of miniature of that in the free world.

The first to make a selection was a fresh-faced boy nearing manhood whose ebony skin bore no marks or scars, a rare enough condition among the slave class. Like the rest, he squatted at the borders of Abe's display, running just his fingertips over the peddler's wares. Like the rest, he murmured admiration or surprise at this and that. Abe sat on the lowest step of the big house's kitchen steps, watching and listening, lulled by the murmurs and gestures into a kind of sleepiness. He noticed the boy's hands lingered over a porcelain teacup whose saucer had been cracked but not broken during Hart's various falls and charges through the countryside. Violets with tiny green leaves were painted on the side of the cup and in a twined circle around the edges of the saucer. Cracked or not, it was a pretty piece of work. The boy picked up the cup and turned it over several times, seemingly enchanted. He poked the fellow next to him and whispered, "Mama'd plain love this, don't you think, Thomas?" Stirring himself, Abe said, "I can give you that set at a discount, lad, considering the damage done en route." Heads popped up all around. A dozen black faces stared at him. He lifted his hands, palms turned upward to the heavens. "What is it, people? Why do you regard me so?" One of them, a slight old woman who, thanks to a lifetime of hard labor, possessed huge arms and hands so muscled they looked to belong to some other body—a man's, perhaps, or a working beast's—spoke up. "No one's ever offered us a discount, sir, on goods broken or whole," she said. "Not even you last year when you come by."

Abe blushed, his head went down, studying the ground. "I was tightfisted then," he said. "Now, I'm something different." While they returned to fondling his goods, selecting only a few for most were too rich even with a discount, he realized that he'd spoken the truth. He was different this year. During his first foray into the foothills, his only concern was knocking off his debt to Uncle Isadore as quickly as possible, and yes, there were occasions he'd made outrageous deals in his own favor, even at the expense of those as poor and miserable as the slaves before him. He felt shamed over his greed now. He could only think it was love that had changed around his head and softened his heart. Yes, he thought, warming to the idea, it was brave, inde- pendent Marian who'd made a *mensch* out of him without even trying. Thoughts of Marian always ended lately with the mystery of Dark Water. He decided to find out what the slaves had to say about her. Slaves, he'd been told, always had their ears to the ground. They knew many things their masters did not.

First, he needed to find a slave he could persuade to speak to him openly on the matter. He decided the boy who bought his mother a teacup would do. After the others finished purchasing what they could afford, he asked the boy to help him pack things up and load them on his horse. Once that chore was done, he mentioned to him that he was curious about a person who was much feared in these parts, a certain Dark Water. He needed to know more about her should he find himself in peril as he made his rounds through the countryside. "Why I might give something as valuable as another of those teacups for the right information," he said. Abe took a teacup out of the pack in which he kept china items wrapped in cloth and unwound its covering slowly at the boy's eye level. "Hmm?" he said, pointedly. "Hmm?"

The boy was thrilled, no doubt, by the chance to earn another teacup adorned with violets. He looked to be about to jump out of his skin over earning treasure for the sake of a little information. His hands shot forward. Abe held the cup just out of his reach.

"Tell me about this Dark Water first."

"Dark Water is a murderess," the boy said in a rush, his hands yet outstretched. "She murdered the master's son but covered it all up and made sure her daddy's black slave caught the blame. That man ran for his life to Echota. That would be the in the Cherokee Nation. It's their capital, like Washington is to you all. But also, it's a city of refuge. Do you know what that is, sir? It's a place where low-down murderers can spend their evil lives in each other's company without fear of arrest."

Abe nodded. He knew of such cities. Jews had them in ancient times. It was a revelation to hear that Cherokee had them too. He'd heard of Echota. It was a far place from the Rupert plantation, some two or three hundred miles south over the mountains of North Carolina, through South Carolina, and into Georgia. His rounds took him no place near it.

"But," the boy continued, "there's stories he died in battle trying to win his freedom, which is the Cherokee way. They say his ghost must be trapped down there or else surely he'd come back and haunt Dark Water to punish her for his troubles. They say he was much betrayed, havin' been loyal to her once upon a time. She was the flower of her day and men trailed along after her like puppy dogs. Him included. Who knows? If the rumors heard at master's table are true, President Jackson fixes to boot all the red men from down there, and their slaves too, even the ghosts. Maybe that vengeful spirit'll show up here soon. Then again, maybe he's still alive. Maybe."

All the while the boy spoke, Dark Water took most strongly the shape of Marian in Abe's mind. Why? he wondered. Why does my heart allow the persons of the beautiful murderess and my beautiful Marian to intertwine so perfectly? Was it intuition? Or was it as foolish as expecting a native woman to love him? He thanked his informant, gave him his second cup as payment, and, as he'd teased the boy some, threw in the teapot that went with. The boy fumbled a bit trying to hold everything in his small hands. Abe gave him wrappings and a sack to carry the lot home. Afterward, he asked, "Do you know, does this Dark Water have a Christian name?"

"All them all do nowadays." The boy sat on the ground to wind scraps of cloth around his booty and place its pieces gently in his sack. "Let's see, it's Mary, I'm thinkin', or maybe it's Margaret." He polished a saucer with a wrapper and a bit of spit. Abe fixed him with an urgent look. "Try to remember for sure," he said. The boy screwed up his mouth for a minute and studied the sky above. At last he said, "No, it's Marian, yes, that's surely what it is. Marian."

A piece of Abe's soul rose and fell with the sound of her name. He took a deep breath to steady himself, then remembered to ask, "And what was his name, this slave of Dark Water's father, who is likely dead?"

"Jacob, sir, like him who wrestled angels."

"Jacob," Abe muttered, "Jacob." The name echoed in his thoughts constantly over the next two months while he completed his rounds and sold out his wares. At the same time, he filled his mind with Marian's kindnesses to him and his horse. Why, she'd been the very soul of humane concern. How could she possibly have committed such vile torture as murder by flaming arrow? Could he trust the testaments of a German farmer or a young slave boy bribed by a teacup? Seized by a jealousy he could not name, he longed to discover the hows and whys of Marian's link to the true perpetrator, the cruel slave, Jacob, who'd followed her like a puppy. A man would have to be very close to her indeed to have murdered on her account, if that was what happened. With a fat wallet and bags of coin in his saddlebags, he thought over and over, Jacob, Jacob, until the name became a torment. After studying his map well, he made a decision. The hell with the distance, he told Hart, and turned the horse toward Echota, the city of refuge, before heading back to his uncle's camp.

IN ECHOTA

What Abe knew of Echota, he knew from Clive Burrows, Uncle Isadore's man who sold there. Burrows had not told him that it was a refuge for criminals, but what he had told him was just as fantastical. According to Burrows, Echota, as capital of the Cherokee Nation, was a vibrant model city inhabited by civilized natives. It was a place where law was written, advocacy nourished by mind and treasure, where a newspaper was printed, where society congratulated itself on its wise path of adaptation and conciliation to the European invader, its abandonment of the old ways, its hopeful embrace of the new. At the time, Abe had doubted the elder peddler's descriptions, thinking them the typical exaggerations in which all their kind indulged when telling a colleague of their adventures on the road. They certainly flew in the face of what the other peddlers claimed, that Indians were brutes and primitives no matter the tribe or what clothing they chose to wear. Thinking on it, he realized in the time since their conversation he'd observed at least two kinds of Cherokee. One, mostly in the upper towns in the mountains, clung to the old ways. A second, in places near settler communities, were more or less civilized. Then there were individuals like Marian, sent abroad for education and display. Some returned to their old lives in disquiet, being neither traditional nor European but half and half. Others embraced European ways and married whites. Still others lived apart like she did.

But what Clive Burrows told him was something else altogether, representing a higher degree of assimilation than anything Abe had witnessed. Abe considered that the Cherokee of Echota were like *conversos*, those Portuguese Jews who swore allegiance to the cross to avoid torture, death, and expulsion from the land of their birth but who nonetheless prayed in secret in the sacred tongue of their fathers. Slowly, generation by generation, the Hebrew they murmured in shuttered rooms shed its meaning until only a handful of empty rituals remained. Eventually they prayed on their knees to Jesus all the week long and lit candles on Friday nights before taking a bit of bread and wine, but without comprehension. He pondered whether a similar fate would befall the Cherokee.

He also wondered if murderers seeking asylum in Echota lived together away from law-abiding citizenry or if they lived in common without stigma. Burrows told him there were few white people there, a missionary or two, a schoolteacher. He imagined the people of Echota kept slaves in small numbers, like most folk who didn't have plantations to run, maybe keeping a woman for kitchen help or a strong man for the heavy work in running a business. But why grant a slave refuge?

In London, there were slaves in the great houses, usually owned by men who'd made their fortunes throughout the Empire but most often in India or the Americas. It was fashionable for great ladies to flaunt their possession of enslaved footmen or ladies' maids, often black children gussied up in livery, wearing turbans that trailed exotic plumes and paste gems. They were more than toys but less beloved than milady's carriage horses, who were sold away with far less frequency and better comforted in their old age. Of the free blacks in London, many were runaways who lived in the worst circumstances, huddled together in fear of recapture, their movements about the city accomplished in the dark and in stealth. The Jewish ghetto was far from theirs. Abe himself had but glancing knowledge of black people before he came to Uncle Isadore's camp, and the ones he'd met in America through trade were universally slaves of the laboring kind, as far apart from London's tokens of wealth as stardust from the soot of a debtor prison's hearth. Even when he sold to them, he learned little of their hearts and minds. He saw they were shy of him, not knowing who he was, or what to expect. Because of his connection to the woman he loved, the idea of Jacob intrigued Abe mightily, yet he was alien to him, an unknown entity. The very idea of his life and death mystified. He hoped people in Echota remembered him well enough to answer all his questions.

After five days, Abe rode through a forgiving mountain pass, then along the Coosawattee River toward Echota. The Coosawattee was a broad river, its banks thick with trees and rocks and not much else. Every once in a while he came to an old campsite with a mound of refuse piled up next to logs half-buried in river sand, which he judged had been used by a Cherokee fishing party. As he got close to the city, he saw plantations in the distance, black slaves like so many crows dotting the landscape as they bent in the sun. They worked fields, or stirred steaming vats and sawed wood, all the various labors required to keep up fine estates. He noted smaller homes too, new ones jutting out from the sides of hills cleared of pine. He checked and rechecked his maps, thinking he'd wandered from Indian territory into white. It seemed not, but he was confused. Where were the huts, the tents and longhouses? Where the naked children playing at barbarous games?

When finally he entered the city of Echota, he nearly fell off his horse from twisting and turning about to take it all in. It was yet another bright sunny day. Glittering mountain light fell upon crisp manicured lawns, cultivated flower beds, clean streets, and immaculate two-story buildings painted in brilliant whites and yellows, arranged not in the haphazard assembly of the ragtag structures of Uncle Isadore's camp town, but in the kind of precise and dignified order that bespoke thoughtful planning and execution. In the middle of the town was a large public square, landscaped, bordered by a white picket fence, sporting a round, covered platform for public meetings and concerts, also benches and tables for the enjoyment of residents. Riding by him in the streets were Cherokee men with clipped hair, wearing tailored clothes and fine leather boots. They rode mounts under English saddle. Women walking along the well-swept wooden sidewalks wore fashionable dresses, bonnets, and gloves. Were it not for their chiseled faces, the high cheekbones and black eyes, the copper tint to their skin, Abe would have been certain he'd landed in a white man's town, and a wealthy one at that. Clive Burrows had not exaggerated. The European-styled men who had come to Marian's cabin, surprising him while he plucked fowl, were not half so finely attired or mannered as the least of these geniuses of imitation. He felt the dirt of his trek to Echota on his skin, heavy as a weight. He decided the first thing he must do was find a bathhouse or a hotel to clean himself up before he approached men better dressed and groomed than he to inquire about a refugee slave.

While Abe regarded with wonder the best hope of the Cherokee, more than a few Cherokee regarded him. Young boys jogged after him, racing to be the first to come alongside, and when two succeeded he queried them. "Boys," he said, "is there a hotel in this town?" They shook their heads in the negative. He halted Hart and the boys halted also. "Then where can a man clean up before he conducts his business?" he asked. The boys shrugged. "In the river," one said. Abe sighed, turned his horse, rode long enough to find a stretch of the river that was more or less private and washed himself in the cold waters of the Coosawattee while Hart grazed. He changed into the freshest of his shirts and brushed his britches with the same brush he used to groom his horse. All the while, he knew he was being watched and knew too it was the same racing boys, who perhaps intended to rob him. For all he knew, they had already.

Once he was dressed and as polished as he could get on the road, he made a show of going to a line of bushes to pee. He loosed his britches, leaned right, then left as if undetermined of the direction of his stream. The leaves of the bushes swayed in tandem with his movements—or rather against them—despite the fact that there was no wind. Abe smiled, then in an abrupt movement, pushed his hand into the leaves and grabbed a young Cherokee by the collar, hoisting the child in the air. Though the boy's face screwed up, his mouth twisting at its center, a vortex of discomfort, he uttered not a single sound. A brave one, Abe thought, just before the boy's compatriots dashed from the bushes to rush at his calves, kicking and biting them until he howled and fell, dropping his captive in his descent. The boy scooted up before Abe hit the ground.

There, from the dust, he stared up the noses of a ring of five panting, triumphant lads, none of whom were older than nine or ten. Each clearly debated in his wily mind whether to beat Abe further or let him be. While they hesitated, Abe got up and calmly brushed the dust from his clothes. He lifted up his pants legs to the knees to assess himself for marks and cuts, continuing to affect an unperturbed air. "So," he said at last, "had your fun?" None spoke. He continued. "When I check my saddlebags, will all my goods be there?" To a boy, they scowled, angrily, but still did not speak. Thinking he'd hit a nerve, Abe went to his kit and inspected everything. Nothing was missing. "Alright then," he said. "What were you spyin' on me for?" Again, none answered. Abe found himself irritated by their silence more than he was humiliated by their beating. He cursed under his breath, turned his back on them, and mounted Hart. Just as he parted his legs to give Hart a bit of a giddy-up, the boy whose collar he'd grabbed spoke. "We meant no harm, sir," he said. "We don't get many strangers here." Another boy, the runt of the group, chimed in. "Especially white ones."

This made sense to the peddler. As a boy growing up in a London ghetto, he knew the excitement a stranger in their midst caused. He'd joined a surveillance party or two of his own back then. Now that they were all friends, so to speak, he thought to ask the boys what he'd come to find out. "I've traveled here looking for information about a man, a black man. He was a refugee and his name was Jacob. Do you know of him, lads?"

The last was a superfluous question. At the name Jacob the boys exchanged a furtive glance, their chests rose and fell in unison, then in unison they dissembled, each in his own manner. One made a circle in the dust with his boot, another crouched, intensely interested in a particular pebble, which he picked up and examined closely, a third turned and studied the opposite shore of the river, and so on. Abe wrinkled his brow, mulling over their reactions. The boys seemed to fear speaking about the man Jacob. Perhaps he should not have asked so directly. Perhaps the man Jacob was even still alive. "Now, there's a thought!" he said aloud, startling the boys, who took advantage of his pursuant meditations to scatter into the brush. Abe continued to puzzle things out. If Jacob were yet alive, perhaps the boys sought to protect him from strange white men, in which case he'd best be careful how he approached further inquiries in town or ranks would close and he'd get no information at all. It felt a good strategy to pretend to be a messenger carrying an important message from a friend. Why not from Marian herself? He could tell a lot from the reactions of whomever he spoke with on that score. But he must be cagey, as cagey as his rascally mates had been back home when they set a trap for some unsuspecting booby. He would have to employ a technique they'd taught him. He thought of it as the Mile End Lie, paying tribute to the place where the Jews Walk of London ended and the sumptuous new homes of the middle class began.

The second time he entered Echota he went directly to the largest building on the street, and as it happened, the building he chose was the courthouse. He tied his horse at a hitching post and went up the steps inhaling the rich scent of fresh paint. Inside, he was met with a functionary sitting at a desk, quill pen in hand, scribbling in a ledger. His shoulders caved inward as if he'd carried a terrible burden from childhood and never quite set it down. Abe coughed. The man looked up, then froze, his pen in midair. So it was not just the boys, Abe thought. White men appearing out of nowhere in Indian territory was always cause for alarm. He made the first move, putting a smile on his face and going forth, his hand extended. "I am Abe Sassaporta," he said, "a friend of Clive Burrows."

The Cherokee stood, extending his own hand across his desk. "I am William Blackclaw," he said. "Clerk of the Court of Echota, capital of the Cherokee Nation."

They shook hands.

"I hope all is well with Mr. Burrows?"

Abe reassured William Blackclaw of the senior peddler's health and after a preamble of praise for the beauty and cleanliness of Echota, he told the clerk of the court he was looking for a man named Jacob, once a slave of the family of a woman named Dark Water, a man rumored to be in residence in Echota as a refugee. There was no question William Blackclaw was surprised by the inquiry. He blinked. He licked his lips. His jaw clenched. "And what sort of business might you have with this man?" he asked. Abe's heart quickened. He'd played the game well. Judging by Blackclaw's response, he was now certain Jacob yet lived. What a coup! he thought triumphantly. What a coup! At the same time he assured himself of the slave's resurrection, a fire flared within him, a fresh, hot desire not to just learn about this Jacob, but to see him, to speak with him, to discover all he could about Marian's role in the murder of Billy Rupert from that singular source. He dissembled. "I am honor bound to bring him a message from a dear friend," he lied.

William Blackclaw muttered "I see, I see" while going around his desk and putting on a frock coat that hung on a brass hook near the front door. Telling Abe to please make himself comfortable for a few moments, he hurried out the door. Abe watched the man's progress through an open window whose curtain fluttered gently against him in a sweet afternoon breeze fragrant with jasmine and pine. Blackclaw moved with determined purpose to a building kitty-corner to the courthouse and disappeared within it. He emerged in company of a severe-looking gentleman with a broad, bold face whose thick black hair was styled in the manner of an English dandy, short at the sides and swept up and over at the crown of his head. The two men chatted out the sides of their mouths while they crossed the street. Their eyes drew a bead on Abe's window, forcing him to draw back and away so they could not see him. After they reached the courthouse and entered it, all three men found themselves face-to-face nursing brittle smiles, insincere tones, and the kind of florid phrase that always connotes mendacity.

"How d'you do? How d'you do?" said the man pressed into service by William Blackclaw, presenting his hand for a good shake. "I'm told you come to our fair capital bearing tidings for a resident of ours, a man we much cherish and wish to protect. Forgive my zeal in wishing to shelter him, but as I say he is much valued here. Ah! I have not introduced myself! I am John Ross, humbly encumbered with the title Principal Chief of the Cherokee Nation."

How odd, Abe thought. The man had the look of a European in more than dress. But he understood his title to be equivalent of that of president or prime minister or even king, and so he clasped the chief's hand with two of his own and bent low from the waist over them as a sign of respect.

"Chief John Ross, I am honored to make your acquaintance," he said. "I am Abrahan Bento Sassaporta Naggar, a simple peddler, who brings tidings from a loved one of this Jacob. I wish him

no ill, only blessings. I beg indulgence but my oaths to Mari—
Excuse me, the sender of that message has held me sworn to
secrecy on her—excuse me, his identity."

Abe's half-utterance of name and confusion of gender was
entirely manufactured in the hope that Jacob's watchmen would
be more forthcoming if they thought a woman sent him regards.
It worked. The words "Mari" and "her" were but a heartbeat out
of his mouth when he noted that the lips of both the principal
chief of the Cherokee Nation and those of his clerk of the courts
tightened. Aha! he thought. The connection between his Marian
and this Jacob of theirs was now unquestionably confirmed by
their anxiety. Soon he would know much more, including why
the fiction that Jacob was dead had been spread far and wide. But
had he gone too far? He hoped the price was not their closing
ranks around the refugee. In the next moment, the men recovered
themselves, releasing their tension with supercilious smiles.

"Let me send a scout to find him," Chief John Ross said. "He
could be anywhere. Please wait."

The chief departed and William Blackclaw made efforts to
assure his visitor's comfort. He ushered him to a straight-backed
chair near a window and brought him a flavored water, although
flavored with what Abe could not tell, along with a fancy bis-
cuit on a plate suitable for high tea back home. After he ate and
drank he waited, and while he waited Abe viewed the civilized
Cherokee world, or at least the world Echota wished him to
know. He was most impressed. A certain gentleman introduced
as Elias Budinot came in wearing a visor and arm guards that
protected his sleeves from the ink that stained his fingers. Apparently, he was the founder and editor of the Cherokee newspaper,
The Phoenix, published in both English and the new alphabet

the man Sequoyah designed. He asked William Blackclaw for a list of pending newsworthy cases due to come before the court and questioned him on those that were. A Major Ridge appeared next, a man dark as a slave, white-haired, with hands raw and red as joints of meat. Like his name, he had the air of a man of battle. He walked flat-footed and heavy, his arms slightly raised as if prepared to strike. He took no notice of Abe until William Blackclaw introduced him in both English and Cherokee ending with the phrase "who seeks our Jacob to deliver a message." Once that intelligence was out, Major Ridge stared at Abe with eyes on fire, stepping up to close the space between them, stealing the air with his great pulsing nostrils. He spoke in Cherokee and Blackclaw translated. "Our Jacob you seek?" he asked.

Abe nodded. The man leaned in closer yet until Abe could smell the starch of his collar. He said nothing. It took Abe some doing to remain calm in the face of that scrutiny. But he managed.

After the silent inquisitor left, Blackclaw said, "The Ridge has the manner of a man born on campaign," then he smiled as if this explained everything. Abe began to grow bored and restless. Perhaps an hour or two passed. He left the clerk's office and took Hart to a livery, where he removed his coin from the saddlebags and stuffed it into his money belt securely that it not clink and rattle when he moved. He strolled the streets, popped his head into the tavern, which was empty, and returned to the court-house. Late in the afternoon, William Blackclaw packed up his desk, grabbed at his watch fob, glanced at the time, and frowned. Once he left, Abe stayed on waiting. Hard as his chair was, he fell asleep.

Some time later, the courthouse door crashed against the inside wall, waking him. Though there was yet an hour before dusk, the room had darkened and was full of shadows. Abe blinked. A young voice spoke out of the darkness. "I will take you to him," it said in a thin, reedy tone that cut through the fog of Abe's awakening.

It was one of the boys who'd accosted him that morning. His mouth was open, his nostrils flared, his chest heaved, and his clothes were stained with sweat. He shifted his weight from one foot to another impatiently. "Now," he said.

Outside the courthouse were two more boys he recognized from that morning. One held Hart, who was freshly bridled and under saddle. The other held a blond pony not more than 12 hand high dressed only in a blanket and rope halter. "Your horse has been fed and watered," the boy holding him said. Hart nuzzled his fist and the boy opened his palm. "He'll bite you if he thinks you've got something there," Abe warned. The boy shrugged. "He already has." The one who had awakened him mounted the blond pony while Abe mounted Hart. The other boys handed the first a double sack joined by rope, which he slung over his mount's withers. "It's not a long way," he explained, "but it's some distance. We need provisions." And he was off, his pony trotting determinedly down the street with Hart after him at a choppy clip.

They rode north with the mountains at their right hand for hours. It was a starry night with a three-quarter moon that bathed the way in an eerie light, making phantasms of trees and filling the brooks and streams with water sprites. Unseen owls chanted in anapestic hoots. The lad never once turned around to speak to Abe, seemingly dead focused on his role as escort, although at one point he removed his shirt and wrapped it around his head. This went on for two days. By checking his maps and figuring their speed, Abe thought they were somewhere in Cherokee territory by Tennessee. It would take him a week to get home. He began to doubt he was being led anywhere at all. Either the boy or the chief had surely hoodwinked him, he thought.

On the third night, at an hour Abe thought surely they would stop and sleep, they came to a settlement surrounded by wooden walls like those of a stockade. They entered its gates and rode down a street gone derelict, grown over here and there with weeds and bushes, studded with rocks. The street was lined with a row of blazing torches as if travelers requiring their light had been expected. By torchlight, Abe saw a smattering of buildings, not more than five in total, ghostly structures with sagging roofs and crumbled porches. Piles of sharp, shattered brick from toppled chimneys lay along their sides like the unraised quills of porcupines. Only one of the structures was lit from within, and it was there that the boy halted. "You go in now," he said. As soon as Abe dismounted and tied Hart to an ancient rail, the boy abandoned them, cantering off on his pony away from the torchlight and into the night. Hart shuffled his feet and twisted his neck in their direction. He seemed to want to follow them. Abe patted his poll. "I'll be just inside, my friend. Be patient. I fear the boy has taken us on a dodgy journey. Why would Jacob be here, in this godforsaken place? No doubt we'll be off soon. Though God knows how long it will take for us to find our way again."

So low were his expectations when he entered the house, it gave him a start to find not pranksters lying in wait to scare him off but rather a well-appointed room with hooked rugs and a tufted settee in front of a fireplace framed in tile. Perpendicular to the settee was a long table draped in linen and surrounded by wooden chairs with scrolled backs. Against one wall was a bookcase with beautifully bound books edged in gold. This was perhaps the strangest sight of all. If he were in a slave's home, who was this slave who could read? Surely not the slave of an Indian chief. His neck craned all about right and left, up and down taking it all in, and he could not help but ask himself aloud, "What is this place?" An answer issued from a doorway that led to an unlit room beyond, an answer unexpectedly voiced in an accent touched by London. "It is my home."

Abe whipped his head toward the voice. At the doorway, a hulking figure stood, obscured by darkness. Leaning to one side against the doorframe, it looked to be a fairly large man. Abe made out the line of his frock coat, his great boots, and the irregular halo of his wooly head. "Are you Jacob?" Abe asked, trying to keep the excitement from his voice. He held his breath, waiting for a response.

"Yes," the man said.

Until this point, all day long and all night too, Abe felt he had been held captive in one way or another by every Cherokee he'd met the last few days. His patience had been tried over and over throughout his long wait at the courthouse and longer journey to this moment. Perhaps it was simply a desire to seize control of events, but he decided to keep up the fiction with which he had inaugurated the events that led to his arrival at this island of luxury in the wilderness.

"I have a message for you," he said. "From one Dark Water, known as Marian of the foothills."

Immediately on hearing her name, Jacob cried out in a deep, anguished groan and leapt forward into the light. He put his hands on Abe's shoulders and stuck his face close to him. Abe nearly shrieked in fear.

"Who did you say sent you? Who?"

Abe's lips moved but no sound emerged. The man who passionately bore into him was a monster and a puzzle both. He was black-skinned, but a deep magenta gash scored the length of his forehead and two more his left cheek. The right side of his face was smooth and well shaped, his features handsome, even dignified. The eye was brown with flecks of gold, his mouth lush and full, his profile heroic. However the left side of his face was as grotesque as the right was noble. Where his left eye should have been was a twisted purple knot of scar tissue. On the same side, his cheekbone was pushed up and in by unknown calamity. The left side of his head was sparse of hair four inches in from his temple and then the hair sprung forth in clusters of white whorls like those that covered the rest of his head. The left side of his mouth twisted downward, and on his neck above the collar of his frock coat were jagged scars without number. His entire body tilted to the damaged side, which Abe soon discerned was due to a crippling of his left hand and leg, both foreshortened by crooks of the bone. The monster shook Abe's shoulders twice to snap him out of dumb surprise.

"Have you never seen a veteran of battle?" he barked at the peddler. "Have you lost your tongue? Who sent you, I asked. Who!"

Abe swallowed and said, "Dark Water, known to me as Marian of the foothills." The monster stared at him and then released him. He paced back and forth in an irregular, limping stride. Thump-tap, thump-tap, twirl about, thump-tap, thump-tap. His head bent downward in thought, his good hand grasped the deformed one behind his back.

"It is impossible," Jacob said at last. "She thinks me dead."

But he did not contradict him. At last Abe was certain beyond the slightest doubt. Dark Water and Marian were one and the same. Stuck now with his fiction, Abe kept it up.

"Someone must have told her otherwise," he lied.

The monster Jacob was in his face again.

"Tell me. What is the message?"

Jacob's good eye seared into Abe's with unrelenting demand. He had to come up with something or perhaps be killed. He remembered the first lesson he'd learned with the boys on London's streets. If you want a man in the palm of your hand, look to what he wants most, then give him a version of it. What would an exiled murderer want? He took a chance.

"She has forgiven you," he said, hoping the man would not ask next what she had forgiven him for.

Jacob rocked on unsteady feet. Clearly, forgiveness was the last thing he expected. He fell backward onto the settee, buried his face in his hands, and softly wept. Touched by the man's surge of emotion, Abe sat next to him, on his good side. "Thank you, young sir," the man said. He dropped his hands, leaned back on the tufted cushions, looked up to the heavens, then sighed a long, ragged sigh. He wiped his good cheek and eye with his sleeve while Abe watched, dry-mouthed, unable to anticipate what might happen next. Then Jacob said, "We should have a drink." He got up, left the room, and returned with a bottle of bourbon and two stemmed glasses of cut crystal on a tray. "Here's a habit I ne'er had in the old days," he said as he poured them each a belt. "How sweet Dark Water would grumble at this! Let's toast her anyway! Here, young sir, let us thank God and cheers to the forgiving heart of my sweet lady!"

Abe did not know if he was more amazed at being given fine liquor in precious glassware by a white-haired, hideous slave who was a murderer and refugee to boot or the fact that the same man had utilized the word "sweet" to describe Marian. The Marian he knew was many admirable things, but sweet was hardly one of them. Still, he clinked glass against glass, and he waited for his chance to interrogate the man—but gently, so as not to rile him.

"And how do you know her?" Jacob asked. One half of his face was alight with wild pleasure and crazed curiosity, the other half quite darkly dead. His tone was cordial, even warm, but Abe feared him. He looked as if he could turn beastly in an instant. Unsure what might set him off, he stretched the truth to breaking yet again.

"I am a peddler and I met her on my route. My horse and I were injured traveling by her cabin this spring and she cared for us both until we were well. I vowed to repay her kindness and what she asked was that I come to Echota and deliver her message, and so I have done, although what this place is, I do not know."

"It is old Chota, which, as you can see, was largely destroyed by the settler troops in their war against the British and then finished off after the settlers murdered Corn Tassel, that chief of Cherokee who came after Oconostota. After that, the clans moved their capital to Echota, or New Chota, but they left me here to care for the sacred graves of their dead. Yes, everyone is here. All their remains or some token thereof if the bones are elsewhere. Old Hop, Standing Turkey, Dragging Canoe, Stalking Fox. They're here, each one of 'em."

"Then how is it you live like this?" Abe's hand gestured over all the fine objects in Jacob's possession.

"The Cherokee love me for the things I have done. They bring me gifts often."

"And what have you done?"

The handsome half of Jacob's face smiled. He refilled their glasses, then shrugged modestly. "Oh," he said, "there are the things I did for Dark Water and the things I have done since for the nation, both in battle and here in Chota."

"What are all these things?"

"Ha, ha! You wish to hear the story of Jacob of Chota, do you? Ha, ha!" His laughter was at first sharp, then trailed off into a long, rolling sound with more than a touch of madness to it. He turned full face to Abe. The mad, rolling sound and the man's disfigurement combined to send a cold sweat down the peddler's spine. "Sit back, young sir, and I will tell you!"

Despite his fear, which increased with every swallow of the drink the mercurial Jacob imbibed, Abe's mind and heart burned to know how the fate of this pitiful person and that of his Marian were intertwined. He sat back.

JACOB

I was born a slave," Jacob said, "but not to the Cherokee. Ah, no. For them, I was a prize of war." The man's chin rose, as if this were a point of pride for him. "It was during the years of Dragging Canoe's war, which you might know as the Chickamauga. My mother belonged from the age of thirteen to a Georgia planter who was also my father. It was just the three of us on the farm along with his sister whose husband was dead, all of us working the rows and bringing in harvest when the season came. We lived as one family. Though my mother and I were slaves, no one remarked upon it. It escaped my notice at that tender age, out there in the backwater. I know my heart has always been different from other slaves. I lack the fear most have. And the humility.

"One day, Mother and I were walking to a neighboring farm with a basket of pies, as a holiday was coming and it was our gift. Usually, we would go visiting with our master, my father, him toting his rifle, but that day he was occupied with fixing a blade of his plow and we went alone. We walked unhurried through field and woods. I was just a tot and my legs short. Mama had no desire or need to carry me. We felt safe walking slowly there, at a pace I could manage. I recall we sang. What was the tune now? Oh, yes, 'High Frolickin' Tulips,' which was a ditty our master, my father, made up while in his cups. It was a funny song, and we liked to sing it. Little did we know that while we sang all the woods were swarming with Corn Tassel's men on the lookout to avenge his murder by a party of homesteaders from east Tennessee."

Abe interrupted. "Who is Corn Tassel?" he asked.

Jacob regarded him as he might an idiot child.

"Why, I just told you! Chief of all the Cherokee, that's who! An honest man, with no hunger for blood, respected by all, murdered by homesteaders under a flag of truce! Did they teach you nothing before you set out into Cherokee land?"

Abe made a small, noncommittal gesture with his open palms. He didn't see why he should be expected to know the name of a chief who'd been dead decades but neither did he want the man to stop talking.

Jacob sighed with dismay and continued. "Looking back, I wonder what was in my mother's mind. If she didn't know about Corn Tassel's murder, she must have known where she lived. It was an untamed land of no constant borders, traveled by greedy white men, as well as Cherokee, Creek, Chickasaw, and Choctaw too. Nearly everyone was seeking some sort of revenge—white men against Indian, Indian against white. How could she take a child on such a jaunt in such a time with nary a care? There is no answer. The point is we walked straight into the arms of a war party whilst singing, 'O *frolickin' tulip, where have ye been?*' One moment we were laughing, playing at nonsense, and the next we stared at the tips of dozens of arrows pointed from every direction at our vital parts. The men who drew them were not like those gents at Echota who sent you to me. No, they were warriors on horseback, both their mounts and their bodies painted in symbols of protection and for the drawing of blood. Some had scalps dangling from their war belts, fresh scalps dripping life."

"How terrifying for you," Abe offered. The other man shrugged.

"It happened long ago," he said, as if he were well over any such shocks. "Life is brutal in the calmest of times. In war, more so. But when you think on it, really not so very much."

There followed a quiet between them. Jacob seemed lost in recollection. Abe regretted interrupting him when he'd only just begun his story. Luckily, the man heaved a great sigh and continued.

"As I thought about it over the years, I realized it was the color of our skin that saved our lives. Had we been white and free, we might have been murdered, mutilated on the spot. Instead, we were seized as a commodity, sent to the back of the war party with its booty of horses and mules to be herded into Cherokee towns for disposition among the worthiest of them. Yes, for all that happened since, I've come to judge that the single moment in my life when it was good to be a slave.

"My mother was given to the bird clan and I to the deer. We were separated by clan and distance but could still see each other from time to time, at meetings of the General Council or at the annual games. In the beginning I missed my mother and wept for her. But if I could talk today to that poor child I was, I'd tell him, 'Stop your whining, it's not the worst slave arrangement! For all of that, you're a lucky chap!' I was the houseboy for a great lady of the clan, you see, a widow woman who had no children and grieved over it. I was petted and spoiled, as much as any young lad might be who'd been born by right and privilege to a grand station in life. After some years, when by chance I would meet the mother of my blood, I treated her with arrogance, which was a great sin, I admit, and no doubt the author of my cruel fate. Unlike me, she'd not been treated well by her masters, who'd worked her like a beast. I was proud and forgot, in fact, that I too was a slave, which forgetfulness turned out to be my undoing.

"The clans had gathered in this very place, old Chota, for a General Council. This was in former days, just before women left the corn to sit at spinning wheels, when Cherokee men had no business in the fields, and all a boy's talents were honed for the skills of his clan, for hunting, and for war. At the games, boys were tested. I was allowed to compete against sons of all the Cherokee as a privilege extended to my adoptive mother and I did so with a special passion, to honor her, whom I loved, and to prove I was the true son of her spirit. There was a footrace I won and at the finish line was my blood mother. She had become bent and ugly with hard work while I had grown proud and strong. She put out her arms to me to congratulate me on my victory. I was ashamed to acknowledge her in front of the princes of my clan. I curled my lip and nodded my head to her, but very slightly, and walked on to be embraced by the cheering members of the deer clan. I can still see how her face went blank, how she shrunk into her clothes. It pained me, but I made my heart hard. I told myself not to care."

For a time, Abe ceased to listen to Jacob, who rattled on about his boyhood achievements, his honored place in his adopted mother's household. Instead, he studied the man's ruination, considering it a just price for cruelty to a mother who had lost him through no fault of her own. Honor thy father and mother. The fifth of the Ten Commandments. Commandments one through four were about man's obligations to Ha-Shem. The fifth was the first about his obligations to his fellow man. It was that important. His own mother had sold him to Uncle Isadore, but did he stop honoring her? Of course not, although lately his letters to her had been few and far between. He must fix that, he thought, at the earliest opportunity. His ear returned to Jacob.

"I achieved manhood. From the time I was fourteen my desires were fierce. At the touch of a green leaf, the caress of a warm breeze, I became frenzied. I needed a wife. My deer mother noticed. That was when she bought Lulu for me." Jacob paused. He stared into space a bit, then poured himself yet another drink.

"Lulu. Poor Lulu. She was a girl fresh from the islands, hijacked by our warriors from traders bringing her inland to a rich settler who'd purchased her off the block in Charleston. She wanted me no more than she wanted to swim with snakes. The hillsides frightened her because nowhere could she see the sea. She desired only her mother back on the sugar plantation. For my own reasons, neither did I want to marry her. I told my clan mother I was insulted. I who had won prizes at the games, I who could run faster than the fastest of the deer people, should marry a slave! A slave who was no one! Our children would belong to no clan! My clan mother spoke to me then, plainly, without softening her words. Although her eyes were full of water, she shed no tears as she said, "Jacob, my love. You are as dear to me as my favorite horse, as the dog that warms my feet during my winter's sleep. I have protected and fostered you, it is true, because you are dear to me. But you are not of my blood, you share not my clan nor are you my heir, who is my sister. You are, alas, a slave because that is what the Great Beings made you. Forgive me if my favor has led you to think otherwise. You will marry who I tell you to marry." That day was a misery of my life, believe me. One that pains me still. At first I thought to rebel. Then Lulu was brought to me and I found her winsome. My lust overruled my pride.

"So. Lulu and I were wrapped in blue blankets and brought before the Council fire. I gave her a basket of deerskins and she gave me a basket of corn. Our blankets were removed. We were wrapped in a single white one and then everyone feasted. Time went by as it does. We lived with my deer mother and served her in the same way others served and revered an honored mother. We lived like everyone else. My wife was the only external sign that I was not free. We had no children. Some said it was because Lulu's womb went sour against me. But I think it was my seed that had no wish to sprout in her. Obviously, Lulu and I never twined our spirits but we came to accept each other. At first I thought that was all a man could ask."

Jacob paused, his breath came slowly. Abe wondered if he should prod him to continue. He looked to be lost in the past, in that marriage to Lulu, perhaps stewing in regrets, but just as he was about to offer his own thoughts on love, such as they were, the man picked up the tale.

"We were married ten years when my foster mother died of the smallpox. It was a great shock to everyone. First because no one had died of the white man's disease in many years and second because it was only she and four others who came sick. All of them were sent to a rocky place high in the mountains to die, lest they infect hundreds. My wife and I were also to go, to care for the sick until we died ourselves. But at last my clan mother proved her love for me. She insisted we stay with our village and at the proper time be given to her sister.

"All this came to pass. There was a day when news reached our town that everyone in the mountain place was dead and a party was dispatched to make sure they were buried and their place of death purified by fire. The next day, Lulu and I were packed up with the rest of my foster mother's belongings and taken on a journey to her sister, who had married a man from the wild potato clan. I wore a suit of European clothes and Lulu was in a typical serving girl's dress. Both costumes had been purchased from a trader for our presentation to our new owners to underscore our role and value. I, who was used to deerskins that brushed against the body like a second skin, hated them. Their fabric itched. They were hot. Each item was either too tight or too loose. It was the final blow to my honor. I cannot express to you the shame I felt to sit on the back of a wagon next to a sack of skins and pots, dressed up like a white man's doll, riding out of town under the cold gaze of my youth's companions, fellows I'd thought were my brothers if not by blood then at least by affection. To add to my suffering, Lulu sat beside me in tears, shaming me further.

"I was by then twenty and four years and while I could no longer ignore that I was a slave, I knew in my heart who I was and what I was worth. I was an expert hunter and my skill at running made me a favorite messenger among the people, even over the clan chief's son. My biggest dread was that I would be put to work for which I was not suited. Lulu, I know, was concerned her marriage to me might not be respected, that she might be prey to whomever we must now serve. Yet neither of us attempted to escape along our journey, nor did we speak of it in the night to each other. We knew if white men found us our fates could be far worse than anything we had experienced from the Cherokee. Several days passed as we traveled north by wagon, sticking to established roads, the old ones made by the Indian nations for trading with each other. It was a long and tedious route. At last we arrived at our new home. Two things about our new people were significant. The first is that they had one foot in the white man's world. The second is that they were parents to Dark Water."

Without explanation, Jacob fell silent. Given his disabilities, he rose more gracefully than Abe thought possible, and left the room and then the house. Abe could hear him pace, thump-tap, thump-tap, thump-tap, back and forth across the front porch. He rose himself to lean against the open doorway and watch the slave maneuver across the length of the porch, then swivel on one leg and pace back in the opposite direction. The effect was disturbing, like a twirling magic lantern, a phantasmagoria where one Jacob appeared, handsome, vibrant, alive, and thoughtful, then at the swivel, the monster Jacob supplanted him, his body twisted, his features horrific, moribund. The flickering torchlight from the street heightened Abe's discomfort until he reached out and touched the man, placing a hand on his good arm to stop him. It surprised him to note that Jacob trembled beneath his frock coat. Looking into the man's good eye, he realized it was deep emotion and not some damage to the nerves that agitated him. Abe's mouth dried. He was about to discover details of his beloved's life that had been hidden from him. "Jacob," he tried, "what happened between you and Dark Water's family?"

Jacob's eye had a faraway look. He turned toward Abe without speaking, without perhaps even seeing him.

"Ah, young sir. They loved me and then for a while they hated me. Because of her. Ah, everything is because of her."

"Tell me."

"Yes, yes, I will." He sniffed, removed a handkerchief from his pocket, blew his nose loudly, and wiped his face again. He glanced over at the place where Hart was tied to a post. "But we should put your horse up with mine. I think you will be staying the night."

Impatient as he was for the history about to be revealed, Abe agreed. It seemed Jacob required activity to calm himself, and besides, Hart had stood quietly for a long time, a state that could not last much longer. He nibbled at the knot that held him and looked to be considering methods of escape. The men took him around the back of the house to a three-stalled barn, where a dappled horse was comfortably confined along with two goats. Jacob's horse and Hart made acquaintance peaceably while Abe stripped him of saddle and gear, brushed him a little, put him in a stall next to that of the dappled horse where Jacob had laid fresh hay, and filled a bucket with water. The two men watched a bit to see if any equine disagreement might erupt, and when it did not, they made their way back to the house. All the while, Jacob talked.

"It was an accident of fate that the day we arrived at our destination was the very day of a great celebration. As we approached the farm of Dark Water's father, the road became crowded with Cherokee all traveling to the same place. They entered quietly from the woods at frequent intervals, appearing without warning to join our burgeoning group. The people were dressed in what I knew were the formal costumes of the nation. The men wore tunics and robes, leggings sometimes of buckskin, sometimes of blue cloth, and turbans. The important ones of them wore gorgets around their necks and long earrings. Others wore bells and feathers. The women were in gowns of doeskin that fell to their knees and blouses pointed like handkerchiefs along with many beaded necklaces. Their moccasins were like short boots. Although they both walked and rode on horses, not an item of European clothing was to be seen among them, which meant to me that their purpose was not only festive but of some importance beyond merriment or thanksgiving. To watch our companions on the road study us and judge us by our clothing unsettled me. I wanted to rip off my jacket, my shirt, that damned cravat, and put on my Cherokee clothes but of course I could not.

"Soon there emerged from the woods a grand plantation. Row upon row of cotton, tobacco, corn, and other vegetables, fruit trees, whatever this good earth can offer, lay on either side of the road, acre after acre. Black men and women worked them, their sweating backs bent perpetually in hoeing or picking. It was impossible to see their faces, for in all the time we rode by them none rose to watch us pass. Lulu and I grabbed each other's hands for comfort, as we wondered if we too would soon be pressed to hard labor. Finally, I was thankful for the trader's clothes we wore. With any luck, they would make us appear too refined for the fields. I ran through my mind all my skills and talents, trying to determine which would most appeal to such an estate, and I know Lulu thought of the cooking and spinning she had learned as a child of the islands. At the first opportunity, we would tell my deer mother's sister what work we were best suited for. Lulu told me later that as we came up to the great house along with the hundred or more celebrants of we knew not what holiday, her hand had gone numb from my squeezing it so hard.

"Once we arrived, our driver pulled the wagon up to the back of the great house, which was the typical plantation house you see in those parts, seeming to rise up from the center of a lush garden like a painted flower. It was made of brick and wood with a long porch in the front and stairs with wrought iron handrails. A Cherokee woman in a fringed buckskin dress with voluminous sleeves came out the back door to take account of the wagon's contents, instructing a cadre of black children where to take what. When she came to my wife and me, she said, 'There must be something in the house I can use you for. For the moment you may rest. It is a holiday here, for slave and freeman alike. Phineas!' she called to one of the children. 'Look after these two and look after them well. Later on, I'll decide how to dispose of them.'

"The child Phineas gestured for us to follow him to the row of slave houses. We rounded to the front of the big house, where we were interrupted by an extraordinary sight. Out of a great cloud of dust, a carriage appeared. It raced down the entry road. It was a marvel, an elegant, rich man's carriage rarely seen in the high places. It shone like the back of a raven at noon. Lanterns sprung from the four corners of its roof. The design of its cab boasted precious wood carved into marvelous curlicues at its hood and baseboard, all of it painted in gilt borders so that these alone dazzled the eye. Its doors were emblazoned with a gold-and-vermilion coat of arms. It was drawn by four galloping horses and a white man in livery drove it. It halted. Many of the people had gathered in the front gardens. All eyes were upon the carriage. Its door opened. The first to disembark was a white man, a tricorner hat trimmed in white fur upon his wigged head. He wore a three-quarter-length jacket embroidered all over with many-hued poppies, a ruffled shirt with long cuffs, tight knee-length britches of satin, and silk stockings resting in buckled shoes. He was like no creature I had ever seen. I imagined him a bird of some kind, a bird that had somehow lost its wings and been forced into the visage of a man by trickery or sorcery, but he was not the only stunning sight that afternoon. No, for after he departed the carriage, he held the door open with one hand and doffed his fur-trimmed hat with the other, bowing toward a person yet within the cab. Lulu and I held our breath, expecting we knew not what when from out of that dark chamber stepped the most magnificent woman I had ever seen, or will see, I am sure. She was a native woman of tender years, with black glistening hair arranged in the English style of the day, rolled and coiled about a copper face as lovely as the dawn, black eyes, strong nose, crimson lips, and her body! Ah! Her body was as ripe as the fields we had passed. Her flesh was molded by the confines of her English dress. Then as if she could stand it no more, the woman moved away from the carriage and raised her arms to the heavens. Her eyes, oh! Those eyes! How they flashed like the sun and stars combined as she lowered her arms to her hair and fiddled with it. Her hair fell down her back while hairpins scattered everywhere like arrows. Next, she loosed her bodice and her skirts and freed herself from them while the people about began to cheer, loudly, and chant in the way Cherokee chant when they are exuberant with joy. There she stood, in a circle of her cheering, chanting people, seven and eight deep they were, and she removed her shoes, her pantaloons and the coverings of her breasts, until she stood before us naked, whereupon she planted her feet, her face raised to the sun, radiant with delight, her eyes closed against its brilliance and shouted out a prayer of thanksgiving. 'Great thanks, Father Sun,' she cried out, 'for at last I am home!'

"The people cheered and chanted without cease. Dark Water's arms fell. She hugged herself and shook with laughter, the laughter born of a pleasure that excites and devastates. The woman who earlier met us at the back of the house then rushed forward in the company of several other women. They covered the naked beauty with a blanket, guiding her indoors. A man, whom I found out later was Dark Water's father, stepped forward. He wore trousers and a loose shirt in the Cherokee style, as well as many beaded necklaces and a tall hat that trailed the feathers of birds of prey. He announced that the feasting should begin. The Cherokee went forth to the tables where the feast was laid out. The popinjay from the gilded carriage joined them, but shyly although many extended him welcome. And after a time, Dark Water reappeared in the company of her mother. She was dressed modestly in her people's clothes, still startling as ever only at her ease. The people rushed to her side, enveloping her like a cloud until I could no longer see her.

"This was my introduction to the woman you know as Marian of the foothills. I had happened to arrive on the day of her return from her year in England. Her return, as I have tried to describe to you, was magnificent both in her appearance, in her pleasure, and in the elation of those who received her. How could I not love her after that? Any hope I had to possess her was doomed, I knew it. But from that moment, she lodged in my soul nonetheless, a nettle of bliss. Whatever else happened between us, I know that day was absolutely authored by the gods of fate. Ever after, I have loved her and prayed for no greater glory than to serve her. But life is odd, life is curious. It always answers our prayers but often in ways we never expect."

Again, Jacob paused. They had entered the house. He left Abe alone while he retired to the kitchen to prepare a supper for them. Abe gave himself to the tufted cushions of the settee, leaning back as his head swam with the images Jacob had given him, images of Marian young and naked, adored by all who saw her. Perhaps most of all, it seemed, she had been loved by the man in the next room clattering pots and crockery. The man who was half-monster, and who loved her still—that was plain to see. Abe dared to imagine Jacob whole and in his prime. Had Marian loved him back? Had she made the vows to Jacob that she repeatedly denied him? Why? What could a slave have offered her that Abe himself could not? Jealousy plagued his conscience, filling him with a sense of guilt that he should feel less than kindly toward a man who, from the looks of him, had suffered inconceivably. His mind shifted to other questions. Exactly who was this Englishman who had accompanied her on her journey to her home?

Jacob returned with two bowls of steaming stew, setting them on the dining table and gesturing for Abe to sit. "There's only vegetables and barley, I'm afraid," Jacob said while refilling their glasses yet again. He gestured toward his damaged face. "After this, it became difficult for me to chew and I've learned to do without meat." Abe took up his spoon and sipped. Perhaps he was hungrier than he knew, but the stew was quite good. "It's very tasty, Jacob, and doesn't need the meat," he assured, without bothering to explain that he'd dietary restrictions of his own, an explanation that led to long, arduous discussions in the pagan world and insulting ones in the Christian. In London, everyone knew he was a Jew by looking at his yarmulke, his beard, his fringes. In America, identification was often obscured. There were so many accents, so many types of dress from so many countries, who could keep them straight? Most settlers and farmers were of the same class, no matter where they came from and status was often determined purely by skin color. For his own well-being, he went along with custom, tucking in his tzitzit, trading his yarmulke for a cap, and rarely declaring himself. Life was easier that way.

The two men settled into eating. His thoughts distracted by jealous imaginings, Abe sipped at his meal while Jacob, due to his deformities, slurped noisily. Neither spoke again until the bowls were empty. Then Jacob pushed his chair back and continued from where he had left off.

"By a stroke of luck, Lulu and I were assigned positions within the household staff. Lulu found her place in the kitchen. Later, she was made attendant to the lady of the house. I was trained by the old man himself to be his valet. Now, that was amusing. Neither Chief Redhand nor I knew much about what it was a valet did. We only knew that grand men had them. I took care of his wardrobe, but not personally. When things were torn or stained, I gave them to one of the house women and she took care of it. He polished his own shoes, as he liked the smell of leather. Mostly, I walked behind him everywhere, carrying whatever needed carrying—even light objects, such as his lunch wrapped in a handkerchief if we were inspecting the crops, or an empty basket were we to go to the orchard and bring home a few pieces of fruit. The thing of it was Chief Redhand was a fake—he was no chief at all. He'd made a great fortune as a young man, selling beaver skins to the English. During the war with the Americans, it turned out he had a genius for finding the things an army on the move requires: fresh horses, victuals, and the like. This made him even richer. The whites acknowledged the gold he had amassed and called him chief. The people, because they are kind and saw that it pleased him, called him chief also but often with a smile. When the war ended, due to an accident of the new treaty, the Cherokee Nation managed to keep that portion of the land he inhabited. At the same time, men like Major Ridge and James Vann rose to prominence in the nation, along with men of mixed blood, modern businesses, and white man's ways. Chief Redhand bought one hundred slaves and installed his family in that big house he built. He purchased an overseer who knew what crops the Americans wanted and where to sell them. He turned hunting grounds into farmland and he prospered. But he was always in his heart a native of the hill country, and he wore his new ways lightly.

"The year before I came to them, he'd sent his daughter to England to civilize her. She was an untamed thing, a child of nature, more at home climbing a tree for birds' eggs, gathering medicinal herbs and plants, fishing, hunting, and riding than sitting in a parlor tatting cloth. After we became friends, she told me she tried to run many times in the days before they took her to the ship bound for London, but always her eldest brother, Waking Rabbit, or Edward as he became known after the chief made his fortune, found her and dragged her back. During the crossing she wept daily. Her heart longed for home. Not only that, she was kept in isolation for her safety's sake. The captain knew his sailors had noticed her and would have ravished her given half the chance. More than once, she thought to throw herself in the ocean. But after landing, she was installed in the home of an earl who looked to show her off to his friends and so increase his popularity. She realized soon enough how little would be expected of her in the English kingdom and she calmed. The earl had homes both in town and in the country. When she was in residence at the latter, she was able to put on the clothes of a boy and wander the valleys and hills, which kept her from despair. When she was in the town, she was celebrated for her beauty and men bowed to her. She found their attempts to seduce her laughable. She made a game of enticing and refusing them, just to pass the time. Then, after an eternity, her year was over. As I've told you, her return home was a triumph for her. She was the jewel of her clan. Not just for her beauty, but for her skills. From childhood, she was a genius at riding, at hunting, with the bow and the knife both. Everyone knew that when she was grown, she would become a *gighua*, a Beloved Woman, with a place on the General Council, honored by all. They say the year she was gone, the very land had suffered without her. The winter had been overlong. The summer, a summer of fire. Her people had missed her. She had missed them. She thought nothing would ever separate her from home again."

"Who was the Englishman who accompanied her?" Abe asked.

Jacob's jaw flexed. He waved his good hand dismissively. "A nobody. A painter looking to capture some scenes of the new country and its original peoples to make his name back home. We all posed for him. He insisted the Cherokee dress in the old costumes for their sittings, which irritated Chief Redhand. He

103

did it because he hoped the man would marry Dark Water. There was little chance of that. She found him ridiculous."

Abe wondered if the painter—who certainly must have created the painting he'd found under Marian's bed—was also the author of the letters she kept. It occurred to him that the black man in the portrait was Jacob, the black woman no doubt Lulu. He thought of the letters a little more. Why would she keep the letters of a man she found ridiculous? He thought to probe a bit more on the subject.

"Maybe that's just what she told you, Jacob," he said.

Jacob slammed his fist against the tabletop, rattling the candlesticks, the bowls, the crystal glasses, and the bottle of liquor.

"No!" he said. "I was there! Ridiculous was exactly right! How we laughed together about him! I was there, I tell you! Ridiculous!"

Because he was envious of the painter, because he'd had too much to drink, because he was yet young and not done with recklessness, dark emotion overrode Abe's finer sensibilities. He dismissed what Jacob said. He failed even to regard the strength of his reactions. He pushed a little harder.

"How can that be?" he asked, eyebrows raised in innocent conjecture. "When I was with her, I saw a painting of Dark Water with her family and you also, I must assume. Surely it was one of those you mention. It had a most prized place in her cabin. There was a box of letters that was somehow connected to the painting too, as I recall, although I didn't think much of them at the time. Perhaps they were from this painter?"

Jacob gave him his full face. One eye brimmed with rage. The good side of his mouth, reeking fumes of bourbon, snarled. On the opposite side, everything remained as it was.

"No! No! No! They can't have been! When finally we were able to get him back to England—and oh, what a trial that was!—there was nothing more between them. Nothing! It was me she spent time with, teaching me to read, to write, to speak like the English! Oh, golden hours! Not his! Mine!"

Jacob inclined his neck backward, imploring his God, no doubt, to deliver him from the idiotic skepticism of his guest. In the next stinking breath, he succumbed to the intoxication his anger had inflamed. His good eye rolled back in his head and he fell forward onto the table, his torso landing with a whack on the tabletop. Abe poked him in the shoulder. Nothing. The man's gone 'til morning, he thought. He stood and found himself unsteady. In his head, he heard his mother's admonitions. *Never drink with gentiles*, she'd say. *It will end badly every time.* Hoping he would not suffer too much in the morning from his indulgence, he staggered to the settee, collapsed, and fell into a deep, drunken sleep.

Morning came in bright shafts of light streaming through the open door of Jacob's house. Abe groaned and lolled his head against the tufted cushions, his back stiff, his stomach queasy. Jacob was gone, but the mess of the night's meal was yet strewn over the table. He got up with difficulty and made his way to the little barn, where he found his host feeding the animals. Jacob greeted him with good cheer, seemingly unaffected by the night's excess.

"Good morning, young sir!" he said. "You look some the worse for wear. No matter. We'll have a tea I make from flowers and herbs. You'll soon feel tip-top."

They went back to the house and cleared the table. Jacob brought in tea with bread. After a short time, Abe felt wondrously revived.

"If only the tea restored the memory," Jacob announced. "I can't recall where we were last night in my story." He shrugged. "Have you any idea?"

It might be best, Abe thought, to skip the painter for now. It was the murder he'd come to investigate. Why not take advantage of Jacob's foggy recollection?

"You were telling me how the son of Teddy Rupert was killed."

"Ah." Jacob looked around the room. "The matter that brought me here. The murder of that dirty, nasty creature." He slapped the table but not in the violent manner of the night before. Here was a gesture of finality, not anger. "I'm sorry, but I cannot tell you that. I have made vows."

"To whom?"

"To her. Of course to her. She would have to release me."

Frustration rose from the peddler's gut. This vow between Jacob and Marian made his journey to Echota less profitable than he'd hoped. Yes, he'd learned a great deal he didn't know before, but hardly as much as he wished. Much of what he'd learned he could have asked her directly. Instead, he'd wasted days that delayed his return to her. What bond could Marian and this monster share that would inspire such fidelity? Yes, Jacob loved her. He'd admitted as much. But could she possibly have returned his affection? Had they been lovers? And what of his ruination? Had his injuries been sustained in a battle with Billy Rupert or elsewhere? He had to know. So he asked.

"What happened to you, Jacob? What caused your scars and crippling?"

Immediately, he regretted his inquiry. It was rude, perhaps hurtful to whatever pride the man had left. But his scruples were irrelevant. Jacob was long past pride. His face, so ugly and so handsome at the same time, betrayed no emotion.

"When a fugitive is a resident of a city of refuge," he said, "he cannot be molested nor threatened by any man seeking justice or revenge against him. But for that, he must be at the front in whatever war is declared from the time he is absorbed by that city until his first kill. Afterward, he is absolved of his crime. He may go free. For me, my chance at redemption was the Creek War, where I served with the Cherokee at the Battle of Horseshoe Bend under General Jackson. It was a great victory for Jackson but not for me. Perhaps one of my arrows stopped our enemy, I couldn't know. Just look at me. I should be dead. I fell early in the battle and the Creek set upon me, burning my face, gouging my eye, crushing my limbs. At the worst moment of my extremity, I had a vision of my sweet lady. I saw her face as I was about to enter the arms of death and she told me to return to life. I've always struggled to please her and so I did." The good half of his mouth smiled. "What a life, eh? Should I tell you to thank her, young sir?"

He laughed a hearty, healthy laugh, not the anguished laugh of the night before. But it was his words, not his laughter that struck Abe as most significant. The slave murderer was asking him, in his way, to carry his story back to Marian, to deliver a message that he was alive, if not exactly well. That meant Jacob would not be going to her himself. A wild, self-indulgent thought struck the young man's mind, hot and sharp as a bolt of lightning. If Jacob had been Marian's lover, he would rush to her now that her blessings had been delivered. If he chose to remain where he was, then his devotion to "his lady" had never been of the carnal sort, or if it had, it had faded beyond reawakening. How obvious! How marvelous! Abe made certain by asking him directly.

"Don't you wish to tell her yourself, Jacob?"

"Oh, young sir. I am never leaving Chota. Never."

Abrahan Bento Sassaporta Naggar felt all ill will toward the man wash away from his heart and mind. Whatever Jacob meant to Marian once upon a time, he looked to be staying exactly where he was, and whatever had transpired between them would remain in the past. The Englishman, whoever he was, had returned to London twenty years before. Abe's heart swelled with delight. As far as he knew, he was the last man standing. Marian would remain his and his alone.

AT UNCLE ISADORE'S CAMP TOWN

There was much for Abe to ponder on the way back to Uncle Isadore's camp. First he prepared an announcement to his uncle that thanks to a beneficent God and a miraculous season, he was able to pay off his debt. This was a delight. Next were multiple rehearsals of the far more glorious speech that would win Marian's agreement to join him in a place where the treacherous world could not reach them. Abe's visions of that euphoric event changed according to the day's weather, as he imagined her assent to his plans in the rain, in the sun, in the fog, in a shower of turning leaves, in the day, and in the night. Always, matters ended in an avalanche of sighs, the most ardent of embraces, and the deepest kiss. With utter confidence, he puzzled over the logistics of transporting Marian and their possessions into the virgin wilderness. Hart had an earful of his practical concerns. As they neared the camp, his plans took definite form.

"This spring, I managed through my skill at packing to burden you with a bonanza of wares, dear Hart," he said, leaning forward to pat the sturdy horse on his neck while they walked the woods, "a load happily made lighter quickly, first by the accidents and misfortunes of our starting out, and then by my equal skill in salesmanship." The horse snorted agreement, as if remembering. "Perhaps when we set out for our new lives, you might pull a cart or a wagon of some kind, with Marian's mount as your teammate, eh? You two can haul everything and us too. What do you say to that, my boy?"

Apparently, Hart found the idea unappealing as he suddenly broke into a rapid trot that stole his rider's breath and thought. Abe did not try to slow him down, knowing by now that when certain moods struck the beast, resistance was useless. Better to trust his good sense and hope for the best. By the time he slowed again, the peddler was elated by both the thrill of their jaunt and the proximity of the camp. They halted by a clear, cold stream, where Hart took a drink and Abe freshened up, combing the hair that stuck out from under his cap with his fingers, washing his face and hands. He separated the commissions the retired peddlers expected from his hoard, stuffing that bundle of coin and bills in his trouser pockets, then remounted and straightened his back. Proud and happy, he rode into town with his head high, nodding to the people he passed, all of whom seemed to regard him with a curious excitement. He attributed their interest to the handsome figure he cut astride the noble, high-stepping Hart, who tossed his head and whinnied their approach. He rode directly to Uncle Isadore's office, tied Hart to a post, and, slinging his saddlebags over his shoulder, ascended the front steps and threw open the door.

As usual, Uncle Isadore sat behind his large, imposing desk imported from England, an enormous dark affair with thick legs each terminating in the claw of an eagle strangling a ball. His winged chair had a back as high as a king's throne and was covered in a rich purple damask. There was a bookshelf behind him stuffed with ledgers, a hooked rug on the floor, oil lamps here and there, as well as a few uncomfortable chairs for visitors. Everything about the room was designed to intimidate. Until this moment, the design had worked on Abe, but suddenly all fear was banished by the young man's joy of accomplishment, and love, and hope. He felt a surge of affection for the bent, bearded figure holding a quill in his ink-stained hands, sitting in a stream of light from an open window like a patriarch of legend. With exuberance, he swung the saddlebags from his shoulder and slammed them emphatically on the desktop. A spiral of dust motes ascended like smoke to form a halo around his uncle's head.

"Uncle! I am home! I am triumphant! Count your money, pay me my salary, and declare me released from obligation!"

He stood back, rocking on his heels in anticipation. Uncle Isadore looked inside one of the saddlebags and scooped out the moneys within. A thick spray of coin glittered in the light. Fans of cash enfolded the coin in a soft, voluminous embrace.

"I am amazed, my lad," Uncle Isadore said. There was admiration and warmth in his tone. Abe smiled, basking in avuncular appreciation. "I was impressed beyond measure by the wares you collected, but this! Nephew, you are one revelation after the other, a true branch of the family tree."

He rose from his desk and walked around it. He put a hand between Abe's shoulders, then clapped him on the back. "Good fellow," he said, "Good fellow. I know I was hard on you when you first arrived. You must understand I had my reasons. This life is not for everyone. The strong survive, the weak are swallowed up. I took you on because your mother wrote me that you lacked direction and that you'd fallen into idleness, perhaps even petty crime. I did it for her before she saw you in the hulks then off to Australia."

Abe interrupted him to defend himself. "Uncle. You cannot know what it's like in the ghetto these days. It's likely changed since you were there. Without a few games up his sleeve, a lad would starve, and his mother too."

He could not tell if Uncle Isadore believed him or not. The older man waved his hands about, dismissing his excuses.

"Be that as it may, I was skeptical, I will admit! I was not sure if I might not have to ship you back to her. But the past is past. You've proved your mettle. So!" He paused to catch his nephew's eye and hold it. He raised his bearded chin in preparation of a grand announcement.

"I'm going to give you a promotion!" he said, smiling. "No more wandering about. You know that shop I've just built in Greensborough? No mere trading post but an emporium, the first of its kind, highly anticipated. I'm thinking I must do no less for you than make you manager. Eh? Eh? After all," he concluded with a wink and a nod, "you are my blood."

It was not the reception Abe had imagined. Like every father-less boy that ever was, praise from an older man, his chief, you might say, a man brimming over with paternal authority, was a drug to him. He inhaled deeply, greedily, taking it all in with delight. Yet he demurred.

"Uncle," he began, "your offer humbles me. You might well ask yourself, how would I, a pup, a greenhorn, an ignoramus of all things American not two years ago, succeed so? I'm telling you, it was because I had a motivation. First, to be free of debt . . ."

Isadore laughed, clapped him once more on the back, then sighed in amusement, as if Abe had delivered a fine riposte.

"Free? You think you're free? Oh, my lad, yes, you've made a fortune but your debt is not yet paid."

Abe's jaw dropped. His brow wrinkled. Stunned to silence, he waved his hands over the pile of money on the desk. His uncle grinned at him and nodded his head encouragingly, ready to hear what great joke might come out of his nephew next. After a few torturesome moments, the old man showed mercy.

"Forgive me, Abrahan. I have a surprise for you, a marvelous surprise!"

He took Abe by the shoulders and turned him toward the corridor that led to his camp-town living quarters. With a great flourish of his arms, he gestured welcome to a dimly seen figure who advanced slowly into the light. "I present," Uncle Isadore said, beaming with the self-satisfied pleasure of a master of surprise, "your mother!"

Susanah Naggar Sassaporta, a short, stout woman of forty years, dressed in old-country black, a mantilla pinned to her well-dressed wig, her plump little hands stuffed into black lace gloves, her great browned-butter eyes running over with joyous tears, stretched out her arms as she toddled her way into those of her beloved and only child.

"Mother!"

"My son!"

Uncle Isadore came up behind them to hug them both together. There were damp eyes all around. Abe inquired about her health and her journey. Susanah waved all that aside and reported on the welfare of the friends of his youth and the gossip of his old neighborhood. She told him she'd been waiting weeks for his return from his rounds. How worried she'd been! What had taken him so long? Abe blushed and muttered something about rains and overflowing tributaries, which was the best he could come up with on the spot. Later, they settled at table to a dinner Susanah prepared, featuring as many Ladino delicacies as she could create out of the foodstuffs on hand. She'd brought spices from home, saffron, cardamom, paprika, and piripiri. Their aromas did a trick. The men were effusive in their praise. Combined with a bottle of Madeira she'd also packed away, they sunk into a haze of nostalgia and familial warmth. Abe thanked his uncle for bringing his mother to him. The drink enlivened his veins and his nerve. "Although," he dared to continue, "I'm not sure the price of such a delightful surprise should be the renewal of my debt!" His mother sat at the head of the table and the men on opposite sides. Abe took up his mother's hand, kissed it, and asked, "How much more have you decided I owe you?"

Isadore raised a palm and patted air. "Now, now. You mustn't feel you're in a hurry to pay me back. Debtors are debtors but family is family." The merchant took Susanah's other hand and kissed it also. "I could hardly allow this dear woman, my beloved little brother's widow, to withstand the rigors a strong young man could endure on the crossing. Nay, I secured for her a private cabin on a fine French vessel transporting dignitaries to Washington. From there, she rode a carriage, stopping at the best inns along the way. Yes, I spent three times the price of your journey, my lad!" Abrahan Bento Sassaporta Naggar blanched, a fact that did not go unnoticed by his uncle. "Don't worry, nephew, your salary as manager will be handsome and we'll negotiate additional commissions on your bottom line. That will be a treat, eh? I look forward to witnessing your skills in haggling! Susanah!

This boy of yours is a marvel to judge by his rapid advancement. We are all so proud!"

Abe's head swam with a confused mass of contradictory emotions. He loved his mother. Whenever his thoughts left the subject of Marian, they often drifted to her. He'd worried about her welfare without him, missed even her nagging. Watching her bustle about serving dinner, hearing her hum his childhood lullabies over the pots in the kitchen, seeing her dear features cast in teary jubilation moved him greatly. At the same time, he felt his reunion with Marian drift further and further away. Their escape together into the frontier, just a few hours ago so close he could reach out and grab it with one hand, retreated to a spot floating above a distant, murky horizon. A grain of desperation lodged in his throat, making it difficult to speak.

Uncle Isadore continued. "Now, where should you live? Obviously, we cannot have your mother in the barracks. And my humble abode here in the camp is too small for all three of us plus the housekeeper. You are needed in Greensborough, and posthaste too, I might add. Even as we speak, the shelves are being hung, the townspeople gather at the windows ogling our every move in preparation for the grand opening. Oh, my lad, we are going to make a fortune, a fortune! So. What I have decided is that you, your mother, and I shall live together in my house in Greensborough until one of your own can be built. I suggest it be large enough to accommodate the wife and children you will have one day—one day soon, I might add, if I judge the light in your mother's eyes correctly! Of course, this will add to your debt as well, but, my lad, you will be with your mother and me in Greensborough a long, long time. And I remind you, I have no heirs but you. None. It will all work out in the end!"

Throughout this speech, Abe's mother clapped her hands, raised her eyes to the heavens and muttered "*Baruch Ha-Shem*" at every new turn in Uncle Isadore's road map of the future. Meanwhile, the grain at Abe's throat swelled to a sizeable pebble. What was he to do? How could he rend the tender flesh of their reunion by shouting "No! No! No!" as he burned to do?

With cloaked impatience, he waited until his uncle had retired, leaving him alone with his mother. The two sat near the fire, their hands clasped, knees pointed toward each other like lovers. He brought her hands to his lips for a tender kiss, then gave her the deep, soulful look that worked wonders against her will when he was a child.

"Mother," he said in as velvety a tone he could muster, "I left you as a boy and here in these United States of America I have become a man."

She agreed.

"Oh, my darling, beloved son, I can see that! Your face has lost its fullness, you've a lean look about you now. Your shoulders— who would have thought it possible?—have grown broader yet. Your hands"—here she kissed his knuckles briefly before putting her cheek against them—"are no longer the smooth hands of a city boy, but the rough ones of a man who toils. And there is something else, something in your demeanor, in your very walk that speaks of maturity." She took her cheek away from his hands and gazed up at him in melting adoration. "You are the image of your father. If I died tomorrow, I should die happy to join him, having left you as his mark upon the living world."

"Mother! You shouldn't say such a thing! Even in jest."

She nodded vigorously. The mantilla danced. "I'm not jesting. I mean every word." Without pause she went on to extol the virtues of her late husband, Abrahan's father, praising his industry if not his luck, as they were never rich, and praising also his piety, his fidelity to the laws of Moses. "I'm not sure how you can do the same in this half-formed place," she finished up. She glanced at his waist, registering that his tzitzit no longer dangled from it. She frowned at that, but then looked up at his head and noted his ever-present cap. She sighed and continued. "I'm hopeful that you at least say your prayers three times a day, eat only of the meats we are allowed, cease work on the Sabbath, and keep the holidays."

Abe blushed. He'd tried hard but succeeded in doing maybe half of all that and as the years of his sojourn in—as his mother put it—this half-formed place wore on, so his resolve wore out. At the same time, he knew he was different from the godless men at the camp and the Christians also. "I'm still a Jew," he said, dismissing her concern with a wave of his hand. He introduced a subject more urgent, the one that pressed a thorn into his heart. He spoke in a low voice in case his uncle was listening from the next room. "Look. Mother. I appreciate Uncle Isadore's offer to me. It's a great honor. But I've a different vision of my future here. It's a big country, big enough to host a million dreams. Let me tell you mine."

Alone together since his boyhood, they had always been confidants of a sort. He told her everything, or rather everything he thought prudent. There was the first time he came home with a fistful of coppers after guiding a stranger through the streets of the ghetto, for example. He took the visitor the long way around three times over as his mates had taught him to do for the sake of a larger tip. He'd given his mother all the proceeds but neglected to tell her the details of his earning them. On this occasion, he thought, maybe he should tell her everything. Like he said, he was a man now. His fate was his own. He didn't expect her to embrace every aspect of his plans straightaway. But he was pretty sure she'd have an open ear and listen to reason.

He had her attention. She leaned forward to hear him better. Her features were alert and open, her hands clasped tightly in her lap. "There's a woman," he began, and her browned-butter eyes widened, her mouth grinned, her head nodded encouragement, and again the mantilla danced. "I love her. She is my destiny. She lives in the countryside, in the foothills, where she is alone, without male protection, although I'm not sure how much she needs it." His mother's cheery expression slowly crumbled. Her brow creased. Abe regretted his description. Why had he expected his mother to consider a woman on her own in the wild without a father, brother, or husband with anything but suspicion? He pressed on, quickly. "My desire is to take her west, to start afresh, where memories of the past will lift from her soul. . . ." His mother leaned backward while a hand went to her mouth to pinch her lips. Damn his hide! Another misstep! He pushed on. "And I want you to come with us. Without a doubt, without a doubt. I was going to send for you once we were established, but no matter. Now you'll come along at the beginning. It will be an adventure, Mother. Think of it!"

By this time, Susanah's hand had formed a fist with which she beat her breast while her eyes rolled up toward the ceiling. "What fresh hell is this?" she implored the heavens. "Why have You done this to me?" Her son reached out to steady her, his features full of concern. What a fool he was! To think his mother, a woman of little imagination, would take his news calmly! He would have prepared her had Uncle Isadore not stolen that option from him. He would have written brilliant letters in which he revealed, bit by bit, his domestic ambitions. He would have created in her mind a wholesome image of Marian as a loving, accomplished daughter-to-be. Instead, under the pressure of his mother's physical presence and Uncle Isadore's presumption of authority over his life, he'd bungled everything. In the midst of his remorse, his mother shuddered beneath his grasp. Frustration erupted from her through clenched teeth, making her voice more serpent's hiss than human inquiry.

"I don't suppose there a chance on earth this shameless cast-off from her people is Jewish?" she asked.

"Mother, she is neither castoff nor shameless," he said firmly, although as soon as the words were out of his mouth, doubt flickered over his face as clearly as light at a breaking dawn. He considered, Marian had granted him her favors without trouble. There remained much he didn't know about her, including why she lived alone and the details of her relations with her people. For all he knew, she'd been driven from them by a band of angry wives. Aware how easily his mother could read the tenor of his thoughts, he took a deep, defensive breath. He shored up the only thing he did know: he loved Marian to distraction. His features acquired a madman's intensity. There was nothing to be done. He'd opened the subject, he'd got in the thick of it. Maybe it would be better if the whole truth were laid bare. Like pulling a tooth or ripping a soiled bandage off a wound, some things were better done quickly. Let the consequences be out in the open and then they could begin dealing with them. What was the worst that could happen? That his mother and uncle might banish him? Well, alright then. At least he could get back to Marian without further delay. He could write his mother letters. She'd come around over time rather than live without him. He was certain of that. Distressed, disappointed, yet undaunted, Abe went for broke.

"She is Indian," he said, "a Cherokee."

It was too much. His beloved mother puffed up. Her neck grew longer, her chest swelled, her nose, her mouth, her eyes somehow enlarged. She got up, covered her ears, then quit the room, slamming doors as she went.

The next few days were the most miserable he'd spent in America. Self-loathing suffused him. He recalled how he'd criticized Jacob's arrogance with his mother. Honor thy father and mother, he thought. What a hypocrite I am. He'd been an idiot to think Susanah, a greenhorn who could not know how the New World worked, the way it encouraged a man to break free of the chains of the Old, would support him. He'd completely ruined their reunion out of selfishness. How much better it would have been to move slowly with her, bit by bit! But no, his reckless stratagem had won out. What a disaster! His mother had gone cold on him. He trailed after her, pleading his case while she froze him with stony silence and frigid stares. He persisted. Her response was shivering fits and tears. As might be expected, she enlisted the aid of his uncle, spilling all the details of Abe's fixation to him. Without delay, Uncle Isadore cosseted him in his office, warning him that his amorous plans might kill his mother, and who could live a happy life with his mother's blood on his hands? "It's all doomed, you see, so best snap out of it, lad," he advised. "Mind, I'm not entirely unsympathetic. I understand your predicament. What you've got is a good case of American fever. It's not a shameful thing. It happens to many new arrivals. They step off the boat, look around, and breathe

the air of liberty. It intoxicates. It infects. A man believes he can divest himself of the past with nary a care and begin anew, however he likes, here in the native land of crackpot fantasies. Take it from an old hand, one who cherishes you as a son. Freedom comes at a price, always! When the fever breaks and the fantasy shatters, many a broken man is left. This Cherokee woman of yours. Believe me, she is using you and will dispose of you rudely when she is done."

Abe resisted all argument. He made his rounds of the old peddlers and dispensed their commissions. Quietly, he bought up a few items he'd need for his new life in the wilderness and stored them away. At last there was nothing but familial obligation to hold him back. Up until his mother's arrival, such responsibilities seemed light and careless things. No longer. Daily, he suffered a barrage of his mother and uncle's criticisms and pleas. He chafed at their attempts to control him as mightily as Hart ever did against his. But with an honest son's devotion, he waited to leave the camp as long as he could bear, hoping they would notice his intransigence and give up. They did not. They redoubled their efforts.

One night he entered his uncle's office with new points of view he felt might convince him to support his chosen path. But from outside the living quarters he heard the two of them, uncle and mother, plot against him. Flattening himself against a wall just outside the entry, he eavesdropped on Susanah Naggar Sassaporta's latest ploy. "We should bring young Ariella Levy here as his bride. A good Jewish girl who's not married yet. He always liked her. He told me once the joy of his life was the day she consented to hold his hand. I know my son. He won't be able to resist. Nor could he hurt such a darling creature by disappointing her." Uncle Isadore agreed. "Yes, yes! For all his faults, he's a gentle soul. He would not break a young girl's heart. It could work! We'll tell him in the morning."

Abe withdrew, stunned by this most unexpected twist of fate. How could they do this to Ariella, an innocent girl? How could they do this to him? He sat as long as he needed to recover himself, then, after obtaining a paper and pen from Uncle Isadore's desk, he wrote the following note:

"*My most beloved mother,*" it read, "*I think it best to allow you a little more time to consider everything we've discussed. I remind you again that when I left London, I was a boy satisfying his mother's wishes for his future. But here in this new, bold country, which struggles to discover its identity and purpose under the Eye of heaven, I have discovered myself. I am a man in love, Mother, and the last days have changed nothing. I will do everything and anything to preserve and protect the object of my affections. I am off now to speak to her and, hopefully, to bring her back here, to your side, where you two will be, if not mother and daughter, sisters. Yes, sisters. Why not? When you meet her, Mother, you will find her much like yourself, yes, yes, in industry, in independence, for have you not both survived a hostile world on your own? After you have so bonded, we'll talk about where we three shall live.*"

The letter went on like this for some pages. Abe grasped a thousand straws inventing fresh persuasions for the future comity between Marian and Susanah Naggar Sassaporta while justifying his immediate withdrawal from the camp. After a warm and loving conclusion, he encouraged her to make herself comfortable in Greensborough until his return. As an afterthought, he scribbled an additional note to his uncle informing him that he was not abandoning his responsibilities toward his mother or his new debt, merely delaying both. He wished him well on his new retail venture in the town and suggested that his mother might be of some use in the store as well as in the old bachelor's home. He stopped short of reminding him that he'd got his mother over the sea without consulting her son and, without consulting that son further, he'd figure out what to do with her now she'd arrived. But he thought it.

He went to the stables to fetch Hart. He found both horse and Irishman awake, the former as he never slept much, like the rest of his kind, and O'Hanlon because he was at hard labor caring for a poor mare plagued by dozens of hives from an allergic attack. He covered her hide in a mixture of mud and something that smelled sweet, like peppermint, swabbing the stuff over each lump while whispering in her ear, "Poor girl, poor girl. Help's here now. . . ." On seeing Abe, his voice went boisterous.

"Well, look who's arrived at last! The wanderin' hawker too busy to visit his mount days on end. It's much surprised I am the beast looks as well as he does despite you."

Abe grunted in response, not in the mood to explain himself. He gathered his horse and belongings, brushed Hart down, and saddled him. The horse interrupted his efforts more than once to nibble lightly on the brim of Abe's cap.

"I see he likes you well enough," O'Hanlon said.

At that moment, Abe felt the only friend or family he had in the world was the horse beneath his hand. "We like each other," he said. He led the animal out the door and mounted up. "Thank you for caring for him, O'Hanlon. I was at family business and time got away."

O'Hanlon grinned. "I've seen your family business. Your mam's a fine woman. She'll be tossin' the black soon enough, don't you worry. There's plenty in these parts be thrilled to have her."

Abe regarded him as he might the most brainless twit. Imagine. Susanah Naggar Sassaporta snapped up by some American bumpkin! Never, thought Abe. Never! He dug his heels into Hart's side, giving O'Hanlon a tip of his hat as fare-thee-well. They trotted into the night, rode a few hours and rested, rode a few more hours and rested again. Unlike his last trip to Marian's side, there were no extraordinary events, neither screams nor scent of smoke nor blood in the air. When the daylight came, all was quiet and beautiful around him. The trees barely rustled. Birds sang sweetly without the piercing caws and death cries of predators and prey. Cicadas chirped. The sun rose red in a cloudless sky while dew glistened from the blossomed heads of wildflowers. The mountains in the distance were like a great gray cloak draped across the earth in folds of protection. It was the perfect setting for the fancies of a young man in love, on his way to his beloved, escaping the bondage of family. He imagined Marian tending her animals, shucking corn in the front yard. She'd jerk her head up at the slightest unfamiliar noise, scanning the horizon, hopeful of his approach. When she saw him, she would rush to him, her arms would enfold him. Unable to wait, they'd make love on the grass under the gaze of the sun. Such daydreams warmed him. His cheeks were always flushed.

At last he was but a few minutes from her cabin. His heart raced. His body tensed. He emerged from the woods and crashed immediately into one of the secret, protective barriers they'd erected together all around her home, setting off a loud clattering of bones and pieces of pottery as alarm. Hart spooked into a sidestep. His hooves found a second trap. A yet louder ruckus rang through the air coupled with a cry of equine panic. The horse reared, flailing at air with his front legs, struggling to free his rear hooves where the contraption's vines wound tight around his ankles. Abe held on to his neck to keep from sliding off his back while a barrage of arrows sped past his ears. "Marian!" he yelled. "Marian! It's me! Abe! Your peddler!"

Hart's legs crashed to the ground. Understanding that his movements only entrapped him more fiercely, he went still. Abe righted himself. Marian ran to their side and the two were reunited in a flurry of apology and excuse.

"I forgot about the traps," he said.

"I wasn't expecting you. There've been more raids," she explained.

"Hart's usually more steady," he offered.

"I could have killed you!" she cried out.

All the while, they worked to free Hart. Once all was well, both quieted and regarded each other.

Marian seemed older to him. She wore her cares upon her brow, there was a gauntness to her cheeks and in her limbs that he'd not discerned before. Her breeches looked worn. There were new patches at the knees. Abe felt a keen desire to relieve her of all concern, to make her smile. He dismounted, took her hand. They led Hart to the place where her horse and goats grazed, removed his tack, and, for the time being, left it in a heap on dry ground nearby. Arm in arm, the couple proceeded to the cabin and once in it, embraced with the comfortable passion of old familiars. Abe was the more ardent lover of the two, but he did not notice. Afterward, they lay in her bed side by side, looking up at the rafters, when Marian confided her most recent troubles to him.

"For a time this summer, the settlers made raids against my people daily. In our villages, in our fields, even at the Christian churches some embrace. Our warriors take revenge, as they're allowed under the white man's law. Did you know that? In our treaties, it says we may punish those who violate our lands however we see fit. We are a nation. The United States agrees we have the same right of self-defense every other nation has. But it doesn't work. My life's trials have taught me all revenge inspires is more murder and treachery." Her chin lifted in a prideful way. "In this cabin, I try to live a good Cherokee life and ignore the settlers. For many years, I've been too well hidden for anyone's notice. But now there's gold down in Georgia, on Cherokee land. The governor of Georgia tries to squeeze us out by law. More Cherokee flee their ancestral lands at the point of his guns every day. Meanwhile, the settlers and gold hunters swarm everywhere, in Georgia and even here, looking in every stream, in every cave for that rock they worship more than God. Three found me this summer."

"What happened?" Abe asked, thinking more of the revenge on Billy Rupert that he suspected had led her to isolated independence than her recent encounter with settlers. She shrugged as if the answer should be obvious.

"They approached me, guns drawn. I killed them with my hunting bow. The traps had warned me. It wasn't hard. Afterward, I scalped them and burned their flesh. I hung their scalps from the trees and I put their bodies near my fields to scare off others. So far, it's worked." She lifted herself up and, leaning on an elbow, touched his face with her free hand. "I confess, I've been on alert ever since. The enemy feels too close. I don't sleep. Otherwise, I would have seen who you were and not shot at you.

Having shot at you, I would not have missed." She patted his cheek, then laughed in a way not without bitterness. "Forgive me. Or thank my tired eyes for your life."

It was a lot for Abe to take in. Never before had he felt so much the callow youth, lying next to a woman who spoke easily about death and the maiming of one's enemies. It was a nasty, vicious world they lived in. Everything in it warred with everything else. The mountains warred with the valleys, the rivers with the oceans, bear with fish, fox with porcupines, men with the earth, men with men. London was a hard place. As long as he had eyes, a poor boy growing up there knew the sting of clever cruelties before he could speak. But in America, brutality came stripped of refinements, of civilization's analysis and rationales. No one knew yet what America might become, who would survive to tell the tale. In this feral corner of it, Abe's money was on Marian, not himself. He dared an important question. Her response would pave the way for his later proposals. He closed his eyes, hoping.

"Have you thought about leaving this place, going somewhere the settlers and gold are not?"

"Give up my land? After I've killed for it? Ridiculous." She yawned. "Abe, I'm quite fond of you. I've grown used to you. Your company is pleasant. I can use another pair of eyes and hands, especially now. But keep up such questions and I will have to banish you." She made a gesture of dismissal as regal as any duchess. Then she smiled and reached over to pat his cheek.

How could he not have known this would be her answer? Abe's awareness of his inexperience deepened. He wanted to approach the subject of his trip to Echota. Along with planning their future together during the trip to her cabin, he'd also thought a great deal about whether or not he should tell her about tracking down Jacob. He decided he must or else the shadow of the man would ever lie between them. That the slave loved Marian was evident. But he needed to know what he meant to her, and there was only one way to find out. Well, he thought, here we are cozy and happy. Might as well leap into the breach now.

"Marian, my travels took me to Echota this time," he began. She leaned up on an elbow, interested. "It's a brilliant town. I met many leaders of your people. Fine men. While I was there I came across a curious man who knew you. Actually, he knew you as a woman named Dark Water, which I assume is your tribal name?"

She nodded. "What was curious about him?" she asked.

Abe took a deep breath and plunged in.

"He was a black man, a slave, scarred all over from battle he told me. He was called Jacob."

The name was barely out of his mouth before she pounced on him like a cat, holding him down with her body while her hands gripped his naked shoulders as a hawk closes its talons on its prey. Her face hovered inches above his own, the eyes bored into him, her nostrils flared. Her mouth looked a dark, angry wound studded with the points of sharp, white teeth. "Who said he was Jacob? Who told you this lie? Who?" Her breath was hot and fierce. Each word seared his flesh. "Tell me where this liar is that I might kill him."

In a halting manner that did not please her, Abe started from the beginning, trying to give her time to calm down. He told her the countryside buzzed with rumors concerning one Dark Water, whom he'd discovered was Marian herself. She nodded once impatiently as if to say, *Yes, yes, we all know that now.* He continued, describing in detail his trip of discovery to Echota and meeting Chief Ross and the Ridge, the last a name that curled her lips into a snarl. She hissed a Cherokee curse through clenched teeth. He paused in confusion, wondering at the source of her venom until she gave his shoulders a shake to focus him. "Get to it," she said. "Get to this man saying he is Jacob." When he got to the part about Jacob's house, about his appearance from out of the dark, about his ruined face, the weakness of his arm and hand, her grip loosened, little by little, until she released him. Slowly, she got off his chest to slide from the bed to the floor, where she crouched with her head in her hands. Her voice was soft, heavy with sorrow.

"Jacob," she said. "My Jacob is alive."

He called her true name. "Dark Water." She picked up her head, looked to the rafters, her cheeks tear-stained, and murmured again, as if she had not heard him, as if he were not there, "My Jacob is alive," before burying her head once more in her hands. This time, her shoulders trembled.

Abe had no idea what to do. He'd never seen her in a vulnerable state. She looked cold. He left the bed, walked around it, and sat beside her on the floor, draping a deerskin about her shoulders. She leaned over onto his chest. He put an arm around her and let her weep. After a while, he said, "Talk to me. There seems to be much I do not know, and only you can tell me of it." She dropped her hands, dried her eyes against her palms, and did exactly that.

DARK WATER OF THE FOOTHILLS

At first there was an eerie detachment to her telling that frightened him. Her voice was flat, her body limp. Her eyes stared ahead, void of expression. She looked soulless, an empty husk. It was as if her spirit had traveled to the past and was locked there in the reliving, robbing the present of vitality.

"I told you before that I was sent to England the year I was sixteen. The day I returned home, Jacob arrived to be in service to my family. I didn't notice him for a time. I had missed my people and the land. I was busy, renewing friendships, visiting my aunties. My family's plantation was large and fruitful. There was always much going on my father must attend to and Jacob was most often at his side. I confess, I was resentful of the father who'd sent me into exile and I avoided his company.

"So. I was overwhelmed with joy to be back where I belonged. Bright Star was still alive in those days and I rode her daily, reacquainting myself with the foothills. Lord Geoffrey Tinsdale, who'd escorted me home all the way from London, rode with me. Lord Geoffrey claimed to travel with me to paint portraits of the Cherokee, but I knew it was because he was

in love with me, poor fool. He was a fine painter and a finer
horseman, I'll give him that. I was young enough then to think
such skills a mark of character. It pleased me greatly to show
my visitor the glories of our waterfalls and wildflowers, of our
lakes held fast in fog's embrace, of eagles and hawks, of the
mountains beyond the hills, standing like sentries to our paradise. Nothing is more delightful than to see appreciation for the
things you love blossom in another's eyes. I had him dressed in
buckskin that he would know what it was like, how superior to
his silks and satins and, I admit, for a kind of revenge against
my year of corsets, crinolines, and buckled boots.

"During my exile, the countryside had changed. Settler communities had sprung up where none had been before. Not so
many, mind you, but enough to cause me concern. Here and there,
in places my people had cultivated or where they had hunted for
generations, settler farms suddenly stood, proud and permanent,
clustered one after another without regard for the boundaries
they violated. Once, we were shot at as we rode close by a settler
farm for a better view. Lord Geoffrey's mount was grazed at the
shoulder. I was infuriated."

Dark Water stood up, slipped a long shirt over her head, and
paced while she spoke, making strong gestures, cutting the air
with her hands. It reassured Abe to see her reanimated.

"And Jacob?"

"Oh, yes, I've not told you about Jacob yet, have I? Well,
I went to my father to demand retaliation against the settlers
who'd shot at us. That was the day I first saw the man you met
in Chota.

"They were in the parlor of that awful house, the place my
father built with the intention of turning us into white men, may

131

it burn to the ground. The same place I was meant to inherit one day from my mother with my white husband at my side, breeding half-white children who would forget their ancestors as quickly as the white world would allow them. Why I thought I would receive satisfaction from my father, I don't know. I was still young. That must be it. He sat in a wing-backed chair, drinking tea from a china cup, which he held in two hands like a bowl. Jacob stood behind him, holding a peach and a paring knife. He cut slices of the peach and handed them to my father, one by one, as if the great chief were a small child not to be trusted with sharp, shiny objects. I was yet trembling with anger from the afternoon's incident. My shirt and britches were stained with the horse's blood, as I'd ministered to his wound before storming into the house. To see my father amidst all his finery, behaving like some feeble peer of the bloody English Crown, enflamed me further. I say it was the first day I saw Jacob and this is true, but I did not truly see him yet. For me, he was a dark form without humanity, a liveried piece of furniture, so blinded was I by anger and the ignominious sight of my father in his ruffled blouse being fed a peach.

"You must understand, when I was a small child, I was raised in the old ways, as a proper Cherokee, in a Cherokee village nestled in the forest, schooled in the arts of my clan. I learned the skills of women and, because it was my nature, those of men as well. But all the while of my growing up, my father was building his white-man's empire, constructing that house, clearing the woods to make fields where he could plant far more than we could consume. Everything he did was an abomination to my mind. 'Chief Redhand!' I near shouted at him. 'Wake from your slumber! The enemy is upon us, infesting the land the Great

132

Beings entrusted to us. They creep about us like ants hunting apart from the hive, ready to summon their fellows, and now they dare violate our guests.' I told him about the settler who shot at us and damaged Lord Geoffrey's mount.

"For a long time, he did not speak, but sat in his wing-backed chair, his slippered feet crossed at the ankles. In silence, he sipped his tea. His gaze seemed to be upon me, but the heavy lids of his eyes were half-closed. His mouth opened, then closed. His lips pursed. He remained silent. I felt imprisoned in that quiet of his. I was like a fire contained by rocks, unable to spread, a flame that burns upward to lose its heat and become only smoke. I'm ashamed to tell you, my frustration grew so that my eyes soon filled with girlish tears.

"'Daughter,' he said at last. 'That land where you found the white settlement was given them by the Council. It's a small piece and all they will ever get. Keep your distance from them. Or if you must draw near, use your English manners. Someday those settlers may be family to you unless we find you a more suitable white husband elsewhere.'

"I was shocked beyond speech. My lips trembled, my hands shook. It was then I looked into the dark, still eyes of his man, Jacob. I suppose I searched them for evidence that I was not in some dream state, a nightmare where my father could betray me, could betray the clan of my mother with commands of not just reconciliation but union with the men I hated most in the world, white men, the interlopers, men without manhood who plowed the earth like women. And what did I see in Jacob's eyes but tears that matched my own. Yes, this stranger, the lackey of my father, wept for me. His pity unnerved me. I quit the room.

"I went directly to my mother and complained to her. I don't know why I thought she would help. She was a hard woman. Despair likely drove me to her. Mothers are powerful among the Cherokee and she was my only hope. I thought she might stop my father's plans. I forgot it was likely her plan too. Perhaps it even originated with her.

"She sat in her dressing room and another slave, the wife of Jacob, I discovered later, brushed her hair. I collapsed at her feet and buried my head in her lap. I told her of the shooting incident and my father's reaction. But I had no satisfaction there. 'Your father is right,' she said. 'We must compromise. It is the only way.' I grabbed her knees with two hands. I shook them. I said, 'You too would have me marry a white man? Who would take my inheritance from me?' She patted my head the way one does a dog. 'Better my property goes to your daughter one day than to the soldiers,' she said. It was too much. 'No, no!' I cried, then howled like the dog she took me for.

"Suddenly, she reached into her pocket and pulled out a sharpened fishbone, an instrument all Cherokee children know as a mother's most harsh tool of punishment. Most of us feel its swift sting once or twice while growing up, perhaps when we have done something very wrong or even dangerous. But on this occasion, my mother struck out at me repeatedly as if she could wound me into submission. She scratched my neck, my arms, even my face until I was a mess of blood trails everywhere my skin was exposed. I was defiant. 'Go ahead,' I taunted her. 'Your petty torture can't hurt me!' She complied. Over and over she scratched me, thinking, I'm sure, that sooner or later I would cry out and beg for her to stop. But from the first cut, I'd stiffened my limbs and sealed my throat. It was easy. At that moment, I hated my mother and hatred is a drug that dulls all other feeling, even pain. When she exhausted herself, she let me slip to the floor and left, telling her slave, 'Clean up that mess.'

"I admit Jacob's wife was kind to me. She brought me water. She washed my injuries and dressed them so that they healed quickly, without scars. I was numb with anger and despair. I did not speak to her, not even to thank her, or to mention the multitude of marks I saw on her own arms, more evidence of my mother's swift hand at discipline. Lulu was a good woman. I can't believe she deserved such punishment. She did not deserve what happened to her later on either, and more or less at my hand. I will repent for her sake for the rest of my life. But the past is past. There's nothing to be done to change it.

"Over the next weeks, I kept myself apart from my family, from Lord Geoffrey too. He began leaving me letters, shoved under the door of my bedroom, but I didn't see them. Those weeks I lived in the woods, under the sun and stars. I prayed to Father Sun and Mother Moon for deliverance from my parents' designs for me, for the strength to defy them, and for the courage to live as I lived those happy weeks, on my own. I made myself a crude hut out of branches that had fallen in a storm. I hunted with sticks and rocks to feed myself. I went naked when I was hot and covered myself in mud when I was cold. And all the while, I knew there was someone watching me. There was no question about it in my mind. I felt eyes upon me even in my sleep. It occurred to me that my father had sent a spy to report on my activities. I knew when he was there. I knew when he left to make his reports. One day, I grew tired of this surveillance. I made a trap to catch the spy and be done with him. It worked. By nightfall, a cry rang through the forest, a human cry, and I laughed and ran to where my prisoner dangled from a birch tree, strung up by braided vines wrapped around his left foot. It was the slave Jacob, twisting and turning and grunting while he hung from that noose like a beast. I watched from where he could not see me, enjoying his humiliation. He was dressed not in his livery but in buckskin. It was like humiliating my father himself.

"Then, just as I was about to reveal myself and free him, Jacob did a most remarkable thing. The movements I witnessed had purpose. While I watched from my secret place, he twisted harder and harder to gain momentum. Mind you, the strength this required was phenomenal. Every muscle of his body strained. Soon he was swinging in an arc that had him close to the tree's trunk and once he was close enough, he grasped it in two hands then pulled his torso up to the branch from which he hung. Taking a knife from a scabbard on his belt, he cut the vines and, once he was free, straightened his legs while yet grasping the branch and lowered himself to the ground. I was very impressed and even more so when he ran off toward my family's plantation with the grace and speed for which my clan is celebrated.

"Perhaps it was an effect of my prolonged solitude in the forest or even of rebellious desire, but from that day on thoughts of Jacob preoccupied me. He was young and handsome in those days. His face was noble, especially about the mouth and eyes. His body was perfect. I considered his agility, his strength, and his compassion for me the day my father refused my plea for revenge against the settlers. I considered myself nearly as much a slave as he, and that too inspired my fancy. I began to wait for his sessions of spying on me with eagerness. When I felt him near, I struck poses, went on parade, so to speak, to seduce him. I could feel his anxiety and the periods of his watch over me grew longer and longer. At last I decided my prey was snug in my snare. I went home to my parents' house but not for their sake. I returned for his."

Dark Water continued describing the fever Jacob provoked in her. As she spoke, her demeanor softened, her features took on a kind of glow, her voice sweetened. Abe was locked in torment. Jacob was, she told him, her first passion. A knife plunged into his gut. "There is no love comparable to a woman's first," she added. "I will love him forever." The knife twisted. The feelings she described for Jacob might have been his own for her. She was his first passion. He was convinced there would never be a love for him comparable to the one he held for her. Resentment grew in him with her every sigh, every blush in recounting the bliss of her youthful affection.

"Can you believe it? I had never even kissed a man before. Girls my age had husbands, children for years already, but at seventeen, I was pure. When I was very young and the others played at kissing games, I was too proud to join in. I wanted to save myself for the bold warrior who would be my destiny. Now I knew at last what it was to desire a man, and that man was a slave. Today, under our Constitution, the punishment for marriage to a Negro slave is twenty-five lashes. Had he known of my fixation, my father, who tried so hard to be white and to be accepted as one of them, would have lashed me himself with or without the blessing of law. My behavior would have ruined everything he worked for, everything he built. In the eyes of the clan, it would be a great disgrace if it became known I wished to commit adultery with a married slave. It would ruin my reputation and no honest Cherokee would have me later on. White prospects would be insulted by even the hint of a match. I considered none of these things. I considered only his face, the muscles of his legs, and the broad, calloused palms of his hands.

"In the beginning, I was content to be in the same room with him. Proximity to Jacob was my greatest pleasure. That I might be near him as much as possible, I extended my father a false reconciliation. I wore the dresses I'd brought back from London. I rode sidesaddle to accompany him on his rounds about the plantation. I told him if I was to be a landowner's wife, I must learn the business of civilized land management. But while my father conferred with the overseer of the orchard or of the corn-fields, I hung back to stand behind him and brush purposefully against the body of his valet, to revel in his heat against my back. For months, nothing more happened between us. I languished. My desires pestered me while I was awake and robbed me of my sleep. As it had to, one day my patience wore out. I manipulated a moment when I could be alone with him in a darkened cor-ridor. It was evening, the hour at which Jacob left my father's chambers for the night. He carried a single candlestick that cast little light. I approached him in my pantaloons and chemise, my feet bare, my hair free. On reaching him, I blew out his candle, took it from him, and placed it on the floor. He did not resist and the music of his hot, tortured breath sang in my ears. Seizing my chance, I put my arms around his waist and pressed against him. We kissed."

"It was the most glorious moment of my young life," she told Abe, her gaze beyond him, focused on the golden past. "A great emptiness had been inside me and now, with that one kiss, it was filled up, no, more than that, it overflowed with warm, honeyed love. . . ."

He could tolerate her rapture no longer. Jealousy ate at him from his toes to his scalp. "And what about Lulu?" he asked to hurt her. Her eyes turned to him slowly, as if she'd just noticed he was there. He watched with satisfaction as her mouth tightened. "What about his wife? What happened to her?"

"I don't know exactly." Her voice had gone quiet and low.

He twisted a knife of his own. "Why?"

"That very night, he took their wedding blanket and ripped it in half. 'You're divorcing me?' she asked him, and he told her yes. She packed up her belongings immediately and left their quarters in the big house for the communal ones of unmarried slaves. Maybe she knew what was between us. She never asked him another question. She just left."

"You said before something happened to her. That you have guilt over it."

"I . . ." She sat on the bed as if suddenly weakened.

"Tell me!"

She bit her lip and continued. "They say she was brokenhearted and allowed herself to be much abused by the slave men and by the Cherokee also. Eventually, she ran away. One of our hunters found her bloodied dress on the banks of a river. Hanks of her hair were scattered nearby along with two fingers, chomped and bled dry. We all assumed she'd either been eaten by some beast or murdered by some white man or both."

She paused and lowered her head. When she raised it, her eyes were freshly damp.

"My friend," she said, unaware perhaps that her next words would stab him quick through the heart. "I must go to him. He is alive! Oh, what a miracle! Everyone told me he was killed in battle. But he was not! I must be reunited with him, my one, my only love."

My only love. With that phrase, Dark Water demolished his world. All his plans for their future crashed into the fiery pit that was her eternal, burning love for a hideous old slave. Abe could not understand the why of it. Why was Jacob his triumphant rival, the thief of his paradise? How could she choose him over me? he wondered. How could she leave me for that wreck, that monster? Abe had given up everything for her. He'd rejected a sparkling future in Greensborough. He'd wounded his mother. He would die without Dark Water. He must stop her somehow. But how could he do that? There was only one way. He must trot out the biggest Mile End Lie of all.

"But he's not alone," he lied. "Lulu isn't dead. She lives in Chota with Jacob. They seemed happy. Oh, yes. A devoted couple, you might say."

Dark Water's mouth fell open. She stared at him in silence while the lie sunk in. Without a word, she rose and dressed. Hunting bow and arrows over her shoulder, she left the cabin, mounted her mare, and walked her into the woods. Abe was too ashamed to call after her. What was wrong with him? Why had he said such a thing? He sat for a bit, hating himself, then went to her larder and gathered victuals, thinking he'd make her a good dinner and confess on her return. When she understood he'd only lied out of a desire to keep her, a wrong one, yes, but one as powerful as any desire she shared with Jacob, she'd have to forgive him. The meal grew cold without her.

For days, he waited for her return, plagued by regret. He milked her goats, he ground her corn, he stood by her front door under the moon and the stars begging the heavens to forgive his selfishness and make her appear, there, by the tree line, game slung over the mare's withers. He rehearsed the confessions he would make at her feet, if only she came back. He swore to his God that he would never again pursue finding out if it were Lord

Geoffrey who killed himself over her, or why Jacob slaughtered Teddy Rupert's son, if only he could see her again. Days without her became weeks.

During those weeks, he searched for her in all the places she had shown him. He came across the corpses of the marauders she'd killed, flesh gone, picked to the bone. Their scalps hung from nearby trees, dry as pods of milkweed in autumn. He found her fields, where wireworm and rot had overtaken the bounty she'd nourished for years. Hard frost had seized their roots and showed no signs of letting go. Standing there in that frigid ruin, all but the last drop of his hope in finding her died. More startling was what he found near the brook where she liked to bathe. Locked in a thin sheet of ice near the shore was her quiver of arrows, identifiable by the signature cluster of feathers attached to their ends. Just beyond, the brook joined a swift river. Heart in his mouth, he followed the river along the shoreline until he came to a doeskin boot, just her size, lying there awaiting discovery. The boot was drenched in frozen blood gone crimson-black with age. There was a trail of small puddles of black blood that led into the brush before they vanished, erased by time and incident. Abe assumed the worst. Certainly she was dead. If she'd an ounce of life left, he reasoned, she would never have abandoned her fields and her animals. Given her absence, the blood, the boot, there was no other explanation possible. Grief married guilt in his heart. His great love was dead and his rash jealousy had killed her.

For seven days he mourned her as Jews mourn. He ripped his sleeve, sat on a stool in his stocking feet, and recited *kaddish* for her. Every day was a day of weeping, of blaming himself, of begging Marian's shade for forgiveness. He ate only bits of dry bread he found in her stores and put a layer of sharp stones under the coverings of the bed to mortify his flesh while he slept. On the eighth day, he circled the cabin three times on foot, then saddled his horse and rode out of the foothills, taking Marian's goats and most of her weaponry with him. Just before he left, on wild, tearful impulse, he took a knife and cut Lord Geoffrey's portrait of Marian out of its frame, rolled it up, and stuck it in a pocket of his saddlebag to have a piece of her with him always. He traveled to Tobias Milner's farm that he might leave the goats there and wander the wilderness, ready to submit to whatever punishing fate a life without Marian had in store for him.

TOBIAS MILNER'S FARM AND, EVENTUALLY, GREENSBOROUGH

Though only a handful of months had passed since his last visit, Abe found the Milner family changed. The eldest girl, the plump, pretty Bekka, no longer lived with her parents and sisters, having married a settler some eighty miles off, a man who'd advertised for a wife in the very issue of the *Carolina Patriot* Abe had last brought them. Her mother had arranged a meeting and although the gentleman was fifteen years older than the girl, he possessed a sizeable farm, he was Lutheran, clean, well mannered, and, as a special bonus, German. The wedding took place within a fortnight of their initial meeting. Her first child was already on the way.

Judith, the second girl, was pledged to marry a schoolteacher from Asheville, which suited her notions of intellectualism and poetry. Her father told him Judith's fiancé was a short, lumpen man with a shirt full of food stains, but he excused him these flaws as he made her happy. Their courtship was whirlwind, the wedding imminent. Abe did not see more than a whisper of Judith during the several days he spent at the Milner home, as she was occupied with preparations for her future life. When he did see her, he found her much self-satisfied.

The youngest daughter, Hannah, had finished growing up. Her cheeks were more pronounced, as was the point of her chin. Her waist was narrower, her hips rounder. No more an impetuous girl reaching toward the future with both hands outstretched, clawing at possibility, she had witnessed her sisters' intoxication with domesticity and sensibly withdrawn. No man would have her out of scarcity of supply. She would rather die a spinster, a servant to her aging parents' needs, than attach herself to the first convenient man who came along. She told Abe as much on his first night back with them. They sat on the rear porch of her father's house, a place her parents had quit minutes before with much pointed yawning, thinking it might be provident to leave the young ones alone for a bit. As safeguard, their bedroom was on the floor above, directly over the porch, where they could easily keep an ear on them.

"You see what they're doing," Hannah whispered as soon as they were gone. "I've nothing to do with it, I promise you. You're a charming man, Mr. Sassaporta, smart, handsome, and very successful too, they say. Indeed, successful enough to be generous! Who else gives away a little herd of goats found by the wayside? But I'll not take the first man that comes along. No matter how Mama and Papa push."

Abe raised an eyebrow. His heart was heavy and sore. Since he'd arrived at Tobias Milner's farm, he'd tried to mask the deep melancholy that pervaded his being. It was a heroic task. Each falling leaf, each withered vine that caught his eye brought him fresh pangs of loss and guilt. That night the air was crisp. Winter felt a breath away. All of nature seemed to coalesce in mortal imagery to underscore his misery. Daily, he unfurled Marian's portrait and spoke to it, asking her shade for a sign of hovering near him in the netherworld. When none occurred, he rolled it up again and, with much grave ceremony, tucked it away. He imagined his future as that of a frontier bachelor consumed by trade, that in finding no other pastime now that love's door had slammed in his face, he would wind up much like his uncle. But the ripe young woman next to him was one he'd imagined in the past quite liked him. She'd extracted promises from him, addressed him by his given name. Just hours before, en route, he'd decided he would be kind if condescending to Hannah in order to discourage what he anticipated were her expectations. Now, by her own unvarnished word, she rejected him out of hand. It was a sharp, unexpected blow, so quick on the heels of Marian's rejection. He played the role of ardent lover to soften it.

"Miss Hannah!" he said. "I have no doubt that even in this backwater suitors will find your door as the hound unerringly finds the soft, beating breast of tender quail. You are, if I may be so bold, delectable. A prize." He stopped to register her blush. An inadvertent clattering from the second floor dispelled the evening's mood. Hannah went her way, Abe went his.

Over the next few days, he intensified his pursuit of a woman he did not love but, falling victim to his own palaver, realized he quite desired. After losing Marian, he needed a woman who might love him, someone through whom he might find redemption, out of his devotion and fidelity. The lovely Hannah fit the bill. Her head, at first turned against him, slowly swiveled in his direction until at last she faced him full-on. She was irresistible. He uttered pledges and begged the same from her. When she acquiesced, her skin warm, her breath short and quick, her eyes downcast, he clutched her to his chest, fondling what he might, and vowed to marry her come the following spring. They decided to keep their plans secret for a time so as not to overshadow Judith's big day.

"It's not such a bad idea," he told Hart on their way to Uncle Isadore's camp. "Life is long, a man must live. She may not be Marian, but she's quick-witted, pretty, and good. I can make a life with her. I'll be a model husband. It won't be a chore."

The horse snuffled in what might have been either agreement or derision. Once he drew far from the Milner farm, Abe was left with his own thoughts and found them drifting to Marian, not Hannah, although the use of such daydreams escaped him. If he had a switch, he'd have flagellated himself to get his mind back to where it belonged, to a future he might actually possess, not one marred by the absence of feminine affection and filled with suffocating guilt, but one bursting with the affection of a young bride, a mother-in-law's goodwill, and perhaps, given time, the worship of daughters. With no penitential instrument at hand, longing for Marian continued to bedevil him. What if she were not dead? Where had she gone? he wondered. The best image he conjured was of a wounded Marian secreting herself deep in some woodland lair, bathing in waterfalls, sleeping in caves, until she recovered. The worst was that she'd gone to Chota, perhaps to make amends to the wronged Lulu. On arriving there, not only would she be reunited with Jacob—the passion she'd expressed would surely overlook his deformities, perhaps even deepen itself—but she would learn she'd been deceived in the matter of Lulu's residence there. She would never know how deeply Abe regretted his lies or of the insurmountable temptation to base envy that provoked them. She would hate him forever.

When the latter scenario implanted itself in his mind, he made rigorous efforts to envision the former but reflection on the idea of Marian bathing in waterfalls, streams of water coursing down her breasts to her loins, provided torment of a different kind. He assured himself he was right the first time—his Cherokee lover was dead. He then forced his thoughts in Hannah's direction. Sometimes it worked and his tension eased.

By the time he reached Uncle Isadore's camp town, Abe felt too drained to face his family straightaway. It was the end of the day. A cold, biting rain kept the streets deserted. Abe rode undetected to the stables, where he dried his horse's dripping coat with a scraper made of bone and brushed him down. Finding a free stall, he settled him in it, providing him hay and water. He bid Hart good night, slung his saddlebag over his shoulder, and prepared to retire to the peddlers' barracks. Head down, he ran, head to chest, into O'Hanlon the stable master, just as he had his first day as novice mounted salesman. Each man stepped back and regarded the other.

"Ah, laddie," O'Hanlon said, "you look like shite."

Abe's mouth twitched, his eyes narrowed. He had no energy for banter.

"It's been a rough day's ride," he said, and made to brush past the taller man. O'Hanlon put out a hand to stop him.

"It's been a rough number of months since we've seen you," he said. "Your mam's been frantic. Rumors of you scalped and rotting in a ditch came to us a week or more ago. In two days' time a search party was to take the dogs out to look for you. And all the while, you've not been dead with your eyes picked out by buzzards, but by the looks and stench of you, livin' the rollickin' forest life. With whom, I wonder?" He stuck out his nose for a

dramatic sniff of Abe's shirtfront. "Must be that wanton Cherokee sprite I hear so much about."

Abe's pent-up grief, frustration, and guilt melted into a hot
fury. He growled in anger, leaned forward, and went up on his
toes as if he might in the next second throw a hothead's sucker
punch. In a flash, his hands were caught in the Irishman's great
red claws. They were given a single, irresistible twist and Abe's
back was pressed against the man's chest, his left hand pulled up
between his shoulder blades. A muscular arm locked around his
neck. "Now, now, laddie, no need for violence," O'Hanlon said,
setting him loose with a push forward so that Abe knocked into
the stable's brick wall. "Fine thing for you to say," Abe muttered
back at him, massaging an elbow that had hit the wall hard.
O'Hanlon put a gentler arm around his shoulders. Ignoring
Abe's flinch away, he gave the peddler a brief squeeze, a manly
hug. "Now, you're the one who looked to be comin' at me first,
weren't you?" he said. "Look. I understand how a man might get
his head turned 'round by a pair of pretty hips, but to vex a sweet
woman like your mam, oh, that takes a hard heart. Don't blame
me for risin' to her defense. Come to me rooms. We'll share a
drop and call each other friends." Abe had nothing better to do.
He might as well drown his troubles.

The stable master's quarters were Spartan, clean and poor in
ornament. Freshly polished bridles gleamed from hooks on the
wall. Spotless spurs were lined up in sparkling pairs on a bench
underneath. The place smelled of leather and woodsmoke. There
was another scent in the air, familiar yet illusive. He could not
identify it. Short glasses were filled, raised, drained, and refilled.
Rain beat steadily against the roof. Abe felt oddly cosseted,
comfy under O'Hanlon's wing despite the room's bare design

and their tussle in the stable aisle, feelings he attributed to the whiskey and his host's mellowed temper, which grew expansive and sentimental by the third glass.

"Abrahan," he said, giving him a moist, mawkish grin, "I know you gave your mam the best of you before you came to the New World. Then gone you were, young and on your own. A man's got to choose his own path and here's the place to do it, 'tis true. But now Susanah's come across the wide sea. She too has her desires and, God bless her, they're simple ones. She wants to rest her weary soul within the bosom of a family, she wants grandchildren. I ask you, lad. Does not this good and giving woman deserve a daughter-in-law she can at least converse with? What can she say to a Cherokee raised from the mud up? Surely you can devise a way to keep your wild love at arm's length, if you know what I mean, and find some lady hereabouts to soothe a mother's heart. I happen to have it on the best authority those native girls don't mind sharin' at all."

Aghast, Abe didn't speak for quite some time as he absorbed the mysteries of O'Hanlon's speech. Why had he called him Abrahan? These days only his mother and uncle did so. Even the Milners had adopted use of his American name. And when had O'Hanlon and his mother come to a first-name relation? He'd called her Susanah, had he not? Why would his mother confide her hopes and dreams to this big, ham-fisted Irishman who presumed to give him instruction in the deception of a wife? What was the smell that nagged at his nostrils? The drink made his head loll about while he worked to identify the scent. At last he had it. It was piripiri sauce, that piquant pepper recipe that flavored the most common of his mother's dishes, made from the spice mixture she'd brought with her, ground up and dried, in little vials all the way from London.

What was it doing lingering within the walls of a stable master's quarters? His mind buzzed with the implications his imagination inspired. Oh, no, oh, no, oh, no, he thought. He had chased after romantic reverie rather than stay home to guard his mother's virtue. And here, in this crude place, she'd been compromised. Fresh guilt flooded his brain, tears sprang to his eyes. He pushed himself away from the table where they sat, nearly knocking both chair and table over. He struggled to his feet, fists raised, and blurted out, "What's going on here? What have you done to my mother, you giant bastard! I don't care how much bigger you are than me! If you've defiled her, I will kill you!"

O'Hanlon stood also, towering over him. He patted the air with his hands. "Now, now. Calm yourself, my boy. Your mam and I have become friends, yes, but that's all there is to it, more's the pity. I don't deny I would die a happy man if there were more, but there's not. Your uncle has moved to Greensborough permanently to take care of that new store of his. Your mother stays here waiting your return. Nothing could move her on that. Each day she prays for your safe return, even in the face of the vilest reports. Three times a week, I drive her back and forth to Greensborough that she may assist your uncle in the running of the store and keep the spot he'd planned for you open, so to speak, by tending his books and inventory, reminding him that nothing is better than family in business, a fact of life I agree with wholeheartedly. During those transports, we talk. Talk! Where's the harm in that?"

Abe felt there was plenty of harm in it, but the whiskey clouded his wits and tied his tongue. They had another drink, then parted, barely comprehending each other's farewells. Abe staggered to the barracks and collapsed. When he woke, his first thought was not the demon hammering at his temples but his mother. How ashamed she would be if she knew he'd developed a habit of getting drunk with slaves and Irishmen! After a stop at the bathhouse, he changed into his freshest clothes before heading to his uncle's office, where O'Hanlon assured him his mother was in residence. Once there, he knocked on the door rather than walk right in. He felt his appearance would be less of a shock that way. The door opened. His mother stood just inside the threshold. Immediately, her eyes grew large and wet, her hands slapped her cheeks, and she cried out thanksgiving to her God and clasped him to her bosom, rocking him back and forth as if he were yet a child at the breast. At last she pulled him into the building and shut the door behind him. Her first words were "You have returned alone? Your wanton Cherokee sprite is not with you?"

True to O'Hanlon's prediction, Abe's mother had tossed her widow's black and now wore a blue dress with yellow piping about the neck and waist. The mantilla was also gone. Her hair was twisted back and piled high on her head. He realized she'd used the same words to describe Marian as O'Hanlon had the night before, which caused him fresh unease. How close were they anyway? Still, her question needed answering. "No, Mother, she is not," he said. "In fact I've given her up and found instead an American girl I think you will much love. I am promised to her. Her father owns a farm in the foothills near abouts."

Susanah's face registered a flicker of confusion. *One love out the window and another rushing in?* her features seemed to ask.

"Her name is Hannah Milner."

Between her given name and surname, Abe's mother jumped to conclusions thinking her future daughter-in-law was that rare gem in the New World, a nice Jewish girl. She kissed his cheeks twice each in succession and praised him to the skies for his wisdom and pure heart.

"Of course, she is one of us," Susanah said, still holding his face in her hands. Abe had learned to be more cautious. He was not going to make the mistake he made with her over Marian by telling too much straightaway. Let her eat by bites what she would not swallow whole, he thought. "With a name like Hannah Milner, one would hardly think otherwise, no?" he said. She searched his eyes. He did not blink. "Good, good, good," she said. "Does your uncle know the family?" By the grace of whatever angel smooths the way for liars, Abe was able to truthfully answer, "I don't believe he does. They have a modest farm. It's not large enough to be of his ken." His mother shrugged. "Alright, then. He will soon enough."

Without inquiring further about Marian, about what might have happened between them to end things, his mother thanked God again and set to making him a sumptuous lunch in celebration.

Once they were seated at table, Abe asked his mother the question that had tormented him, drunk and sober, since the previous night.

"Mother, what's going on between you and Mr. O'Hanlon? He appears to be intimate with your thoughts and concerns."

Susanah Naggar Sassaporta blushed in a girlish manner her son had never before in all his twenty-one years witnessed.

"Nothing to concern yourself with, my son."

He locked her gaze and stared at her, hoping to cause a crumbling of the defensive walls he imagined she and O'Hanlon had concocted together. She withstood his scrutiny. He put away his suspicions, made blessings over bread and a hearty soup, and ate lunch. After a few delicious mouthfuls of the tart savor of home, he considered, Why shouldn't O'Hanlon appreciate a good meal as well? If he and his mother shared a plate together now and again, it didn't mean his intentions were less than honorable. He liked O'Hanlon. But he felt protective of his mother. He could not stop thinking that it was his job to watch over her in the New World. Of course, he'd abandoned her to traipse after poor Marian. One more thing to feel guilty about, wasn't it? he told himself. Well, no more, no more. Time he grew up and behaved like a man.

It was not long after that he took a postprandial snooze in his uncle's bed. Later that night, mother and son made plans to travel to Greensborough together. They expected to remain there providing they could satisfy Uncle Isadore that Abe had come home completely reformed, his wild oats sown, that nary a backward glance would tempt him from the family trade in future. It was good, it was very good, Susanah opined, that he'd returned with the promised hand of Hannah Milner, may a thousand blessings rain upon her head. They could tell his uncle that Abe would soon be settled into a married man's boots.

Abe expected to drive the wagon loaded with goods from the company warehouse to Greensborough, his mother sitting up front beside him. But on the day they were to depart, O'Hanlon insisted the art of driving was not as easy as it looked and that he would be doing the honors himself. Abe and Hart could travel behind. "You'd not want to endanger precious cargo, would you, lad?" the Irishman asked. Abe had to admit he made sense. Uncle Isadore would have four kinds of fits if Abe misjudged the team's readiness on a turn and lost even a small portion of dry goods, sundries, or farm tools. He agreed to the proposed arrangement. But they were not long into the trip before he judged by the way O'Hanlon and his mother put their heads together from time to time, the way she leaned into him whenever the terrain was remotely perilous, or how they laughed together, sharing what looked like a thousand intimacies, that the cargo O'Hanlon found most precious was Susanah Naggar Sassaporta.

Greensborough was a prosperous, rapidly growing town. There were four other stores besides Isadore's. Each had carved a niche for itself, one in haberdashery, another in canned victuals, a third in hardware, and a fourth in used and often broken things offered at a great discount. They were small, cramped, with no allure beyond utility. By contrast, Sassaporta's emporium was majestic, built to service a city far larger than Greensborough. But then, Uncle Isadore said, it was built for the future. It housed three times the space of the others combined and was stocked with goods of all kinds, including many imported items and ones produced by factories up North. There were potted plants in brass containers at the entrance, and on the main desk where the register sat, a bowl of cut flowers was freshened daily during the pleasant months to be switched out for pinecones and fragrant chips of wood in winter. When mother and son arrived, Uncle Isadore was on the floor chatting with customers. Seeing them, he clapped his hands and affected a joyous reunion of family hugs, happy banter, and prayers of thanksgiving. Isadore congratulated Abe on his impending nuptials, which he'd learned about from Susanah's dispatch sent ahead by courier while she and her son readied the wagon.

Behind this flurry of welcome, the stable master stood back, hat in hand, presumably to pay his respects to the boss. He waited a good while. Isadore wanted Abe to meet the patrons clustered about, lists in hand. He was introduced as "my new manager," which caused Abe to stand just a bit taller. The customers swarmed over him with congratulations and curiosity. There followed a tour of the premises, including the stock room, where Isadore's men transported goods from the wagon. There was also a vacant room. "What's this?" Abe asked, knowing his uncle was not one to waste space. Isadore smiled, put an index finger to his temple, and tapped three times. "A secret," he said, "to be shared when your mother and I can speak to you in private on it." So distracting and grand was all this activity that Abe nearly failed to regard his mother's farewell to O'Hanlon. But when he'd chanced to look toward her, he noted the two standing together, the Irishman's face, serious, mournful, damp eyes glistening. Suddenly, O'Hanlon bent his head over his mother's hand. Susanah's head bent also, apparently that she might study the stable master's thick red hair. Her expression was invisible to him, but Abe judged that the two were positioned far closer than custom required. Isadore called out, beckoning to Abe that he come meet an important customer who'd just arrived. Abe turned his head to smile and gesture he'd be right there, then glanced backward. His mother stood alone. The Irishman had gone. He wondered if distance would cure what might be between them.

Later that night after a meal prepared by Isadore's cook, the family gathered in the drawing room to discuss what should come next. Isadore insisted that despite his debt, Abe must add to it and break ground for a home in which to install his new wife and the family that would surely follow. "I have just the man to build it, a gent who can provide both the plans and labor," Isadore said, his chin raised high with a patriarch's pride.

"But you'll not need that room for your mother so quickly, God willing." Abe raised an eyebrow. Susanah covered her mouth with one hand and again dropped her head. "Aha! Aha!" Isadore continued. "Can't you guess? Your mother has consented to become my bride! What think you of that, my son?" Abe was surprised at first and then he was not. In the ghetto back home, men often married the widows of their brothers. On certain occasions, it was more than custom. It was religious law. He put a hand under his mother's chin and raised her face to him. "Is this what you truly want, Mother? Will it make you happy?" She blushed like a girl and nodded. Abe's chest warmed. His eyes teared. His mother, a bride again. He acknowledged Susanah and Isadore were a natural couple, logical, normal, like himself and Hannah. The age of Dark Water and his father was over. They would be forever honored, forever mourned, but new beginnings beckoned. Were the possibilities of renewal, of rebirth in America limitless?

"I congratulate you both," Abrahan said. It was even sincere. Next, the matter of the vacant storeroom was revealed.

"Rubber," Uncle Isadore said. "It's to store the rubber." He paused as if he'd delivered a sacred pronouncement and waited for the key word to sink into Abe's consciousness. Abe gave him a quizzical look. Isadore repeated himself, louder this time. "Rubber!" Abe raised his palms to heaven and shrugged. His stepfather-to-be grew impatient. "Haven't you heard, son?" Abe shook his head. "Oh, yes, I forgot, you've been traipsing about the Indian hills, where civilized news is scarce." Susanah put out a hand to touch Isadore's arm in warning. *The Indian crisis is over for this family*, her touch seemed to say, *best not bring it up*. Isadore shut his eyes tight and gave his own head a quick, hard shake as if casting all Indian thoughts out of it. His jowls wobbled like jelly. He opened his eyes and resumed.

"Rubber is all the rage!" he roared. "First in London and now here. Futures in rubber have hit the roof on the exchange! Factories all over New England produce boots, overalls, even shirts of rubber, along with pails, pans, and pots! There's a new process, you see, courtesy of a Mr. Goodyear. I've convinced all the Sassaporta Brothers traders from Florida to Maryland to carry rubber with yours truly as the chief wholesaler. Imagine! Everything can be waterproof now thanks to elastic gum, or, as we in the trade say, rubber." He laughed, enjoying the warm flush the words "we in the trade" gave him. "Just think, it's cheap enough to sell to the most parsimonious farmer. Oh, they'll eat it up! I've ordered hundreds of pounds of rubber goods to feed them. Imagine! We'll have labels made up with the motto: 'From the Jungles of Brazil to Boston to Your Door, Compliments of Isadore Sassaporta and Son'! Ah, that fortune I promised you will extend until the fourth generation even should you raise indolent beauties and impractical scholars!"

The old man's excitement was infectious. He continued to extol the durability and versatility of rubber. Flattered by Isadore's sudden impulse to include him as the "Son" on the store marquee, Abe considered the implications of introducing a new and functional product into the waiting world. Immediately, his mind turned to the best ways to approach the market to ensure a grand success. If he were the architect of a sales scheme in which the whole family empire made millions, he might lobby for a territory of his own with the corporate founders in Savannah and win independence as well. He hoped his uncle had ordered some small rubber item, a child's rain cap or a ladle for sipping well water, something they might offer at next to nothing or—why not?—for free as a promotion. That night, rather than mourn Marian or list the reasons why he should love Hannah instead of a Cherokee ghost, he considered the properties of rubber, how best to create excitement about it, what advertising he might design to put in the windows of Sassaporta Brothers stores throughout the Southeast, and how to train the sales force of peddlers to spread the word. He dared daydream that one day he might be appointed by the headquarters in Savannah to his own territory, which he would add to Isadore's, making he and his stepfather the most powerful merchants of the firm. In the morning, he thought, How good work is for a man. Without it, heartsickness would kill us all.

Early that December, Isadore and Susanah married, courtesy of a traveling rabbi who wintered in Durham. There was no one to paint Susanah's palms with henna, no wedding dress of velvet and pearl. But enough of Isadore's Jewish peddlers were raised up out of the camp town to provide a fiddler and drummer along with men to dance to their tunes. The people of Greensborough, most of them descendants of the founding Quakers and kind to a fault, were eager for a chance to celebrate a happiness at the advent of a cold, dark season. After the rabbi chanced to explain to their leaders the custom of *shevah brachot*, they feted the couple for seven nights, showering them with visits, gifts, and baked goods. Abe was feted as well, as he lodged at a different Quaker home each night of that first week while Isadore and Susanah held court in their home together. It escaped none of the Jews' notice that such generosity from gentiles would have been a miracle back in Merry Olde and felt pretty much a miracle in America as well. All agreed the couple was starting out well blessed.

Notable for their absence during the festivities were any of the Milner family, who had the excuse of weather and the difficulty of travel in that time of year. Truth was, had there not been a drop of ice or snow in the foothills, the Milner family could not have attended. Abe made sure they were unaware of the event, having taken the precaution of removing their invitation from the mailbag of the intrepid postman who trekked to Micah's trading post at least twice over the winter months. Once certain he was unobserved, Abe ripped the purloined envelope up and burned the pieces. He told himself he did this to spare his mother concern during her preparations for matrimony. The truth was he feared her reaction to the news that his bride was of the Lutheran faith.

Neither did O'Hanlon, who'd been invited as a friend of the family, attend. Isadore attempted to encourage a change of heart in him, but the man was firm that he could not leave his horses during a time of year all were in danger of slipping and breaking limbs. Susanah told Isadore to quit his suit. O'Hanlon obviously did not consider the celebration of their marriage a priority.

In the spring, it was Abe's turn to marry. He traveled to the Milner farm during the winter thaw to formally request Hannah's hand. During his ride there, he grew increasingly anxious, wondering if he'd made the right decision. Had his heart's wounds over Marian, so eager for healing, taken him down the garden path? He enumerated Hannah's virtues to himself. She was sweet and smart, a hard worker, so her mother bragged. She made him laugh. What else could a man want? When he arrived at the Milners' front gate, she burst through the door and ran to him, auburn hair flying, her skirts lifted against tripping. His heart leapt. How lovely her calves, he thought. How beautiful her hair. Her face is as pretty as a china doll's and all afire with happiness just from the sight of me. Me! How brilliant it is to be loved and desired! Tender feeling toward her suffused him. He had a notion that maybe Marian's spirit had guided him to this moment as a sign of her forgiveness. With aching heart, he thanked her.

He dismounted Hart and embraced Hannah there, in the open, for all to see. How easy it was to yield to the warm pleasures of her flesh! He looked up. Tobias and Esther stood at the doorway all smiles and nods of encouragement. "Someone's been sharing secrets," he whispered into Hannah's ear. "How could I not tell them? You've made me so happy, they guessed!" By nightfall, a date for the wedding was settled. Two days later, Abe took his leave of Hannah reluctantly, all his doubts assuaged.

Abe rode back to Greensborough past streams rushing with melted snow. Nesting birds cried out in songs of mating. The sun coaxed tiny green buds from the barest trees and bushes. He happened across a solitary pink-and-yellow flower whose name he did not know and the sight of it, pushed up from barren rocky ground, its petals sparkling with dew, affected him unexpectedly. His eyes smarted. His throat closed up. Marian, he thought, Marian. I need to say goodbye once more. He turned Hart about to ride to her cabin. All along the way, which was half a day's ride, his heart trembled, as he realized that his hope she might still be alive had never completely forsaken him. As he rode closer and closer to her, that hope grew. He spoke aloud while he rode, saying, "Forgive me, Marian, forgive me. For your sake, I renounce Hannah Milner, I renounce my stepfather and mother, I renounce the fortune that is coming to me and all the white man's world, if only you would forgive me. Henceforth, I will be your slave."

When he arrived at the outskirts of her homestead, it was plain to see that everything remained derelict, yet still he dismounted to approach her cabin, now covered in wild vines, with humble reverence. He knocked on the door. Immediately, as if that door had waited half a year to deliver to him alone a mortal message, it fell off its hinges. Inside, forest creatures and insects had made dozens of nests in the room where Abe and Marian once negotiated the sale of gunpowder. Curtains of spiderwebs obscured the windows. The picked bones of one animal were strewn amid the dried droppings of another. After staring at nature's mess for a long, melancholy while, Abe turned about and remounted his horse. He vowed to weep no more for Dark Water of the foothills, to never again entreat the ghost that lived in the Englishman's portrait. A shadow fell over a chamber of his heart and closed it down.

On his return to Greensborough, he related to Isadore and Susanah the details of his visit to the Milner farm. He told them the bride's price they had settled on and the date in early May on which Hannah and her family would arrive in town for the wedding. The elder newlyweds noticed the change in his demeanor and found it dear. "He's got oh-so-solemn now he's about to be a family man," his mother told her husband with a tender smile. "May it only spill over into the business," Isadore joked. And it did. With a fiery intensity, Abe drafted a marketing plan to boost sales of rubber straightaway. He had a flyer printed with the company slogan "From the Jungles of Brazil to Boston to Your Door, Compliments of Isadore Sassaporta and Son" as a heading. Underneath were hand drawings of boots, hats, tarpaulins, and pots. Between the drawings were printed testaments to the waterproof and insulation properties of rubber.

At the bottom were the words "Coming Soon" writ large. For the flagship store itself, he drew up designs for large posters to put on the doors and change out as the time required. They read RUBBER GOODS OF ALL KINDS, COMING SOON!, RUBBER GOODS HERE NEXT MONTH!, RUBBER GOODS —IT'S ONLY WEEKS NOW!, and RUBBER GOODS—NEXT WEDNESDAY! For extra measure, he arranged for like announcements to appear progressively in the *Carolina Patriot* and the *Miners' and Farmers' Journal*. He then distributed sheaves of advertisements to all Isadore's foot and mounted peddlers to hand out along their early spring routes. He gave bundles of them to the postmaster that his man might drop them off at trading posts. He even thought to find a Cherokee half blood who could write the new Cherokee alphabet and had a portion of those destined for the trading posts printed in that language. Isadore cautioned restraint on that score. "The Indian Removal Act will surely pass the Congress," he said. "Soon all the land east of the Mississippi will be cleared of Indians. The Georgians want this and so does President Jackson. We may expect the Act to call for the tribes to leave their lands voluntarily, but believe me, I've seen how these disputes worked in the old countries. Their removal will be mandatory before long. Only those who can read the writing on the wall will leave right away. The smart ones. The ones who know that life has its way with you no matter what convictions you hold here, in the heart. The rest will leave under the snout of a gun." Abe convinced him to worry about that when the time came. "While on my routes, I made a study of the native heart," he claimed, without revealing his study consisted of a single woman called Dark Water of the foothills. "Some may withdraw to their higher peaks, but they will not leave the land so fast. Not without a fight. Between now and then, if force is made law at all, the opportunities for sales are staggering."

Soon enough, Isadore and Susanah could not open their door, walk down the street, or enjoy a stroll in the meadows near the town without neighbors coming up to them and mentioning rubber. The questions "When is it coming? Is it truly waterproof? How is rubber pliable for one use and hard as a rock for another?" rang in their ears everywhere they went. The two were proud to bursting of their son. In early April, the rubber arrived and flew off the store shelves. Everyone for miles about had to have at least one item made of the miracle stuff. Isadore placed an order with the factory in Boston for replacement rubber goods that doubled the original amount. At the end of the month, the Milner family prepared to make their way to Greensborough for the wedding, just as peddlers were trickling back to the camp town to restock for the late spring sales season. Rubber invoices bulged from every pocket. Abe could no longer hide the truth about Hannah's lineage from his parents. One night as he'd come from the building site of his future home where the matters of paint and wallpaper were put off until his bride might choose them but where everything else was nearly done, he decided the moment had come to tell them their new daughter was born a Christian.

Isadore's jaw dropped at the news. After a few painful seconds, he sputtered, "What barbarous news is this? I have the rabbi coming from Durham in two weeks' time and now you tell me? Susanah, do you hear him?" His wife's mouth worked, her eyes blinked back tears. Speaking quietly, oh, so quietly, she shocked them both. "It's a new world, Isadore. What can we do? He will have whom he will have. She sounds a good girl and her parents have not complained that she wants a Jew. Did not similar unions take place on occasion in London? At least he's not converting the way those London Jews would to cement a mixed alliance. In the meantime, he's come a fine man, an honest steward of your business. We have much to be thankful for out of him. If our son wishes to marry a gentile, he will be no different from the patriarchs of old. Did not Abrahan make Hagar his wife? Did not Solomon have a princess of Egypt as his queen? When the children come, I'll be there to make sure they know they spring from Abrahan, Yitzak, and Yacov." After a long stretch of quiet, Isadore nodded his head from side to side. "You make a good argument, my love. Life in America undermines the old ways a thousand times a day. If she's ok by you, she's ok by me." Abe embraced them both, overwhelmed with gratitude.

The night before the Milners were due to arrive in Greensborough, Abe went to his parents to thank them again for their support on the question of his choice of bride. It struck him that he was on the threshold of an eternal union with a young woman he much admired but barely knew and reminded himself there was nothing unusual about that aspect of their arrangement. Only second marriages like Isadore's and Susanah's were commonly matters of knowledgeable choice. For men his age, love began as an urge for family or an expansion of land or business. Whatever came next, people made the best of things. He had no desire to avoid his situation. Every fiber of his being told him this would be a good thing, that this marriage was the next best match to one with Marian, who was, in any case, dead, but why his mother had approved the idea remained a nagging mystery. So on the night before his bride and future in-laws arrived, he said to her at a moment when they were alone, "Mother, why do you sanction my union to a gentile girl? When you first came to America, I had the idea only a Jewish daughter would please you. In fact, I half expected last fall to return home and find Ariella Levy waiting for me." His mother clucked her tongue and, reaching up, brushed the forelock away from his eyes. "My dear son. I confess I tried. But Ariella was already promised by the time word got to her family. No, my change of mind is based on my own heart's adventures since I arrived here, events that taught me tolerance in these matters, although I'll speak no more of them to you. Now that I'm married to your uncle, it would be shameful to do so. The whole *megillah* is not for a son's ears."

O'Hanlon! thought Abe. O'Hanlon was her route to comprehending Hannah. *O'Hanlon!* He wondered if the reason his mother refused the Irishman was out of loyalty to her people, or because she truly preferred Uncle Isadore. It was hardly a question he could ask. Without pretending to comprehend the marital decisions of others, he fell to examining his own. Once again, he decided there was no fault he could find in Hannah. None at all. But, ah, he thought, the stuff of Sassaporta marriages is complex!

The second of these unions went exceedingly well at first. The families were cordial, even warm from the first hello as if Christians had always loved Jews and vice versa. After the first family dinner before the wedding, Isadore announced that he would forgive all Abe's debts, including those related to the purchase of land and the building of the marital home, as a wedding gift.

Abe's jaw dropped at the news. Tears of gratitude sprang to his eyes. Until that moment, to be debt-free felt a whimsy, a dream, and a farfetched one at that. The only way he could envision himself free of obligation to his uncle and stepfather was to imagine him dead and his mother twice-over widowed. Fantasies of financial independence thus inspired tremendous guilt and he rarely entertained them. But in a single pronouncement, Isadore Sassaporta absolved him. Esther Milner's eyes sparkled with grateful tears on her daughter's behalf while she rushed to kiss the merchant on his bearded cheek. Susanah clapped her hands and kissed Tobias Milner's shaven cheek in kind and they all laughed while a teary Abe raised his glass of tea and toasted, "God Bless America!"

The night before the nuptials, Abe took the portrait of Marian, which, true to his vow, he had not studied since his final visit to her cabin, and hid it under a floorboard of the new house. The Indian Removal Act had narrowly passed Congress days before. While the president might or might not be successful in his negotiations to have the tribes remove themselves from the Southeast voluntarily, he at least had authorization from the people to try. It was 1830, a date to remember. A new American era had begun. If things went according to Jackson's plan, the United States would no longer be hindered by patches of Indian territory everywhere she wanted to spread her wings. Abe considered the pushing out of Cherokee a tragedy, queerly related to the tragedy of his lost first love. But the destiny of nations and the passions of a Dark Water could not be stopped by such as him. There, he thought, nailing the floorboard down, that's it. The ultimate vestige of a great love gone. Buried. Past. The page is turned, the book closed. If the sun rises tomorrow, there'll be a future for me and it will be good.

The next morning was particularly bright and clear. Abe and Hannah married in the town square under a trellis of dogwood and wisteria, which Isadore and Susanah viewed as nature's most glorious *chuppah*. The mayor of Greensborough officiated. Farmers from here and there, Isadore's peddlers, and the

tradesmen of the town all attended. There was feasting and dancing. Even the Quakers among them deigned to take a step or two.
The wedding night was extraordinary. Abe's breath was stolen
by the contrast of a virgin's passion weighed against the caprice
of a mature woman. Where Marian had been casual, if generous,
Hannah was hungry for his sex and strove with every muscle
and sinew to give him pleasure without knowing in the slightest
what men might like or women deserve in kind. Her eagerness
near overwhelmed him. More than once, he whispered to her,
"Slow down, my love. Slow down." She obeyed instantly for as
long as she could stand and then she was at it again, grasping,
straining, heaving against him. Later, when he collapsed against
her breast, panting with exhaustion and release, he glanced up
to see her smiling at him in the most gleeful manner, her mouth
stretched wide, her eyes large and merry. He asked if she found
him ridiculous and she answered, "Far from it, my husband. I'm
only thinking how different love has been for me than for my
sisters. Both instructed me to close my eyes and think only of
Jesus when you came to me, that our union should be the worst
five minutes of my life, but something I should get used to for the
sake of family harmony. Oh, those poor silly geese!" Her body
shook with laughter. He found her so adorable in her mirth that
he kissed her deeply again and again when their second exploit
of love occurred without either expecting it. It was an event both
agreed was a good omen of the highest degree. In fact, for the
first month of their marriage, nothing transpired between them
that was not delicious, ecstatic, and unworldly in its deepening
layers of sweet emotion, until the happiness of those early days
was broken by the stench of spoiled rubber, carried into the store
one day by a party of disgruntled Cherokee.

FROM GREENSBOROUGH
TO CHEROKEE COUNTRY

Melting rubber stinks in a particular way, and the open windows and doors of Sassaporta and Son caught a breeze that ushered that horrid stink into the store. Those on the floor coughed at its arrival or covered their nostrils and mouths with handkerchiefs. At first there was great confusion. Had the earth erupted and expelled the reek of hell? Had rotted corpses fallen from the skies into the street? Then the Cherokee in charge strode through the door, his men bearing baskets of ruined rubber, and the malodorous air suddenly had an undeniable source.

There were five of them in all. The Cherokee was a tall, imposing figure in a white man's frock coat and trousers, but bare of chest in the heat of summer. He wore a beaded cross belt beneath the coat, one with a red background overlaid by designs of blue and white, in which a pipe and tomahawk were inserted. Another belt of similar configuration circled his waist. The butt of a pistol stuck out of it at one hip while a deerskin pouch dangled from the other. Around his neck, a silver medallion in the shape of a half moon threaded on a rope of rawhide hung level to his heart.

He wore English boots with his trousers tucked into their tops, and under a broad-brimmed Quaker-style black hat, his hair was cut short. The other four men were black slaves dressed in worn hemp tunics, drawstring pants, and simple moccasins. Each held in arms bulging with effort a large basket filled with a heavy, stinking black substance. At a gesture from the Cherokee, they dropped the baskets on the floor and stepped back.

Abe had the misfortune to be behind the front desk that day, his stepfather having accompanied his mother on a social call. Hannah, who'd been in the back taking inventory, came out holding a perfumed cloth to her nose to see what repellent odor weighted the air. She arrived in time to hear the Cherokee's complaint and witness the backs of customers fleeing the emporium floor as quickly as they could without appearing to panic.

"You have sold us demon's spunk for coin and skins," the man said. "Like every demon, it was beautiful when first we saw it, but now it melts and reveals its true nature. It despoils our homes, our fields, and our hunting grounds. You may have it back. But first your men must come to our homes in the mountains, to our fields and our hunting grounds and take it away as the rain will not wash it and the sun cannot burn it off. You will return our coin and skins as well."

Having spoken, the Cherokee lifted his chin and folded his arms across his chest, his right hand very close to the butt of his pistol. Abe stood silent with his mouth open while his mind swarmed with the disastrous ramifications of what he'd just heard. Rubber melted. Once it melted, it adhered. It stank. Unbearably. Would all the rubber they'd sold, all those hundreds of pounds, suffer a similar fate? The sun in the mountains where many Cherokee lived was stronger during the day than it was in the middle towns and foothills, but the lower ground would soon catch up, within weeks, as summer took hold. If all that rubber melted too, Sassaporta and Son was ruined. *No,* he prayed, *no, no, no, no, no.* The Indians must have done something queer to it. How to find out? His wife, dear Hannah, whose parents had taken home dozens of rubber items after the wedding, stood behind him, poking his back to prompt him to speak. When he did not, she dropped the cloth from her face and took over.

"Sir," she said, smiling sweetly, addressing him with uncommon respect. "Why don't you and Mr. Sassaporta retire to the offices back there and discuss the matter in full? I am sure we can accommodate you, but this is all something of a shock and we need to understand exactly what's happened, don't we, dear?"

Abe awoke from his miserable stupor. He gestured to the back rooms and even bowed but very slightly. "Yes, yes sir. Follow me." The Cherokee dropped his arms and prepared to do so. Hannah interrupted his movement. "But please, sir, might you have your men there remove the baskets? They can leave them behind the store, in the livery area, until we determine what to do." An order was given, Hannah's request accommodated. But for a round of disturbed whinnies coming from the livery once the spoiled product was deposited there, all was exceedingly quiet as the Cherokee and Abe settled into the office at the back.

Abe sat behind Isadore's desk, the Cherokee sat in the red leather chair opposite. With the energies of a Joshua, Abe marshaled his resolve to appear in-charge, accommodating, and civil. He was well aware that the man sitting across from him was a generation older than him, by his demeanor, a leader of his people, accustomed to obedience as his birthright, and that his grievance against Sassaporta and Son was probably just. At the same time, this odiferous debacle had the capacity to spiral out of control, especially if the melting occurred to all the rubber they'd sold. He didn't yet dare contemplate what difficulties he and Isadore would be in if the rubber they'd convinced the family franchises to purchase had also spoiled. For now, he was primarily concerned with his neighbors. If the local whites learned he'd been especially generous to the initial complainant, the Cherokee, they would expect, no, demand even more. While hope dimmed, he longed for there to be something wrong with the Indian's story. All this would simply go away if only he could trap the Indian out in a lie or even a small exaggeration that somehow exonerated rubber. With these thoughts and a thousand offshoots of them running through his mind, it was all Abe could do to plant a pleasant look on his face and nod for the man to begin.

"It is as I tell you," the Cherokee said. "The rubber first melted when we laid it upon flat rock in the high places. The traders told us this rubber comes from bleeding trees. Our *gighua*, our Beloved Woman, told us we must thank the tree spirits for giving their blood for our use. We spread out sheets of it, those tarpaulins your men sold at the trading posts, and on the sheets we laid the sacred crystals our priests use for divining that as Father Sun rose and set, they would capture a portion of His eternal light and this new thing might be blessed. Instead, as you can see, it melted and released its poisonous vapors into the air. It sticks to the rock and only by hardest labor can we scrape most of it off. There is a remnant that lingers like a scar upon the earth."

Abe chose to display empathy. Apology felt dangerously entangled with compensation, which had yet to be determined. Empathy was safer. "It's a terrible thing you tell me. Terrible," he said. He opened his palms, pointing them upward as if entreating the heavens. "A most unfortunate event."

"Hmph," muttered the Cherokee. He continued. "It is a sacrilege. The stuff sticks not only to the rock but to our priests' crystals. We put them in holy fire and still they are streaked with blackness. The light inside them is trapped. It cannot be seen, nor read for signs. We have had to find new crystals and to purify them. For a time, our priests could not read omens at all. Then there are the other things that melted."

Baruch Ha-Shem. There were other things. Abe's heart sank to the pit of his stomach and sizzled there as if fried in a vat of bile. His head felt light, almost dizzy. "And what are these other things, if I may ask?"

"Hmph," muttered the Cherokee. "You may ask. Everything has melted. The pots, the spoons, the boots. Oh, yes, the boots. On one occasion, they melted on a fisherman's feet while he slept in the heat of high noon by a riverbank. He was stuck there for some time. He could not get his feet out of the boots nor the boots out of the ground. When he did not come home as expected, his wife sent out his elder sons looking for him. When they found him, they cut his boots from the earth and then his flesh from the boots. Hopefully, he will walk again."

There were other stories of the rubber disaster in the high places of Cherokee country. None were as gruesome as the man who required cutting from his boots, although the rest were disturbing on their own. Yet no matter what the human cost in life or treasure, what seemed to bother the Cherokee most was the defilement of the crystals, an event he kept returning to, relentless as the chimes of a clock, and the defilement of the forest and mountainside. "Everywhere there are piles of it in the spots people have managed to leave it. Sometimes, it remains where the people put it in the hours before they were about to use it but then it melted at the last moment and became unwieldy. In other words, it is next to their house or in it. Wherever it sits, it contaminates either by scent or by its thickness and its ugliness. You have done this. You must clean it up."

It was at this point, when the Cherokee had summed everything up, when Abe was ready to give the man whatever he asked, that Isadore burst in, his hands flying through the air in gestures of welcome to the Cherokee and in warning to Abe, that one might be becalmed until they'd talked and the other quieted before he gave away the store. Without delay, Isadore demonstrated his experience in dealing with unhappy customers by affecting an air of cordiality and formally introducing himself, then introducing Abe as his son, and lastly, with a little bow before settling in the chair Abe vacated, he asked, with humility and respect, "And I have the pleasure of speaking with whom?"

The Cherokee, who was by now becoming impatient, lifted his hand long enough from the butt of his pistol to shake the one the elder Sassaporta extended. "I am Edward Redhand," he said. "Eldest son of Chief Redhand, whom you may know as the neighbor once upon a time of Theodore Rupert, who took over my father's land after the death of his son, William, as recompense."

Abe paled, swayed on his feet a little, but the others did not notice. Inside his skull, the Cherokee's words reverberated. The man before him was none other than Marian's brother.

"Yes," Isadore said while Abe struggled to recover himself, "I recall that incident. Very unfortunate. I recall your people appealed to the courts on the land issue and, after some years, were denied.

You removed yourselves, as I also recall, to the Unicoi mountain peaks, no? Yes. A small contingent of your people remained here, I think, until recently, when for some reason you came down from the mountain and collected them. I heard you did this in anticipation of the Removal Act. This is what I heard."

Abe wondered how it could be his uncle knew so much and he so little about the movements of his departed lover's family. Had Isadore any idea that Edward Redhand's sister was the wanton Cherokee sprite his mother reviled? New torments afflicted him. His mouth went dry, his head swam. His heart left his belly in a single leap to reassert itself in his chest where it pounded like a steel hammer against his rib cage. He sunk onto the stool next to the desk, the one Isadore stood upon when he needed to reach the highest levels of shelving behind him. What would the Cherokee say if he knew the young man sitting there, his back pressed against the wall that he not keel over, was the catalyst of his sister's death? Worse, what would he do? Did Edward Redhand even know she was dead? It was well known that news traveled swiftly through the mountains from Indian village to Indian village, at rates and by methods no white man fully understood. Surely by now it was common knowledge among her people that she'd disappeared. Surely they at least must presume her dead. He had time to think these questions over while the Cherokee repeated to the older man his tale of what happened to the tribal rubber and his stepfather responded to his visitor's demands, time enough for Abe to come to a thick fog of acceptance for whatever might come next, whether ruination of the family business or his torture, perhaps death, at the hands of an avenging brother. When Isadore finally spoke his name, he turned his head to him expressionless, numbed to fate.

"Abrahan, I want you to travel with Mr. Redhand to his village in the mountains and assess the damage that's been wrought in this most horrible manner. You understand, Mr. Redhand, that I must have a witness to the destruction you describe before we settle on compensation." Marian's brother shrugged. Of course you shrug, Abe thought, you'll have me as hostage. Not that I deserve less. "In the meantime, I will communicate with Mr. Goodyear in Boston. It is his product, and in the end, it will be him what pays!" Isadore slapped his hands on the desk with finality and everyone stood. He shook the Cherokee's hand once more. "Let the lad bid goodbye to his wife first," he finished. "He is newly wed." At this, the Cherokee lifted an eyebrow. "Hmph," he said. He went outside to wait for Abe and ready his men for the return trek.

As soon as he was gone, Isadore's congenial manner evaporated. He grabbed Abe by the shoulders and, spittle flying, said in a quiet, urgent voice, "Inspect every inch of his land! Closely! Draw maps, take notes! Interview the purchasers of the melted rubber! I need to determine if this will happen to all my rubber, or if somehow the Indians got hold of a rotten batch. I need enough evidence to threaten Goodyear with a lawsuit, and oh my, I need to cancel that reorder, which is probably as we speak on its way south by train. Dear Lord, this could ruin us. Ruin! Quick, go say fare-thee-well to Hannah and be off!"

Once Abe turned to leave, Isadore grabbed him again. "But don't take too long. The last thing we need is parties of angry Cherokee riding into town, scaring away all the customers. If we are to mitigate their losses somehow, keep them peaceable, the Cherokee must be at the front of the line. If the farmers hereabouts start complaining, that may be hard to do. Yes, yes, son. Whatever it takes, I will try to make this right. I've worked too hard and too long to win the confidence of my neighbors that I'll not end things as 'that Jew who stole our money.' Ruin or not. The Quakers are good people, but they too will want a piece of our hide."

Abe collected Hannah and led her to the livery that he might tack up Hart. She'd had her ear to the back room and knew everything. As soon as they were alone, she said, "This Edward Redhand is the brother of that Dark Water we spoke of! Remember? The one my father warned you of, the one I spied, hatter mad, as a child! Oh, the nightmares I had of her!" Hannah shuddered and grasped him around the waist from behind while he tightened Hart's girth. "He may well be as savage as she, no matter how he dresses or how well he speaks. Please, be careful, my love. I swear, I'd rather have you poor and whole than rich and mutilated by a Cherokee brute!"

Abe felt as if his head were already on a spike. Impending punishment for his sins threw in stark relief all the wrongheaded ideas he'd entertained since he'd arrived in America. Fresh awareness washed them away as surely as a deluge cleanses a gully of loose rock and refuse. He knew now he'd lived the past years inside a mist of whimsical thought and naïve feeling while all along harsh reality nipped at his heels, getting ready to bite. There were signs of calamity everywhere, yet he'd blathered along, utterly unaware. What was he thinking? Could he ever have been so young? Why had he ever been so sure Marian would love him? What blind dreams he'd entertained on her behalf! Her world and his, while overlapped, were as far apart as London from New York, and Lisbon from both. Why had he thought he'd never love another when this dear woman whose tears wet the back of his shirt had so effortlessly delivered to him a month's worth of nightly bliss despite his broken heart? In a matter of minutes, he was to march off into the unknown with a suited, shirtless Cherokee who had every reason to hate him and every opportunity for cruel revenge at his disposal. Envisioning a dark and justifiable fate, deadened by guilt, he told his wife, yes, he'd be careful, and gave her an embrace that, while long and lingering, felt empty and hopeless to him.

Abe rode around to the street where Edward Redhand waited in a two-horse wagon, his slaves sprawled about its bed, catching a rest. "Hitch that horse to the backboard, and sit up here with me," the Cherokee said, and Abe did so.

Their trek into the mountains was arduous. Abe knew the range they traveled was known by the Cherokee as the Unicoi, or White, Mountains for its thick fogs. Often, it was near impossible to see clearly as far as one's outstretched hand. Their progress was slow. Abe grew anxious and tried to engage his companions in conversation to ease his nerves. Edward Redhand was not terribly convivial, preferring silence to Abe's chatty attempts. He tried also to engage the black men in the wagon bed, but these were no more forthcoming than their master, giving him only the yessirs and nossirs slaves are wont to employ when a freeman not their master addresses them. They talked among themselves both in Cherokee and an island patois Abe did not understand, so it was possible their comprehension of English was limited. When they stopped for the day, Redhand hunted for small birds and mammals, and one of the slaves roasted the game over the fire. One of the birds wasn't consumed by the men, but instead Redhand raised it to the skies in offering and then incinerated it. After dinner, he and Abe slept in their bedrolls, while the others slept on the bare ground. At breakfast, the slaves heated up round cakes made of cornmeal that they carried with them. One night, Redhand scraped a length of bark off a walnut tree, crushed it, and placed a walnut powder in a nearby stream to drug the fish that they might be more easily caught in the morning. Abe awoke just after dawn to the sounds of slaves splashing about in the cold mountain waters, catching dull-witted trout with their bare hands. That morning, breakfast was a feast. When they were three days into their trip, the heir to Sassaporta and Son found himself lulled by the pure air, the breathtaking vistas of green woods, rushing springs, soaring mountains, and his companion's silence. He reasoned that if Edward Redhand knew his sister was dead, he could not possibly know his lie had driven her to it. Abe would have been long dead and the fact that he was not gave him confidence. He found Marian's brother admirable on many accounts. He seemed much like his sister. He wished they could speak openly to each other. That they could talk about Marian, share their memories. He could not help himself. He brought her up, in a way.

"I've sold goods to this Rupert family who won your father's land," he said. "I only know rumors about what happened between them and your people. I'm sure you were probably in the right, no matter what townsfolk and settlers say." He moved his head side to side philosophically, in imitation of every wise old man he'd ever met. "I'm telling you, money and power make men perverse. Over to the Rupert plantation, even the house slaves have airs."

Edward Redhand pulled the wagon's team into a dead halt, securing the reins. He turned and looked at Abe with narrowed eyes, mouth and jaw sternly set. Abe swallowed but held his gaze. "What do these townsfolk and settlers say?" Redhand asked. Abe hemmed and hawed until he thought of something to report, then spit it out. "They say a slave belonging to your father murdered the Rupert son, who was a spoiled boy growing quickly into a bad man. This slave—a Jacob, I think?—then took refuge at Chota." His chest heaved with excitement at his recklessness, but the other man did not react, either to his condition or his evocation of the name Jacob. His eyes remained narrowed, his voice slow and deep. "And why would this Jacob," he asked, "this slave of my father, murder the boy if he had not yet finished becoming bad?" Abe responded without hesitation. "That's the part I'd love to know," he said. "I heard it had something to do with a Cherokee woman, perhaps the slave's lover." Redhand's mouth pursed. He cocked his head and looked at Abe quizzically, as if well puzzled. "Do you know her name?" he asked. And Abe, telling himself in for a penny, in for a pound, looked up at the blue sky as if searching there for his memory. "I think it was . . . let's see now . . . I think it was Dark Water. Or—and I know this sounds crazy—but maybe . . . let's see, an *m* name . . . maybe Marian too." Edward Redhand reached forward to unwind the team's reins from where he had secured them on the wagon's brake post. He lifted them with one hand and took up a whip with the other. "Dark Water?" Abe pretended to think. "Yes, I'm sure that's it." The Cherokee raised his whip. "Or maybe Marian?" Abe wrinkled his brow. "I think so."

Crack! The whip sliced the air and landed not on the horses' flanks but on the side of the wagon wheels, its sound nonetheless driving the beasts off at a wild pace through rough woodland paths. The cab and bed bounced dreadfully as it sped over rocks and crashed through puddles, which sprayed upward wetting the men as high as their shoulders. The black men held on to the sides of the bed for dear life. Abe held fast to the edges of his seat. Behind them, Hart's lead snapped at the sudden jolt forward, yet he galloped alongside fighting to keep up. All the while, Redhand laughed like a madman. "Ha, ha! Ha, ha! Dark Water, I think!" he cackled over the terrible sounds of the wagon racing over unruly ground. "Ha, ha! Maybe Marian? Ha, ha!" They coursed through a rut that was deeper than any of them surmised. The wagon listed to one side so far it nearly tipped over. The men in back rolled with the list to land in a mass of legs and arms against the cab's right side. Abe twisted so far he banged a knee, when sheer momentum twisted him back or surely he would have been thrown off the vehicle and landed against stone and tree. At last Edward Redhand had had his fun. He slowed the wagon. Abe and the slaves suffered coughing fits from the dust raised by a riotous ride. The Cherokee breathed normally.

"Oh, titmouse, titmouse," he said. "My sister named you well."

Abe struggled to catch his breath before dissembling.

"Your sister? What are you talking about? And why should this sister know me or name me thus?"

"Hmph. Don't you remember me, titmouse? I remember you. You sat in front of my sister's cabin on a stool plucking birds. You were covered in turkey feathers. It was the day I came with my friends to collect her and bring her up to the mountain peaks. She would not come. She was not ready. Not yet."

Not yet. The words came loud to him. They rang in his ears more intensely than the revelation that Redhand knew who he was. *Not yet. Not yet.* That could only mean that Marian was still alive. He sat back against the bench of the cab taking in the revelation.

"And you, married, titmouse? So quickly? She'll be surprised to hear that. After your eternal pledge." Edward Redhand chuckled then halted the wagon once more. "Come. Get out. From here, we go on horse and on foot."

Dozens of conflicting emotions ran through Abe's body, making him both shaky and confused. He was exhausted, disoriented, terrorized, relieved, overjoyed, guilty, anxious, and irritated. In frustration, he asked, "Why do you keep calling me titmouse? Why does she call me titmouse?"

The Cherokee alighted from the wagon while the slaves unhitched the team and secured Hart. Redhand mounted one of the horses. His men loaded whatever provisions remained on the other. "The titmouse," Redhand said, "is a harmless little bird. It has a tuft on its head, like the hair under the cap you always wear."

Abe mounted Hart. His eyes smarted with embarrassment and hurt although he fought not to show it. "So. Your sister finds me harmless and small, is that it?"

"No. It is for the other thing."

By now, Abe was exceedingly annoyed. "What other thing?" he asked sharply. Redhand raised an eyebrow at his impatience. "The titmouse has a certain call," he said. "It begins loudly and then fades away so that he may trick his enemies into thinking he has flown away. In the stories we tell our children, he is a deceiver who aids a great witch."

"I don't understand."

The other man sighed in the way fathers do when young sons are stubborn or thick.

"The titmouse is a liar," he said. "She is calling you a liar."

"Oh."

Suddenly, the earth opened and swallowed up the mortified soul of Abrahan Bento Sassaporta Naggar. His spirit descended deep inside the mountain into a fiery pool of shame, becoming smaller and smaller while what was left of him climbed higher up the mountain toward the sun. Hart grew restless sensing his rider's diminishment. Abe's legs went limp around him. The horse whinnied in a way that was mournful, distressed. After a time of riding in silence, the only sounds about them the movements of the horses and slaves who walked behind, for even the birds and the creatures of the wood were still, Redhand unexpectedly took pity, although perhaps his pity was more greatly extended to the horse carrying a man whose spirit had left him than the husk who rode him.

"When she calls you titmouse, she laughs," he said. "It is not said in anger."

Abe's head snapped up. His back, though suffering a world of penitential weight, went rigid as his soul returned to it. He asked Edward Redhand the only thing that mattered. "Where is she?" The Cherokee shrugged. Then beneath the bowels of the earth, the mouth of hell opened. Hell itself belched into the atmosphere the scent of all the exhalations of the multitude who writhed within its tortures. It was the scent that sprung from the pit where what molten rubber could be scraped or shoveled had been dumped.

Abe examined the pit for depth and breadth. Dusk came but the moon was full and there was plenty of light at first. Abe was shown where homes had been abandoned to escape the stench of the black gum puddles the mountain sun had made of that miracle substance before which the financial geniuses of the northern cities had bowed. Cherokee women wept, pointing to ruined gardens and putrid streams. Children scowled at him as he passed. Abe was humbled and stricken with fresh guilt. He asked Edward Redhand to whom he should appeal for forgiveness. Redhand informed him their *ghigua*, their Beloved Woman, would accept his remorse.

After the horses were relieved and put up for the night, he was taken to a place a short distance apart from the village. A great cloud descended over the mountain, making it difficult to see the way. Edward Redhand and two other men, by their dress and ornament Cherokee of some stature, led him bearing torches that he might see through the thick mist. Still, he stumbled. They came to a cave and halted. The torchbearers entered first, then gestured him to follow. Deep inside the cave down a long corridor of stone was a round, open space. A figure there beckoned him to approach. He complied. Drawing closer, he could see by its shape the figure was female. She sat on a kind of throne made of interlocking tree limbs. Her breasts were barely covered by a gaping, sleeveless robe the color of milk. Her head was down but her hair was dressed so that it stood out on its ends like rays of light. Lit torches were placed in sconces set in a semicircle behind her. Through the gray-and-purple darkness, they were like stars set around the moon. Her head lifted as he approached and he saw she wore a mask, like that of a sorcerer. It was in the shape of a beast he did not know, which unnerved him. When he reached her, he bowed from the waist.

"Great Mother," he said, "I have seen what the rubber has wrought and although I do not know how it is to be accomplished or assessed, I promise you there will be compensation."

The woman pulled herself up from the throne by leaning on a thick staff whose finial was carved into the shape of a stag head and from which flowed leather ribbons decorated with many colored beads. He saw that one of her feet was swathed in bandages. It looked twice the size of the other. She waved the Cherokee men away, waited until they stood guarding the entrance to the cave with their backs to them before she spoke. The sound of her voice knocked the breath out of him.

"Why should I believe you, titmouse, whose words are as dried leaves in the wind?"

She removed her mask. It was Marian. Marian was alive. Abe fell to his knees and babbled his amazement and regret. He confessed his sins. He kissed the hem of her robe. He would never lie to her again.

DARK WATER OF THE MOUNTAINS

Abe did not grovel long.

"Get on your feet, titmouse," she said. There was warmth in her tone despite the insult of address. "I have no anger toward you at present. I've come to understand why you lied to me. You were trying to save me, were you not? From the pain of seeing what Jacob has become? So many people have lied to me about him. My father. My mother. Under their direction, my brother also. Everyone in this village has lied to me about Jacob. Why should you be any different? Come to me. We will go deeper into this cave. I would like to lean on you. I've grown weary of my staff."

She put a hand on his shoulder, he put an arm around her waist. "Carry a torch," she said. "We'll need the light." With his assistance, she hobbled down a corridor of sheer stone without the wooden reinforcements common to mines. Its formation was either natural or carved out so long ago it might as well have been. Under the glow of his torch, graceful images of deer, hawks, and rabbit appeared on the walls, then vanished into the dark as they passed. After a short time, they arrived at a new opening of the rock, this one much higher and broader than the room with the throne. A bench, a table, a raised wooden bed fashioned out of interlocking tree limbs much like the throne and topped by a down mattress, two wooden chests, a fire pit, which was alight and occupied with heating a caldron suspended from a metal rack over a low flame, a stack of bowls, and other utensils were positioned about. At one end, the rock face dropped sharply off into a gorge through which a spring ran, while overhead, the rock face soared. As it was night and the mist had settled over the mountain, Abe could not determine the height of the ceiling, but it seemed infinite, and appeared to have an opening, perhaps quite small, at its center. The smoke of the fire snaked toward it as if a draft pulled it there. He helped Marian to the bench, where she sat and leaned forward, her elbows on the table, her clasped hands supporting her chin.

"Come sit by me," she said, "and I will tell you what happened to me. Were you distraught when I did not return to the cabin? Yes, of course you were. I wanted you to be. The English have a saying about hating the messenger who brings bad news. I hated you a little for telling me that Lulu was alive and lived in affection with Jacob at Chota. I hated you a little more when I found out it was not true. After everything I told you about how I loved him, why did you wish to hurt me with that news? It was a long time before I discovered the lie of it. Before that, I suffered."

"Forgive me, Marian. I was jealous."

She laughed. Her laughter echoed throughout the cave like a thousand bells chiming all at once. It mocked him.

"Really? Were you? I wonder if you can even know the meaning of the word. If for you jealousy was a race of mites beneath your skin, scratching at you until a bitter canker rose up on your tongue, for me it was an inferno that enflamed my very blood and consumed my senses. I was mad with it. I could not understand why Jacob had forsaken our vows to each other, that as long as we lived there should be the most sacred fidelity between us. From the day we first loved, no other man touched me until I was told he was dead, and after I thought him dead, throughout all the years since, what my body enjoyed, my heart ignored."

Abe was taken aback. He, who had loved her devotedly, passionately, did not represent anything remotely similar to a violation of her vow in her mind. He was an inconsequential event to her, a means to an end, a convenience, a tool, and that was all. He realized he understood nothing of this woman and listened more closely, seeking answers to the riddle of Dark Water of the foothills.

"For days, I tore through the woods, wailing. Branches ripped my skin. Thorns caught in my hair and pulled it out without my notice. I frightened my horse. She fled from me. I had not mourned like this since the year after Billy Rupert was killed, when I thought Jacob had died in battle, when I mourned him as a woman does her husband. I did not wash. I let my hair hang loose. I did not change my dress and cared not what I ate or when. My tears were like acid. They burned my skin and made me blind.

"That was how I walked into the river that belonged to the Catawba people before the white man drove them out. I waded into the waters close to a place where the falls could hurtle me headlong into rock. I had no idea how close they were. I did not hear them. I could not see. To this day, I believe I did not wander into danger intentionally. But perhaps I did. Isn't it more likely though that I only wanted the burning of my skin to be soothed? Who knows. The water was very cold, the currents were swift. After a time, my body went entirely numb. Without thinking, I gave myself to the river. I let myself drift in her arms, I don't know how long. Sometimes, I lay flat in the water. Other times, I got turned all about, somersaulting past deadwood. My ribs cracked against both the riverbed and debris. It didn't matter. I had given myself to the river. In my mind, I reached back to the time when Jacob and I were together and I floated there, as if in a dream, unaware of the present, unafraid of what came next. It was then I learned a most remarkable thing. The heart's will to live can die but the body ever fights to survive.

"After a great tumble down a wall of water, I became stuck, I don't know how. My foot wedged between two rocks, in a place close to the shoreline. For a while, the waters battered me back and forth like a reed in the wind. I swallowed much water. I coughed. I was nearly done for. I fell forward, ready to die, when a powerful spirit, dwelling until that time silent, watchful at the base of my lungs, leapt forth, roaring his refusal to succumb. Ai! I can still hear his voice shouting into the void! Suddenly, at his command, I ripped my foot from its stony trap, at the expense of much flesh and blood. I threw myself forward, landing on the riverbank. From there, I dragged myself into a cluster of huckleberry bushes, or perhaps that same spirit carried me, I cannot know today. And although it was long past the season for fruit—it was at the birth of winter, remember?—I watched, half-dead, astonished, as one of the bushes, a bush who had pity for me, suddenly bore fruit, pushing through its dead branches green leaves and clusters of beautiful, juicy berries, blue as the night sky. Giving thanks, I ate mouthful after miraculous mouthful, gaining strength until I could get myself, somehow, by another miracle or else I don't know how, to the boundaries of the old trade path. Then the fourth miracle. Four is a sacred number for us, did you know that? I should have expected something magical to happen next. And this is it: by the grace of Mother Moon, certain Cherokee found me that night and brought me here, to my brother, for healing. The people exulted, for they have always loved me, and put me here, in a cave of the ancients, to recover. Waking Rabbit, whom you know as Edward, then told me the truth about Jacob's life. He'd only recently learned himself that he was alive. For many years, only a handful of people outside Echota knew. The people there had protected him, keeping the secret that he had survived because he asked them to and because they were respectful of his bravery at Horseshoe Bend and of his service at our ancient burial grounds. Once you visited, he released the people of Echota from their vows of silence. Word spread. By the time I was found, my brother knew enough to tell me my titmouse had lied.

"Can you imagine my bittersweet happiness when I came to know? Poor Lulu, who thanks to you I'd thought miraculously alive, was truly dead, and my darling, who I thought long dead was suddenly alive! Now I wait until I am healed enough and then I will go to him, to my Jacob, and we will live the life that has been denied us nigh on twenty years."

Throughout her story, Marian looked straight ahead at the wall of rock beyond with a singular determination as if the force of her mind could paint images of her recollections there. Now that it was over, she turned to Abe. Her eyes were ablaze, her entire face, haloed by spiked hair, shimmered with a delirious vision of the future. She looked half-mad to him. It occurred to him that the period of mourning she described when she'd thought Jacob dead at the Battle of Horseshoe Bend must have been her state of being when Hannah stumbled across her fields at the age of four. He wasn't sure if he should ask her what sprang next to his mind, how wise it was to do so, or if, like one who walks in her sleep whose slumber should be left undisturbed, he risked shattering her by asking, but he asked anyway.

"Did Edward tell you how Jacob is nowadays? I mean, what happened to him?"

"Happened. Do you mean that he has lost good use of one leg, an arm? That his beauty, which I loved, is ruined?"

He nodded, watching her carefully for the smallest crack in her resolve. But there was none. She smiled, lifted her bandaged foot a little, and said, "We'll make a fine pair, won't we? Shuffling around old Chota together, chanting prayers to the dead. Oh, titmouse, titmouse. Why did you ask me? Did you think a love such as ours could ever dim from such a small thing? One of Waking Rabbit's men told me you married a pretty girl with hair dark red like autumn leaves and pink cheeks. Would you abandon her if suddenly she were ugly or crippled?"

Abe opened his mouth to attest his fidelity to Hannah, but he hesitated just enough to undermine what followed. "Of course not," he told her, blushing, as it felt quite odd to discuss Hannah with her. "She is my wife!" Marian raised an eyebrow and pursed her lips, scolding him. "I hope she is more than that," she said. "One blanket can keep two dry in a pleasing rain, but not in a torrent."

Abe squirmed in his seat. Would this woman always make him feel an idiot, an inferior? Would she always hover above him, an all-knowing force, seeing through him, chastising him, instructing him? Would they ever be simply a man and woman together, friends perhaps, brother and sister even, anything beyond this imbalanced, tortured relation? Once he'd thought there were a thousand points of congruity between them. Were they not both children of exile, seeking freedom from their oppressors, both rebels, adventurers in their separate ways? But now he realized that while he'd left the Old World and forged an identity that rejected much of it, one he reveled in, Dark Water strove with every ounce of her considerable strength to hold on to everything she knew of her past and the past of her people, that her past, their past, was, in fact, where she found her strength. A flash of shame went through him. The past was the strength of Jews also, but he'd pushed his heritage aside in his hurry to live an American life, to make his fortune, to marry a gentile. Worse, despite all that, despite his marriage to Hannah, despite the lovely future he'd mapped out for himself and his bride, despite the fact that this Dark Water of the mountains, his Marian, was soon to be reunited with the monster Jacob and happily so, he found himself wanting her as much as he ever had, more even. What impossible pain! His fists clenched where he'd placed them on the tabletop. His breath, belabored now, echoed through the heights and depths of the cave. The heat from the fire pit felt uncomfortably close and he broke into a sweat. His once beloved who did not, never did, love him regarded him with narrowed eyes.

"It's time for you to go, Peddler. We will talk in Council tomorrow about reparations for the rubber damage."

Peddler! Peddler! Would she ever bother to learn his name? Anger built up in him so that his desire twisted into a hot, thorny knot at his core. He could bear it no longer. His voice became

191

weighted with a kind of whining command, his questions more like the barks of a small dog.

"When? When do you intend to go to him?"

His pique meant nothing to her. She rose from her table and limped alongside it using one hand against the wall to balance herself until she reached the caldron, where, taking a bowl and ladle, she served herself a fragrant helping of savory stew. She did not offer Abe any. She set her bowl on the table before returning to her seat. Once she was settled, she answered him.

"Soon. In a matter of weeks. He's waiting for me. We've sent more messengers back and forth to each other than John Ross and Chief Pathkiller. He begged to come to me but I insisted he wait. Our law prevents him from traveling here without abandoning the sanctuary that brought him to Chota. My mother might enslave him again out of spite. After all we've been through, I would not have him jeopardize his life."

"Let me take you to him," Abe blurted out impulsively, without any forethought whatsoever.

"Why?"

Abe did not know why exactly himself. But the idea had come to him like a lightning bolt. Hannah always told him one should embrace such feelings. They were often divine in inspiration, she said. Alright then, he thought, I will pursue this queer spark of the brain. If I am late getting back home, Hannah will understand when I tell her of it. I'll say it was under her direction in a way. As he analyzed things, he warmed up to the idea. His argument took on an impassioned flair.

"If I do, you can go sooner," he said. "I can look after you along the way. Why should you and he spend a moment apart that's not necessary?"

"Peddler. If that's what I wanted, I could have one of my own people accompany me. No, I want to go to him as whole as I can be."

"Please, let me do something for you. I owe you it."

She did not respond but set to eating her stew, holding the bowl in two hands and bringing it to her mouth. Abe pulled an ace out of his back pocket.

"Alright, then. If you are concerned that he will love you less infirm . . ."

Dark Water slammed her bowl back on the table so that the contents splattered about.

"How dare you!" she said, eyes blazing.

"Prove I'm wrong. Let me take you."

A few heartbeats of silence passed between them, combative heartbeats, no one backing down, then Dark Water laughed and slapped a hand against the tabletop. It was a sign of agreement. Favor blossomed between them and they made a plan. They would travel to Chota together in two days, after Abe had an opportunity to meet with the Council and settle on a claim against Sassaporta and Son. As the clan's *ghigua*, Dark Water held a powerful seat on the Council. She was the peace chief, the one who settled arguments. She promised him fair if not generous treatment. Only after they'd worked out the details of the journey to Chota did she offer him stew, which they ate together, quietly, as in olden times. Afterward, he helped her to her bed and left her there unmolested, which made him feel virtuous.

Edward Redhand was at the mouth of the cave. He was alone. His men had left. He looked as if he had not budged during Abe's audience with his sister but remained motionless under the moon, patient, immoveable, silent, keeping his own counsel, not the master of time nor its slave, but its partner. "I will take you to where you will sleep," he said.

Abe followed him to a house finer than the other homes of the village, all of which were log homes, each of three or four rooms. The great house was twice as large as that. Its windows were glass paned and had curtains. There were flowering bushes in clay pots at its door, stones laid in decorative patterns in its yard. Two indistinguishable young Cherokee sat in rockers on its porch. They stood when Abe and Edward Redhand approached. Redhand introduced them as his twin brothers, Black Stone and White Stone. Everyone shook hands and they all entered the house.

They waited in a large foyer with hooked rugs and finely crafted tables upon which cut flowers in painted ceramic bowls were set. After a short while, an elder Cherokee woman entered, followed by her black slave. The woman was tiny, wizened, her skin the color of dark honey, bright golden butter, and copper all together. She was dressed extravagantly in a black taffeta dress of antique design with ample skirts and many flounces. As if the dress were not ornament enough, she wore a white lace dickey pinned to her breast by a ruby set in gold. Her white hair was arranged in a thick knot at the side of her neck, and a black square of cloth sat on the top of her head in the manner of the death's cap English judges wear with a tasseled point coming forward over her brow. Her slave was a tall, heavyset woman in middle age, her thick waist and belly obvious under a sackcloth shift. She wore a frayed blue bandana around her head. Tight gray curls poked out all around it. Her face was broad, her features large, fleshy, and impassive. Her ankles were swollen, spilling over the sides of her moccasins. She was twice the size of her mistress.

The lady of the house extended a hand toward Abe while Edward Redhand made introductions.

"I present my mother, widow of Chief Redhand, and mother of Dark Water, White Stone, Black Stone, and me. Mother, this is that peddler we've told you about, Abe Sassaporta, who is known to our sister and who sold us rubber."

At the word "rubber," the widow of Chief Redhand slipped her hand out of Abe's respectful grasp though she continued smiling up at him with cold, glittering eyes, two pebbles of blackest quartz.

"Welcome to my home," she said. Her voice was low, reedy, the voice of an ancient, one laced with a weary cynicism. "I'm sure you are tired. Daniella will take you to your room." She turned to quit his company, her head high, moving across the anteroom on tiptoe in the mincing steps of a grand lady, although it could have been her age that made her movements so small, so crabbed. It was impossible to him that this was the same woman who'd had strength enough to scratch a young, robust Marian near senseless with a fishbone when she'd rebelled against the idea of marriage to a settler husband. For all her antiquated finery, it was a fact her life had not gone the way she'd wished to shape it. Clearly, she'd suffered over that. He could well believe that this bitter woman would reenslave Jacob. "You may retire when you're done, Daniella," she called over her shoulder. "I'll undress myself tonight."

"Yes ma'am." The black woman nodded in a direction opposite that the widow of Chief Redhand took, waited patiently while Abe bid her sons good night, then, candelabra in hand, led him down a short corridor, stopping at a guest-room door invitingly ajar. Inside, the windows had been open against the heat of the day, but the night air had gone increasingly cool. Daniella stepped inside and busied herself getting a quilt from the wardrobe and draping it over the foot of the bed against evening's chill.

The room was as well appointed as any rich planter's guest accommodations might be. There was a four-poster bed, washstand, the wardrobe, a small writing desk and chair, linens embroidered with delicate flowers, a porcelain chamber pot, and warm, thick rugs. Set on a stone mantelpiece above a fireplace was a silver tray with two small crystal glasses and a decanter of what looked like sherry. Next to that was a bowl of ripe apples and pears. Abe sat on the bed. It felt delightfully soft after nights spent on the ground. Daniella came to the side of the bed where he sat. She leaned over and pulled off his boots, telling him she'd have them cleaned and outside the door by the time he woke. "Might you like a warm bath in the mornin', sir?" she asked. "I can get you a tub and hot water, if you're likin' the idea." He told her he liked the idea very much. She asked if he wanted her to launder some of his clothes. Pointing to his kit, which had been delivered there earlier, he said most everything he had could use a turn. "Anything else, sir?" She stood at the door holding an armful of clothes and his boots. "No, Daniella. I must say you're very thorough, very kind. Have you worked for the family long?" He wanted to talk to someone about Marian, about her younger days when Billy Rupert was murdered, and hoped the slave might be forthcoming. She did not disappoint. "Oh, yes sir," she said. "Since I was a young calf. I come here from the islands. I been workin' in the kitchen from the start and only came to the missus after her Lulu run off. Poor child."

Abe sat up and attempted to sound casual when he spoke

next. "Yes, I've heard something of that Lulu. And Jacob, Lulu's husband, did you know him?" Daniella rolled her eyes. "Oh, yes sir. Everyone knew Jacob. He was mighty hard to miss."

He gestured to the chair by the writing desk. "Why don't you sit down and tell me about them, Daniella. I'd love to know more than what I do." He put a hand in his pocket, pulled out a copper coin, and tossed it to her. Quick as that, she shifted the clothes and boots to her hip so she could safely catch it and shove it inside her dress before he could grab it back. Abe smiled his winning salesman's smile and told her to sit down by the writing desk while he poured them both some sherry. Within just a few minutes and fewer sips, the slave opened up.

LORD GEOFFREY, LULU, AND BILLY RUPERT

Y ou want to know about the olden days, do you, when the chief was alive and livin' like the king of England, yes? I can tell you things was different then. His big house was nothin' like the one you settin' in right t'here. This one'd be the slave common house back then. His big house was the biggest house anyone'd ever seen or slept in and that includes the white folks thereabouts. Had to be grand for those parties a his. He called it politickin'. All the white folk from miles around come visitin' time to time and we made banquets for 'em. Oh, yes, squash soups and bean cakes, corn puddin', roast turkeys stuffed with chestnuts, and venison on a spit. The chief never had a lick of liquor himself, more's the pity, maybe things'd gone better for him if he had. But at them banquets, wines and bourbon and brandies came from spigots like mountain water does from the well. There was dancin' too, fiddlers, flutes, and mandolins in every room. Oncet Mr. Crockett came. Another time, Joseph Vann. You know those men?"

Daniella finished her sherry in one go, then put forward her glass for more. Abe refilled it, thinking he'd landed in a pot of good luck, finding a woman who liked to talk and a bottle to coat her tongue, make it good and slick, all at the same time.

"Crockett I know of, he's that representative from Tennessee railed against the Removal Act. Vann? I've heard his name here and there. Has a shipping line, no?"

"Oh my Lord, well, he's just about the richest Cherokee anyone's ever seen. Only one I know of richer than the chief used to be. Got plantations and steamboats and over two hundred slaves at his command. Mean as can be too, lemme tell you. Meaner than his daddy, James, and that daddy a his was one devil of a man. But Joseph Vann. Why, he'd string you up for a rebellious glance. When I was a girl, the kitchen boss used to say, 'You gals don' behave youselves, I'm gonna sell you to Rich Joe Vann.' And oh my, didn' we straighten up then. Truth is, though, he's mostly white. But for alla that, Mr. Vann, even he come callin' to Chief Redhand with his hat off, that's how my lady's old husband did do."

She leaned forward, crooking a finger that Abe would come close and incline his ear to her. He did so. She looked right, looked left, then whispered.

"I'll tell you a secret. The chief never was comfy bein' that way. He'd smile and shake the hand what come to him, nod his head at the business talk. But soon as all the world gone home and there's quiet in his room, it's off with his fancy pants and he's into his leggin's and long shirt, callin' for his pipe to puff a li'l thanksgivin' into the air that the bloody thing was over. Ha, ha!"

She pushed him back with one hand, chuckling for all she was worth. Abe saw she had no fear of him, which, drunk or not, was exceedingly strange. If she'd had twice the sherry he'd given her, it still would have been strange. Last he'd checked, he was still white. According to the United States of America, despite being a Jew, he was whiter than a Cherokee, never mind that the Cherokee thought themselves on the same level as whites. A black slave should have been circumspect with him, copper coin or not. Had she never been taught proper manners? Was she spoiled with kindness? He'd never thought much about whether the Cherokee treated blacks any better than white folk, so he put a few minutes to it. The men in the barracks back at Isadore's camp liked to joke about the airs Cherokee put on, pretending they were equal to Europeans, keeping blacks under their thumbs to prove the point. He'd heard they mated with them and had children together, but who among the white plantation population didn't do similar from time to time? How was it Daniella spoke with him so freely, mocking her owners, disrespecting their dead? He recollected Jacob's story of the Cherokee mother who'd loved him, encouraging him to think himself free until she proved he wasn't. He considered Jacob in Chota, where he was given refuge despite being black and a slave, by all evidence honored and protected by his betters. On the other hand, there was this Joseph Vann, who'd lynch a black man as soon as slap him, although he, Daniella had pointed out, was mostly white, so perhaps he didn't count. My oh my, thought Abe, the racial lines in the New World blurred considerably up in Cherokee country. One could rattle one's reason trying to figure out what policies were expedient and what policies came from the heart. Yet this was the field in which the love between Marian and Jacob had taken root, given them the hope that they could love each other in peace. If he hoped to ever understand it, he needed to know more.

"There's something I'm trying to figure out, Daniella," he tried. "Chief Redhand's daughter had Lord Geoffrey at her feet, and that Billy Rupert came calling too. What happened there and how did the slave Jacob come to be mixed up in it?"

Daniella held her crystal glass against her chest with two hands. Her grasp looked to tighten, then relax, tighten, relax, over and over again, the fingers twisting, loosening, twisting. "Hmm," she said, "hmmm." Her lower lip jutted out, her eyes studied the ceiling. "Now, that's a precious story you're askin' me for," she said. He pulled two more coppers from his pocket and placed them in his open palm. Her gaze bored into him while the rest of her features went impassive. He added two more. Her hand shot out to grab the money. It disappeared inside her dress before he finished closing his palm.

"Alright. Now, where to start? That Lord Geoffrey. My, but he was a sad man to start with. Always looked like he'd et a bowl of gloom for breakfast. Eyes like a beaten dog. Even when he was with Miss Dark Water, or Marian as he liked to call her. Maybe his eyes looked pitiful especially when he was with her, because what'd he ever do besides traipse around behind her holdin' her gloves or her hat or whatever English confinement she looked to be free of. Oh, sure, every day he'd sit awhile somewhere he liked the light and paint his lily-white heart out, but after that he'd be tuckered and take his tea and a nap in his room. Unless of course Miss Dark Water had need of him. Then he was on his toes and runnin'! There was a time after she got home from England that they'd go ridin' together every day but then she had a fight with her mamma and daddy, and she took to the woods for a bit. That was the end of their rides. Poor Lord Geoffrey. After that, he got gloomier still. When she came back outta the woods and stayed to home again, she'd disappear for hours at a time and he'd go lookin' for her, glidin' around corridors of that big old house like a ghost, sad and swift. One day he found her rootin' on the floor of the game house with the slave Jacob, who don't you know was her true love. Oh, yes, lip to lip and limb to limb they was. But you know about how they loved, don't you? Everybody in this village knows you know that."

She reached out and squeezed his hand while a look of sympathy crossed over her broad, bland features. Abe blinked. Everybody in the village knew the darkest torments of his heart. She'd said so. He had no doubt it was true. Humiliation seized his throat and wrung it dry. How pathetic was the story they told of him that he'd won pity from a slave? She held out her glass. The sherry was half gone. Dry as he was, he didn't dare take more for himself lest there weren't enough left to inspire Daniella to finish her story. Filling her glass, he encouraged her to continue. "And?" he said as pleasantly as his suffering would allow.

"Oh, not much more to that man, was there? They say Dark Water and Jacob didn't even stop their business when he caught 'em. I like to think Jacob probably didn't know. But she did. They say she looked up from the floor and stared right in his eyes, then closed them and kept on goin'. He left in the next few days, as soon as he could book passage back to England and arrange a carriage to take him to the port. But after he was gone, came the letters. So many of 'em! He musta written two, maybe three a day. Then they stopped and after that came the news that Lord Geoffrey was dead, hung from his daddy's game house by his own hand. They say Dark Water didn't shed a tear."

Abe wondered if all of those who gossiped about Geoffrey killing himself also knew that Dark Water saved his letters and his portrait. Why would a woman preserve the memory of a man who meant so little to her? Was it guilt? Seeing his attention had wandered, Daniella leaned forward and tapped his knee. "But it's the Billy Rupert part you bought the right to know, isn't it, sir?" She leaned back again in the chair, smiling and tapping the sides of her glass, her lips pursed in amusement. "Yes," he said. "Yes, it is."

"Billy Rupert. Billy Rupert. Such a worthless lad to make a ruckus out of. Let's see, where was I? Oh, yes, Jacob and Dark Water were able to love but in secret. The Cherokee don't care how their men mess with black women. Why look at Shoe Boots, they even made his half-black children citizens equal to all after he pestered the courts. But who is Cherokee and who is not passes through the mother in every other case, so that blood they want pure. Things was a bit easier then, but not much. Today, only white or Injun can marry with the ladies, you see, without punishment. There's the twenty-five lashes—"

"Yes," Abe interrupted. "I've heard that. Twenty-five lashes if a Cherokee woman marries a black slave."

Daniella nodded. "Uh-huh, so you know. Now. Once Lord Geoffrey was gone, Dark Water's parents looked about for a rich white to marry her. It shouldn't have been much of a chore except she was known all over for bein' willful. In those days, many whites wanted to marry Cherokee women as a way of grabbing onto their inheritance. They had no love of the people. They were the intruders, the ones who wished only to steal the land and make it their own. Marriage was a heap easier than drivin' 'em off with a torch and gun.

"The chief's plantation was close to the one Teddy Rupert made, only the Rupert spread was spankin' new then and not rich like it is today. His people was from Canada. They knew nothin' of the plants and trees what grow best here, nor did they know the climate or how a crop got the blight. The chief helped 'im. Gave 'im fruit trees, fig, apple, and lemon, tole 'im how to protect 'em in winter. He gave 'im all the kinds of potatoes the Cherokee know, which are five. He taught 'im how to make the best bed for the corn and the cotton and the squash. He gave 'im vines from his own bean field. What didn't he give 'im? In the first years, Teddy Rupert was stunned grateful. He brought the chief the first fruits of his harvest and other presents. After the chief moved us from the village to the big house, Teddy Rupert, his wife, and that bastard, Billy, come visitin' often. The men smoked the wild tobacco while the women played flutes and sang for their pleasure. How Elizabeth Rupert must've hated those visits! Later on, we all discovered what was in her true heart, but even then there was somethin' about her I did not like but could not name.

"Billy would hunt with Wakin' Rabbit, with White Stone and Black, but Dark Water ignored him. Oncet she was gone off to England, he was gone off to Boston to become a gentleman. He returned shortly after she did, fat and red-cheeked, full of airs and foolish gestures. If you could have seen 'im! He'd be takin' a handkerchief and holdin' it in two fingers and wavin' it all about when he spoke. He'd grown a habit too of blowin' out the corner of his mouth to a thatch of hair that fell over his brow, makin' those blondie wisps fly when he wanted you to think he just said somethin' important. Lord Geoffrey, who was still with us then, said even the English was not so ridiculous.

"But then Lord Geoffrey was gone. The chief and my lady turned their sights to Billy Rupert as a husband for their girl. Now, his mama bragged that Billy Rupert was goin' into the law and for the chief the next best husband to an English lord was an

American lawyer. Who better to help the nation to thrive among the whites? Cherokee leaders was near every day in the courts up to Washington to represent the nation. Just as they are this day. Anyway, Billy Rupert came callin'. Dark Water laughed in his face. The chief ordered her to suffer more visits from 'im. And that she did but only so no one would suspect she had a lover, much less who that lover might be. Mind you, all the slaves knew what was up and what was not, but the chief and his wife, maybe her brothers too, why they were as ignorant as rocks on the subject. Soon enough, you couldn't keep Billy Rupert out of the house. Wakin' Rabbit took to stayin' in the high places just to get away from 'im. He told my lady he sought a wife out of the paint clan and spent many hours away from home wooin' maidens. Sometimes, because they begged 'im, he took the twin boys with 'im too. No one wanted to be in the house when Billy Rupert was there. Which is why, I've always been thinkin', he started nosin' around the slaves.

"There was gals in the slave quarters didn't mind the company of men, even if it meant a lot of it. Some of 'em were gals lost their babies to the traders or maybe their true loves. Others never got over bein' taken from their mamas too young. I guess those gals figured if they weren't gonna have a regular life, they might as well have one that got 'em somewhere. The poorest man'll find a bit o' ribbon, or a square of lace, maybe a li'l silk or satin, somethin' sweet like that, no matter what trouble it takes, if it's what'll get 'im some sugar from a pretty gal. It's nothin' I'd do and no path I'd raise a boy to follow. But I'm not judgin'.

"So anyway, among all those brokenhearted songbirds, there was one sang her sad song like an angel from above and that was Lulu, the one Jacob threw over when Dark Water turned his head away. That Lulu had strong legs and high breasts, a long neck, the kind a man liked to lay his head against just for the silky touch of it. Sum up, she had a body and a nature made for forgettin' all your cares and woes and there was many who went to her to do so. Maybe it helped her forget some too.

"Well, before too long, Billy Rupert noticed her. Took to usin' her, and not kindly either. Whenever Dark Water was out with Jacob, you could be damn sure Billy Rupert would be botherin' Lulu. One day, that poor gal could take no more. She put a knife from the kitchen in her clothes. I know this 'cause I'm the one gave it to her. I had pity, you see. I thought she was gone to kill her own self and I warn't judgin', but it was Billy Rupert's heart her blade sought.

"They were alone in the common house. Everybody else but a young girl nursin' a fever was at their chores. Ellie told us all what she'd seen while hidin' 'mongst her bedclothes. Billy Rupert put his hands on Lulu. She saw her chance and took it, jabbin' with all her might at his chest. Dammit all, he seen it comin' and it missed. He went into a rage after that. He got the knife from her. Dragged her outta the common house by her hair and into the woods and there he cut her up good. Cut her face. Cut her belly. Cut her left breast clear off. He woulda kept on goin', but a work crew come down from the fields just after and they spied him runnin' away and her layin' there bleedin' and weepin' and nearly dead.

"Lulu got bound up and she lived alright but in the meantime Jacob tracked down that Billy Rupert and killed him. Killed him with flamin' arrows. They say Dark Water dipped the arrows in pitch, lit 'em, and handed 'em to 'im, one by one. They done it together, they say. I don't know about that. Nobody knows for sure, 'cept them two and the dead. There was no one didn't think Billy Rupert had it comin', but there was still hell to pay. Oh, yes, sheer hell to pay. But who should do the payin'?

"The Ruperts didn't know about the murder of their baby boy for a bit o' time. Likely they thought he was in the town, sportin' about. Or even still at the chief's plantation, doin' what he did. Now, to get what happened next, you have to understand Dark Water was the princess of her people. Everybody loved her. She was the best of the old ways and yet she knew better than any of 'em the ways of the new, havin' been in England and all. When she was gone that year, the crops failed. Everyone thought it was because she was gone. When she returned, the world bloomed. So understand, no one wanted to see her suffer 'cause of this, especially since Billy Rupert had it comin'. Then Jacob came forward confessin' all. She did too, with some crazy story took all the blame on her own head, but no one believed her. That was when she left to live away from the people. Never before had anyone doubted her word. It was too much for that one. She was hoppin' mad at the clans, her father, and 'specially Jacob himself. He's the one what stole her word and took her power away. But she could hop spittin' fire if she wanted to, everybody'd rather Jacob pay the price than their own dear.

"An' he did. Off he went to Chota, where at least he could live. Least until the Battle of Horseshoe Bend, or so we all thought. Old man Rupert wanted his hide, but that Elizabeth Rupert, Billy's mama, cared more about the chief's land than the fair livin' head of her own son. She saw opportunity and grabbed it, went to the courts to git the chief to sign over his plantation to pay for what his slave did and dang me, I'm not sure how it happened, you'd have to ask Miss Dark Water or my lady that 'cause

I'm sure I don't know who else knows, but the courts failed 'im and he gave the land away. Broke his heart too. He was never the same after that. Why, he just clammed up and faded away, bit by bit, 'til there was nothin' left to 'im and the first strong wind of winter carried him off. An' that's it. There's no more story I got except the long, cold tale of how we all got up here to the top of this mountain, and I'm not sure that's a story you care much about anyways."

Abe was silent a long while, absorbing everything she told him. He was silent so long, Daniella fell asleep and started to snore, which startled him into awareness. Waking her, he helped her pick up the clothes and the boots. He took up the candelabra and helped her to her room off the kitchen, as she was unsteady on her feet. Once he got her there, she flopped onto her cot in one great abandonment of gravity and consciousness, rattling the floorboards. "I don' know why they say that," she muttered when, out of kindness, he bent to remove her shoes as she had his. "Say what?" he asked. "That Jews are nasty greedy," she said. "You been awful generous and nice to me."

"You're welcome," Abe said, and covered her with a sheet.

Despite the fine feather bed, his sleep was poor. He awoke every hour or so with a mind full of questions whose answers were elusive, just beyond his grasp. Who had killed Billy Rupert? Was it Jacob alone? Jacob and Marian together? Or Marian on her own? Why had she kept Lord Geoffrey's letters and portrait if she didn't love him? When he'd met Jacob, Jacob was over the moon when he told him Marian had forgiven him some great sin. What was that sin?

He was so tired the next day at Council that he promised the Cherokee everything they asked. Sassaporta and Son would return all the money they'd paid for rubber product plus 5 percent more to compensate for damages. He had no idea where the money would come from. If he had to, he'd sell the house Isadore had given him as a wedding present. But where would he find a buyer? Where would he take his pretty little wife? To Tobias Milner's farm, where they could sleep in the kitchen like slaves and wayfarers? Such thoughts did not improve the next night's sleep.

It was with a pounding head and ragged heart that he started out the next morning with Marian to Chota. His body was exhausted, his mood was dark, he'd no idea why he'd wanted to take her there in the first place. When they started out, several men carried her down the mountain on a litter to a place where the trail widened. There, they hitched Hart to a waiting wagon and placed Marian, Hart's tack, and a variety of Marian's possessions in it. Edward assured Abe the trade routes could accommodate the width of the wagon wheels and that even a novice driver could handle the terrain. Abe sat grumpily up front while Marian sat in the back, where she could stretch out her leg with the bandaged foot. She hummed happy songs, as cheery as the first spring day when flowers suddenly poke themselves up from the dirt, their green buds crushing all memory of cold and bitterness. Part of him wanted to tell her to hush up.

"You're very quiet, my friend," she remarked when she'd tired of singing.

He wondered if he was supposed to stop the wagon, get down on his knees in the dirt, and thank God that she'd not called him peddler or titmouse but friend. He grunted instead.

"My mother told me the welcome drink was gone this morning," she said. "If your head's aching, I can point out a leaf along the way to better it. When we stop to rest the horse, we can brew a tea. Willow might do the job, or crape myrtle, though to find the latter around here would be a chore."

It irritated him that she'd turned into a chattering magpie all of a sudden. He understood she was excited, that their journey represented the revival of love's hope after twenty years of despair, but he liked his Marian more, well, Dark Water. He grunted again to encourage her to please shut up. But she continued.

"I'm very grateful now the time's here that you're taking me to Chota, that I didn't delay," she said. "You were right. It was a stupid idea to wait. I don't know what I was thinking. I guess it was an issue of my pride. Ha! My pride! Why haven't I learned, my friend? Why after all that's happened, after half a lifetime of regret, I haven't learned to abandon my pride?"

"It's a large part of who you are," Abe said.

"Really?"

There was something flirtatious in her question, the way she said it. Who was this girlish woman he found himself in company with?

"I wouldn't know you without it," he said.

Hart made a snuffling sound as if in agreement. She giggled. Giggled!

"Jacob wrote me that when you went to him, you told him I forgave him. What did you know of that?"

"Nothing. I guessed."

"Huh." She was quiet for a time. Abe offered a small prayer of thanksgiving. Then she started up again. "Maybe I should tell you. Would you like to know?"

Razors scraped along the nerve ends at his neck. He wanted her quiet, the job of transport done. Since they came down the mountain and were now on the west side of the Unicoi range, it wouldn't take much longer to get her to Chota. But the trip home would be at least a week. He'd have to travel through Tennessee north and up and over the mountains again, across half the state of North Carolina, to get to Greensborough. He wished he could close his eyes and be there already with a woman who lived to please him. He wanted away, far, far away from the one who lived to give him agonies, by buckets or teaspoons as the occasion allowed. But still, he said, "Yes. I want to know that very much." Because, damn him, he did.

Of course, she went quiet then. He waited. Gnashed his teeth. Waited some more. At last, patience destroyed, he barked at her. "Well? What was it? What did you have to forgive him for?" She sighed, three times, with long pauses in between.

Finally, she spoke. "You paid Daniella too much," she said. "She would have told you everything just for the drink." He bit his tongue to keep back all he thought to say. She continued. "It's a village, you know. Before the cock crows, everyone knows everything that's transpired in the night. It's not easy to keep a secret in a village, or on a plantation, for that matter. And when two people love, as much as they try to hide it, everyone near them with eyes in their heads can see it. When they're in a room together, a fool can see the way their skin shines, the way the muscles go taut. If that room is full of people, somehow they always manage to stand near each other, where a hand can brush a hand, or the breath of one caresses the neck of the other. Even the blind can feel their heat. Jacob forgot that. I was so young, I didn't know it. Our lack of caution got us into heaps of trouble.

"First there was Lord Geoffrey. He knew. He mentioned his suspicions to me several times, in that cloaked way the English have. You know it. He'd say, 'My, but that Jacob fellow does a smashing job of taking care of you for your father, doesn't he?' and hold his breath, staring at me, waiting for a reaction. I'd do my best not to blush, but I'm sure my feet tapped against the floor, or my skin shivered, something I know gave me away because I couldn't help myself, you see? What can I say. Despite my evasions, he found out the truth somehow and left us. I know Daniella must have told you what came next."

"Yes," Abe said quietly. *He left us.* Was that all she had to say about a man's grisly death at his own hand for her sake? Would she have said more had it been him in Lord Geoffrey's place?

"Billy Rupert was another story altogether. Even as a boy he was cruel. I remember when we were all young together and his father would bring him when he visited my father. This was before the plantation, when we lived a normal life. My brothers and I would take Billy Rupert with us when we hunted and when we played games by the river. The things that delighted him repulsed us. He would pull the wings off insects and pin the legs of frogs to the earth, then watch while birds of prey came and plucked their innards out. He was a horror and we hated him. But years went by. He acquired an education and learned to hide his cruelties. He also acquired a future inheritance while his father expanded his properties. My father and his decided we were a perfect match. Their plantations could be joined at the price of purchasing just a small strip of land from a family of newcomer Germans. What could be better?

"Jacob and I living together in the foothills could be better. Sensing that the dogs of fate were on our trail, I told Jacob, 'Let's get married somewhere. It doesn't have to be a Cherokee wedding. We can marry at a trading post, some frontier town where no one cares who marries who.' He hesitated. He said he could not expose me to a slave's life on the run. I told him that would be a low price to pay for paradise. He kissed me, he fondled me, he lay deep and long with me to tell me, oh, how brave and dear I was but he could not allow it. He would not have me suffer such pain out of love for him. So we went along in our mist of loving until the world came crashing in.

"We were in the wood one day, loving as we might. Afterward, we strolled along the riverbank dreaming of a future together. I'd taken my short bow and arrows as an excuse to spend time with him. I'd told my parents I was bored and left to hunt what might cross my path. They knew my habits and thought nothing of it. Anyway. As we walked, arm in arm, I told Jacob I would convince my mother to free him. Who better than he? He was raised Cherokee. He knew our ways, he respected them, there was no man closer to the true blood. Once he was free, we could marry without encumbrance. Then, in the midst of our daydreams, out of the wilderness came the cry of a woman. Her cries were cries of terror. We ran forth, thinking some poor girl had fallen prey to a pack of wild dogs. But no. It was a woman fallen prey to Billy Rupert. And the woman was Lulu, once Jacob's wife, whom he'd always liked well enough but failed to love.

"An atrocity lay before us. Billy Rupert's pants were around his knees. He had a kind of dagger in his hand, a sharp curved blade with an ivory handle, and he hovered over a sometimes whimpering, sometimes crying-out Lulu, who was bleeding on the ground. His arm swept up and down as he sliced at her, cackling like a crow while he did so. Oh, he had an abundance of pleasure in his actions. Jacob did not hesitate. He roared. Roared like a great bear. The very leaves of the trees trembled with his anger. He rushed forward to stop the man. There followed a tussle between them. Jacob was unarmed. The wild slashes of Billy Rupert's blade cut my love's arm, his leg. For a time, I did not know who would be the victor.

"So. What else could I do? I withdrew my arrows and placed them in the bowstring, one after another. I took out Billy Rupert's eyes first, then placed several in his heart, next for the joy of it, I pierced his root, just for the pleasure of seeing this beastly, dying man double up and cry out in misery for his manhood, now lost, lost by my own hand. In all of two minutes, the life of Billy Rupert was over and I could not help but think, None too soon, none too soon.

"Jacob cradled Lulu in his arms. He wept. He cried to her, to Lulu who may have heard him, maybe not. 'Forgive me, forgive me. For leaving you unprotected,' he said. And then he shouted at me, 'Get help! She will surely die!' This I did, running through the wood, unheeding of the stones beneath my feet, the brambles whipping at my thighs. How small my little wounds seemed to what Lulu suffered! A band of our warriors heard my cries for help. They followed me back, back to the place where Lulu lay, in Jacob's bloody arms, near breathing her last. They picked her up, took her to the medicine man nearest us that he might save her life and heal her with his crystals, powders, and smoking sticks. A conspiracy was forged at her bedside between the medicine man, the warriors, Jacob, and me. Together, we concocted a story of what had happened. My mother would learn her girl had been ravaged by a bobcat, that her life hung by a thread. My father was told his valet wished to nurse her who was once his wife, as an act of kindness, which he admired and permitted. In this way we were able to keep secret what had happened until weeks later, when Billy Rupert's body was discovered mutilated by beasts, the sun, rain, and insects.

"In the meantime, Lulu's life was spared but her once-beautiful face was ruined as was her body. Jacob was most kind to her. He sat with her, keeping watch. He fed her. He changed her dressings and bathed her too. Of course, I was conflicted over this. He had little time for me. I was young. I was jealous, bitterly so. Every minute he spent with her I spent weeping, tearing my clothes, or beating whatever objects were close at hand with my fists out of frustration and rage. But I also shared his guilt. If he had stayed with her, if I had not encouraged Billy Rupert to court me as a way to disguise our love from the world, Lulu would not have caught that man's brutal eye. When Jacob said to me, 'If we had parted and this happened to you, would you not want me to take care of you?' I had to say yes. So I buried my jealousy and took to visiting her in her sick room, to bringing her presents of flowers and the little sweet cakes Daniella made. In this odd way, in looking after her, our victim, Jacob and I grew closer still.

"After Billy Rupert's body was discovered, there were only theories of what had killed him, thanks to the degradation of his flesh. Only Jacob, the warriors, the medicine man, and I knew the truth. None of us would tell. My people loved me. Several of the men had known Lulu well enough to be grateful for Jacob's revenge. We were safe. But here's what happened. Lulu's body recovered, but her mind did not. As soon as she could walk, she went to the river and got herself killed, ripped apart by man or beast, at least that's what everyone thought. It made sense. No woman used to life in those parts would walk out in the dark, with no weapon, no protector. It was as if she didn't care about herself anymore. Didn't care whether she lived or died, and death found her.

"Jacob grieved for her. He felt her hideous end came from his hands. I tried everything I could to dissuade him, to bring him out of himself, but he sank deeper and deeper into a dark and terrible void of regret. He loved me still. He clung to me. There was no question of that. We loved as passionately as always we had, but there was no lightness to it, no sweet joy, instead there was a solemn tenderness, a grave, affectionate need that was satisfied only by an ecstasy washed in tears."

Marian paused for a long while. Abe considered the differences, large and small, in the story she told him and the one Daniella had told him nights before. It occurred to him that the events in question had happened a very long time ago, that it was natural they should change with time and the telling. The love affair of Marian and Jacob had become legend among her people and legend was often a shifting thing. But here he was receiving a firsthand account, the best he'd ever get. For all his malcontent, he found himself demanding more.

"What happened then that Jacob wound up in Chota without your forgiveness?"

"Oh! He confessed!"

"Yes, Daniella told me. It was an act of honor. You blamed him for that?"

"Hmph. How hard is it to understand? The thing of it was, he didn't need to. No one was going to betray us. Life would have gone on. My mother was so impressed with his selfless care of her maid, she spoke of freeing him, which would have cleared the obstacle for us to marry. But his guilt and grief got the better of him. In a fit of misery, he confessed. His breaking point coincided with a great General Council of all the clans in Chota, during which matters vital to the nation were discussed. A vote was to be held on entry into the war the Americans fought against the British and their allies, the Creeks. I believe you would know it as the War of 1812. While the clans argued, Jacob painted his face for mourning, chanting a prayer older than the Earth itself. He dressed in the Cherokee clothes he wore in my auntie's day, in that time before he came to the plantation of my father. He wore the decorations he'd won as a boy in the annual games. Then, in the midst of the war vote, he burst into the Council House. There he confessed to the murder of Billy Rupert and demanded punishment. As soon as word came to me of his betrayal of our vows of silence, I ran to the Council House and threw myself at the mercy of my people as well, confessing my own part in the murder of Billy Rupert, which was greater than his. Jacob denied I was even present. I called him a liar and told the world of our love.

"You can imagine the riot that erupted. For two days our case was discussed. The warriors who had protected us were released from their oaths. But Jacob had got to them somehow. They supported his story, that he acted alone. I was infuriated. I repudiated my clansmen. I vowed if they did not accept my version of the facts, I would leave my clan forever, to live alone in the foothills until Jacob might be free.

"In short, I was ridiculous. No one believed me. Jacob was taken under the protection of Chota, because he was considered a hero for having rid the world of Billy Rupert. He resided in a stockade, where he would live until he could be sent into battle, to the front, which was the only way one who has taken a life could be redeemed. Twice a day during his confinement there, he wrote letters to me, begging my forgiveness. For some reason, they alienated me yet more from him, perhaps because they touched my heart and threatened to weaken my resolve to abandon my clan and make my own life in the foothills. In the end I realized, before I could do that, I must see the love of my life one more time. I decided I would be cold to him, to put my own wall between us rather than merely suffer the one he had made. I went to the stockade to visit him, but not before stoking my anger over his betrayal. I was prepared to be cruel. I told him I was leaving. He asked where I would go. 'I need to know,' he said, 'so I can find you when I have killed an enemy of the people and been set free.' I turned my back on him. As I left him, I called back that it was not necessary for him to know. Because he had broken our pact of silence, he was a cursed man. He would surely die.

"What demon held me in his grip that I spoke so? I regretted my words almost immediately. Yet, I left Chota and my people. I found no peace. I wandered the Cherokee world. My spirit fluttered about, halved, rootless, unable to achieve rest. I was in a state of complete wretchedness and then I heard from a passing stranger, a member of the paint clan who happened upon my lonely camp, that Jacob had died in the battle of Horseshoe Bend. The death he described was an ugly one, but it was also the death of a champion. Major Ridge's men had stolen canoes to bring our warriors across the water and into battle. Jumping in the first of them, Jacob made a solitary foray against the Creek lines, ahead of all the others. Once on land, he shrieked in the bravest, most bloodcurdling manner, and ran with glorious speed into a storm of knives and arrows. His courage, I was told, served as an inspiration to his war mates. His very name became a war cry and whatever Red Stick died that day died with Jacob's name in his ears. But it was unlikely he killed any enemy himself. A great irony, no? And this is what I thought true until the moment you told me he was alive in Chota and living with Lulu who, according to you, had been miraculously restored to him."

She sighed yet again musing on all that had happened in the lives of three young people so many years ago. "Later on, no one would tell me that he lived because I had said that he would die but even more because Jacob himself would not allow it. Do you know why he ran so fatefully into that barrage of Creek death? He told me in a letter just last week. He said he was sworn to give me what my heart desired. If I thought he should die, he would give me that terrible wish and in a way that would make me proud. My gods, my gods. When I heard that . . ." She smiled and shook her head. "I guess we both have had too much pride."

Her story was done. She remained quiet for a time, enough time for Abe to absorb her history, to realize once again that he'd never had a chance with her. Unlike occasions in the past, he felt neither jealous nor resentful. Surely his brief life with Hannah had something to do with the mitigation of his feelings. But more likely it had to do with acknowledging his inability to measure up to the exploits and fiery emotions of a Jacob or, for that matter, a Marian.

Abe halted Hart and told her they would rest awhile. He helped her descend from the wagon bed. She asked that he pass her her walking stick that she might hobble a ways apart to relieve herself and wash up in a nearby stream. When she returned, they ate a little of the cornmeal cakes that had been packed for them and watered Hart after he finished grazing. They spoke little during their short repast. Too much had been divulged already. What conversation passed between them was inconsequential, confined to speculations about the duration of their trip, whether the clouds ahead indicated rain, and the like.

At last they approached Chota. The quiet between them deepened. Marian's back arched, her neck strained as she studied the horizon looking for landmarks along a route to a place she had not visited for decades. Nature had had her way with certain trees and rock formations. Unfamiliar growth had replaced or obscured them. For these reasons, once they were upon Chota, it took her by surprise. There was a turn in the road, the crumbled buildings of the old town appeared, and she gasped. Her hands flew to her chest, where they joined as if she were in an act of prayer. Her breath came hard and fast. From somewhere in her throat a high-pitched whine, a sound not entirely human, emanated. To Abe's ears, it seemed to sing "*Jacob, Jacob, Jacob*," and then they were within the town and in the distance the man himself could be seen leaving his house, throwing his body across the porch.

As they drew closer, the whine at Marian's throat rose up and flew out of her mouth, crashing into the sweet mountain air with the piercing majesty of an eagle's cry. She grabbed at Abe's shoulder from behind. She shouted to him, "Stop! Stop! I would walk to him!"

So Abe stopped and helped her out of the wagon while Jacob slowly lumbered toward them, step by painful step, his arms lifted and spread wide for her, even the shortened, crooked one. "My love!" he cried. "My love!"

She sobbed and hobbled toward him, crying out alike, "Jacob! Jacob!" At last, they reached each other. Tears coursed down their cheeks. Her hands went up to his ruined face and she kissed it all over while he gathered her in close to him with such hungry, aching intimacy that Abe could not watch, and turned away.

EXODUS

GREENSBOROUGH, WHERE DEBTS ARE PAID

Before Abe set out for Greensborough the next morning, Marian left the house to immerse herself seven times in the river as a gesture of thanksgiving and as purification to prepare for the new life she'd wrenched from the clenched fist of fate. While he waited for her to return that he might bid her fare-thee-well, Jacob made him breakfast. Abe had spent the night in the bed of the wagon rather than restrain the lovers' reunion by his presence. He moved the wagon twice to pull it far enough apart from the noise of them that he might get some rest. When they weren't moaning and, at intervals, screeching, they sobbed, laughed, sang. Even on his wedding night, Abe hadn't made such a racket. Understandably, he was both intimidated and sleep-deprived afterward. His conversation with Jacob was stunted by tired bones and an envious heart.

"We are indebted to you, young sir," he said. "Last night, in our joy, we blessed the day you rode up to my lady's cabin. If you had not been taken with her, you would not have told the great lie that led us here, to this moment of sublime delight."

Abe had no desire to be reminded of his great lie, much less frame an acceptance of gratitude for it. "Don't be indebted. Please.

Don't be," he said, his irritation, which Jacob misinterpreted for modesty, leaking through his words. The slave's good eye widened with surprise as he thump-tapped over to him, a bowl of grain cereal softening in hot milk in his unharmed hand, a large silver spoon tucked between his bad arm and his side. "Here you go, sir," he said, putting the bowl and spoon in front of him. "This'll start you off good on your journey." He sat down in a chair next to him, put his elbows on the table, and cradled his chin in his hands. He smiled, nodded. "You like it?" Abe considered himself fortunate that the man sat with the unmarked side of his face toward him. Even so, the white of his hair, the lines around his handsome eye and mouth underscored that if Marian was older than Abe, Jacob was again older than she. It disconcerted Abe to think that he'd been unable to compete with the ghost of an old man. Ha-Shem, get me out of here, he thought. I want to be home again in the arms of my pretty wife with hair dark red like autumn leaves. Jacob had not quit staring at him.

"Yes, yes, I like it well enough," Abe said finally to put an end to that happy smile and nodding head. Putting a hand on the tabletop. Jacob hauled himself up. "Good. Now I'll make you something to take with you for your journey. For my lady, I've put up birds I haven't cooked in years! Ha, ha! Cold quail and white potatoes should do you well. I'll pack some beans in a tin vessel also, if you've a mind to cook over a fire at night."

Abe surprised himself. "Wait," he said. "What will happen for the two of you now? Will you stay here?"

"Ah, That is a good question, very good. Personally, I would like to leave, to go to Echota, where my lady can live with more comfort. Or perhaps near her brothers and mother. She will not admit it, but I know she loved living in her cave in the mountains, surrounded by her people. She'd been without them for so long, you see. But first, I must convince her."

"Why does she need convincing?"

He shrugged, then tilted his head left and right like a rabbi who ponders a prickly distinction of the law.

"To tell you the truth, it's hard to get her to think of going anywhere. Her family would like her back in the mountain place. But she won't go. She says her mother blames me for the death of her father because my actions led to Chief Redhand's final miseries. I would not be welcome there. Her mother will never free me. If we go there, I will live as a slave again.

"Now, if we go to Echota, she fears Billy Rupert's mother will hear of it and take revenge, even though our law prohibits blood vengeance there. She says it doesn't matter that the Ruperts won the chief's property by blessing of the white man's court, the mother will still want my death. My lady Dark Water believes any agreement with the whites is as light as smoke. She trusts none of them. Except you! Ha, ha!"

Abe doubted that, but he answered Jacob's lopsided half grin with a weak one of his own.

"I suspect you have your ways of swaying her, Jacob."

"I have arguments, absolutely. My lady Dark Water doesn't know Chief John Ross, for one, the man who has been most kind to me. She lumps him in her mind with Rich Joe Vann, Major Ridge, and even Stand Watie. She thinks them cruel, selfish men. Now, why does she do this? She does it because these are the men who have led the people out of the old ways and into the habits of the whites. To her, they are all the same, traitors to the ancestors. I tell her Chief John Ross is different from the others. Whatever he does, he does to save the land and the people on it.

Much of what he does, he does with a sad heart, even when it comes to men like me, to black men, to slaves. He believes in the old ways of having slaves. Do you know how it was back then, before the white man came?"

"No, Jacob," Abe said. "I barely know what goes on today."

"Ah! In the old days, the Cherokee treated their slaves fairly. It was nothing like the slavery you see today. Free man and slave worked together side by side, not one holding a whip while the other labored beneath it. They married together if they wished. They did not enslave by the color of a man's skin. Their slaves were conquered nations, Creek or Seminole, Iroquois. After a time, slaves might be ransomed, or freed out of affection or respect for deeds of loyalty and bravery. To be a Cherokee slave was not as good as being adopted by the people, but slaves were not chattel in the same way black men are under the whites. For Chief John Ross, this slavery by race is an evil thing. He does it because it is one more way of living to force the whites to see the Cherokee as equals. Then perhaps they would stop trying to push us out of the land and across the great river. Men like Rich Joe Vann, they find the white man's way more . . . more . . . comfortable. They like to hate the black man. It suits them. It is in their nature. Oh!"

Jacob's hand suddenly cupped his ear.

"List! My lady returns. She sings her way home."

Marian's voice came to them in the lilt of birdsong riding the back of a balmy breeze, warm and buoyant. The two men left the house to stand on the front porch and watch her approach. Seeing them, she waved, smiling brightly as she shuffled along more gracefully than in the past, but still leaning heavily on her stick. She carried the cloth she'd brought to dry herself and in it she'd placed the bandage that had been on her foot, which now sported a moccasin to her second foot's short, fringed boot. It was the first time Abe had seen her injury unbound. Her ankle was misshapen, bent outward in a peculiar way, while at the heel, the soft skin of the moccasin bowed inward, indicating a chunk of flesh was missing there. From the looks of things, he wondered if she'd ever be whole again. Unable to bear the thought of Marian damaged in this manner, a manner he found particularly vile when he recalled the glorious goddess of the foothills who'd first invaded his heart, Abe felt a powerful hand pressing against his back, pushing to get him beyond her and on the road to home. His role in her mutilation was almost too much to contemplate.

The lovers meanwhile limped past him to nuzzle cheeks, noses, and lips. When they were sated more or less, they turned about to face him while holding hands as if the idea that they might stand near each other and not touch was unthinkable. Regarding them, Abe's eyes welled, although he did not understand exactly why. Too many emotions pulled and shoved within him, stealing his breath. If he did not get apart from these two and very soon, he might suffocate.

"Well, I suppose it's time for me to depart." His voice squeaked, which humiliated him. "I should get my horse."

"I'll get him for you."

Jacob turned to make his way toward the barn where the livestock was kept before Abe had a chance to dissuade him. He was alone with Marian. He could not look her in the eyes. He studied the horizon instead.

"It looks the weather will hold up today, don't you think?" he said in as bright a tone as he could muster.

"Yes, you should have a good day to travel." She came closer to him, put her hand on his arm. "My friend, I want to thank you for everything you've done for us, for me. I don't know what the future will be for Jacob and me, but at least we have one now." She sighed. "I was a broken person before. Today, I am complete. My greatest wish for you, our benefactor, is that you find with your wife the unbreakable bond my love and I share. If there is ever anything we can do for you, we shall move mountains to do so."

Abe had no words for her. Jacob arrived with Hart in hand. After packing up and hitching him to the wagon, Marian of the foothills' peddler looked hard and long at the couple standing on their porch, arm in arm, leaning into each other, each with a hand raised in fare-thee-well. He waved also, then turned his back on them with some sadness, thinking he'd never see them again. In his heart, he wished them well. Hannah waited for him. He would return to her with renewed zeal to forge a true union between them. The shadow of old love would not diminish the bright promise of the present.

In good time, he came to the place where the litter bearers had left them to travel alone to Chota. He unhitched Hart, saddled him up, and continued on, leaving the wagon behind as prearranged. It felt good to be free of that encumbrance, good to be astride the horse again. He tapped his heels against Hart's belly. They picked up a trot, then a canter.

It was a hot ride. Over the two weeks he'd been in the high country, sun-drenched, heavy air had taken hold in the mountain valleys along his route. Hart foamed up several times a day. They took frequent rests to cool him off, respite Abe was grateful for himself. Great patches of fog obscured their trail, forcing them to wait until it lifted. They rested near cool streams, watered and bathed under gentle waterfalls. Every so often, a putrid scent drifted to them on humid air. Invariably, it emanated from some rubber object, now melted and in a state of malodorous decay, discarded by whoever needed to plain get rid of it and then far away. Abe worried in what state he'd find the family business.

The third day of his trek, they encountered a mass of violent thunderstorms so dangerous and dense, he decided to alter their route. He headed farther south than he needed just to get away from them. A bit lost, he looked for the worn thoroughfares of the low, rolling foothills. Before long, he located the common route on the eastern side of the Unicoi, the one established by the Cherokee ancestors and used since that time by traders, armies, miners, settlers, and adventurers. Its terrain was beaten into a civilized hospitality, free of rocky patches and other natural obstructions. Abe breathed relief. They walked on. Things went smoothly enough until they were near a branch in the road that offered a choice between yet farther south and due west or east. He spied a great cloud of dust at the horizon advancing toward him. Hart raised and tossed his head at it. To be on the safe side, Abe took him a ways inside the tree line in case whatever it was that caused such a disturbance of dirt and debris was something they'd rather not encounter hair to hide. The cloud grew larger the closer it got. Abe tied a kerchief around his nose and mouth to keep from coughing. The horse stretched his neck high, trying to catch a draught of clean air. Abe petted the root of his mane in long, firm strokes to steady him. They waited.

A wagon train approached. There were ten, maybe twelve conveyances. Many people, both on horseback and on foot, walked with them. The wagons were large, drawn by teams of four and six, and burdened with possessions. Buckets, farm implements, chairs, mattresses were tied to the outside of the frames, and inside the beds were larger, heavier items, such as trunks, wardrobes, breakfronts, even spinets and stoves. Children and old ones perched on top of the furnishings, also pregnant women and the sick, whoever could not keep up the pace on foot. There were also goats, cows, squawking chickens and geese in cages. It struck Abe that here was a group leaving well-established homes for western parts with no intent of returning. During the days when he'd fantasized of going west with Marian, his constant concern was how to strip themselves down to spare essentials for ease of motion over unknown ground. Yet these people traveled in a completely opposite fashion. Everything they valued was with them. Not only that, they were Indians.

Even without their copper complexions and angled cheekbones, their thick black hair, their chiseled noses and mouths, he would have known them as Indians. They had the quiet, sober aspect of most Indians he had known. While some of the children tussled and played together, the adults were uniformly silent, grave. He wasn't sure they were Cherokee, although the route they took was established by the Cherokee eons ago. Their clothes, though European, had flourishes that signified their origins, certain feathers and colors of beads as ornament, the earbobs of men, the cut of their shirts, the head coverings of the women, that sort of thing. It wasn't that Abe was an expert in such matters, but he'd spent enough time with the Cherokee to notice subtle differences. He wondered if they might be Creek or Chickasaw. What was not questionable about them was that they'd left their homes with time to pack. If they were in exile, it was a voluntary one, heading to the Mississippi, he figured, and across it in accordance with the new Indian Removal Act. He wondered next if these peoples were cowards or lacked the attachment to the land that Marian had. On the contrary, they might be the ones Isadore spoke of, the clever ones who wished to claim from the new territory the best it had to offer while taking with them the best they had acquired before the US government drove the rest of their kind into the West in penury and under the gun. Abe kept Hart quiet and under cover. To impose himself on these solemn people felt akin to bursting into a synagogue with trumpets and drums on a high holiday.

He and Hart traveled on. They came across another caravan of Indians, this one less populated but just as burdened with housewares and livestock. When they drew closer to areas where farms and settlements were established, a riot of war whoops startled them back undercover. Ever wily, horse and rider crept through the forest, evading the tumult's source. From a safe distance, they witnessed crazed caravans of roaring white men charging through the wilderness along roads that led to abandoned native farms in the lush, cultivated valleys and on hillsides scored by terraced fields. Abe's vantage point gave him a wide scope of vision. His eyes followed the marauders to the places the Indians had left, each one of them racing to be the first and to claim the most. They were terrifying, exuberant, exhilarated. Where the Indians had been full of dignified, tragic grief, these were grave dancers, frantic, aggressive, hopping mad with avarice, barbarous in both their greed and contest.

Abe was repelled, ashamed of his race, and then calmed himself. He was not white like them, not really. He was a Jew. He was apart from them. All his life he'd been reminded by the English that he was different, fit only for commerce or a short list of trades, best left to live with his kind, out of the sight of Christian men. Yet in America, they accepted him more or less, he'd felt liberated here, he'd married a non-Jew after all, without much comment from anyone. But was he safe only for now? In the hundreds of years the whites had known the Cherokee, Marian's people had felt as secure in the beginning as he did at present, surely even more so. It was all confusing and disturbing. The more he contemplated the land grabs he'd witnessed, the more he questioned. Similar thefts had been suffered by Jews throughout the diaspora, wherever Jews had resided for however long. Could he be certain his own property would always be protected? The simple answer was he could not. And yet, as long as America wrestled with issues of Indian removal and black subjugation, he felt uncomfortably confident that it would take them a while to get around to the Jews. Or would it?

At last they entered familiar territory. They rode past Marian's ruined cabin, her shed torn down, her front grazing land marked by rows of corn and cotton planted by an unknown usurper. He rode along the outlands of the Rupert place, imagining the days when they belonged to Chief Redhand, and from there, he rode past his own in-laws' farm, where he did not stop. Another two days of travel, days made longer by heavy late-spring rains, and he rode into the streets of Greensborough in the early evening under a pelting, blinding downpour. He took Hart to the stable behind the store, untacked him, checked his feet for stones, then bedded down a stall with dry straw before leaving him there, properly cooled and towel dried, with hay, a bit of sweet feed, and water. "Good job, my dear," he said to the horse, thanking him for making their trek and getting them through. Hart nickered and gobbled the feed. "What a good-hearted soul you are." Abe bid him good night. He pulled down the visor of his cap against the elements, then took to the wooden side-walks built half a foot above the coursing streams of rainwater on the streets. When he got to his house, there were no signs of life within. Concern drove out all other thoughts. If the last weeks had taught him anything, it was that the path of love was fraught with fateful episode. What if something had happened to his bride? Worried, he went on to Isadore's house, knocking on the front door. Hannah answered.

"Husband!" she cried out, slapping her rosy cheeks with two hands before dragging him inside and gripping him in the fond-est embrace. "I've been so worried!" She held on to him, unmind-ful of his sodden, trail-worn clothes. He freed himself from her grasp only long enough to raise a hand to her chin, which he lifted that he might kiss her deeply.

There were coughs behind them. Abe looked up. His mother and stepfather stood in the arch that led to the drawing room. Both beamed, both clasped hands over their hearts in thanksgiv-ing. Beyond them, bright hooked rugs, soft couches, and easy chairs glowed in the lamplight. The warm hearth beckoned.

"My son! You must get out of those wet clothes! Isadore, bring him something!" his mother said. Hannah and Abe sepa-rated, looked down, and laughed to acknowledge how wet they had both become. After short, loving greetings to the elder cou-ple, the newlyweds retired to the parental bedroom to change what needed changing. Once behind a door that shut, they made quick, hot, and happy love before returning to the others. Spir-its were poured, glasses were raised, toasts made. In the dining room, a buffet of tasty victuals was laid out. They sat to eat. Talk turned, almost immediately, to business.

Abe reported his promises to the Cherokee. Isadore shrugged, then tilted his head left and right as Jacob had when they discussed convincing Marian to move to Echota. "I hope I can do what you have promised, son," he said. "So many considerations have come up. The neighbors, for one. The settlers hereabouts and beyond for another. Let's face it, everyone who purchased rubber will want a refund. *Baruch Ha-Shem*, the weather has been off and on. Not all our customers have lodged complaints yet. But they will. I'm still waiting on further response from Goodyear's lawyer not only about refund on the goods we sold but also about the down payment of the reorder we canceled. I've had only a perfunctory communiqué from the man, which said something about blood from stones. If we carry on with a lawsuit, we'll use up resources we won't see back for years or maybe ever. Whatever judgment may come is uncertain. We must face facts. We convinced all of Sassaporta Brothers outlets to take on rubber. The members of the family headquarters are in equal straights. Compensation to our customers as well as damages will be up to us alone." Abe, until that moment drifting into a fog of cozy respite after a long and difficult trip, bolted upright in his seat and spoke harshly to his stepfather. "It's not possible that I disappoint my Cherokee!" he said, pounding the table with a fist. "They are ill-treated everywhere of late and I will not add to it!"

His family sat back, surprised by his passion on the subject. "What is this?" his wife said, folding her soft hands over his hard, clenched fist, which she stroked to soothe him. "My love, my love. How are these Cherokee 'yours,' first of all? How are they separate or superior to, say, my parents, who have also been hurt by this plague of rubber you so espoused?" Abe looked at her with jaws flapping wordlessly. He floundered about, looking for an answer that would please her, when his mother rescued him.

"My son, like my husband, is an honorable man," she said. "All of his customers are dear to him and his fortunes rely upon his honesty and reputation with them, that's all, daughter. Don't worry too much, Abrahan. We will do the best we can and then we will work harder to restore ourselves. You'll work hard too, won't you, Hannah?" She turned brightly toward her son's wife, deflecting her question as expertly as a diplomat in the court of a Spanish king. Isadore looked to his Susanah with admiration. "Alright," he said, "it's settled. The best we can with what we've got and no more. And now, to bed."

None had objection to that idea. To bed they went, each in their own homes, for one couple to discuss the economic implications of Abe's negotiations, and for the other to find the kind and genial gestures that cement a passion yet untried.

THE FALL OF SASSAPORTA AND SON

———————

Quakers," Isadore always said, "are good people." Abe could not disagree. It was well known they were honest, prayerful, and kind. They'd accepted the Sassaportas among them without comment on their beliefs or heritage. They also accepted the Catholics, Presbers, Moravians, Lutherans, and Methodists of Isadore's camp town, the missions, and farms about. Quakers always treated the Cherokee with common decency. He'd heard gossip there were Abolitionists in their ranks who held secret meetings and, it was rumored, helped fugitive slaves escape to free territories. But these were rumors only. No one held enough animus against the Quakers to investigate closely whether these honest, prayerful, and kind people truly broke the law. Also, they'd founded the town and were in the majority.

After the rubber melted, Sassaporta and Son discovered something new about Quakers. When they demanded justice, they didn't hold back. They were fierce. Daily, furious Quaker farmers and townspeople barreled into the store with scythes, whips, canes, and even burnt-out torches in hand, slamming such onto the front desk as if they might not receive proper attention without proof of potential aggression. They decried the faulty goods they'd been sold, declared the promises of its excellence indisputably betrayed, and refused to budge until Isadore gave them legally binding notes that they would be made whole. When all the claims against rubber were in, a process that lasted until mid-fall that year, Abe and Isadore took stock of their holdings and determined the best they could do and remain in business was provide a thirty-five-cents-on-the-dollar refund and open a room of free merchandise for complainants to peruse to make up the rest of what was owed. Many of the items in the free room were quality, high-demand goods, ones either made in Isadore's work camp or lots paid for on delivery from the manufacturer. Other items were pretty much useless junk that never sold, novelty items, and goods damaged in transit. Customers grumbled but accepted the deal. After loading up on the choicest of wares in the Sassaporta and Son free room, they displayed their dissatisfaction by withdrawing their business and patronizing the competition in town with their hard coin, even buying in the used goods store. It was humiliating, Isadore and Abe agreed, but in the great scheme of things it was just. They had blundered. They had squandered their good name. They would have to re-win their customers' loyalty. It would take time, but they would do it.

In order to absorb the cost of refunds and merchandise giveaways, Isadore cleaned out his savings and mortgaged his home along with the land on which he'd built the store. Abe sold his house to the owner of the new lumber mill over on Haw River. He sold it at a great discount in order to sell it quickly. The younger Sassaportas moved into Isadore and Susanah's home, which was just as well, since Hannah carried their first child and they could use the help. It was cramped, there weren't luxuries for any of them, but they managed to eat and keep the store doors from closing for good. As for the Cherokee, Abe sent peddlers armed with flyers for display in all the trading posts, which described the settlements offered to Quakers and any others who'd bought rubber products. The flyers recommended those affected send representatives to Greensborough to collect compensation. Oddly, no Cherokee came to the store that fall and then it was winter, the time of year no one traveled anywhere.

All winter long, Abe wondered why Edward Redhand had not appeared before the mountain pathways turned to sheets of ice. He'd been hoping to see him, to settle matters justly between them as he'd promised, and to hear how Marian and Jacob fared. When he packed up to vacate his former residence, he found a moment when he was alone to lift the floorboard under which he'd hidden Lord Geoffrey's portrait of Marian, her family, Jacob and Lulu. Now that he knew who was who and what was what, he studied faces he recognized from life. There was Black Stone and White Stone, the twin brothers he'd met on the porch of Marian's mother's mountain house, looking much the same. Her mother looked entirely different. She had more flesh about her, and in her native clothing her posture was softer, less grand lady than contented matron. Her hair was not yet white and there was a warmth in her eyes rather than the icy-cold glitter he'd encountered. Like his brothers, Edward looked much the same, just younger. Abe realized his original opinion of the expression captured on both Edward's and Marian's mother's face, that they were possibly angry or suspicious of the painter, was a false one. Now that he was accustomed to Cherokee people, he realized Lord Geoffrey had simply captured that gravity, that self-possession they all displayed. If he'd misinterpreted their painted aura, it was out of ignorance and because of an enormous contrast in the representation of her family and the representation of Marian. One was realistic, unemotional, the other an aching hymn to lush, impossible beauty. The chief looked proud and stern to Abe's eyes, but then they'd never met. Lulu was indeed a winsome creature with the long, elegant neck Daniella described. Jacob's appearance, however, gave him pause. Despite his many viewings of the painting, he'd not paid much attention before to the man's likeness, partially because of the smudge over his face, which obscured it somewhat. But having come to know the man more intimately, he wanted to determine just how he looked before he had been ruined. Taking the canvas in two hands, Abe squinted at it, held it far away, then up close. He took it to a lamp and held it under the light, where he made a startling discovery.

The smudge was not a smudge but an indent of sorts, a pattern of tiny lines pressed into the canvas either by a sudden extreme pressure while the paint was still fresh or one applied repeatedly for a very long time. It occurred to him that if one filled in the impression of tiny lines with small grains of something dry, the pattern might be identifiable. Taking a handful of the sand Hannah had put in a box of breakables to protect them during their move, he shook a thin stream over Jacob's face and gave out a little gasp. There was only one interpretation to the indentation of the tiny lines possible. They had been made by a pair of lips pressed against the painted face of Jacob the slave, first while the painting was new and then over and over and over again during a period of twenty years. Abe wasn't sure why the idea stunned him, but it did. All the time he'd known the portrait, all the time he'd kept it, he'd assumed the smudge to be just a smudge and that the letters nested with the portrait in Marian's treasure box were most likely from Lord Geoffrey. Now he wondered if indeed they'd been from the much-kissed Jacob, written during that period in the stockade before he'd gone to Chota. He'd claimed it was Marian who taught him to speak proper English and also to write. Abe wished he'd taken the letters from the derelict cabin too. Sighing his regrets, he rolled up the painting and stuck it under his shirt until he could find a new hiding place in Isadore's home. As the weather was cold and he'd a jacket on over the shirt, the secreting of Lord Geoffrey's masterpiece into his marital bedroom—an area at the back of the kitchen closed off by makeshift draperies—presented no difficulties. No one was home. He wrapped the painting in a square of protective linen lining a drawer, then stuck it behind a large, heavy wardrobe. With effort, he pushed the furniture hard against the wall.

During that winter, the family heard from a new group of malcontents. A much smaller one, it's true, but one no less vocal and demanding of recompense. For whatever reason, perhaps the benevolence of the protected hollows they called home, this group had not found their rubber melted in summer. Instead, it went dry, brittle, and cracked broken in winter. Once more, Sassaporta and Son was forced to open the free room and let the disgruntled have at it. "We'll have to close up shop if another onslaught of the rubber cursed knock on our doors," Isadore confided in Abe. "We have to start making a profit somewhere, or else you and I will both be hitting the trails in the spring." Abe hoped he exaggerated but he feared he did not.

Hannah's pregnancy was worrisome in a season when life was already full of burdens. In the first months, she couldn't keep a morsel down. Susanah suggested she eat cold ashes from the fire, but it didn't help. Her complexion went sickly pale, there were dark rings beneath her eyes. She grew haggard and weak, though she bravely soldiered on. At night, Abe rocked and soothed her with songs and kisses until she fell asleep, then he spent hours awake, adding up debts and subtracting resources, wondering how he was ever going to keep the wolf from the family door.

By midwinter, Hannah could eat again, but just as she appeared to be regaining her strength, her back bothered her and she began to have fainting spells. Twice in the next months, spots of her blood stained the bedsheets. Susanah, who'd had some experience as a midwife's assistant back in Bethnal Green, advised Hannah to spend her time in bed until the child came. The young mother obliged. She lay in bed all day in a room shut off from light and air as protection against winter's icy touch, filled with unwholesome daydreams of losing the child. Abe tried to comfort her, but there were days he could not. He'd come to love her for her beauty, her energy, and her pluck. The pregnancy had drained her store of each. Her anxieties seemed to him endless and intractable. There were days he told her he must be gone to work overlong in order to complete an inventory or restock the shelves. But it was winter and business was exceedingly slow. What he aimed for was a little time without her. "She drives me mad!" he'd complain to his mother. "I cannot help but feel the child is a test of our love and we are both failing completely!"

Susanah consoled him. "She'll be back to herself in form and temperament once the child is born and so will you," she assured him. "But until then, maybe it's good to work a little late now and again. Don't worry, I'll look after her."

He'd go, insisting to Hannah on his way out the door that yes, yes, he loved her, he'd worry about her all day, and yes, yes, he'd return for lunch, but he wouldn't have time for a lingering one, what with the pre-spring orders and invoices to complete. Once he hit the street, he walked rapidly to the store, nearly running, only dimly aware that he was not running to work but fleeing from a helpless, frightened wife and his growing fear that he would prove unable to take care of either her or the child, should it survive. Often, he thought of Marian and Jacob, of the infinitely greater trials than his own they'd faced with stoicism. His thoughts left him both envious and ashamed.

There came a day in early March when Abe sat tense and idle, wondering if business would ever pick up. Hannah had come to term. She could deliver the child any day, so his mother said, which put him on pins and needles. He worried about money constantly. Isadore studied his accounts in the back room. Every so often, he'd hear the elder man mutter, "Ay, yi, yi, yi, yi," which did not encourage. It was a time of year business should be picking up, when farmers planted their fields, when cows began to calve and horses foal. Everyone needed new clothes after winter had worn their old wardrobes out, but the haberdashery section of the store gathered dust. Even the bin of cloth and leather scraps favored by those looking to patch rather than purchase new, and the shelf of buttons, needles, and threads, were left untouched. Bored, uneasy, and depressed, Abe left his stool with duster in hand to brush off the windowsills. He glanced across the street to where people filed in and out of the storefronts of the competition. Something was wrong. Everyone seemed in a hurry. All heads turned north. He followed their direction to see what was of such universal interest.

It was Edward Redhand, riding into town astride a massive black stallion. Behind him were the Stone brothers, Black and White, one astride a chestnut mare, the other a black-and-white paint. The Redhands were dressed in European style, more or less, but their mounts were outfitted as Indian horses were in the old days before the tribes were civilized, with blankets and hemp halters. The men bore arms. Pistols and hatchets were stuck in their braided belts, bandoliers of bullets crossed their chests under frockcoats. They held aloft spears streaming with feathers and fringe the way corsairs on parade bear ceremonial swords. Neither man nor equine was decorated in war paint but yet they were terrifying.

They terrified especially Abrahan Bento Sassaporta Naggar. Here he was, a breath away from fatherhood, partner in a business that teetered on the edge of collapse, a maker of promises he'd pushed so far to the back of his mind he'd forgotten he'd made them except in nightmares, and trotting down the road, heading directly to him, were the avenging angels of Cherokee justice, arrived, no doubt, to collect on a debt he could not pay. He swallowed, he gathered courage. He prayed Ha-Shem was not so cruel He would leave Hannah a widow with an infant child by the end of the day. His prayers gave him courage. He worked up a smile of welcome and exited the store to stand at the entrance next to the freshly planted flowerpots.

"Edward," he said. The lead horseman dismounted, tied his mount to the hitching post, and approached. "I've been expecting you."

"I am here."

"So you are."

Edward extended his hand. Abe shook it. He nodded to the younger men, saying, "White Stone, Black Stone," although he had no idea which was which and wondered suddenly why he had never been told their Christian names. There followed a short silence, a fractional one, perhaps two, two and a half seconds longer than it should have been, but yet that hesitation was enough to lend an awkwardness to conversation. "How is your mother?" he thought to ask. Redhand shrugged a little and looked straight ahead, over Abe's shoulder and into the store. "Old." Abe prattled on. "It happens to us all, don't it? If we're lucky. Growing old, I mean. Well, I hope aging is gentle to her. And your sister? She is well, I hope?" Redhand glanced at him with narrowed eyes. "Hmm. Well. Yes," he said. He lifted a hand waist high, palm upward, and raised his eyebrows. *Are we going to stay out here all day?* his pose, his expression asked. Abe blushed and ushered him inside. The twins dismounted as well.

Once they were in the store, the two customers on the floor took one look at the Cherokee bandoliers, at the spears trailing feathers, and left the premises. The gentleman tipped his hat, the woman kept her eyes downcast. Soon enough, Abe and Redhand stood facing each other in the empty store. The two Stones quietly entered to stand behind their elder brother. It feels like the prelude to a duel, thought Abe, with Isadore, unaware and muttering in the next room, as his second.

"You know why I am here," Redhand reached into his side pocket and withdrew a tattered rubber settlement flyer, now many months old.

Abe swallowed. He could not do this alone.

"Uncle Isadore! Could you come here, please?"

The squeak of wood against wood as Isadore pushed his chair away from his desk in the back room resounded through the empty store. There followed his great sigh, the loud shutting of a book, and the shuffle of the elder shopkeeper's tired feet.

He pushed back the curtain that provided privacy to his office chamber and saw the party waiting for him. Surprise swept over his features, yet he gathered his wits and smiled broadly.

"Why, Mr. Redhand! We had despaired of seeing you again when you did not come forward last fall to make your claim! Good to see you, good to see you."

"I am here now."

"Yes, yes, I see."

Redhand waited for Isadore to make his offer. He was pre- pared to wait a long time. He stared ahead at the wall of the store. He did not move a muscle. Neither did the twins. Isadore studied him, trying to determine his wants. Abe held his breath, waiting. Just as he was about to purple, his stepfather said, "Mr. Redhand, how I wish you'd come earlier. Our resources just now are very slim. We can pay you twenty cents on the dollar and offer the remainder we owe in kind." Redhand looked at him directly for a time as if measuring Isadore's word. He looked away again.

"The paper reads thirty-five cents. I remind you, you prom- ised more in the mountains."

Isadore put a hand on the man's back to guide him to the free room. "My dear friend, that was six month ago or more. We have been wiped out by this debacle of miracle substance. But here is the place we keep for the purposes of settlement. Take what you wish. Even beyond the eighty percent."

The camp peddlers held that Indians will take any worthless thing if they find it pretty or if it's manufactured. They often bragged of the wild trades they'd made with one or another unsophisticated tribe. Colored glass for beaver pelts, a child's music box for gold nuggets. Most of these stories Abe discounted as rubbish, but as he and his stepfather stood back watching Marian's brothers examine the poor excuse for merchandise the Quakers and settlers had left behind after their zealous grabs at compensation, he found himself wishing the stories were true. No such luck. After striding the length and depth of the room, fondling various wares, lifting them to the light, bracing others against his knee, Edward Redhand turned to look at Abe and Isadore with bemused disbelief. He pointed his spear and made a wide sweeping arc with it.

"We would have to clear this room four times to make up what you owe us. What need have we for a loom with missing pedals? An iron sieve with holes conjoined? A hollowed gourd with a breach in its bottom would work as well. The rest you have here is no more than toys for children. A hatchet without a handle. A fork with only one tine. A teacup with half a saucer. Cherokee children do not play so much as white ones. They must grow up faster than that."

Isadore's mouth twitched. "You are very late coming to collect."

Redhand's mouth twitched also. He held up the flyer and crumpled it pointedly in his free fist.

"There is no deadline on this paper. Nor in the promises made to me."

Abe could stand no more. It was his own word at stake in these deliberations, his reputation among Marian's people. That word looked to be sliding into the mire along with the word of so many, from the duplicitous Andrew Jackson to the gold-hungry Governor Gilmer of Georgia. He could not let that happen. He could never go back to being Marian's titmouse no matter what the cost. It was time he assert himself as a man. Wasn't he the "son" in Sassaporta and Son? Didn't that mean he had as much say as Isadore in negotiations? He coughed for attention and spoke up.

"You're right, Edward. Let's sit down and review what it is we owe you exactly and then you may take what you like from the main floor. No one is buying anyway. We have plenty of stock." He glanced over at Isadore, who regarded him with knit brow. Whether his look was one of confusion, surprise, or anger, Abe couldn't tell. He didn't care. Meanwhile, the Redhands filed into the back room. The deal was struck for good or ill.

It took several hours to hammer out the details. In the end, the Cherokee took what they could comfortably carry, packing the chestnut and paint with clothing, tableware, kitchen and gardening tools, needles, thimbles, buttons, and shoes. There were heavier items, plows and yokes, the younger men lobbied for, but Edward refused, reminding the twins they'd descended the mountain expecting more coin and few goods. Though the settlement was just, they were unprepared. Whatever they took had to be carried back up steep, rocky paths. "There is no wagon or wheelbarrow waiting for us to help in the ascent," he cautioned. "No longer can we leave goods on the trail until we can return for them. There are more white men swarming the hills this spring than ever before. They would steal what we leave behind before we can get back." They prepared to leave. Abe took Edward aside.

"So," he said, "your sister and Jacob are well, you say? Where are they living? Still in old Chota?"

"For now, yes."

The phrase struck Abe as odd. "What d'you mean? 'For now'?"

Edward studied him as a physician studies the sick, with acute attention, with curiosity, and with pity. When he spoke, there was a quiet, paternal quality to his tone, as if he were instructing a child who, through no fault of his own, was ignorant of many things that mattered.

"Our world, the Cherokee world, has been under siege since the first white man arrived. We fight them. They fight us. In the past, we give them land to make them go apart from us, to leave us in peace. They are to pay us for the land but they make the payments difficult to collect or they do not pay us at all. We fight their wars, hoping for peaceful alliance. Andrew Jackson promises war's rewards, then repays us by stealing land, our property, and our slaves. Always, the whites want more land. They raid our villages. We raid theirs. We adopt their ways to win respect as a nation. First we are a nation in their eyes, and then there is gold, so we are not. Surely you know all this?"

It irritated Abe that Redhand would speak to him this way. He struggled to keep annoyance out of his voice, but he failed. "Yes, yes," he said. "The worst laws against you are in Georgia, where the gold is. Our sales force there is not permitted to deal with Cherokee anymore, not without a writ from the state. It's ridiculous. That law will not stand in the courts. You'll see. It will be reversed." Even as he reassured the man with regard to the fate of his entire people, a judgment he based on his immigrant's faith in the benevolence of a country that had been good to him, Abe doubted himself. What he said next was more an effort to convince himself of his words than to convince his listener. "I understand, I can see that the white man rules over blacks and attempts to rule over the Indians. I'm not a fool. But this is a new country. It's not all settlers and missionaries. Every day it changes, it grows." His optimism was met with a skeptical expression from Marian's brother, who knew too well the dire consequence of American growth. Abe's brow wrinkled as he sought within himself a clarification of his stated beliefs, beliefs that had come to his mind as suddenly as rain on a dry day, before he'd had time to consider them. "Good change will come. Isn't that what John Ross and the others work for, day and night? And as for the slaves . . ."

His voice trailed off. Neither Abe nor Edward Redhand had ever lived in a society without slaves. There was an Abolition movement gaining strength in the North, but not in the South, where Cherokee and white man alike owned men as easily as a pair of gloves and needed them too, to achieve their goals. Abe wasn't sure what he was about to say. That slaves might one day be free? All of them? Ridiculous. As ridiculous as the land grabs the Georgia legislature barreled through daily, writing laws governing the disposition of ancient Cherokee territories, laws that all the good Quakers of Greensborough swore would never hold up in federal court. Both men sighed. Both men shrugged. They fell silent.

"I am not so hopeful of the future as either John Ross or you, Peddler. I fear worse times are coming, not better ones. Our medicine man fasted and bathed in the river. He had a vision. The soldiers will come, the land will turn to smoke, and many will weep. Only our ghosts will remain in the forests of our fathers. The only security for my people is in the upper towns, where they can hide." Edward said. "One day, Dark Water will know this and come back to the caves and village of our mother."

For reasons he did not fully comprehend, Abe's eyes watered, his throat went thick with bitter fluids. He coughed. "Yes, security," he said. "Security is the thing, isn't it?" He cocked his doubtful head, wondering where Marian marked security on her list of priorities. Defense, yes. But failing to stand her ground? Someone pulled at the hem of his jacket. In a kind of daze, he turned about, looked down, and saw a young boy with an earnest face, a fringe of ginger hair poking out from beneath his round black hat, a young boy who said, "Sir. I am sent to tell you your child is coming. Now."

"Now!" Abe slapped his hands against his cheeks. "I must go," he said, "I must go!" Yet he stood rooted to the spot.

Edward Redhand nodded. "Yes, I think you must." He mounted his horse, picked up a trot, and gestured to his brothers to follow him. The Stones had waited astride their mounts while the other men talked, keeping so still that Abe had forgotten them. They trotted out of town after Edward with the same aloof dignity they'd displayed on trotting in.

Their sudden departure startled Abe out of his shock. Without further delay, he ran toward his uncle's house, his heart full of more emotion and contradiction than his mind could bear. He ran about to the back of the house and threw open the door that gave to the kitchen and his marital bed. The privacy curtain was drawn. Bloody cloths were heaped in a bucket next to the bed. Another bucket held a thin sheet of something slimy and brown-colored, sitting in a pool of more diluted blood. He saw the buckets first, which panicked him. He dared not raise his eyes and chance to see her, his Hannah, spread out on the bed, legs raised and parted, the child straining through between them. He paled thinking he must, he must look up, except if he chanced to see such a thing, he might never touch her again.

There were shoes around the bed. Two pairs of women's

shoes, one pair of men's. All had feet in them, but he was too frightened to look up and see to whom they belonged. Then he heard her. His daughter. Crying. Crying in the way newborns cry, in the plaintive bleats of little lambs. His heart rushed to his throat, his face ran with tears, and suddenly he was kneeling by the bed, looking from the tired, enraptured gaze of his wife to the tiny, squealing pink creature in her arms. His jaw dropped. His breath stopped. Never had he seen anything more beautiful than his daughter, not even Marian naked in the firelight or Hannah on her wedding day. She had what seemed to him to be long, slender limbs, tender feet, exquisite hands with elegant fingers made to bear rings of gold and fine jewels. Her chin was gently curved, her nose small and snubbed like her mother's, her mouth was plump and purple. Of the eyes, he knew nothing as they were shut, but their orbits looked perfectly shaped, fringed in impossibly long, silky lashes the same color as the wisps of auburn hair that graced her little head. Behind him, Isadore clapped a congratulatory hand on his shoulder while his mother and the young messenger boy's aunt, a Mrs. Collins who lived down the street, murmured to him the details of the birth. "It went smooth as glass," they said. "Your little girl was hardly any trouble to her mama at all. The water came and then out she slid." Hannah rolled her eyes from side to side as if to tell him it wasn't quite as easy as all that, then laughed. He was so proud of his wife, so entirely delighted, he kissed her in front of everyone, giving her a hearty, happy smack on the lips, then a delirious series of smaller kisses all over her face and neck, stopping only to bestow yet more caresses upon the fingers, toes, and belly of his clever daughter, who had stopped crying having somehow found the teat. He swore to heaven, Hannah, and the child that he would make certain they never wanted for necessity or comfort, that he would crawl through hell on a path of broken glass before he would let them suffer deprivation or harm.

He had no idea how hard keeping that promise the first few years would be. By summer that year, Sassaporta and Son had not recovered from the rubber debacle. There were no signs they ever would. It was not for lack of industry on the new father's part. He created a multitude of advertisements and sale promotions, creating a kind of shoppers' club with numerous free rewards. He went on a buyer's trip to Raleigh, the state capital, finagling with every wholesaler and big retail outfit he could find for the best goods at the best rate. He packed Hart with wares and rode him to the foothill trading posts. None of it yielded much in the way of profit, although it helped them keep the doors open.

Over that year, two new stores opened in town. One specialized in spare parts for agricultural tools and had a blacksmith onsite. The other sold ready-made suits and offered professional tailoring carried out "in the European style." With great reluctance, Isadore rented out the old rubber room to a cobbler, who fashioned boots and slippers there. His hands were tied by desperation and the deal they struck was less than favorable. The cobbler sold his shoes at a profit in the front of the store without having to pay the shop owners a penny above rent. At least from time to time one of his well-shod patrons stopped to buy a trinket or two from the landlord, so there was that to console them.

The town grew faster than anyone had anticipated, and yet Sassaporta and Son continued to flounder, teetering on the edge of bankruptcy despite Abe's brilliant promotion plan of having Hannah and their baby girl bring around welcome baskets to the freshly arrived. Why this didn't increase business was a mystery to him—his daughter, Raquel, was an attraction all on her own, everyone cooed and smiled at the very sight of her—until one of their new neighbors mentioned casually to him that it was too bad what he'd heard on the street about the wonderful emporium that had been ruined by rubber. Then he asked for a discount on a set of shovels. Abe bemoaned to Isadore that the old customers were poisoning their reputation with the new. Isadore sat at his desk, shuffling through papers, scribbling in his ledger. He kept his nose in the big book while he spoke. "Customers suffer from selective memories, Abrahan," he told him. "They forget the credit my peddlers once bestowed in the years of a bad crop or an overlong winter. They remember only the rubber." He sighed grievously and slammed his ledger shut in a gesture that was half tenacity, half defiance. "In a matter of months, we will have to close up shop and return to the peddlers' camp. Business there is also not so good. As the roads improve, more and more people are willing to travel to towns for their shopping. We can always expand the field by catering more to the needs of slaves, but their pennies and nickels won't save us."

The prospect of returning to the camp town was abhorrent to Abe. He could not imagine his dear wife and sweet child living among the rough crew that remained there. What if that was the final destination of their lives? Dear Raquel maturing among lowlifes and whores? Hannah old before her time, bent by care and woe? Himself a disgruntled, bitter failure? *Baruch Ha-Shem.* There must be a better answer.

"What about the trading posts in the upper towns? We can redouble our efforts to supply them. They could well expand their stock and keep the farther-out Indians and settlers from traveling for their needs. Perhaps we could even persuade the family headquarters in Savannah to allow us to reach into Mississippi or Louisiana, in the least settled parts, where others are loath to go. New markets are ever worthy for a business."

Isadore stroked his beard. "It might hurt us as much as help," he said, then threw his hands up in the air. "But any port in a storm!"

"Alright, then. I shall devise a battle plan and lead the charge."

The two men shook hands, unaware that Abe's use of a military metaphor would prove meaningful over time. He made a list of items that could easily be transported, ones he'd never seen in a trading post before, things that might spur a sensation. Isadore wrote to the Sassaporta Brothers in Savannah and secured permission to solicit any territory of Mississippi and Louisiana that was more than seventy-five miles from a town. Abe mapped out all the known posts and ranked them according to whatever information he had on the population type and density of habitation each one served. Then he revisited his lists to further refine what could be safely carried along some of the more treacherous routes. He resisted the decision, but in the end realized that only he could be trusted to make the sales trips, for none of Isadore's dwindling staff of peddlers would be half as motivated to succeed as he was. At the first difficult mountain pass, all but he would immediately give up. "Ah, Raquel," he'd whisper to the child, "I will have to leave you for months at a time and it will break my heart. But more will it break my heart to see you destitute." The child would purse her plump, rosy lips for him and flash him a saucy look she'd learned from her mother, her brown eyes glittering with charming flecks of gold. "Pa-pa-pa-pa-pa," she'd say, and throw her arms around him.

When it could no longer be avoided, Abe packed Hart with

samples for a sales trip beyond the foothills. It was the summer of Raquel's first year. She was at an age when pretty children of jovial nature are equally demanding and adorable. With terrible reluctance, he took his leave from her on the street outside the store. He was on his horse, outfitted with layers of saddlebags piled on top of one another in gradually decreasing size. From a distance, Hart looked as if he had a giant squeezebox draped over his flanks, but good-hearted equine that he was, he didn't seem to mind. Hannah held Raquel up to Abe for a final embrace. In the strong light of a fine morning, Abe noted the cares writ upon his wife's brow, although she smiled bravely at him and patted their daughter's back soothingly. Intense pride in her courage swelled his chest. He leaned forward and kissed them both, then straightened up with his jaw set in firm resolve and rode off.

He was on the road through the summer and into the fall. Sales went well. His store of samples dwindled. He took orders at every stop. But traveling by himself away from his family, surrounded by the wilderness in which he'd spent his most formative years before his wife and child had entered his life, had a curious effect. He became afflicted with a terrible nostalgia for his early days in America. He thought of his first love often and wistfully recalled himself as young, callow, ignorant, and passionate. Everywhere he went in the upper towns, a part of him hoped to run into Edward Redhand or the brothers Stone, to hear news of Marian and Jacob, but chance did not turn to his desires. He could have traveled to Redhand's village, but he felt it wrong to seek him out. If fate denied them a meeting, fate knew best. With effort, he pushed from his mind all things Marian as an act of fidelity to his marriage, for he found no good in thinking of her or her brothers, only a romantic distraction possessing the power to consume his solitary attention bit by bit. With chastened heart, he pressed on beyond Cherokee territory.

Looking to rid himself of the last of his goods before going home, he found himself on strange ground in Mississippi. There he saw his first parties of Choctaw, a tribe he knew to have recently signed expulsion treaties, marching under the guns of soldiers escorting them from the land of their fathers to unknown territories in the West. These were not the wagon trains he'd seen on his way home after he left Jacob and Marian in Chota, those solemn, voluntary processions of tribes in exodus, their transport slowed by a lifetime of possessions, their women and children, their old and infirm riding or walking in as much ease as modern travel allowed, their men astride the backs of fine Indian ponies, providing protection. This lot was the resigned, betrayed by a false treaty full of holes. Their old and sick rode in rude army wagons built to convey boxed supplies. Thirty or more were stuffed into wagons with no covering to protect them from the elements, neither beveled bonnet nor simple blanket set up on poles. Abe saw faces, very old and very young, stretched in extremis and yet no one ordered that the wagons stop to give them succor. In despair, mothers and sons jogged alongside them, working to keep up, able to offer nothing but the hot comfort of eyes that bore witness to their suffering. Behind them, proud women, warriors, and children walked, their heads high, their faces set in determined silence. There was a ruckus, but it came not from the exiled but from soldiers who whooped and galloped about to fluster those who walked, trying to frighten them into utterance, making a game of it until their lieutenant ordered them to cease. From the hillock on which he and Hart paused to watch the rueful march below, Abe attempted to count the exiled. By his reckoning there were nearly two hundred people along with twenty soldiers and a single wagon loaded with sacks of supplies; food, he supposed, and maybe medicine.

This was but the first group of the expelled he witnessed. There were others he encountered on his way home, each in the same state of abject, silent mourning. It caused him to recall Edward Redhand's prophecies of the Cherokee future with a sense of inescapable dread. What would happen to Marian and Jacob, he wondered despite himself, when the same policies that afflicted the Choctaws came to rest at the Cherokee's door? How could she possibly accept a mandatory expulsion? He imagined her anger, her fighting spirit ramming heads against her afflictions and those of Jacob. He imagined her annihilation and groaned lament in the night by his lonely fire. He looked up at the swarm of stars blanketing the mountains and swore upon them as Ha-Shem's jeweled agents of light that, if it came to all that, he would do what he could, however he could, to preserve the life and freedom of Marian and Jacob even if it meant his own well-being. He amended himself almost immediately. Anything, that is, that did not compromise the safety of his dear Hannah and Raquel.

A RETURN TO GRACE BY SUSPECT MEANS

Near mid-fall, when the mountains are the most beautiful, when streams rush, trees go the color of gold and fire, and animals grow fat and dark in their winter coats, Abrahan Bento Sassaporta Naggar returned home triumphant. He'd sold every item in his pack. His pockets were stuffed with orders. His ready cash earnings were not glorious but substantial enough to keep the store afloat in a manner that would ensure solid nights of sleep for the entire family. It happened that he arrived in Greensborough shortly before the Jewish New Year, which was declared by his mother to be a great and wonderful omen of continued good fortune. To cement it, she convinced her husband to hire a traveling rabbi, who would conduct services for them despite the fact that the price of such was a dear percentage of Abe's profits. "It will be a *mitzvah*," Susanah said, "and bring us more blessings." It was exceedingly difficult to arrange at the last minute, but thanks to the use of swift horses and homing birds along with a dollop of luck, the deed was done. Word was sent out. The remaining handful of Jews at Isadore's camp traveled to Greensborough to attend the rabbi's service, along with other Jews spread out over the countryside who'd heard there would be an old-fashioned holiday there. The new hotel was full. Every home with a spare cot was rented out. For the first time the sound of the shofar was heard in the town, attracting considerable attention and curiosity. Quakers remarked that dogs ceased barking, cows stopped lowing, birds stopped singing from the shofar's first blast to its last. More than one admiring farmer contemplated sawing off one of the horns of his ram to fashion a like instrument.

No one loved the shofar more than little Raquel. Now that her father was home and she'd learned to stand up, she clung to his leg at every opportunity. As she was under three years of age, the rabbi permitted her to stand with Abe during the services rather than in the section marked off for women by quilts strung over a clothesline. When the shofar was blown, she dropped the arms that encircled Abe's knee and stood straight and wide-eyed at the long notes, hopped one foot to the other with the short. When it was over, she reached up her little hands to beg her father to pick her up and transport her to a spot near the rabbi. Once there, she pulled on his caftan and begged for more. Everyone, including the rabbi, laughed. After services, the Sassaportas feasted on roasted turkey stuffed with barley, chestnuts, shallots, apples, raisins, and spice all properly blessed by the rabbi. Susanah served honeyed delicacies from the old country and everyone toasted to a sweet year of health and prosperity. Pleasing his elders no end, Abe sat at table teaching his wife the words of all the blessings required before, during, and after their meal. Until then, they'd not been sure he remembered them.

Hannah had only learned the blessing for the candles on Friday nights, and this by virtue of her mother-in-law's efforts, not her husband's. When Yom Kippur came, Susanah noted how

Hannah did her best to fast with them for the first time, taking only a little fruit and water during the day as she was not accustomed to such deprivation. Her parents wrote asking her if at least she and the child might visit them at Christmas, providing there was not too much snow on the byways. Her sisters and their families would be there, it would be a grand family reunion. She replied that she would do her best. Abe promised to take her there, weather permitting. When Susanah overheard Hannah describing to Raquel the Christmas tree and the presents, there was at least no mention of a baby Jesus and from this omission, she took hope that her granddaughter would not be Christianized over her mother's holiday.

Between the Jewish holidays and Christmas, business was slow as it always was in the cold months. Abe pondered mightily trying to devise new sales strategies for the spring, but his bag of tricks was empty. He looked constantly for inspiration, had a few lame ideas, ran them by the family for critique, and accordingly abandoned them. Apparently, he always said later on, one must sift through a lot of dross before finding gold. The key is never giving up. Indeed, the striking of gold is often happenstance.

What happened to Abe was that while taking his wife and daughter to the Milner farm for the Christmas reunion, he crossed paths with a convoy of army supply wagons. He asked the man in charge, a lieutenant of craggy, war-worn appearance, where they were headed.

"Anywhere that ain't Choctaw country," was his reply. "We almost got all the buggers out of our assigned section down there but they's some laggards ran north. We went after to round 'em up and escort 'em west." He took a flask from inside his shirt, drank long and deep against the morning chill. "We got 'em," he said. "And we'd be long home except for the weather and supplies. Now, there's nothin' a man can do 'bout weather. Supplies, though. Somebody's hide should burn. Supplies din't last. Quartermaster couldn't get everything we wanted before startin' out. We was hopin' to get 'em there quick and easy, let 'em hunt their way to food and such. But the weather. The rains was terrible, flood was all over, and then came the snow. Slowed us down. We'd run out of just about everythin' by the time we put 'em on the ferries to cross the river. We bid 'em fare-thee-well and told 'em to get 'emselves to the new territory next to Arkansas, what they's callin' the Oklas—on their own. Good luck to 'em. Bound to be a frigid walk."

There came a fork in the road. Convoy and family parted company but the information imparted to him resounded in Abe's mind like the echo of cannon fire. For whatever reason or reasons, something he would devote his winter to finding out, the quartermaster in charge of outfitting troops charged with Indian removal had difficulty in the requisition of necessities. Perhaps it was a question of funding. Perhaps it was a question of will. Whatever it was, if Abe could get to the right people in Washington, he knew he could convince them that the North Carolina branch of the Sassaporta Brothers trading group was precisely the vehicle that would find what was needed for the next round of removal and at a good price too.

The Christmas visit lasted four days. Tobias and Esther spoiled little Raquel with treats and presents. She played with her cousins, two girls close to her in age and an infant boy. Hannah sequestered herself with her sisters much of the time while their husbands attempted to befriend one another. Gunther and Paul did just fine together. But there was a distance between Abe and the others that could not be breached. He was alien to them and knew it. One night, Bekka's husband and he sat cozy by the fire. Gunther asked Abe if he could feel his horns, which he'd been assured all Jewish males possessed. Abe had heard the question before, but not since he left London. He sighed grievously. "I don't have any," he said. The other man leaned back, squinted as if sizing Abe up, and remarked, "Then why you always wearin' that cap, if not to cover 'em up?" Abe weighed telling him the truth, that he kept his head covered because Ha-Shem told him to, that he had given up so many of his observances in this wild, free country, he had to hold on to something, even something so flimsy as a cap, or he would no longer know who he was. But this would only lead to questions more difficult to answer. "I suffer in the cold," he replied instead. Bekka's husband stroked his chin. "Well, you are a desert people." His observation was uttered with the finality of a man who is accustomed to considering his own judgment and finding it invariably right. Abe let him be.

It was not difficult for him to find ways to spend his time at the Milner farm apart from the others. No doubt they were as uncomfortable with him as he was with them. While they were singing carols at the local church five miles away, he spent his time with paper and pen secured from his father-in-law, and with them sketched out plans for his assault on the US War Department, General Quartermasters Division. While they strung the draft horse's reins with sleigh bells and trundled off to give the neighbors baskets of baked goods, he combed Tobias's stack of newspapers for articles on the removal procedure, taking down the names of the men in charge. While they napped after Christmas dinner, he jotted down the food, clothing, blanket, and medicine requirements for a family of four traveling from Vicksburg to Fort Towson, on the border between the new Indian and the Arkansas Territory. Then he determined the number of oxen, hogs, horses, sacks of corn, dried beans, pumpkins, and onions that might be purchased along the route and how much would be vital before starting out. He figured how many people a mid-size steamboat could ferry across the Mississippi to Arkansas and budgeted what would be required to sustain them after they reached Little Rock.

"Just imagine!" he enthused to Isadore on his return to Greensborough. "We won't have to take credit. The government pays on the spot. We can get all the goods we need from the farmers hereabouts, I'm sure of it. Now that most of the Cherokee have removed themselves to the upper towns, the farms in the foothills are reporting sizeable gains in acreage and projected harvest. They're not sold by contract anywhere yet. We can be the first. All we have to do is supply the army with enough to get them to Vicksburg. We could make a deal with the Mississippi branch of Sassaporta Brothers to resupply the trip from there on. So even on the second leg of the trip, we'll make a handsome commission. Not only that, once we've proved ourselves in '32, there's a final round planned for '33. We can supply that removal too. After the Choctaw are resettled, surely there'll be other tribes we can help relocate."

Isadore was behind him one hundred percent. "We'll send you to Washington come the spring," he advised. "It's not just the War Department men you need to see but the other ones, agents from the Commission of Indian Affairs. They'll be the ones. They'll be your men with their boots in it. You'll have to woo them, we'll have to budget for that. Don't fear. We'll get the money somewhere."

Isadore begged and borrowed to remain true to his word. Outfitted in a new suit, a sleek beaver hat, and a fat purse, Abe visited Washington in the late winter when the roads were more of mush than snow and ice. It was a dirty, difficult ride for him and Hart, but better, the family agreed, than waiting for spring. A keystone of Abe's sales plan was to solicit officials before they had time to think of how to improve the next round of Choctaw removal. When he arrived, he learned quickly that the game of government lobbying is one in which the most useful tools are those of patience and flattery. His backside polished a bench outside the door of the War Department for three days before he was seen by a midlevel administrator more concerned with the cut and crease of his uniform than the tasks at hand. Abe smiled and bowed and saluted, addressing the man as sir. His pitch was a hot stew of the most obsequious flimflam a seasoned salesman can muster. Without spending a penny on the man, he succeeded in obtaining a set of preliminary papers stamped in all the colors and varieties the War Department had to offer, which he then took to the office of the Commission of Indian Affairs. There he sat and waited again, this time under a row of Indian busts that were apparently modeled on a single man who looked astonishingly like Edward Redhand. He'd scrambled to get a seat. The corridors were crowded with Indian agents eager to pester the new commissioner, Elbert Herring, for one favor or another.

Abe was in a state of contained excitement, like that of a duck hunter, still, quiet in his blind while an unsuspecting flock of fat birds glide into the pond under his watch. He asked the fellow to his right what exactly was the name of the new commissioner as if he did not already know it. He plucked the sleeve of another man and asked him how to spell "Elbert Herring," then made a show of scribbling it in his notebook. "Why, thank you, sirs," he said. He made his eyes round, the eyes, he hoped, of a child. "I fear I'm unprepared for my business here. I could use guidance from gents like you." He glanced at his fob watch. "It's rather late, don't you know, but if you're hungry, might I buy you a good lunch? A drink? An early supper?" The agents exchanged a sharp look, one Abe recognized from his old days in the ghetto. If there were such a phenomenon as the Mile End Lie, what passed between the two men was the Mile End Unspoken Collusion. Their gaze traveled in tandem to the door of the commissioner's office, where enough men were clustered to make the chance of seeing Herring before the end of the day slim indeed. Abe made his features open, innocent as he regarded them. "Yes? You'll come?" The men smiled and shrugged. "Marvelous! Obviously, I'm new here. Where do you suggest? Anywhere you like!" The agents pulled at their beards thoughtfully, then tapped the tops of their tall beaver hats. "The Old Patriot would do this time of day, no, Mr. Parker?" said one. Abe did not miss that agents standing near them turned or cocked their ears at the mention of the place. "Oh, yes, Mr. Judson," said the other, "it would do well indeed." Incredibly, as they quit the lobby, other agents parted to make away for them, dispensing Abe's new friends little nods of admiration as they passed.

At lunch—which extended long into the night—Abe learned first that an Indian agent spends so much time in the rough hinterlands, when he is in town he likes nothing better than a swank meal of oysters, prawns, squab, and tender cuts of beef washed down with plenty of Champagne, followed by exotic fruits and port. The Old Patriot, Washington's premiere hotel and dining establishment, had the well-earned reputation of offering all the luxuries a man stuck in the hinterland could dream of, if only someone else were paying. Abe could smell the money the moment he walked through the eatery's door. Stout men dressed in natty suits, their satin vests adorned in brightly stitched brocade, their thick gold watch chains stretched across satisfied bellies, sat around heavy oak tables draped in costly linens. Potted palms in brass pots created corridors and veils between tables as if stationed to provide a privacy everyone ignored.

The central table hosted a man who was obviously the great light of the afternoon. His tablemates fawned upon him, leaning forward in rapt unison whenever he opened his mouth, if only to belch or yawn. Waiters placed silver domed dishes in front of him with bowed heads. They removed the domes with a flourish, then held their breath until the man smiled or frowned at the delicacy revealed. A secretary stood behind him, bending to whisper in his ear and place documents for signature to the left of his plate. Unlike his plump tablemates, the man himself was unexpectedly thin, his face on the gaunt side, his brilliant blue eyes marred by the deep shadows and bags beneath them. Despite the richness of his clothes, the shine of his boots, and the elegance of his surrounds, he looked a simple man with all the world resting upon his shoulders.

On seeing him, Abe's guests, Judson and Parker, nudged each other excitedly. The great light was, they whispered urgently to Abe, none other than Commissioner Herring himself. "What luck!" cried Mr. Parker, sotto voce. "While the others clamor outside his door we find ourselves neck to jowl w'him right here in this choice spot!" Not missing a beat, Abe hastily pressed twenty dollars in coins in the palm of the maître d'hôtel and gave the man a pointed nod in the direction of the commissioner's table.

The maître d' then executed a sharp turn from the far table to which he'd begun to lead them toward one adjacent to the Man Himself. As they settled down to their menus, Judson and Parker used them for shields and, wide-eyed and unobserved, listened to Commissioner Herring announce his intention to tighten the reins of Indian trade now that the Removal Act was in effect.

"Oh my, oh my," Judson whispered to Abe. "Do you know what this means? Very soon gents from Maine to Florida, from South Carolina to Mississippi will scramble to Washington to retain their positions and salvage what they can of a dwindling industry! Look who's there, Mr. Parker! Simpson from Boston, Harrow of New York! A hand's breadth away from us!"

How lucky they were, he continued, to be in a position to somehow pick up their leavings, to learn by eavesdropping whatever the commissioner felt most important in issuing the licenses that remained.

"Oh, we can do better than that, Mr. Judson," Parker said, winking broadly.

By the time Abe's companions finished their soup, Herring rose to leave his table, shaking hands all around. Parker stuck out his foot just as the commissioner's secretary, struggling with an armful of disordered documents, made a move to follow his superior, thereby causing the man to stumble. Papers flew all about. "My dear sir," Parker exclaimed, "what an oaf I am! Allow me to assist you." In an instant, he was on his hands and knees, scooping up papers from the floor. On rising, he put an arm around the shoulders of the commissioner's secretary and spoke into his ear. Just as they disappeared from view, Abe saw the agent's hand reach into his trousers and withdraw a money clip. A quarter hour later, he returned, shaking a scrolled document in the air in triumph. "We have an appointment, Mr. Judson! Tomorrow at ten of the clock to make our case for relicensing, a mere formality I am assured, a mere formality!" Judson applauded his fellow, then turned to Abe. "But you must come with us," he said. "Were it not for you, we'd spend the day tomorrow cooling our heels outside Herring's office like all the rest."

Abe equivocated. He told the men he had no desire for a standard agency license, that he was only interested in a temporary one to serve the removal. In doing so, he could take the burden off men so privileged. That the two before him felt burdened was obvious, he pointed out. Earlier in the day, he'd listened to complaints of bad weather, lame horses, endless wilderness, impertinent Indians, and skinflint farmers. "Yes, it is quite the burden, you know. There are times I think it's not worth the trouble anymore," said Judson after his second dish of prawns. Parker agreed. "Well, then here's an idea," Abe quickly offered. "Might I not serve as subagent for you? You could delegate trade to me both during and after removal and so expand your influence. No need to supply me. All I'm after would be the right to trade my own goods. I'd do it for, oh, sixty percent and the rest in your pockets for the privilege. I like the frontier you seem so weary of," he told them, working up a good blush to underscore his persona of greenhorn rube. "I'm something of a nature buff. Have you ever seen the rolling hills of Wales? Ah! Magnificent, I tell you. The Blue Ridge puts me in mind of them."

In the morning, when Abe and his new mates arrived bleary-eyed at the lobby of the commissioner of Indian Affairs, they were met first with curiosity and then with great interest, once the story of their night of indulgence and proximity to power made the rounds. Abe found himself with numerous quick friends.

For the next week, he dined with as many agents as his stomach and liver could tolerate, sometimes dining twice a night at tables of ten or more, paying tabs at hotels and restaurants across the city. He was the master of the glad hand, the high commander of the delicate bribe. After ten days in Washington, he returned home not only with a subcontract to supply the army in the second phase of Choctaw removal but with a fistful of limited licenses to trade with Indians under the new restrictions and regulations. He had bribe money left over unspent too.

All the way home, he sang songs to Hart, happy songs, songs of security, songs of comfort restored to his wife and daughter, songs for which Hart seemed to keep time, bobbing his head right to left, jogging in rhythm to his tunes as if they were dancing. Within the year, Abe imagined, his family could move back into a home of their own and none too soon either. Raquel grew by the minute and ran riot around Isadore and Susanah's place, ever threatening to topple furniture, sentimental knickknacks, and glassware. Isadore's house was close to the street. Abe wanted a place with an expanse of yard, front and back, for his little jewel to play in. Maybe, he dared dream, there would be more children in due time. True, the turn business looked to take meant he would be on the road more than Hannah was bound to like, at least until he could recruit drivers. He wondered how many peddlers were still up to snuff in the old camp town versus how many lived there in penury, drinking the last of their days away, swapping stories of the glory days before one too many settlers came to farm, before the roads were built and the old trails improved. He knew the arrival of a man with a pack on his back no longer engendered a village worth of excitement but caused the more cautious farmers to lock their doors and shutter the windows quick as you please. He halted Hart long enough to jot down a reminder to sit down with O'Hanlon for an honest view of what was what, an assessment of whom he could trust to take care of new business in the upper towns, and who could manage the procurement of army supplies.

He arrived in Greensborough in the early morning. The sun had just come up, gold and red, streaming light. Abe entered Isadore's house bathed in its rays, his bright, shining face, bursting with happiness. His daughter turned a corner, screamed out, "Papa!" and nearly knocked him over as she slammed into him to wrap her little arms around both his legs, her smiling face pressed into his knees. Isadore and Susanah came out from the kitchen, where they had been eating breakfast with the child. Their faces lit up when they saw him. "My parents," he said, "I have returned with a wondrous tale to tell!" It was obvious from his demeanor that he had been successful, that their troubles were over. They joined Raquel in hugging him welcome. Then Hannah came out of the kitchen, her hands wringing a dishtowel as if it were an enemy's neck. The three who embraced him immediately tensed.

"So. You're back."

Her tone was ominous. Her mouth was set in a straight, grim line. Her eyes were drawn 'til they were nearly closed, the brows above them scrunched together to form a solemn wave of displeasure. Shrinking back from her mother, Raquel let go of his knees to hide behind them. She huddled against the back of his thighs, stuck her thumb in her mouth, and twisted her hair. Isadore backed away from the scene in mincing steps. Susanah remained at his side as a mother always stands by when her child is in peril. She pinched the back of his neck hard to warn him that he must be alert in the face of impending doom.

"What is it, my love?" he asked his wife. "What's wrong?" He held out his arms. "Are you not happy to see me?"

"Huh," Hannah muttered, and gave him her back. She went to their room off the kitchen and sat on the bed, waiting.

Confused, he followed his wife, wondering what he could have done to upset her in absentia. His Hannah, his sweet Hannah, had never been angry with him before. Never. When they'd parted, she'd been as loving and affectionate as ever. It was a mystery, a conundrum. As soon as he entered the bedroom, however, the mystery was solved, the conundrum cracked. Hannah sat in the middle of the smooth, crisp bedclothes, their borders stitched with sunflowers by her own hand. Her shoulders curled inward, her face was red, her eyes brimmed tears, her lips were clenched to still their tremble, and at her side, spread out flat to cover a good portion of the bed, lay Lord Geoffrey's portrait of Marian, her family, Jacob, and Lulu. She waved a shaking hand over it.

"This is your great love, I hear," she said. Her voice was high pitched and wavered with upset although she spoke quickly, with determination, as if she'd practiced her speech a hundred times. "I've discovered from your very reluctant mother this is a woman you loved to near ruin once. Perhaps you still do. Perhaps you see her during your travels, for all I know. You're certainly gone often and long enough. Why would you keep this hidden from me unless you cared for her still, perhaps more than you care for Raquel and me?"

Abe fell on his knees, grasped her hands, and bowed his head to kiss her knuckles. They felt hard and cold beneath his lips, which terrified him. He spoke in a rush of words, uttering the first phrases that came to mind as he instantly and fortuitously intuited that to hesitate would be disastrous.

"My darling! How can you say it? This painting is a relic of the past, that's all. Yes, yes, it's a woman I knew long ago as Marian of the foothills, a woman who was once kind to me and who earned my gratitude and affection. But all this happened before we loved. . . ." He chose not to mention how very briefly before and plowed on. "Never, never would I betray you and our daughter for her memory or her person in life. I assure you I did not see her this summer past nor did I look for her. She is in any case a woman in company. She has a lover of very long standing to whom she is passionately devoted. I'm barely an afterthought in her life. I know this well. How I pray you will know it too."

He stopped speaking, breathing heavily from the outpour of feeling that accompanied his speech. His wife straightened her back and lifted her chin. He dared look up at her, making his features open and sincere to inspire mercy. Feverishly composing fresh argument in his mind should he need it, he watched her lips twitch as she examined his explanations under the harsh light of wifely judgment. But her heart proved kind, subjecting him to only the slightest of tortures before embracing him with forgiveness. "You allowed me to be in ignorance of your friendship with her, a woman so important to you that you would keep mementos," she said, though in a milder tone than her original accusations. "And then you hid the painting from me. By most women's reckoning, that would be a guilty act." Her gaze was steady, searching his expression for any hint of mendacity. He decided discretion was in order and gave her the truth but the smallest possible portion of it. "I was unsure how you felt about the Cherokee," he said. "God knows, your father reviles them. Our love was so new I dared not speak of it." Her back went straighter still. "You thought me unloving toward any of God's creatures? Abrahan, this is a fresh wound." His heart leapt. When she used his full name, it was always in affection. "Forgive me," he pleaded, kissing her face and neck all over, "forgive me for being in such terrible fear of ever losing you, my beloved, my darling, my sweetheart, my bride."

His petition had the desired effect. Putting her arms around him, Hannah raised him up, then coyly fell back on the bed to submerge him in a frenzy of absolution. Hoping his parents had done the sensible thing and taken Raquel on a long walk, he succumbed happily to marital pardon and strove with all the imagination he had in him to express to her through his hands, his mouth, the strength of his back, and the ardent need of his sex that she was all of those things to him—that is, beloved, darling, sweetheart, and bride. Though the morning was yet chill, they threw their clothes off into a heap on the floor and kicked off the sweetly embroidered comforter along with Lord Geoffrey's portrait as well. In the midst of the most intimate embrace, they moaned loudly in tandem, then heard through a fog of passion and as if from very far away, the hurried patter of feet. In the next heartbeat, the front door opened and shut. They laughed and kissed and continued what they'd been doing until they were done.

Afterward, they lolled about in the bed, drawing the comforter back up around their shoulders so that only their feet stuck out its end. Abe made good on his protestations of love by continuing to stroke and pet her under the covers while murmuring endearments. "How could you doubt my fidelity to you, Hannah?" he said after a time. She stretched out in the sensual way satisfied women have, with confidence, with generosity, flirting with the idea of another go. Her skin glowed. Her hair had come undone. It framed her face in a mass of charming curls and love knots.

She turned a bit and reached down to the floor, picking up the painting, then holding it up over her chest with two hands. "Well, you have to admit this Marian is quite beautiful." Abe took the canvas and tossed it back on the floor with bravado to prevent her from recognizing Edward Redhand's likeness, which would surely reanimate her doubts. He also wished to prove a point. "It's a very old work," he said. "She must be in her forties now." Knowing that Hannah considered any woman remotely near Susanah's age to be ancient and thus unable to rival her, he nuzzled the sweet hollow between her clavicle and throat with warm content when her next words hit him like a hammer aimed directly at his temple.

"Oh my Lord. Then I bet that was her after all!"

Abe's head reeled. "What'd you say?"

"Well, there was a Cherokee so like the painting who came in the store just last week, only much older. I thought, Oh my goodness, she could be your Marian's mother. Imagine, I found the painting when one of Isadore's men came by to help me with the spring cleaning and moved the wardrobe as I thought to dust behind and underneath the furniture. After your mother blurted out that the Indian in the painting must be that one you'd been so in love with, I stared at it so much I memorized her features as if they were those of our own sweet child. When I told your mother that I thought your lover's mother had been in the store, she said I was mad, that I was so distressed I must be seeing signs of her everywhere I looked. But on the other hand, I thought she would say anything to calm me before you returned home again."

Abe propped himself up on one elbow. There was no time for artifice. He put a little more urgent command in his tone than he'd have liked, but luckily she ignored it.

"Describe her to me," he said.

"Well, as I mentioned, she looked very much like the painting, only older by maybe twenty year, plus she had a staff to lean upon. At first I thought she'd a limp, but no, it was really just a kind of stiffness. I think that's why she needed the staff. I recall thinking perhaps she had the gout or rheumatism. She was bundled up, dressed in layers. The first was one of those tear dresses they wear, you know, made out of strips of cloth, and she had a homespun shirt over it, leggings under it, and a buckskin jacket with a long shawl over all. Her hair was covered by a turban like their men wear, and she had gloves too. Really, I could not tell much about her except for the stiffness and the face because they stood out from all those clothes. I suppose she wore so many because it was cold that day and there'd been a little late winter snow in the night. Isadore thought that she might be very poor and wore everything she owned. He'd already resolved to give her charity, but it turned out she was not there to beg. She wanted to know where you were. She and her companion had business with you. We presumed it was a late rubber complaint."

"Her companion?"

"Oh, yes. There was a strange man outside sitting astride a horse and holding one for her. He was big, that's all I could say for sure. Very big. You could not see much of him for the hooded cloak he wore, naught but the tips of his boots and his hands. Judging by his hands, I believe he was a black. It was all very odd. So. What do you think? Could that have been your Marian fallen on hard times?"

Yes, he wanted to say, *yes!* But his heart was seized by a thousand fears both for Marian and for the tender pardon he had just won from his aggrieved wife. He paused, swallowed, and at last was able to speak in a measured, rational manner.

"How'd you know, perhaps it was. Was there any message?"

"Not really. They bought a few items, canned things and blacksmith tools, trading a silver dish for them. Can you imagine? A silver dish from such as those two. We thought it stolen but took it anyway. There was a desperation about them that Isadore pitied. She mentioned they were on a journey and did not expect to be back this way. She said to tell you Jacob and his wife bid you farewell with their thanks."

His wife! Surely that was an exaggeration for convenience sake. A journey. What kind of a journey? he wondered. Was it possible that Marian and Jacob had joined the ranks of the exiled and voluntarily chosen to go west? Or north, perhaps to a free state? Canada? No. Impossible. Not her. Not his Marian. He heard her voice, mocking him: *"Give up my land? After I've killed for it? Ridiculous."* And yet. She'd moved to old Chota quickly enough, where she was so happy he suddenly realized that her terrible injuries, for which he'd blamed himself, had been largely healed. How remarkable she was! How like the fabled firebird in the Talmud, he thought, imagining her as a magnificent winged creature rising from the ashes of a scarred life, soaring up and away, away from trouble, away from him. Abe held his wife a little closer as he felt his world shrink without even a phantom first love in it. He envisioned his Marian, the woman not even Jacob knew, the one that was his alone, leaving his heart, ascending into the heavens, illuminating the night sky in a blaze of light, then dispersing slowly into vaporous anonymity throughout the four corners of the universe. His eyes went damp. He kissed Hannah's shoulder. He took a chance and gave a sentimental whim, a tribute to a dying desire, its brazen voice.

"I'd like to keep the painting," he said, "if you don't mind. It's a souvenir for me, of times past, of my youth."

He held his breath while she deliberated with her mouth screwed up, her gaze upon the wall. At last her face broke into a dazzling smile. She turned to him.

"Of course I don't mind," she said. "I am the most secure of women, aren't I?"

He gathered her up in his arms and buried his face in her hair that she would not notice the extremity of his emotion. "Yes, my love, yes," he said, "you are. You most certainly are."

BEST-LAID PLANS

O'Hanlon stormed into Greensborough in a military wagon. He cracked a whip hard above the flattened ears of his frothy team of four and yelled warning. "Gang way!" he bellowed to startled citizens of the town before he pulled up short in front of Sassaporta and Son. "Laddie!" he shouted to a drop-jawed, wide-eyed farm boy of fourteen who sat on the bench outside the store waiting for his father to finish up business. "Can ye lead these beasts to the stable 'round back and tell the man there to brush and water 'em?" The boy nodded. O'Hanlon flipped him a coin, jumped down from the wagon, and stomped into the store, sending up clouds of trail dust with each heavy step. Abe rushed around the front desk to greet him.

"What news?" Abe asked. "How goes the transport?"

O'Hanlon shut his eyes and shuddered.

"What terrible, terrible sights I've seen," he said. "Oh, dear God, there it is."

He brushed past Abe to a shelf where spirits were sold and grabbed a bottle. Abe ushered him into Isadore's office. Hannah counted stock in the back while Raquel sat at the big desk drawing on scraps of paper. With a perfunctory tip of his hat, O'Hanlon sank into a chair facing the desk and took a long draught from the bottle. He wiped his mouth with the back of his hand. "Beggin' your pardon, ma'am," he said, "but my need is great." Abe quickly told Hannah to take Raquel out and mind the store. She scooped up the child in her arms and left, closing the curtain behind her while casting her husband a final, worried look. O'Hanlon drank from the bottle a second time, then placed the drink hard on the desktop and shook his head so that his whiskered jowls danced. "Brrr," he said. "Never again will I attempt a journey like that without spirits! It's inhumane to ask a man to bear it. Injun and white man alike. It was a horror, I'm tellin' you, a horror." The Irishman fixed Abe with a look of such suffering that the younger man shuddered. O'Hanlon looked a wreck, that much was true. His cheeks were hollow. The flesh under his eyes were like the bladders of colicky cows, stretched so full they pinched his lids together making it appear he could barely see. His hair stood out in spiky clumps below the brim of his hat. The stench of the road blended with the reek of stale fear and loathing rose up from him in a foul wall.

"Tell me," Abe said, bracing himself for the truth.

"Yes, you need to hear the tale, lad. For your part in it and mine, we may well be cursed for the rest of our natural lives.

"Like all disasters under God's eye that befall the fate of men, it started out well enough. Nothing went perfect, but me an' the boys were hopeful and bound firm to make the exercise go better than it went last year when so many died of the cold and of hunger. I took me boys, the livestock, and the goods to the fort in Virginia, where that Mr. Gaines would divvy the lot up into the detachments takin' the Choctaw into the West. Now, may I say, that part I always thought was a wee bit daft. Why take the goods to Virginia and then have to take them back south again? But rigmarole is the way of government tasks, ain't it? Ah, it was a harbinger, let me tell you, yet I paid it no mind at the time. I was feelin' too proud of meself and of you too, bucko, that we were givin' over fair value for the money they paid us. Other agents there gave not the value we were givin'. Used blankets they had, with holes. Scrawny cows so old their shoulder blades rose higher than their noggins. Corn that looked to have spent the summer season in the bottom of the barrel and then got pissed on. But not Sassaporta and Son! Our blankets were new, our cows fat, our corn fair golden as a pale March sun. Yes, I was proud 'til I saw what use our pains would go to.

"First thing the soldiers did was take what they liked for themselves. Yes, there was a good deal of skimmin' goin' on. The quartermaster's men laid up the best of the best in their own wagons and pens. Off it marched to Jaysus knows where. Now, you know me. I'm not a man to keep me mouth shut. I spoke up about it, sure I did. They called me a stupid mick and laughed their arses off."

O'Hanlon paused to take yet another pull from the bottle. His face went dark with anger. "Stupid I may be," he muttered, "but who's lyin' in the cold ground now and who's livin' to tell the horrid tale?" His head fell on his chest. He appeared to remain conscious but in some nether world of memory and frightful vision. The sight of him, just this side of madness, dried Abe's throat. He dared to reach forward and prod the man gently. O'Hanlon raised his head. Abe took the bottle, feigned having a draught himself, then nodded, encouraging him to continue.

"After that, I should have sent the boys home and maybe I

should have gone home meself. But it irritated me, you know, that the soldiers stole what they wanted. I thought to volunteer us to go along for the mission and do what I could to keep 'em honest." O'Hanlon looked as if his own words confused him and then he howled. His howl resembled a long, rolling bout of laughter but underneath was a harrowing aspect that made it something else altogether. At the sound of it, Hannah popped her head in to see if all was well. Abe gestured to her that he was on top of things and signaled her to disappear. She did.

"I'm guessing," Abe said in as gentle a tone as he could muster, "that your presence had no effect?"

O'Hanlon shrugged. "They were as decent as soldiers might be for a while. We picked up bands of Choctaw waiting for us along the roads to Vicksburg, the place we was marchin' 'em to. From thence, they'd be put on steamboats to Arkansas and from there escorted to the promised land. Quick at our backs, settlers raced their horses along the common roads to raid whatever had gone unsold or untaken by the Injuns in their flight. They moved in before the Choctaw breakfast fires were cold. Our own movements was slow. Mr. Gaines, that bastard, requisitioned only a single wagon for each detachment. The old and the sick could ride, but everyone else must walk. This meant children, women heavy with child, others deemed less sick than whoever was in the wagon but still infirm, walked alongside, some of 'em barefoot, and quietly, so quietly it spooked the soul of every white man there, even mine. Still, they ate. They slept under kind stars. It wasn't until we approached Vicksburg, our ranks a thousand strong, that the journey took a hideous turn.

"Some of the people came down the Mississippi, but our lot were on the woodland route. It was late fall and cool and the leaves of the trees what yet had 'em were orange and yellow and red. The days were short and we made our way in the light God had given us, resting for the chill nights wherever the sun fell. The chiefs came to us and asked if they might stop a while and fish in the running streams since the food we'd stored was making the people sick. Or so they thought. Gaines in his wisdom said no and on we pressed closer to Vicksburg and that's when we came head to head with a plague of such strength no man alive has known it. It was the cholera and it had whoever gave it welcome fast as you please in the grip of death. The horses caught whiff of it first. I'll ne'er forget the moment every jack one of 'em stalled and turned 'round, unwilling to walk on into the cursed vale. We whipped 'em. They blew and snorted. A wind came up and then not a one of us could ignore it no longer. What drew off the horses was the smell of rotting flesh.

"We got closer. The outskirts of Vicksburg were scarred by piles of bodies, sometimes ten or twenty high, dumped in the wood, then set aflame to burn the plague out. Never will I forget that pinch of me nostrils, the gag in me throat, as the full scent hit me square in the face. I pray never to smell again what I did that day. And the sight of 'em! Men, women, young, old, children, mere babes, the ones on top burnt to a crisp, and underneath bodies yet smokin', the flesh not entirely consumed. Faces stretched in agony. Charred limbs bent and twisted into positions no man unpossessed can form. Infants with their scorched mouths round and black like tiny holes leadin' to the depths of hell. Over all of it were swarms of flies so thick you could not see your hand before your face should you be so unlucky as to ride through them, and with 'em a buzzin' sound what got inside the ears and stayed there no matter how you pounded your head with your fist or ran away, far from all that carnage and noise and stink.

"Scouts were sent into the city. It was deserted. Everyone had fled the plague. We drew back. The local farmers you engaged to refresh our supplies once we reached Vicksburg were in hiding from the disease and refused us. What they had they were keepin' to themselves. They wanted no contact with us. So we were locked out, runnin' low on everything. While we waited for Mr. Gaines to decide what to do next, we camped outside of town next to the smolderin' bodies of the damned. Then we too started dyin'. A quarter of me boys took sick and in time as many died. Soldiers succumbed as well. But it was the Choctaw what suffered worst. So many dead. So many.

"There were steamboats waitin' on the docks to take the Choctaw across the river to Fort Smith, and from there they were to be taken to their new territories, what they called the new Oklas after their old towns. Gaines offloaded supplies from the boats but just enough to keep souls and bodies together until the plague passed. It was a half measure too late. When it came time for the crossin', near two thousand Choctaw were crammed into a single vessel, the *Brandywine*, with nary a place to lie down so stacked they were, above deck or below, and then the rains started. Many of 'em were still sick and the tides rose and the ship could not dock for the flood that came next and more of 'em died and got tossed in the river, or so I heard from them of Gaines men what returned. God alone knows how many made it all the way to the new Oklas. I fear a paltry few."

O'Hanlon sighed. It was a dark and mournful sound. He sat back in his chair, took yet another drink, and let tears fall down his cheeks, one by one. "I was never a great friend to the

Injuns, Abe. But I was never their enemy either. My heart has been turned now. I'll do those people a good turn whenever I can from now on. It was a terrible dishonor to be part of such events. Neither I nor what's left of me men and me beasts will ever forget it. I believe I will hear the weak little bleats of the dyin' babies and the mournful chants of their mothers for the rest of me life, awake and asleep. God help America on the day comin' when she must pay for her sins." He shut his eyes then. Within seconds, it looked as if he'd passed out or fallen asleep.

Abe let the man rest while he digested his news. The more he thought about it, the fiercer his shame and anger. The travesty O'Hanlon described was not the expedition he'd signed on for. He imagined Marian and Jacob in similar circumstances. In his worst imaginings, both died along the route. How could they not? He took a couple of long pulls on the bottle himself and, as he was not used to the drink, soon trembled with remorse. His features dissolved into a melting plane of regret. He looked blearily about the boxes of the stockroom, regarding the imported treasure he'd accumulated with his government contract moneys. Quality imported goods traded at a profit as fast as a merchant could pile it up. Customers would stampede even a disgraced Sassaporta and Son for such and Abe had been hopeful the treasures he surveyed would bring the store back to health. Now he regarded his imports with disgust. Blood money! Blood money! he thought.

In a drunken rage, he picked up a plate of fine china crafted in England, nested in straw for its transport overseas. More care had been devoted to its well-being than the efforts extended to ten Choctaw children. "Blood money!" he shouted, and smashed the plate against the wall. "Blood money!" he shouted again, smashing another plate, then another, and cups and saucers as well. O'Hanlon snored through it all but Hannah heard the racket and pulled back the curtain to witness him in his mad tumult, smashing away. Fear seized her with two hands about the heart. She grabbed her child. They ran down the street to Isadore and Susanah's house for help. Isadore was out gallivanting with his peers, taking tea at a rich planter's estate where he could play the grand entrepreneur, but Susanah was home. She saw the fear in Hannah's eyes and said, "Stay here. Mind the child. I'll take care of this."

By the time his mother threw open the door of Sassaporta and Son and barreled into the back room, Abe sat in a pile of china shards, head in hands, talking to himself in a voice blurred by the drink. O'Hanlon, until that moment oblivious, opened his eyes. "Oh, Susanah!" he cried out. "How beautiful you are! Happy I am to see you once more!" He held out his arms as if she might fly into them. Susanah shushed him. He ignored her. "Oh, Susanah!" he cried again, stretching out his arms farther, attempting to fix her with a red-eyed stare of great intensity. "Come t'me, lady! Come t'me what loves you!"

Unbowed, she marched up to the man and slapped him hard. Twice. "Stop it! Stop it!" she said. "I am a married woman and you are a thing of the past, you great git!" Abe was yet blubbering on the floor, locked in his own world of sorrow. "Help me here with my poor son!"

Through a cloud of drunkenness and misery, the Irishman slowly grasped his situation. He staggered up and helped Susanah raise Abe to his feet, muttering all the while, "What the feck am I supposed to do now, I ask you. What the feck?"

Susanah told him. "Get my boy home to his wife and put him to bed. I'll take care of the store."

Days passed before the world calmed down. O'Hanlon returned to the camp with his wagon, his team of four, three bottles of whiskey, and all his sundry heartbreak. Isadore, Susanah, and Hannah took pains to bolster the conscience of their devastated Abe. They assured him what had happened was not his fault. He had not been in control of events. He'd done his part with honor. What came next was no sin of his. They could take a portion of their profits from the endeavor and gift it to the Moravians, for those schools they had that trained young Cherokee in English letters and modern means of support. Would that make him feel better? Next year, oh, yes, yes, there would be a next year, for the Choctaw removal had a final phase to come, they would insist on a disposition clause in the provisions contract that made it clear the transportees would have what they needed, even if disaster struck once again.

He was not convinced. Contractual provisions were the flimsiest of solutions. He laughed like a madman when they brought it up. Instead, Abrahan Bento Sassaporta Naggar swore an oath on the head of his second child who was soon to be born: Next year he would do everything in his power to condemn the abomination that was Indian removal. He no longer trusted anyone involved in the process to have a lick of sense or an ounce of compassion. In a fit of principle, he vowed he would not put his name to any removal activities. He would go once more to Washington to expedite the termination of his license and to lobby the commissioner of Indian Affairs for a change in stewardship of the process, as George Gaines was obviously a blockhead, a man of hard and narrow heart. To put some gumption behind his words, he was prepared to relinquish his sublicenses, those he'd won to do business with the Indians that remained in the country, as well. "If it doesn't pinch," he explained to his family, "if it doesn't hurt, then penance is void of meaning. And for our part in the murder of innocents, penance is due." They looked at him helplessly. Hannah bit her lip and anxiously agreed while fearful of the consequences of agreeing. Susanah clasped her hands to her bosom and looked to the heavens but for what purpose it was unclear. Isadore raised his palms in the same direction, saying to his wife, "When did your son become the head of the family?" only he said it not with acrimony but with pride.

For the second year in a row, Abe rode to Washington in his sleek suit and beaver hat. He reversed the order of his visitations, first sitting outside the office of the Commission on Indian Affairs under the row of Edward Redhand busts. As in the previous year, the corridors bustled with men eager to make their fortunes on the back of Choctaw hardship. Unlike the previous year, Abe befriended none. At last his turn came for an audience with the same commissioner's secretary Mr. Parker had bribed in the lobby of the Old Patriot Hotel the year before. He declined an offer to sit in the man's well-stuffed visitor chair covered in red-white-and-blue damask. Instead, he stood tall, shoulders squared before an over-large mahogany desk with heavy scrolled legs and highly polished top, an appurtenance of power meant to intimidate and impress. In unwavering voice, he lodged a protest against the management of the Choctaw removal, providing the gray-haired, mustachioed bureaucrat with a letter protesting the horrors O'Hanlon had reported. Below his summation, every Quaker in Greensborough had signed his name. Abe told the man there were more copies of this letter. One would find its way into the hands of the War Department, others into the hands of the press and of Congressmen Crockett, Sprague, Everett, and Frelinghuysen, the most vocal opponents of the Indian Removal Act, with the hope that it might inspire an effort to repeal the heinous law. He then took his various agency licenses from his breast pocket, ripped them in quarters, and tossed them onto the desktop.

The eyes of the secretary shifted to the side, where his marshal stood at the ready. The man's lips pinched. He opened his mouth, preparing to excoriate his visitor before giving him the boot. Abe didn't wait to be thrown out. He executed a sharp nod with eloquent finality, turned on his heel, and left. Exhilarated, lighter, happy, halfway to redemption, he headed to the War Department.

The War Department corridors were even more crowded than those of the Commission of Indian Affairs. Men were pressed shoulder to shoulder without courtesy or order. From their chatter, Abe surmised many of them were members of the press. He wondered what newsworthy event had occurred. Was there a new war? A revolt in the hinterlands? The massive gold-knobbed door to the war secretary's chambers swung open. Cries of excitement pierced the air. Men pushed one another backward and forward, climbed up one another's backs, all jostling for a spot where they might see what was going on. Officers of the guard pushed the crowd against the walls. Abe stood on a bench to avoid being crushed. Once a narrow passage had been cleared, several men left the secretary's chamber. The remarkable thing was that there was among them a man Abe knew. They were all Indian, but the one he knew was Principal Chief John Ross of the Cherokee Nation.

He called out to the chief. So did thirty other men. The Indians made their way slowly through the crowd, stopping to answer questions from the most prominent journalists. Whenever they spoke, the people immediately hushed. When they stopped, cacophony broke out again, redoubled. Abe left his bench to scuttle along the wall 'til his back found a door leading to a service staircase. He pushed it open, ran down the stairs, and positioned himself behind a wrought-iron railing at the building's entrance close to the brick wall. So secured by stone and metal, it would be impossible to dislodge him. He waited. Within moments, a sea of shouting men flooded the entry lobby. Guardsmen pushed them aside with the tips of their bayonets. The Cherokee walked with their heads high down the interior steps and out the door. Abe extended his hand and pulled on Chief John Ross's coat. The chief turned. His black eyes flickered with a hint of recognition.

All the world around them faded away as Abe said, "Chief Ross, remember me? A friend of Dark Water and Jacob's what came to you at New Echota a number of years back."

He remembered. He nodded. "And what do you want?"

Before he knew what his words would be, Abe blurted out, "I need to know of them."

Chief John Ross turned to a man Abe hadn't noticed before. He was a small man in an ill-fitting suit. The copper color of his skin declared him Indian of some kind, but somehow he had neither the bones nor the carriage for it. "Give him my hotel." John Ross put his head close to Abe's and spoke in his ear for privacy's sake. "You may come there tonight. Nine o'clock."

Abe clasped his hand and gave it a good solid shake. "Thank you, sir. Thank you," he said, before scribbling down on the back of one of his copies of the letter of protest the name and address of Chief John Ross's hotel.

ALLIES

Abe entered the lobby of the discreet, three-storied brick hotel, the Federalist, located in the heart of the capital at a quarter to nine. He looked around. The chief's accommodations were far superior to his own, which were situated in a boardinghouse more than halfway to Virginia, a place frequented by transient salesmen looking for a home-cooked supper and decent bedding for their mounts. While the common areas of Ethel Mae's Rooms were plain and worn, furnished in scraped wooden chairs and threadbare carpet, at the Federalist there was gold flocked wallpaper, multiple crystal chandeliers, oak floors, and an abundance of velvet and brocade upholstery on welcoming couches and chairs that dazzled the eye. His merchant's gaze wandered to the walls, estimating the worth of oil paintings and brass sconces, when he was interrupted in his reverie by a shuffle of feet and gently murmured "ahem." Standing close to his right was the small man in the ill-fitting suit, a man Abe assumed was the chief's secretary. He tipped his hat to him. The small man reciprocated. He gestured Abe to follow him to a corner suite on the second floor.

John Ross sat in his shirtsleeves at a writing desk overburdened with papers. His head was down, his hand held a quill poised tentatively over documents he read with furrowed brow. He did not seem to notice his visitor. Again the small man murmured "ahem," so gently the utterance was more plea than announcement. Chief John Ross looked up.

"Ah, Mr. Sassaporta, here you are." He rose and slipped on his frock coat. "I apologize for my disarray."

Abe executed a little bow from the waist, not too deep a bow, which he worried would appear obsequious, but a short, respectful one.

"Not at all, sir. I am delighted you could find time for me."

They moved to a settee. The small man brought them glasses of sherry. Abe inquired about the chief's negotiations with the War Department, to which John Ross raised his eyes to the heavens and moved his hands to indicate hopefulness. "I believe we are near the end," he said, without clarifying his meaning.

Abe blushed. Were his feet put to a fire, he would confess he had no desire to discuss the current round of negotiations. It wasn't that he was heartless on the subject of the Cherokee Nation's fate. Obviously, he believed that the government management of Choctaw removal was an abomination. They'd been promised moneys, livestock, and western lands in return for volunteering to leave their ancestral home, and what had they got but penury, sickness, and death? He felt he had done his duty when he lodged his protests and washed his hands of all aspects of the removal, denying himself any profit in it. The point was that there was nothing else a man like him could do. Who was he but a humble merchant in a provincial town? Abe's America was one of wholesome geniality, of the good people of all backgrounds who had embraced him. His experience inspired him to trust that, having made tragic mistakes with the Choctaw and after suffering impassioned objections like the ones he'd delivered that very morning, the various men in power would see to it that such horrors were not repeated. He had faith in that. This was the New World, not the Old. America was not Spain or Germany or France, where Jews could be kicked from country to country, their assets gobbled up, their futures left to their own devices, to good fortune or ill. In any event, he had not visited Ross to inquire about the fate of the entire Cherokee Nation. He'd visited to inquire about the fate of one Cherokee in particular, and that of her mother's slave.

"Chief Ross," he began, "if you say you are near completion, then I wish you only the best of luck in securing whatever terms you desire. But I am come to you to ask what has happened to Jacob and Dark Water, who are my friends. I was told that, while I was in this very city a year ago, they visited my place of business and, not finding me there, went on their way. It was reported to me that they were not in the best of circumstances. I'm hoping you can explain to me what happened to them."

John Ross leaned backward in his seat and presented Abe a look of astonishment.

"What do you think has happened to them, Mr. Sassaporta? Our glorious boundaries have shrunk from the spread of an eagle's wing to that of a butterfly's in but a handful of years. In Georgia, where first we met, white settlers are granted what's left of our lands by lottery, dispossessing whoever might be in the way without so much as a warning. We crowd together on territories with little enough game to go around while our most fertile fields are harvested by white hands. Echota is a ghost town.

Our white advocates—our postman, Reverend Worcester!—are arrested for their loyalty. It's a crime in Georgia for white men to help us. Men like Reverend Worcester languish in prison despite your Supreme Court's decisions in their favor. President Jackson, who is bound to be rid of us, sides against the supreme judges and with the State of Georgia, despite the Constitution, which I thought your people held sacred. More the fool me.

"Our ruination is certain. The only thing left of Echota is the printing press, which is in disrepair after the last militia raid burned the building in which it was housed. We prepare to move the capital of the nation to Red Clay, Tennessee, as soon as the buildings we require are completed. How long we will last there, I cannot say. I pray at least until President Jackson is out of office and one more sympathetic sleeps in the White House. It's our only chance. Otherwise we will be on our way to that small parcel of this great continent your government has designed for us—a little corner of land just outside the Missouri Territory and the state of Arkansas. We will sit on a crowded territory with no place to grow, on top of those awarded the Choctaw and Chickasaw, the Seminole and Creek. No nation will be happy. There are other tribes, western nations, who will resent our arrival. It will be only a matter of time before we are all at war with each other as in the old days. I fear then your government will drive us farther, even to the great mountains, then over them, and into the western sea.

"We have not been able to support the old places for some time. These lawsuits gobble up all our funds. If Jacob and Dark Water left, it was only as they were hungry. Except . . ." John Ross put his glass down on the little table in front of them. He paused. When next he spoke, it was in a hushed tone, his voice as soft as the small man's ahem. "They married. Did you know that?"

Abe spoke slowly, embarrassed as he was to have been ignorant of the extent of Cherokee decline. He thought the Choctaw disaster an anomaly. The newspapers he read painted a rosy
picture of other Indians who voluntarily left their lands, of a
benign federal government that helped them relocate for their
own protection against the lawless. This country, he thought. So
rich it opens one's eyes to boundless ambition and blinds them
to the misfortunes of others. All of his earlier assumptions were
thrown into doubt. "Yes," he managed to say. "I believe Dark
Water mentioned as much to my wife and uncle. I wasn't sure
whether to believe it."

"Indeed, they married. Not in the traditional sense exactly,
as they had no clan to witness them nor medicine man to bless
them, but they observed the rituals. They fasted, they purified
themselves in the living stream, they exchanged the proper gifts
and wrapped themselves in a single blanket."

John Ross rose and went to the window, stood looking out
with his hands clasped behind his back.

"You are aware the marriage of a black slave and a Cherokee
is against our law?"

"Yes."

"And are you aware of the punishment the law prescribes?"

Abe's breath was stolen by an image of Dark Water, his Marian, with a back striped by scars. He could not speak.

"Then I'll tell you," Chief John Ross said. "It is twenty-
five lashes against the naked back if the Cherokee is a woman.
Seventy-five if a male. It's a cruel law, yes, but one the people
have voted is necessary to preserve the true blood and make
themselves as good as white in the white man's eyes. Questions
of survival often have dubious solutions. At any rate, I suspect

our friends left Chota not merely out of hunger but also to avoid prosecution. Many of our people love them. Most of the people would look the other way—and I include myself in that number, Mr. Sassaporta, willingly, wholeheartedly! There are few so brave, so faithful to the Cherokee way as those two. But Jacob and Dark Water have their enemies. Bitter enemies who would be delighted to see her flogged. Especially while he wept."

"Please. Tell me."

"I admire the ways of the full blood and those who have resisted my own efforts to accommodate the Europeans. Never have I supported the idea that the white man's ways are superior to Cherokee. But war against the white man does not work. There are too many. To preserve the people, I have dressed them in broadcloth suits and calico dresses, weakened their rituals and encouraged the Christ in their hearts, put plows in the hands of men and spinning wheels in those of women. I knew from my father that the white man would devour them otherwise. But the white man's maw remains open and greedy despite my best efforts.

"When I was a boy, I worked in my father's trading post high in the mountains close to my mother's village. He was a Scot, you see, and my mother also had Scottish blood that flowed with the Cherokee in her veins. I would watch the play of the Cherokee boys from the windows of my father's store and long for their company. To my eyes, they were free and strong and wise in all important things while I was but an apprentice shopkeeper, skilled only in the making of change and the stocking of shelves. My mother and aunties encouraged me to participate in the Green Corn Dance and other celebrations of the people. These were the best days of my youth. When I was allowed to frolic with the others, how good those full-blood boys were to me! They joked with me. They called me Little White Bird, as my mother was of that clan, but they also embraced me. When my father sent me to the Christian school with other mixed bloods, I was the chap most likely to paint my face and rip off my shirt at the first opportunity.

"I first saw Dark Water just after I graduated and was appointed Indian agent. There was a General Council as was held every year, and of course all the people who were not infirm attended. There were the usual practical matters and disputes discussed and a most important vote on whether or not to support the United States in their most recent war, but there were also dances, games of stickball, races, and other competitions. Dark Water competed against the boys and won fame throughout the nation for her skill at running and shooting, and her beauty, of course, was by that time legendary. Like all the others, I longed for her attention. We noticed that after she collected her awards and honors at the competitions, she would rush to place them in the lap of her father. Yet her eyes did not take him in but settled instead on the beaming features of the slave, Jacob, who attended him. We were all jealous. Some swore they saw them touch hands or lean into each other when they thought no one was looking.

"This was the infamous year of the slave Jacob's confession to the murder of Teddy Rupert's son. You know of that, do you not? Yes, I thought you did. And of her foolish pleas for him, her confession, which he denied? Yes, yes. I tell you many of the young men who longed for her, myself included, loved her all the more for the madness of her passion. Who would not desire the devotion of a woman who could love so deeply? Others hated her for it. They felt she demeaned herself and shamed her family.

When Jacob fled to Chota, our city of refuge was all but deserted after your Revolution scoured it. He tended it as best one man could. He labored to rebuild its cemetery. In this way, he earned the respect and gratitude of the nation even before the Battle of Horseshoe Bend in which he was so terribly damaged. But some hated him for being the one who caused the desertion of Dark Water, her withdrawal from her people, that terrible isolation and refusal to take one of them as his replacement in her arms."

Chief John Ross turned from the window to face his visitor. He put his hands together in front of his chest and then opened them again, holding them close to his face.

"After you reunited them, their joy was boundless." He wiggled his fingers in the air. "They say the very leaves of the trees trembled with pleasure at the sight of their lovemaking under the moon and stars. And these, they say, whispered their midnight secrets to the birds, who flew from one town to the next to tell their trees of it, and soon the goats knew and the dogs and then all the people. Lovers among them smiled and felt their own love strengthened in the happy ending of two so challenged and faithful. But those who hated her and those who hated him joined forces and spoke of them as a disgrace. Married properly or not, they grumbled, they were in violation of the law and she, especially, must be punished.

"How do y'think their supporters defended them? They said, they are not young, they are not whole, they will not bear children. Why should anyone care? Even if they should have children—was Shoeboots punished? Or were his babies with his slave made citizens? Ah! How much argument would then occur. Shoeboots bore his children when the restriction against marriage with slaves was custom, not law. He was a man. The issue of men has never been as important to us as the issue of women, who carry the privilege of citizenry and inheritance in their very wombs. On and on and on. Whenever there was nothing else to argue about, the gossips of the towns and villages would argue about Jacob and Dark Water. Even when there was much to argue about, they argued about Jacob and Dark Water to hide from the pain of matters more pressing. Questions such as when we will all be driven from our lands, and who would be the most convincing man to send to Washington to achieve a peace and, if not that, a settlement we could live with. This is the way of man. To seek distraction in the petty and evade the significant."

John Ross clucked his tongue and sat next to Abe once more, falling into his own dark thoughts while Abe, absorbing so much intelligence, kept him company in his silence. The little man interrupted them, offering more sherry. They both refused with weary waves of the hand. The chief took up his tale.

"So. Last summer these two beleaguered lovers came to me at my home in Ross's Landing, you know, that place on the Tennessee River where I have my trading post and ferry business. They came in the night under cover of darkness, rapping at the window of my study, where I worked while the rest of the household slept. I thought them birds, they were so light in their touch. I looked up expecting to see ravens perhaps or some other night birds bearing omens in their beaks. No. It was those two. His features were hidden in the hood of his cloak as was only prudent when he was out of Chota, but she, ah! Who could forget that face? Those eyes that even through the darkness shone like the stubborn embers of a dying fire? That mouth? I signaled for them to approach the front door, at which I gave them entry. Stealthily, we returned to my study and straightaway I asked, 'What are you doing here?'

"Jacob spoke first. 'I am here to inform you, Great Chief, that we are leaving Chota and to give you these keys to the house the nation has allowed me these many years. We have left it intact with all the nation's gifts to me. You may wish to retrieve them.' He reached in his breast pocket, an action that exposed his ruined face. I kept my gaze steady so as not to offend. 'And here is a map of the graves I attended, along with the many keepsakes of heroes who are gone but whose bones are elsewhere or were lost in battle. I know you know where the graves are, but'—here he made a gesture of uncertainty—'we do not know what their fate will be without a guardian.' He finished his speech and stepped back, his head down as his eyes had tears. Dark Water came to stand beside him, her arm around his shoulder.

"I stammered my gratitude. It was difficult, even for me—a man who addresses the president of the United States, his wily men, and all the Cherokee Nation under the most difficult conditions—to take in the shock of how they had fallen from grace." John Ross paused and put his head back against the settee. He looked at the rafters and shuddered. "What I fear the most, Mr. Sassaporta, is that such is the fate of all my people." He gave out a bitter laugh. "Only worse!"

Abe was in a state of great suspense. It erupted.

"What do you mean by 'fall from grace'? Tell me! For pity's sake!"

To his credit, John Ross did not react to Abe's impertinence but resumed his account.

"Simply put, they were in tatters, impoverished. They appeared weakened from malnourishment, exhaustion, and anxiety. They were dirty too. That was especially heartbreaking. Do you know how important cleanliness is to Indians, Mr. Sassaporta? Their condition could only mean that they had been closed to water. Water. For the Cherokee, it is like gold to the whites. A sacred thing. How had this come to be? How had two people highly skilled in living without the conveniences of what the whites call 'civilization' come to such a state? I believe, after thinking about it, that several elements led to their downfall. First, as I mentioned, game is scarce now from the lower towns to the mountain villages. The settlers near Chota hunt everything the Earth provided for our people. The settlers care not if they kill does with child or take the mother bird from her chicks, leaving them to starve. Second, our friends could not be seen together without great risk from both whites and those of the Cherokee who were their enemies. Third, they had what you might call special problems complicated by their impoverishment."

"What special problems?"

"Dark Water was with child."

"Oh!" Abe was shocked. With child! Marian with child! He'd always considered her age a barrier to procreation. Dozens of thoughts cascaded through his mind. That her new child and his would be about the same age. That he might have given her a child in the past. And yet it was Jacob who had done so. Was that what people meant when they spoke of the miracle of life? Was that the holy key to all its mysteries? Love? He struggled to return his attention to John Ross.

"Yes, she was with child but not so far along at the time. Just enough so that when she draped her arm around Jacob's shoulder, the thin clothing she wore, a tear dress and a worn buckskin shirt, emphasized her condition, a condition that put both of them in danger in more ways than one. Hurriedly, I gave them what I could. In the kitchen, I found a couple of sacks. I filled them with as much clothing, food, and coin as the sacks could carry. On impulse, I added a silver dish. I took them to my stables and gave them two horses. Then, because it was coming near the dawn, I sent them on their way before the people of the town rose and found them out. Once they were off, I prayed."

Abe's mind continued to spin. Hannah's perception was right. They were in extremity. His Marian, with child!

"Please, sir, Chief Ross, you must tell me. What happened to them next? Do you know? Where were they going? To her brother's settlement? To the mountains?"

"Immediately, of course, they were going to you, although I imagine it took much time, under the circumstances. After they paid you this visit, which I understood was intended as ceremonial like the one they made me, committed to expressing gratitude and such, they intended to go to the mountains, yes, but not to her brother's. That would be indiscreet. And dangerous. Her mother, who has never forgiven Jacob, is yet alive. I cherish the hope that what I gave them plus what they could barter for the dish would take them somewhere they might find respite and a new home, if only they arrived before the winter took hold."

There was quiet between them then. Abe had discovered what he came to know. Now that he'd time to notice it, he realized Chief John Ross appeared exhausted. The man's head lolled against the settee and his eyes were closed to near slits. Without further fuss, Abe thanked him for his audience and bid him fare-thee-well, offering as a matter of politesse to be of service whenever, however the chief might need him. He also requested that he be informed if there were ever fresh news of Jacob and Dark Water.

The small man guided him to the door. As he opened it, he gave Abe a most studied look, intense and filled with urgency. He then stuffed into Abe's hand a square of parchment, folded over three times. Before Abe had time to investigate it, the small man closed the door behind him, leaving Abe to open the note in the privacy of the vacant corridor. He did so. There was a message, but it was written in Sequoya's alphabet, which he could not read. Placing it in his pocket, he quit the Federalist Hotel for his bed at Ethel Mae's Rooms, where he lay sleepless, reviewing with a weight pressing against his heart all that Chief John Ross had told him. In the morning, he headed for home, relating to Hart all along the way the information he'd gathered on their old friends, pausing many times to sigh, to fret, to imagine calamity. He was a man. He could worry only so long before he put his mind to a solution. After rigorous thought, he devised the best plan he could to find and help them. He made a detour, stopping at the old camp town, where Abe paid a visit to O'Hanlon.

The camp town was much changed. The barracks were gone, replaced by a row of cabins in which married peddlers lived or small groups of bachelors shared a hearth. The streets were not so muddied. The main street had been bricked. Gardens sprouted here and there. The company store had transformed itself into a bright, cheery spot. Mannequins dressed in seasonable clothing flanked its entry. Through sparkling windows, he noted its canned goods with colorful, appetizing labels displayed in escalating rows of shelves next to placards advertising special discounts. Fresh game and domestic fowl hung by their feet from a wire above the front desk. There was a new building, whitewashed and shuttered, with a large bell mounted in a hoop on the front porch next to a joggling board marking the place a school. Children! Jacob thought. They are everywhere these days! He wondered about Marian's child. The weight against his heart grew, expanding like a sodden sponge.

"O'Hanlon, it's good to see you well," he said when he found the man and repaired to his rooms. They exchanged pleasantries. As it was midafternoon, O'Hanlon put out a bit of soda bread and a pot of tea. After a few sips, Abe came to the point. "My friend, do you recall the Cherokee woman to whom I was attached before my marriage?"

The Irishman raised his great red eyebrows and nodded. His lips pursed with curiosity.

"For complicated reasons, she and her husband are hiding out somewhere hereabouts, at least this is what I hope, and I wish to find them. They are in need and I am pledged in heart and conscience to help them. Do you know someone, a tracker perhaps, who can do the job? They are a distinctive couple with a small child. If they are in these hills or mountains, surely they can be found."

Without a word, O'Hanlon put his teacup on the fireplace mantel and went to the top of the stairs that led to the stablemen's quarters below. "Charlie, me lad," he called down, "fetch me Mr. Broken Branch if you don't mind." He stood by the mantel and took up his tea. "We have more than a few Georgian Cherokee with us nowadays," he explained to Abe. "Poor lads are displaced by settlers, homeless and without support. They make good workers but not as salesmen, I can tell you that, mostly as the settlers would sooner shoot 'em than listen to a pitch. So I hire as many as I can to help about."

"I'm glad you do." Abe reached in his jacket and pulled out the note the chief's man had given him. "I hope he reads Cherokee. I may have information that will help in finding these people but it's written in their language."

They waited for Mr. Broken Branch. Wrestling him up took some time. Abe fidgeted, getting up, going to the door to listen for his approach, looking out the windows for sight of the same, at last sitting down again, elbows on a tabletop, head in his hands. O'Hanlon watched him, thinking on matters of love and loss. "And how is your mam these days?" he asked. "Still happy as a clam with your uncle?" Abe's head shot up. "Yes! Of course!" A shadow passed over O'Hanlon's features, giving Abe cause to regret his brash reply. Once love has entered a man's heart, he acknowledged, it lodges there until the grave. They finished their waiting in silence, each man meditating on old delights, unfaded in remembrance, mellow and ripe, until the arrival of the Georgian Cherokee disrupted their reveries.

Mr. Broken Branch was a man in middle age, a full blood it was easy to see, his strong features worn by time and troubles. His hair was clipped beneath his hat, his attire that of a white man. When Abe asked if he could read the note, his chin went up. "We all read, if we care to," he said. He took the note in hand. "It says, 'Look southwest of the brother's keep, though higher up.'" He frowned. "Does this have meaning for you?" Relief flooded Abe in a bolt of energy. He bounded up and took Mr. Broken Branch by the shoulders. "Yes, my man, yes, it does! And glorious meaning too! Now I have a direction to find loved ones I thought lost to me!" O'Hanlon then asked Mr. Broken Branch if he could help find these people. "They are Cherokee," he said. "Their names are . . ." He looked over to Abe, who filled in, "Jacob, a black slave with no surname, and Dark Water Red-hand. Do you know them?" If Mr. Broken Branch was surprised by Abe's revelation, he did not show it but kept his features still and said, "Everyone knows them. If they do not wish to be found, you will not."

Abe was undeterred by the man's suggestion of failure before the search had rightly begun. That night, he gathered Mr. Broken Branch and several of his fellow Georgian Cherokee in O'Hanlon's living room. He made them an offer of five dollars each in gold to search for Jacob and Dark Water, with a bonus promised of twenty more in greenbacks if they were located. He did not consider whether he could afford such a rich reward, but vowed if not he would find the moneys somewhere, somehow. As insurance, he put out a notice to all peddlers who traveled the high places to be on the lookout for the two, described as a black male, disfigured by war, and a mature Cherokee woman of grace-ful and handsome mien, adding that they likely had a child with them. He offered a twenty-five-dollar reward for their location with the caveat that they be left unmolested. The next morning, he arose enthused by the stratagems he'd put in place. His hope was renewed.

Once he'd returned to Greensborough, life as usual asserted itself. At first he waited on tenterhooks for news from his search parties. None arrived. As time wore on, he came to accept not defeat but that results would require patience. He sent out word to his peddlers that the reward was increased to forty dollars, but he won not even a fanciful rumor of Jacob and Dark Water's whereabouts for his trouble. In the meantime, his son, Judah, was born. A rabbi from Charleston was hired for the circumci-sion. Abe was so delighted by Hannah's acceptance of that event, he forgot for a time that other child, alive or dead in a cave in the cold mountains of the high country only to be suffused with guilt later on when the wails of a dark-skinned Indian child came to him in dreams.

The Quakers of the town found his efforts in Washington redemptive. The rubber debacle was at last and finally forgiven. His life turned busy, rich, filled with familial obligations, rewarding hard work, and simple pleasures. Occasionally, at sentimental moments, he took out from its resting place in a box with a bird's beak for a clasp, the small man's parchment, the one folded over three times. He unfolded it and muttered to himself, "Look southwest of the brother's keep, but higher up" in remembrance. Then he muttered the phrase again, adding at the end *Baruch Ha-Shem* as a prayer. Afterward, he'd fold it up again and put it back in its special box where he kept Raquel's first tooth and a lock of Judah's fine, curly hair. Weeks turned into months, months to seasons, with no clues as to Jacob and Dark Water's whereabouts. For all of that, Abe could not give up the notion that one day he would see Marian again.

In 1833, the last of the Choctaw were removed from their land. The weather was clear, the convoys were supplied minimally if not plentifully, and no plagues followed them, only the usual dysentery and croup. When they took the children to Tobias Milner's farm for a visit, Abe happened to read an analysis of Choctaw removal published in one of his father-in-law's periodicals. In three years of transport, the article read, 8,000 Choctaw souls had made it to the new western home, and 2,500 had perished along the way. Now that the US government had learned methods to transport thousands efficiently and safely, the author boastfully surmised, future Indian removals would go smoothly.

He flipped through the pages of the magazine. Another article reported on the Georgia Land Lottery. Georgians boasted of the benefits of swallowing up prime land in full development, gold mines, and entire towns regardless of federal treaty authority. The author quoted snippets of the Supreme Court's Chief Justice Marshall's decision in solid favor of the Cherokee on matters where federal treaty and state law such as the Lottery conflicted. He quoted also President Jackson's famous retort: "John Marshall has made his decision, now let him enforce it!" Abe shook his head at the cynicism of both Jackson and the author of the article. The summation was one that grieved him personally. It read: "In the end, Georgia does what it will. Earlier this year, when Principal Chief John Ross returned to his home from Washington after negotiating for weeks with the War Department on Removal matters, he found a certain Mr. Smith living in his home. He too had been dispossessed by the Lottery."

Abe shut the magazine, unable to read further. He was full of disquiet and complained to his wife of the state of the world. She held him tenderly, then distracted him with a story about the antics of Raquel, who'd attempted to suckle her baby brother that day in a most comic manner. Yet the fate of Chief John Ross disturbed Abe's sleep for a long while. In the end, he buried himself in his daily tasks, deciding that the raising of children with a sense of ethics and fair play was the best remedy he could offer an unjust world, with the hope their generation might grow up to reform it, person by person, bit by bit.

ENEMIES

Two years later, at the tail end of 1835, Hannah found herself about to give birth yet again. As luck would have it, the very day she went into labor, Abe heard at the store that the Ridge family had signed a comprehensive removal treaty without the full authority of Cherokee law. In it all of the Cherokee Nation's land was delivered to the United States for the pittance of $5 million to be paid in allotments over time, payments no one believed would ever be made in full or without significant and frequent delays. Thousands of people would be transported to the western wilds. Abe gasped with disbelief at the bearer of the news. How had the Ridge family managed to override Chief John Ross? "You lie!" he told the hapless fellow, a trader come to fill outstanding orders before the deep freeze of midwinter. "Sir!" the trader protested, putting a hand on the gun holstered around his waist as if to challenge the shopkeeper or perhaps to protect himself in case Abe's consternation took an expansive course. To prevent either from occurring, Abe grabbed his hat and rushed out the door, leaving Isadore to take care of business and clear the air.

Once he was on the street, he had no idea where to go but

home. He burst into the house brimming over with undigested emotion, ignoring the fact that his first two children were not there, having been shipped off to their grandparents for the evening to afford Hannah and Abe a rare night of quiet. It was a good month before her time. Hannah's face, a map of contented smiles, made no impression on him. Instead of recognizing her content, he poured out his dismay at the traitors of Chief John Ross and all his people.

"Why has this happened? What were they thinking?" he asked her who had no idea what he was talking about. "All they had to do was wait for the chief to finish his work. But now they've gone and done it. Placed all the Cherokee riches into the laps of settlers, planters, tradesmen, and miners. All those . . . all those *mamzers* who've been waiting, aching for them for so long, ah! So very long!"

Finished, exhausted, he sunk into the settee facing the fireplace and looked at his wife, his eyes brimming with frustration and disappointment. He expected her to come sit by him, drape an arm around his neck, and console him. She did not disappoint.

"My dear, my poor dear," she said, settling in close to him, one hand over his shoulder, the other braced against her belly, "what are you talking about? What has distressed you so? What has happened?"

He told her. She considered his news and his distress while he continued to fidget and scowl.

"There's nothing you can do," she said. "You mustn't torment yourself. It was bound to happen sooner or later. The people are tired of the 'Indian Problem.' They want them gone, out of sight, so they can enjoy life like Georgians who defy the courts and take matters into their own hands."

Abe's back stiffened. Her pragmatism sounded to him like betrayal. He took to his feet to lecture her. "The people can go to hell," he said in a dark, ugly tone. He slammed a lamp stand with an open palm for emphasis, making his wife jump in her seat. Suddenly, she gave out a sharp, loud cry, grabbed his wrist, and said in wavering voice through clenched teeth, "Oh, no, oh, no, it's time. Get your mother here straightaway!" As he ran off in a panic to fetch Susanah, he decided his anger somehow had brought his wife's labor on and cursed himself.

The delivery was difficult, her struggle long, lasting the entire day, the night, and most of the next day as well. Judging by the faces of the women who bore bloody towels and basins of water as they came and went from the bedroom where Hannah lay, screaming at regular intervals, terrifyingly silent in between, Abe thought he'd lose her or the child or both. In despair, he vowed never to mention the Treaty of Echota in anger again, if only they would live. At last the child arrived, a small but healthy boy.

True to his promise, Abe kept his mouth shut as his neighbors hailed the resolution of the Cherokee fate. When the Quakers said, "It's as the papers say. They'll be better off out west, where there are no white men to trouble them," he did not so much as shake his head. Defenders of the Treaty Party pointed out that the documents were signed out of patriotism because the War Department was losing patience with John Ross and his constant haggling over details. If he kept it up, there would be no more talk of payments for land or allowances in the new territory. There would only be the sharp ends of bayonets driving the people across the Mississippi, they said. Though it cost him dear, Abe neither raised an eyebrow nor a smirk. Privately, he nursed the vain hope that Chief John Ross would succeed in nullifying the Ridge betrayal. Ross had two years to do so before all Cherokee were forcibly expelled. "Two years is a good amount of time," he said to his wife, "and Ross is the man for the job." But he didn't really believe it. Rather, he agreed with Isadore's assessment that once the wheels of progress chugged along with determined direction, they were impossible to reverse. Hannah was also right. He was helpless to do anything about it. He stopped reading his father-in-law's journals. All they did was upset him. When he dreamt of Marian, he awoke depressed, out of sorts, a condition his family could not help but notice. He fought to put her out of his mind for their sake while his hopes of ever learning her fate faded inexorably into the West.

By the time their third child, Gabril, or Gabe as Hannah liked to call him, was learning to walk, Judah was closing in on four, Raquel six. Hannah was exhausted. The children were lively, noisy, the house was too small. For respite, she'd put them outside with Raquel in charge but Greensborough had grown. Their backyard playground had shrunk. The children's shrieks of laughter or petty argument bled through the walls. Their mother had no peace. Everything got on her nerves. Abe realized there was no need for them to live near the store anymore. His function in the family business had become managerial. He no longer worked the floor but spent most of his time at a desk next to Isadore's, writing letters to factories, negotiating contracts, devising sales campaigns, analyzing product trends, tracking the performance of peddlers and trading posts, investigating maps for locations of new stores in the towns popping up everywhere, and a dozen other sedentary chores. So he built them a larger house outside the camp town, a grand, two-story home atop a rolling hill with pillars, porticoes, many fireplaces, gardens, and shade trees. Once a week, he traveled to Greensborough with all his papers and charts to confer with Isadore and, when he did, spent the night with his stepfather and Susanah. The rest of the week he worked out of Isadore's old office in the camp town, a bustling community now large enough to sport an official name, Laurelton, for its stands of sweet bay.

Raquel went to the Methodist school in Laurelton most days, which lightened Hannah's load, as she had been teaching the child her letters and numbers by the family hearth the same way her mother taught her. Once someone else took over that job, Hannah's temperament improved considerably. She cooed her little student out the door and celebrated her return with kisses and smiles. She praised the virtues of Laurelton's one-room schoolhouse whenever she had a chance. There were twenty-seven other students, most of them children of farmers. Only Raquel was from a trading family, which meant that she attended most regularly while the others were often called away to help in planting or shearing or harvest. A handful were younger than Raquel but most were from two to eight years older. Their parents or grandparents hailed from Germany, Britain, France, Italy, and Ireland. It was good for her to know them, Abe and Hannah thought, until it wasn't anymore.

As Laurelton grew, the Sassaporta name became less important. No longer its sole employer, Sassaporta and Son competed for labor and market share. Of all the endeavors the new town supported, only the public stables under O'Hanlon's management remained a Sassaporta monopoly. Still, people were jealous. None of the old hands forgot the leaner days when Isadore ruled them like a king. They spoke behind Abe's back, remarking that he knew nothing of the land or the difficulties of taming it.

He only knew how to exploit those who did. There were rumors that, after the rubber debacle, he was more loyal to the Cherokee than his own kind, and what was that exactly? Oh, yes, he was a Jew. Those types always went where the profit was. What was it the Cherokee gave him? Gold? It wasn't long before little Raquel was pushed in the dirt outside the schoolhouse, tripped when she climbed its stairs, and ignored by her teacher when she hugged her scraped knee and whimpered. Abe took her out of the school and put her back in the constant care of Hannah, who now had her hands full not just with the demands of the older children, but also with the toddler Gabril, who ran about constantly getting into mischief. To keep the peace, he hired the full-blood wife of poor Mr. Broken Branch to help her.

Poor Mr. Broken Branch and his wife lived on the derelict property next to Abe's own. Beatrice, a strong, stocky woman with a broad face and big hands and feet, had most lately looked after an old settler couple who'd died the previous year of feeble hearts, one after the other. Around the same time, poor Mr. Broken Branch had been kicked in the head by a horse he labored to shoe. He had a dent in the shape of a hoof on the left side of his forehead and was only good for the most directed tasks. O'Hanlon gave him a small pension out of his own pocket, but it was not enough. With no place else to go, the Cherokee remained in the servants' cabin of the old settlers' spread, leaving the big house to fall back into nature's cruel embrace while the heirs to the place squabbled endlessly in court. Abe felt righteous about the hire. He could have bought a slave for less than he'd pay Beatrice the first year. He liked the idea that his children might learn something of Indian ways from her, and she was in need. Of late, Beatrice had become more or less a beggar, scavenging in a town where people did not waste so much as a thread. The day she came around the back door looking for day work or scraps, they had a conversation. He asked her about her people. She claimed she had none. "I am away from them so long I can't remember," she said. A planter-soldier, whose name was lost to time, had stolen her from her village when she was nine. He'd needed someone to wash his pots and his clothes while he was on campaign. He told her he took her because she was the right size, she wouldn't eat much. Beatrice was not certain if he was British, American, or French. "All I know is he like children," Beatrice said. "He not like women. When I become one, he cast me out." She shrugged as if such events were commonplace, leaving Abe to speculate uneasily on what she meant. "After that I wander. Mission men take me in. They teach me English and how to read and write a little. I was baptize in the water. I learn to cook and clean the way white men do. One day, I meet Broken Branch and we like each other well enough."

Throughout their interview, Beatrice kept her hands in her lap. Her gaze was without expression, her voice was monotone. If ever a spirit of fire or ice had dwelt in her veins, it was gone now, smothered, beaten off. He considered the indelible twists of fate that had made her so. "I wonder," he suggested to his wife, "if she is what happens to a people ripped from their roots and plunged, solitary, into an alien life. They are left adrift, belonging nowhere within touch or smell or taste of their true blood, whatever blood that may be, and this, you must agree, is a tragedy." Hannah nodded. As long as the woman was honest and hardworking! she thought. The old couple had liked her. That was recommendation enough. Any rumination about her circumstances, how they came to be, was pointless. As a woman with a hundred daily practical concerns, she considered her husband a tender soul who thought too much. Abe was always philosophizing and sometimes came to dubious conclusions. That was his nature. She agreed with him anyway. She wanted help and Beatrice seemed humble and obedient. What else was there to say?

As it turned out, the children liked her. She taught them Indian songs, her only memories of her people. She cooked corn pudding for them and baked yam bread the way her husband taught her before he'd lost his sense. If they were very good and very patient, they found they could make her smile, which felt like accomplishment. As a bonus, poor Mr. Broken Branch fascinated them. They thought there was a magic about him because he was docile but also given to strange pronouncements out of the blue, like a mad wizard or bewitched king from a fairy tale. They took him with them when they went to fish or pick berries or mushrooms in the forest. Often, when Gabe got tired, Mr. Broken Branch carried him home. Once he was in the forest, he always did something unusual.

One day, in the late spring, when the children and their damaged companion tromped through the trees with their baskets and sacks looking for wild herbs and new fruits, Mr. Broken Branch stopped short. The children followed suit. He looked up at the sky and tilted his head. Slack-jawed, they waited to see what he might say. They waited a long time and were about to give up when suddenly Mr. Broken Branch said, "The drums are loud. The words are wrong. They come." He said it the first time in his own language, so they could not understand him. "English," Raquel said, tugging his sleeve. "English, please." "English," Judah said, hopping up and down. "English," Gabe pestered also, pulling on his pant leg. Mr. Broken Branch blinked, then repeated himself in English, "The drums are loud. The words are wrong. They come," and said it again in English after that. Later in the night, the family gathered in front of the living-room fireplace before bed. Abe and Hannah chatted about their day. The children played on the floor with their collection of feathers, stones, and sticks. Suddenly, young Gabe stuck out his little hands before him, closed his eyes, and repeated the Cherokee's pronouncement in his baby's lisp. "Drums loud, words wrong, they come," he said as best he could while his siblings rolled on the rug, collapsed in laughter around him. "Drums loud, words wrong, they come!" they echoed, repeating themselves louder and louder until their parents begged them to stop and explain what game it was they played. They all talked at once so that neither Abe nor Hannah could understand them. "Time to go to bed," Hannah pronounced at last, "before you give your mother a sick headache."

The next day, Beatrice did not come to work. Abe went down to the servants' cabin of his old neighbors' spread to check on her. Neither Beatrice nor Mr. Broken Branch was there. All their personal effects were gone. It was mystifying. No one in the town had seen them leave. A few days passed and they did not return. The family might have put their sudden disappearance down to the sometimes odd behavior of Indians, except for what happened the following week.

Abe was in his office working on the payroll account when the sharp roll of military drums came to his ears, at first faintly, then louder, then louder yet, until the rappity-rap-rap commanded he leave his seat and look out the window. A column of armed irregulars made their way down Laurelton's main street led by a trio of threadbare drummers, scrawny boys, none older than twelve. Behind them were thirty or so men who marched, and behind those, thirty or so men on horseback. Both marchers and riders were slumped over, filthy, trail worn. Some wore caps, some hats with chewed-up brims, others kerchiefs tied up in the manner of Caribbean sailors. They were in buckskin and home-spun. Rifles were slung across their backs at cockeyed angles. Only their boots looked uniform and by the looks of some, a good pair of boots may have been their primary reason for join-ing up. The horses moved at a desultory clop, undirected by their riders. They wandered from side to side of the street at the slight-est distraction. More than a handful were swaybacked. At the head of this motley procession was an army man in US blue, but his jacket was too dirty for Abe to be sure of his rank. He wore a misshapen felt hat, mustard-colored, with a long eagle's feather trailing out the side. A lieutenant, Abe surmised, for no reason at all. When they'd achieved the center of town, the drum-mer boys beat their drums at a faster pace. The leader raised a gloved hand. "Company, halt!" he said, and both drummer boys and irregulars did. Abe went outside to join his neighbors on the sidewalk and wait for whatever came next. People stood, staring, three and four thick. The lieutenant braced his toes against his stirrups, stretched himself upward in his saddle, and looked over the townspeople crowding the sides of the road. He spoke in a loud voice.

"I am Lieutenant Robeson, of the US Army," he said. "My men and I are on our way to Cherokee country to round up them Injuns and take 'em to the place from whence they will go west. Every last one of 'em we're after, and their slaves too. Those what refuse will be taken by force. Those what flee will be hunted down. I do not know how the great state of North Carolina will dispose of their property, but I might suggest to you that those who want it take it and the law will have to answer to you later. All Cherokee who are with you, residents out of the borders of the nation, and I see a few of 'em in among the people here, will have to prove to me that they are US citizens or vital to the interests of those for whom they work if they wish to avoid marchin' with us to Tennessee and from thence to the future what awaits 'em."

He sat back in his saddle. He reached in his breast pocket and pulled out an envelope frayed at the corners and fringed in dirt.

"Now. I have detoured to your town on an errand of some importance to certain folk in Washington," he said. "Is there a Mr. Abe Sassaporta here?"

Murmurs rippled through the assembled. People looked around for Abe. They looked to the right and the left of themselves without success, as he was in the back of the crowd and not a tall man. He pushed through shoulders and approached the lieutenant. "Here I am," he said. The army man gave him the envelope, tipped his hat, and kicked his mount a bit in the sides. "Walk on, Barney," he said, guiding the horse toward O'Hanlon's stables, where a cluster of Georgian Cherokee refugees stood about. On the lieutenant's approach they silently walked forward and queued up behind the drummer boys, though O'Hanlon himself burst through their ranks to deter them, leaving the Irishman robbed of voice and scratching his head. The Indians were told they must produce any weapons carried on their persons, and each one silently offered up a hunting knife. "You'll get 'em back at the place all you all are goin'," Robeson promised. The drums rolled. The soldiers marched off in a cloud of dust with their first group of Cherokee in tow. Soon enough, they were gone.

A vague disquiet settled on the main street of Laurelton while the significance of what had just happened sunk in. After a few *Oh my*s and *What was that*s, someone suggested they form a party to follow the soldiers for the purpose of staking claim to what the Indians left behind. "Better us," he said, "than some government agent who'll give it all to Lordy knows who." More than a dozen men gathered around, making plans.

Abe took the envelope into his office, locked the door, and opened it. It was a letter from Chief John Ross. "As I am sure you are aware by now," it read in part, "the battle for our country has been lost. We are all of us aggrieved mightily, our hearts are riven, our tears flood the ash heap of our hopes. But between tragedy and tragedy, there is no rest. A new battle has begun, the struggle to transport my people to the West in peace, health, and security. To this end, I am on the threshold of securing primary authority to arrange the method, route, and supplies required for their journey. My brother, Lewis Ross, will be the chief purchasing agent for that endeavor although we both admit that the assistance of under-agents who can be trusted will be essential. As we discussed this yesternight, your name came immediately to mind. . . ." There followed a summary of the goods the Cherokee would need, the budget agreed to by the United States for same, and a request for a list of what Abe thought he might be able to supply. Ross estimated 645 wagons; teams of oxen, mules, and horses to pull them; plus victuals and dry goods amounting to $65 per head for 18,000 people would represent a good beginning.

The very idea of such a project was staggering. In the three years since the removal treaty had been signed by the Ridge family, the three years since Chief John Ross fought to prove its illegitimacy to the US government, who among them truly envisioned the scope and complexity of a nation's expulsion? To see its details outlined in even a preliminary manner made Abe's head swim with figures, details, and facts. Of these 18,000, how many were children, he wondered, how many old, infirm? How many were strong, how many spoke English, how many could read? How many could eat a white man's diet and not perish of intestinal disease? If their weapons were confiscated, how would they hunt along the way for those foods more hospitable to their bodies and minds? He considered the eagle's feather that sprung from the lieutenant's mustard-colored hat. Was Robeson aware the Cherokee held the eagle sacred? That it would be an affront to their very souls to march behind that feather to their uncertain fates? Then O'Hanlon was at his door, knocking insistently and calling for him. "I know you're in there, lad," he yelled. "Open up! We must do something about this!"

"In a minute!" Abe yelled back. He'd got to the end of the letter. The final paragraph stunned him as if icy fingers had grabbed his heart and squeezed. "Finally," the letter said, "it would seem our friends and their son were among the first taken. They await deportation at the government stockade near Ross's Landing, where my brother requisitions what is needed for the transport of our multitude. My guess is that the child was held hostage. Otherwise, I cannot believe either of them would leave their aerie home in Tennessee without a fight. He is a handsome little child, I am told, but with a weakness of lung. If you accept my proposal and take supplies to that place, I would ask that you give them my regards and offer in my name any assistance I may be able to provide."

As he read, tender feelings that Abe had long suppressed warmed his blood and sped through his veins, turning the cheeks of his face and the tips of his ears a deep red. His eyes watered. The thought of Marian in a jumble of people awaiting deportation was inconceivable. And soon she would be on the march! His mind conjured a flood of ghastly scenes based on O'Hanlon's report of the Choctaw catastrophe, in which Jacob, Marian, and their little boy—who must be past five by now, like Judah— played the principal roles of martyrs steeped in like tortures. "Open up, lad!" the stable master continued to insist, but both his booming voice and hammering at the door were like a far-off thunder. Enveloped in his sorrows, Abe was deaf to him. When he opened the door at last to stumble home in a fog of distress, he bumped into O'Hanlon's waiting chest. He looked up. The Irishman looked down. Abe handed him the letter and waited while he read. When he finished reading, O'Hanlon said, "You must go and save them." Abe said, "Yes, I guess I must."

In the days that followed, Abe faced down two major challenges. One was collecting enough supplies to fill a wagon he might take to Ross's Landing as a preliminary gesture of goodwill and introduction to the chief's brother, Lewis. Such a trip was completely unnecessary, but it would give him an excuse to travel there without delay to seek Marian and her family out. O'Hanlon agreed to canvass the farms and tradesmen in and around Laurelton for whatever might be had quickly. At first he put up some opposition against Abe's stratagems, arguing that, based on the Choctaw experience, he'd decided the removal of Indians from their ancestral lands was not only wrong in principle but despicable in practice. "I thought you were out of the death-walk business," he said to Abe with the kind of haughty bluster in which Irishmen excel. "I am. The business at hand is for the singular purpose of finding Marian and her family. But I object to your overview. The current transportation of Cherokee will be managed not by greedy and cruel government agents," Abe countered, "but by their own principal chief. Because of that, it will not be the abomination the Choctaw suffered."

Convincing Hannah that he must leave swiftly was far less difficult than he'd anticipated and, oddly, honesty was the trick that won her favor. "I have to leave in the next few days for Tennessee to assist in the Cherokee removal," he told her, and when she crossed her arms over her chest and asked, "Does this have anything to do with that woman?" he could think of nothing to do or say but hand her the letter from John Ross. They were in their bedroom at the time. She sat on the edge of the bed reading while he paced back and forth in front of her, remembering that other time when she'd sat red-faced and angry next to Lord Geoffrey's portrait of Marian, her family, Jacob, and Lulu. When she got to the end of the letter, she picked her head up and looked at him with a soft, kind expression. "My husband," she said, "I am not the child I once was. I find, both to my surprise and yours also I suspect, that I am no longer envious of—what does the chief call her?—your friend. You have proven your love for me and our children over and over and I am convinced that your fond feelings for your . . . friend . . . are but evidence of the goodness of your character and the largeness of your heart. As a mother, I feel for this woman tremendously. Daily, I thank God all my children are healthy. What heartbreak it must be to have a child who is unwell and who must perforce embark on a long and arduous journey! Please go and offer your assistance to that unfortunate family, if you can find them. Perhaps you'll find poor Mr. Broken Branch and Beatrice along the way as well." Abe fell to his knees and kissed her hands all over.

The next week, he was on his way in a one-horse wagon loaded with blankets, cooking utensils, dried beans, and corn. Between the blankets, he secreted a number of hunting knives. He continued to believe Marian and the other full bloods could not survive long without fresh game. How were they to obtain it without tools of the hunt? His act of resistance made him feel neither a rebel nor lawless, but righteous. It excited his flesh, filling him with determination to—why not?—steal Marian and her family from the stockades and deliver her back to some mountain cave where they could live undisturbed until the War Department considered its removal work well and done. Hart seemed to catch a sense of his fervor. Despite his age, which was not yet old but certainly near it, he hauled Abe and his cargo with admirable speed and good humor.

It was the height of summer. They traveled through hillsides and valleys rich with new growth, dotted with plots of cultivation once the property of Cherokee and now the pride of white men busy with expanding them. For miles on end, the sound of trees being felled, their limbs chopped, then dragged away to hastily built mills that churned loudly day and night, filled air that had once been filled with birdsong. "Progress," Abe muttered disparagingly to Hart. The horse snorted response. A plague of heavy rain slowed them down a couple of days, but soon after it stopped, they found themselves on a plateau overlooking Ross's Landing, Tennessee, and next to it, the stockade erected just outside the town's limits. Abe took out the spyglass O'Hanlon had given him for the trek along with a new compass. He was just near and high enough to get a good look into the stockade's interior with his instrument. He raised it to his right eye, eager, happy to have arrived at his destination. Within seconds of observation, he went sick. His stomach seized up. He bent over from the waist. His very heart felt crushed, as if some-one had dropped a massive boulder from a great height directly onto his chest.

The stockade, even at that distance, was a scene from hell. Hundreds of men, women, and children were huddled in small groups together, many squatting in mud with little space to walk between them. Wagons for those obviously sick were spaced in a circle just inside the stockade gate, and these were impossibly crowded, some-times so much so that the old lay elbow to elbow on the wagon beds and children lay on top of them as if the old ones were cush-ions. Beneath and around the wagons were yet more sick. They lay on blankets without so much as a pallet between blanket and mud. Many of the sick were vomiting. Others clutched their guts, their mouths open and groaning. Still others coughed without cease or glistened with the drenching sweat of fever. Nearly all of them had skin covered with red, festering sores. In the center of the stock-ade, a dispensary for food had been set up. Four giant steaming cauldrons held what looked to be a thin soup. Queues of people with bowls outstretched snaked around them in a spiral four and five persons deep while black-robed missionaries, their arms flap-ping like the wings of ravens, ladled out the soup. Reluctantly, Abe put the spyglass down and with tremulous hand, jiggled the reins to urge Hart on, thinking, If she can live it, I can see it. Before he entered the cesspool that was the stockade at Ross's Landing, Abe gathered the knives he had secreted. He placed them in a sack, which he hid among his own belongings in the locked box of the driver's seat. Telling Hart that they must hold steady, neither balk at nor flee the loathsome scene below but somehow embrace it, he descended into the arms of nightmare.

Fifty yards before he got to them, the gates were opened that he might enter. A powerful stench of human waste, rot, and disease was released. He stopped to tie a kerchief around his nose and mouth. Swarms of flies, mosquitoes, gnats, along with every other flying thing that thrives on blood, flesh, or filth coursed through the air in drifting clouds of black and gray. He pulled his cap down low on his brow and lifted his collar against them. Following the direction of the guard at the gate, he picked his way to the command post past people without shoes, whose feet were black with mud, whose cheeks were hollow with hunger, whose skin was full of scabs from scratching at the relentless insects, and yet none accosted him or tried to filch so much as a pot or a blanket from the wagon bed. Instead, full bloods and mixed bloods both followed his passing soundlessly with mournful eyes. From a place where uncovered corpses awaited disposal, the wails of grieving women came in waves that rose and fell like an unholy tide. His eyes followed his ears to the sight of rows of the day's dead lain out one after another. He saw the medicine men, painted, chanting, with no sticks to burn or purses of healing stuff, guiding the souls of the women's loved ones into the next world with their prayers but without even the clear water necessary to purify them first. Hart tossed his head, pulled against the reins. *Get us out of here,* he seemed to say with his strong neck and prancing feet, *get us out of this hive of misery!* But Abe kept him back until they reached the command post, where he wound the reins tight around the brake post, descended his seat, and went forward to the horse's head, which he embraced. Taking off the kerchief that was around his lower face, he put it over the horse's eyes as if he meant to lead him out of a barn on fire. "Be brave, my friend," he whispered to the beast. "With luck, we'll soon be out of here."

"Who's in charge?" he asked two uniformed men who sat smoking roll-your-owns on barrels set up at either side of the command post door. "Captain Willis this watch," one said. He opened the door. His companion grinned, revealing an acute lack of teeth. "You're just in time for the show," he said, and winked. Abe did not bother to ask what he meant. It took every ounce of focus he had to walk into the command post without trembling, to assume an air of authority and control. "Look to my horse, boys," he said, "and there'll be something in it for you. Take heed though to watch out for my goods. I've all of it counted and a list sent ahead to Lewis Ross. If there's something missing, I'll know." The soldiers scowled, affronted by the suggestion they might be thieves, yet their mouths twitched as if they held back smirks.

Abe walked into a scene of disputation. A minister, identifiable by his black frock coat, big-brimmed hat, white ruff, and clerical collar, stood in front of Captain Willis's desk, slapping one hand into the open palm of another, making his point. "Her crime is against nature in the eyes of civilized people," he said. He slapped his hand into his palm again. "And what's more, it's against her own law as well. Their Council voted to abide by the whole of their laws during and after removal. In the name of Jesus, why should she not be punished?" Captain Willis was a fat man in late middle age with round red cheeks and a white mustache as thick as a paintbrush. His snowy muttonchops drifted from temple to jowl like the shields of a Roman helmet. He shifted in his seat. "She's just a woman looking for her husband and child," Wright said. "I hardly think that a terrible crime worthy of extreme measures." The minister huffed and puffed and went slightly blue. "You're a military man, Captain. I am a lifelong servant of the community, sworn and anointed. I think what I understand as disruptive to the social fabric of not only our world but theirs, more cogent, shall we say, than the word of a brave man accustomed to the irregularities of campaign. A number of her own people have come to me to complain."

Sighing, Captain Willis looked to the heavens for the wisdom of an appropriate response and, finding none, searched the corners of the room for the same. That was how he noticed Abrahan Bento Sassaporta Naggar standing near the door. "Ho, who's this?" he asked. Abe promptly introduced himself. Hands were shaken all around. Abe's nerves were high. He got to the point a little too soon.

"I've been contacted by Chief John Ross to assist his brother, Lewis, in supplying the removal," he said. "I have a wagon outside carrying samples of what I am prepared to provide. But also I seek a family friend who is"—he caught himself before saying "imprisoned," which might be impolitic—"housed here. She is known as Dark Water to the Cherokee, Marian Redhand to me. Do you know of her?"

The army man's bushy eyebrows shot up. The Jesus man sucked in his breath and grabbed at his collar with one hand. "Well, yes. As a rather odd matter of fact," the captain said, "we were just discussing her case. It's quite sensitive."

"Her case?"

Abe feared the worst. Marian's strong nature had gotten her in trouble. Of course it would, he thought, she would never take these conditions lying down. Willis got up from his desk and came around to put an avuncular hand on the trader's shoulder. "She's in confinement. Why don't I have one of my men take you to her. She can tell you about it herself." He opened the door and directed one of the men outside to take Abe to Marian Redhand. The sentries blinked. For a long moment, they did not move. Then one stepped forward and gestured to Abe that he was his man. He reached inside the door to fetch a large ring of keys from a wall hook. As the captain returned to his desk and the door was yet open behind him, Abe heard him tell the man of God, "You see? She has her admirers everywhere. This will backfire on you, I'm sure of it."

He was taken to a structure built up against the stockade walls. A crosshatch of split wooden posts filled in the frame of its padlocked door. The soldier unlocked it, then stood outside at ease while Abe ventured within. Inside was a dim, lantern-lit corridor lining a half dozen cells, each one blocked by another crosshatched wooden door. They were dark, windowless, fetid. He peered into them one after the other, making out only shapes and shadows so that he called out, "Marian!" and "Marian!" There came a rustling from one of the boxlike rooms. Suddenly, a pair of hands, dirty, cracked, and red in the knuckles, shot forward to grasp the bars of the last cell. "My peddler! Help me!" Marian said in a rough, dry voice. Abe's heart leapt at the sound of her. "Oh dear God," he cried, "what is this?" He sought and found a key that would open her door. "Oh dear God." He opened it, then froze at the sight of her.

Leaning against a wall with one hand, she stood in the lantern light, a worn and fragile version of her earlier self, her strong body thin, shorter somehow as if the very marrow had been sapped from her bones. Her thick, glorious hair was lank and twisted into knots, her lush lips as dry and cracked as the skin of her knuckles. Her shirt and buckskins were in tatters, her shoes worn so badly her blackened toes stuck through the leather and so did the thickly scarred heel of her damaged foot. A hot lump of compassion lodged in Abe's throat, waking him from his shock. He took her hand and quickly led her outside the jailhouse, where he told the guardsman in words thick with barely restrained emotion that it was alright, he was in charge of her now. The guardsman stared at the helpless woman squinting in the sunlight, assessed the odds of their making it out of the stockade when every gate was locked and heavily guarded, then nodded and looked the other way. Abe found a spot not far off where the man could not hear them talk. Others walked by, Cherokee all. They glanced away from her, purposeful in their delicacy. *Thank you*, he wanted to tell them, *thank you for that*. Marian stumbled. She looked as if she could not stand for long. He sat her down on a tree stump, then took her rough, dirty, tormented hands in his and said, "Marian, Marian, what has happened to you? Why are you locked up like a dog? What have they done to you?"

For all her sufferings, her eyes remained clear and bright. She captured him within their light and said, "First you must promise to help me. Will you help me? Will you help me even at a risk to your own self?" Abe nodded vigorously. She looked up to the skies and thanked the heavens. "Good. Good," she said. "I must have help or I am lost."

"What do you mean?" Abe asked. "Please, explain to me."

She smiled. It was a rueful smile. One of her teeth was missing on the upper-left side, yet despite everything, her smile lit up her face making it beautiful again. It took his breath away.

"Why not? I have the time. They punish me at noon, I hear, and Father Sun yet climbs to his heavenly seat. But please, could you get me some soup? It's vile, I know. The soldiers take our meat for themselves and give us only the bones to boil. But if I am to have the strength for my ordeal, I must have it."

"Yes, yes, of course." Abe elbowed his way through the queue four and five men deep to reach the nearest cauldron. Ripping the ladle from the hand of one of the ravens muttering "Praise Jesus" to each supplicant, he filled a bowl as full as he might, then hurried back to Marian, who slurped the thing whole and sent him back for more before telling him the tale of her disaster.

PARADISE LOST

_____

She began by asking him an obvious question. "How did you find me?" He told her about his misadventure supplying the second Choctaw removal, his trip of protest to Washington, and what he had learned of her fate from John Ross. "And how did you come to this place?" he asked. "I'd have thought you well hidden somewhere in the high places." She moved her head up and down. Yes, yes, they were. "How did they find you? How did they take you against your will?" Marian confirmed John Ross's suspicions.

"Jacob and I were in our cave," she said. "It was one sacred to the old ones. Our walls were painted with images of buffalo and wolves romping under the sun, with the imprints of the hands that painted them, but who these painters were even the old ones do not know. When we found it, we rejoiced. There was a fire pit already dug, as if waiting for us. Birds and deer, mountain goats aplenty to eat. Beyond the living water, fields of wild potatoes and beans planted by ancient hands. We were happy there. Our son flourished. The day our idyll ended, I'd sent him to the stream not twenty paces off to bring us water.

He returned in the saddle of a soldier, who held him before us by his neck, threatening to bash his head against the mountain stone if we did not come immediately with him to the place of our deportation. What could we do? We left with the clothes on our back and nothing else. After a week of walking with other Cherokee as unlucky, we came to this fort."

"I'd like to get you out of here," he finished, "but I'm not sure how."

She put out a skeletal hand and gripped his wrist. "I'm not what matters. It's Jacob and our son you must find. They separated us. We walked through the gates and it was 'Blacks over here! Injuns there!' She made rude, abrupt gestures demonstrating those of callous authorities who'd broken up a family without a second thought. "My husband refused to be moved. I held our son in my arms. Two of them dragged Jacob off. A third ripped my boy from me. That was three months ago. I haven't seen them since." Her eyes filled with tears in the telling. "They are both so vulnerable, you know. I can't bear the thought of either of them without me to look after them. How will they survive? Jacob doesn't admit it, but his infirmities are worse with age. And my boy, he has a cough in the best of seasons. Oh, I wonder daily if they are alive or dead!"

She began to sob. Abe embraced her. Her troubles dampened his shirt. After a few moments, she pulled away and looked up at him. Though they trembled, her cracked and swollen lips pursed in defiance while her eyes blazed with light.

"You don't think I suffered it without a fight, do you?" Her voice chafed like two metal chains ground together. "I have bothered and pestered them daily. The soldiers shrink from me now. They know at the sight of me that I will come and harangue them with the vilest words because words, you know, are the only weapon I have left. And the priests! At first I went to them for help. Foolish me! I thought they were men of charity. No, they are only interested in harvesting souls for their thirsty god. If you want meat, if you want medicine, your soul is their price. 'Kiss Jesus!' their man said, holding a cross to my lips. 'Kiss Jesus and I will help you!'" She shuddered. "Oh, may the Great Beings forgive me, but I did it. I kissed the feet of his idol and asked again. 'Help me,' I said, 'please help me.' And he told me then he could not help, that I must ask Jesus to accept my fate, to beg not for my husband and child but ask rather that the Great Judge of All grant me peace of heart. If I did this, he said, Jesus would forgive me all the depravities of my sinful life and one day I would dwell in paradise.

"Anger took hold of me at his deception. Anger like a fiery brand pressed against my heart. I spit at his cross. I spit at him. I went again to the soldiers but the priest got there first and poisoned their minds against me. The commander here, Captain Willis—that fat, white-haired man who looks so kind, like a grandfather who spoils little ones with treats—put me in my prison cell. He sees me once a week. The guards take me from my cell to his offices. He asks me will I apologize to the priest. If I do so, he can keep him, he thinks, from insisting on my punishment for a life's worth of crimes. But I tell him no. Only if they will give me back my son and my husband. If they do that, I will do even as their righteous whore did and wash their feet with my hair."

"There's something wrong here," Abe said. "I don't think they can lock you up for simple blasphemy. Or for such a slight assault." He paused. He knew the law in an army prison was whatever the

333

authorities decided it was. They enforced what they wished and ignored the rest. "What is your crime exactly? And what the punishment?" Abe asked, although he feared he already knew.

She laughed. Madly, of course, but yet it was still a laugh, a frog's laugh in her ruined voice, to be sure, but yet a laugh so that her face transmuted once again from the mask of torment to one bathed in grace.

"Why, twenty-five lashes, of course. For the great evil of diluting Cherokee blood. For marrying a black slave."

Abe thought, It will kill her. Straightaway, he said, "I'll go to the commander. I'll plead your case. I'll bribe the damn priest if I have to. I'll get you out of this and away from here."

She put a hand on his cheek with the tenderness she'd once displayed to him in the days they spent together in her cabin in the foothills, in the time before he found Jacob, before he took her to him.

"No." She let her hand slip back into her lap. "I would rather bear it and be free. Here's the thing. My people have decided that if we are to remain ourselves through this transplantation at the hands of our neighbors, the only thing that will keep us whole is the law. Some of those who would whip me hate me. I know this. They have nursed their resentments of me for many years, from back in the days when I would beat them at the games and refuse their offers of marriage. Others who would whip me regret my fate but believe only if the law is obeyed will the people survive. 'No exceptions!' they cry on all occasions. 'No exceptions!' To be honest, I understand them! How do you like that? I may suffer from the law, but I'm proud of my people who would preserve it. If the law is unjust, it must be changed in the right way, by Council and vote. We are not like whites, who break every treaty and promise without a care." She paused. Her lips curled in a grim smile. "Of course, just this once I would not object if the law were suddenly suspended." She sighed. Her frail shoulders sunk a little more. Then she shook herself and straightened her spine as if renewing her determination to face her fate.

"Forget saving me from punishment. If you would do something for me, find out where my husband and child are. There are other depots in Tennessee where we are taken. Go to them. Find out for me if my beloveds are there or if they were sent west already. I beg you. I will only live if I can see them again."

Abe agreed to do whatever he could. He would find them, he promised, although he had no idea how he was to accomplish it. He returned her to her jailer and went directly to the command post, demanding answers from Captain Willis, who said, "Don't you think I would give her that information if I could, sir? Here's the problem. We don't list the blacks by name. Our records might say, 'Blacks: fifty men, thirty women, twelve children, slaves all, ferried across the river on July twelfth.' Or, 'Seven blacks dead from fever, left at the crossroads.' The truth is I have no idea where her husband and child are. For all I know they're in the new territory already. Maybe they're dead. In the meantime, I have missionaries and Cherokee both who want to see her flogged. I can't suffer insurrection from either here. If you wish to help her, convince her to apologize to the reverend and beg forgiveness from her people. You have two hours."

For two hours, Abe searched through the stockade for Cherokee who wanted to see Marian suffer, thinking if he could persuade or bribe them to withdraw their complaints, she might be saved. He spoke in English. Many were full bloods who could not understand him. Those who could kept mum. Who were these mysterious Cherokee who wanted her whipped? He began to believe they did not exist, that they were figments of the captain's imagination or the product of the reverend's lies. Still, he searched, desperate, exhausting himself in the summer heat, tormented by insects and the stench that even a brisk breeze could not dispel. Everything he said made less and less sense as the hours flowed through his hands like water.

The time came and the bugles sounded, calling the people to witness Marian's degradation. By then, Abe had only prayer left and Ha-Shem, it seemed, had gone deaf. He stood among the witnesses of stone-eyed Cherokee; soldiers who swayed on their feet as if drunk and probably were; clergymen, some distraught, others righteously expectant; and Captain Willis, a man who had survived four wars and seen worse than the whipping of a willful Indian woman. They brought her from her prison cell and walked her, chains hobbling her feet, constraining her hands, to the center of the stockade, where a post and platform had been set up for the purpose of her torture. One soldier pushed her to her knees and tied her arms to the post so that they reached upward, embracing it. When she was secured, he removed the chains on her wrists while another soldier ripped the shirt from her back. She was so thin. Abe could count the ribs at her back. Her breasts, the breasts he'd loved so, the soft, beautiful breasts on which he'd lain his head in a delirium of pleasure at the age of nineteen, were crushed hard against the post. Captain Willis read aloud her offense and sentence. Abe moved to position himself so he could look directly into her eyes, thinking perhaps it would give her strength. She locked her own onto his, which gave him the strength he wished for her. Throughout her ordeal, their eyes held each other fast, making it impossible for him to weep outright no matter how the scene tore his heart. A strong burly man, a full blood Abe judged, in a fringed buckskin shirt with Indian beading, approached the post and platform, whip in hand. It was a whip with only one business end of knotted leather rather than the cat-o-nine tails Abe expected. He thanked Ha-Shem for that small miracle. Perhaps she might live after all. A drum rolled.

The first lash drew blood but not on her back. As it hit, her back arched, her body pitched forward so that her breasts scraped hard against the rough post, raising thin red lines. By the third lash, tiny rivulets of blood ran down her breasts onto her stomach. There were wide welts on her back but no breaking of skin. It took ten lashes for that. Abe could only think the man who flogged her restrained himself out of pity, but by the end of things, when her flesh, ripped raw and open, ran with blood from shoulders to waist, he revised his opinion. The drum rolled again. It was over.

Her body collapsed against the post. Slowly, her eyes shut. Abe looked away from her for the first time since the torture began and found, to his surprise and pleasure, if such can be had at a moment of horror, that most of the Cherokee had turned their backs en masse from the scene before them in protest, refusing to witness the needless cruelty inflicted on their Beloved Woman. Not all of them protested. There were a number who leered at her crumpled form along with the soldiers and the clergyman from the commander's office, their eyes glazed with a kind of lust. But the lion's share of them did not.

Captain Willis, the clergymen, the whip master, and the soldiers quit the scene, leaving her strung up. Several Cherokee rushed forward, scrabbling at her bonds with their fingers uselessly until Abe got to her and cut her down with his knife. Women bore her away, followed by medicine men. Abe went with them. He held her hand when she was stretched out on the ground, his tears fell over her body, which the others tended as best they could with what they had. He learned the supplies of the medicine men were alarmingly low. There was much illness and they were not permitted to leave the stockades to forage for new herbs and plants to make their potions and salves. They washed her wounds with the cleanest rags they had, which were yet unclean. They used what medicines they could spare to soothe them and spare her a portion of pain. When she was able to speak, her first words were directed to Abe. "Did you find them?" she asked. Her voice was a feather of noise brushing against a wall of hurt. He feared the truth would kill her. "Yes," he lied. "Heal now, and we will go to them."

It was night by the time Abe returned to where he had left his horse and wagon. Hart was greatly distressed and sweated up all over. There was foam at the places where the harness touched his hide and also between his legs and over his belly. Abe wept. "I am so sorry, old friend," he said, "forgive me." He took him outside the gates and found water to cool him with, sweetgrass for him to eat. The goods in his wagon had been ransacked by the soldiers guarding them. There were a few blankets left that had been dirtied with heavens-knew-what. He brushed them and put them over his horse that he not chill. "No more of this," he told the horse. "Even the brother of the principal chief cannot assure goods will get to the people. No more."

Before dawn, he reentered that hell, bribing the guardsmen with coin, telling them to turn a blind eye when he exited again

with precious cargo. This was easier than he expected. They were
not unobservant. They knew what cargo he meant. But now that
she'd been whipped, none of them cared much about Marian's
fate. He returned to the place he'd left her in the care of the
women. She was unconscious but breathing. He took what powders the medicine men could give him, a paltry collection, they
indicated in broken English, as they must hoard what they had
left for the sake of the children. He gave his secret store of hunting knives to those who had tended her, and loaded her into his
wagon bed, covering her with what was left of the blankets. With
his heart in his mouth, he smuggled her out. They rode the rest
of the night away. At first light, he held her naked in his arms as
he waded into a clear forest stream to wash her broken body.
He burned her bloody clothes and gave her his shirt, wrapping
the rest of her in blankets. He tried to make her a soft bed of
pine needles and green leaves. She remained barely conscious,
mumbling sometimes in Cherokee, making little sense in English
when that language found her tongue. Twice a day, he mixed the
medicine men's powder with water and wet a cloth, sponging the
mixture over her back. To soothe her pain, he brewed the leaves
of wild willow into a tea, as she'd once told him to do for a headache. It seemed to help.

The second day they traveled, someone followed them in
stealth. He'd heard a slight rustle, turned his head expecting to
see a squirrel or rabbit, and caught the briefest glimpse of fringed
buckskin disappearing behind a rock. The hair on his neck
prickled, his skin drew beads of sweat that rolled slowly down
his spine, but no one molested them. The third day the disrup-
tion repeated itself. He knew that a small number of Cherokee
continued to haunt the mountains and foothills and evade the

soldiers but it would do no good, he decided, to pretend whoever followed them was benign. He halted Hart, checked on Marian in the back of the wagon, then took up his rifle, cocked it, and fired a shot in the air. Two figures suddenly ran from behind the nearest tree into the thick of the forest beyond. Abe's jaw dropped. He thought he knew them. "Mr. Broken Branch!" he called out. "Beatrice!" but they were either not those two or were far, far gone.

Two days later, he reached Laurelton and gave the care of Marian over to his wife. Hannah took her in with wholesome heart. Who could not pity this battered woman, no matter what her husband's feelings for her had once been? Three weeks later, Marian came back to herself. Her first words were "Where are they, my friend? When can we go to them?"

Again, he lied. "When you are stronger," he said. "They are already in the new territory. I've had word. They made it, against all odds. You want to live to see them, don't you?"

Hannah said, "My husband is right. Eat your lunch. The stew will help you heal all the faster. You'll like it. It's from a recipe taught me by a Cherokee woman who was once with us."

Marian smiled at them both. A world of joy enlivened her blood. "My friends," she said. "My dear, dear friends." She ate. Between mouthfuls, she told them, "I am glad I named my son what I did," and then she laughed. They asked her, and what was that? She said, "He is Sleeping Bear in Cherokee, but for English"—her eyes sparkled and she laughed again—"for English we wanted him to have the name of a person beloved by us. His English name is Abrahan." Abe marveled. It was the first time he was absolutely certain she knew his name.

Little by little, while she recuperated, he embellished his lies about the fates of her husband and son to the point he'd begun to believe them himself. If he'd not told her his stories, he was sure she might die. They gave her a reason to live. Accordingly, he told her Jacob and his namesake had been removed that summer and lived now in the new territory. Their journey had taken sixty-four days. Many had died, but the dream of finding her again kept them alive. The air of the high plains was good for the boy. He breathed easier there. Her husband was unable to write her, he lied further, the postal system had not yet been set up, but he'd sent word through Lewis Ross's men that he loved her and waited for her, that he would build her a new home with her own garden and a little pen for goats.

The day his lies unraveled arrived after she was whole again, strong and healthy. He came upon her while she was in Hannah's garden with the children. She wore a dress his wife had given her. It was a blue color that set off her copper skin, bringing out the gold beneath the red. She'd not yet gained back all her proper weight. The dress hung off her at the breast and the waist but she looked strong. Her back was straight, her arms muscled. Even the old stiffness Hannah had noticed on Marian's visit to the store while Abe was on the road, the vestige of her foot's injuries, was gone. His son Judah clung to her skirt. They had grown fond of each other. While Raquel and Gabe pulled weeds from Hannah's vegetable beds, Marian taught Judah Cherokee names for the bugs he collected in a little tin pail. Hearing his father approach, Marian looked up, kissed Judah's head, and sent him to his siblings.

"I'm glad you're here," she said. "I owe you much, my friend. My life, in fact. But I'm in good health now and it's time for me to go. My family waits. I've read the newspapers your O'Hanlon leaves you. Five of the thirteen detachments John Ross set up for transport have not yet left for the new land. I will join one of them and be with my family before the worst of winter."

Abe grabbed her hands. He stared at her with eyes wide with fear, wondering how to tell her that most likely her family was dead. His mouth opened, his throat worked. No words came.

She studied him, perplexed. She tilted her head. Her brow wrinkled up.

"Marian," he tried at last. "Jacob . . . I don't . . . he is . . ."

Understanding dawned over her features. Then clouds came and darkness fell. She slipped her hands out of his.

"Oh, titmouse, titmouse," she said quietly. "You don't know where they are, do you?"

His voice was a whisper. "No," he said.

She shook her head and clucked her tongue. His very soul shrunk inside his skin at her remonstration. Then she turned and walked away from him, away from the house, toward the old couple's property next door, the property gone wild while heirs bickered.

"I tried, Marian!" he called out to her back. "I tried everywhere. They were not at the other forts! If I'd told you the truth—oh, forgive me for saying it aloud—that they are likely dead, you too would have died!"

She stopped and turned again to answer him.

"And what would have been wrong with that? Our ghosts would be together. We would wander the Upper World, hand in hand. But listen well and I shall tell you. Jacob and Sleeping Bear are not dead. I know this. If they were, their ghosts would come to me and ask me to join them. I know this as well as I know the titmouse cannot help but lie."

She gave him her back for good and walked into the high grass. He wanted to follow her, but his feet would not move. He was as rooted as a tree to his wife's garden, where his children played.

PARADISE REGAINED

It was the hardest winter in memory, a winter of ice storms, blizzards, weeks of sunless skies, unrelenting cold. When Abe thought of the final 13,000 Cherokee marching off that winter into the arms of frigid, hungry death, he was robbed of all peace. John Ross had spared the remnant of his people the disaster of the warm-weather removals, in which hundreds out of several thousand died of summer diseases, by begging the United States to cease operations until the weather had cooled and vectors slept. But how could he or anyone know that instead of the mild chill of a southeastern winter, that year a glacial evil would sweep down from the north and seize 4,000 people, including Chief Ross's own wife, around the neck until they were dead? It was as if the land itself refused to let them go. Abe grieved for Marian every day, convinced she was one of the removal's dead. He remembered her last words to him and asked her ghost for a visit, just a short one, so he could beg her forgiveness. Otherwise, he feared his life would be blighted forever.

Hannah and the children suffered for his sins. That winter, the husband and father they loved for his good humor and kindly ways withdrew into a solitary sadness, neglecting his work, neglecting them. He sat in Isadore's old office, windows shuttered against daylight, without burning a lantern or feeding the fire O'Hanlon made for him each morning. Hannah brought him meals he would not eat. O'Hanlon brought him whiskey he drank too quickly until the Irishman decided it did him no good and brought him no more. His wife sent a desperate message to his mother, who braved sleet and ice to visit him, but even Susanah's arguments neither consoled nor moved him. Isadore made an impression, reminding Abe that he was getting old. He needed him. The business was too large for an old man, a tired man, to keep track of alone. If Abe did not get back to work, their business would fail and his wife and children would be destitute in the end. So he started working again, keeping the books, making orders, analyzing payroll, but when his chores were done of a day, he sat in his office in the dark, letting the fire die as before.

Spring came and the enlivening of the earth failed to cheer him. The flowers his daughter picked for him brought tears to his eyes but little joy. His family began to learn how to live with him and yet without him when out of the blue at the start of summer the letter came. Hannah knew who it was from the moment the postman handed it to her. It was a thick envelope from the Indian Territory and his full name was written over it in a fine, well-trained hand. *Abrahan Bento Sassaporta Naggar*, it read, *Laurelton, North Carolina*. Hannah could almost hear Marian's laugh when she wrote that. Almost.

She put on her coat, her hat, and bundled up the children. She hitched Hart to the small buggy and hurried to Abe's office that had been Isadore's. All the way she considered how her love for her husband had grown over the years. Once, she had been bitter and jealous at the very mention of Marian Dark Water Red-hand's name. Now the Cherokee's letter was a precious lifeline giving her hope her husband might come back to them. She burst into his office with Hannah, Judah, and Gabe in tow, everyone chattering, throwing open the shutters, letting in light. Her husband, slumped over in his desk chair, blinked and slowly stirred himself. Hannah gave the letter to Gabe, who scrambled up into his father's lap and handed it to him. He stared at the thing, opened it, then his face came alive and the world blossomed. This is what the letter said:

My Dear Friend. May this letter find you and your family healthy and whole, especially your wife, who was so kind to me, and your son, Judah, who gave me solace when I had not my own boy to hold. I hope they have forgiven me for taking leave of them without proper good-byes. I know that you think of me. When I was on the trail and the North Wind howled greeting to me in the night, your voice was hidden in his beard, but I found it out of all the others. "Marian Dark Water Redhand!" it called out. "Forgive me!" I looked every-where for the West Wind to ask that he carry a message back to you but I could not find him. So here I am to tell you of my fortune and in it I pray you find what you seek.

After I left you, I went back to the fort at Ross's Landing, where the people who were yet there made preparations to go to the new territory. Things had changed at the stockade, but not much. We were resigned. There was rare need for the soldiers so there were fewer of them. No one wished to escape, or if they did, none tried. I discovered I was not the only one separated from her family. There were others. We banded together, a clan of outcasts who had lost the most important possession of all, our flesh and blood. We were ashamed, defiant, but none of us abandoned hope of finding what was ours again. Each day we spent in the stockade was another day we could not seek our beloveds. All we desired was to get on with it, the march and the search twinned in our hearts. Among us were old ones and children. We took care of one another as best we could, hoping somewhere another took care of our own.

The day came when my detachment was on the move. The omens were not the best. The sky was gray. There were bolts of lightning in the hills that set trees afire. Hail fell too, pelting us with balls of ice. The Spirits were angry with us for leaving them, we told each other, so we said to them, "Come with us. The whites will not love you as we do. Come with us." Only the North Wind heard our invitation. He swept the trail ahead of us with his snowy robes and made paths with his boots of ice. He gathered up the souls too weak to follow him, leaving their bodies behind like the broken limbs of trees that litter the frozen ground after a storm.

We were hungry, we were so cold the only warmth came when we lay together and the heart of one beat against the heart of another. Storms came without cease. The wagons got stuck in snow or slid into boulders and trees. Often, we stopped for days until the skies gave us small respite and we could move again. Many people died, and so did the beasts who pulled the wagons. We wept for them. Our tears froze on our cheeks. We stopped to butcher and eat the beasts, oxen and horses both, because it was all the fresh meat that we had. It made us sick. In that cold there was nothing to hunt. The streams were frozen, the fish slept at the bottom of riverbeds unmolested. The birds were silent. Without their song, we could not find them.

One day, our leaders thought to change our route. They looked for a place to cross the Great Rivers. There were ice floes all through them. Some places, they were frozen over completely. They tried to convince us we could cross on foot. Every Cherokee knows the western rivers take souls to the resting place of the dead. It has always been so. Only those tired to madness of our journey wanted to cross the river this way. The first of them broke through the ice and disappeared. No further attempts were made.

How many of us fell to our knees and did not rise? How many while holding their children in their arms? Only the moon, who witnessed our sorrows, can count them. You cannot know what it is like to pry a crying babe from his mother who has gone stiff by that sole embrace colder than that of the North Wind, the embrace of death. But I did it. More than once I pried babies from their mothers' arms as I prayed somewhere someone had taken my own child and nourished him under her wing. Sometimes, you know, I thought I saw him, my boy, as a little dark form on the horizon coming at me, his arms outstretched. At first I was happy and lifted my own arms in welcome. Then I would tremble inside, hoping he was not a ghost who would melt into vapor once we met. Always, he disappeared before I knew what was what. Still, I had reason to hope he was alive, the strongest hope. I do not know if you will believe what I tell you next but trust me. Every word is true and it fed my hope, that burning hope, for your namesake.

There were bodies sometimes we came across. Bodies abandoned by those who marched before us. Abandoned by the orders of soldiers who would not allow the dead's loved ones to take the time to bury them. They were covered in leaves gone brown in the cold, then often snowed upon. There were mounds of them here and there along the way. Some of us rushed to them, brushed the snow away to see if we knew who lay there, unblessed, but the bodies were rotted beyond recognition.

One night, our march ended until daylight came again. I laid down with my band of outcasts near a mound of the dead. We asked their forgiveness, then stole some of the driest branches that covered them to make our fire. Our bellies rumbled but we had little to eat. We melted snow over the fire. When it was hot, we threw into the pot a single potato cut into small pieces and a few bones from the squirrel we'd shared days before. It was the last of our stores. On the morrow, we would be beggars. But what can you beg from those who have nothing? From families who must care for themselves first or die? I confess that night I despaired. I separated myself from my band and laid down next to that mound of the dead. I prayed to join them. I closed my eyes. My ear, my cheek were pressed against the icy ground. Then the wind howled against the side of my face that was exposed to the air. Inside it, I heard a voice murmur to me. "Open your eyes, my love," it said and I knew who it was. "Open your eyes," it said, and I did.

Yes! Yes! It was my husband, my Jacob! He lay next to me, his arms around me although he gave me no warmth. "Beloved, at last you are here!" I said. He smiled at me and then I realized that he was young again, and whole, as handsome as the day I first kissed him in the dark outside my father's room. "Oh, you are dead! Am I dead also?" I asked this with eagerness, hoping that my suffering was over. He smiled again and laughed, that big laugh of his that echoed against the walls of our cave in days gone by. "No, dear one, you cannot die. What would our son do without you?" My heart leapt. I struggled to my feet. He stood also, if ghosts can be said to stand. "Where is he?" I asked. From out of the woods, a woman walked toward us. She called out. Jacob turned his head to her. "He is in the West, waiting for you," he said with his head turned toward that other. The woman, whose face I could not see, said, "I've found them, tell her to come here." Jacob beckoned to me to follow him, which I did although the closer we got to the tree line, the fainter his image became. He was like smoke drifting up through the air while the woman became more defined, larger, and suddenly I saw she was my mother, also young, dressed in buckskins, and that she was pointing. I looked in the direction she gave me and saw in a nest of pine needles covering a hole in the ground a family of rabbits, five of them, their little chests rising and falling in slumber. My hunger returned to me. It gnawed at my belly, reminding me I was yet alive. I made a prayer, a quick one, thanking the rabbits for their lives, and then I took a nearby rock and killed them all, in five swift strokes. Their warm blood ran over my hands as I picked them up.

I walked back to my band of outcasts with my bounty, then turned in guilt that the sight of fresh meat had made me forget the ghosts of my mother and husband. I caught one last sight of them, fading into the night as they climbed on the backs of stars into the heavens, and they were hand in hand, all peace made between them. I would have perished from loss then and there despite the meat except that Jacob's words, "He is in the West, waiting for you," rang in my ears loud as the echo our laughter made in our happy mountain cave.

What do you think happened next? The rest of the trail was hard and many more were lost, but the vision of Jacob and my mother, their promise of my living son, kept me at it until at last, in the third month of the English New Year, our destination was reached at the fort near Arkansas. Crowds of Cherokee were there to greet us. Everyone looked for family and clansmen. I'm afraid I was enfeebled by then. I was placed on a pallet in an area designated for those in dire condition. Imagine my joy when I spied walking toward me my brothers, Black Stone and White, with Waking Rabbit, whom you know as Edward. I could no longer walk myself. It had taken everything I had just to get to the fort. They wrapped me in blankets and carried me home with them. It was some distance away, a mean place of rough tents and wide-open space, our new paradise. They told me not to worry, better land lay beyond, things would get better, we could make a home here, US money promised for our old homes was on the way but slow to arrive. I didn't care. All I wanted was Sleeping Bear. Abrahan, my son.

I grabbed at my brothers, whichever carried me at the time for they took turns, asking, "Have you seen my son? Do you know where he is?" They exchanged looks and put me off, saying, "Soon you will be at rest. Then we will talk about your son." I feared the worst. But I clung to the idea that my mother and my husband, his father, would not lie to me about Abrahan, about Sleeping Bear, my son. At last they brought me inside a tent and lay me down on a narrow bed made of pine logs and a mattress stuffed with hay. A young woman I did not know brought me bread and a joint of chicken with sweet spring water to drink. I pushed it away. "No, no, I want only my son!" I told her, and then the entrance to the tent moved and crisp air flooded in. There, bathed in a shaft of light, was my boy, my Sleeping Bear, my Abrahan, my son. He ran to me, his mother. We have been together ever since.

My foolish brothers thought the shock of seeing him would kill me, so they kept him from me until I was safe, at rest. I know I was near extremis when they found me, but I could have told them he is my only strength. During his trail, I learned, this dear boy watched his father die. Jacob had carried him part of the way, despite his old injuries. But it cost him dear. He grew weak quickly. He caught a fever and, within a day of catching it, lay down and died. My son sat with him, weeping, all the day long. Then, at night, a ghost-woman brought him by the hand to a living woman, who took care of him until he reached the promised land. She was a woman of the deer clan who had her own son die in her arms of typhus and so my son was precious to her. I am certain the ghost-woman was his grandmother, who never met him in the flesh, protecting him despite his black skin. By yet another miracle, when my son and his foster mother arrived here, my brothers found them easily, almost by accident. I like to think his father's spirit had a role in that.

Now we are here together, regaining our strength. I wish you could know little Abrahan, my friend. He's a very handsome lad, brave like his father. But also he is just a bit like you. Sly, smart, devoted. Though his lungs are weak, his chest is big and round, his legs thick and short. When I catch him doing something he should not, he tries to hide it, though he learns he cannot, day by day. My brothers, his aunties, and I will make him strong and straight, have no fear. His foster mother lives with us. She teaches him too. He will not shame you.

Of course, I will grieve his father the rest of my life but I know I will see him again and that makes it all bearable. Often, I think upon the nation's past. How could I not? We all do here. We dream of our mountains. Of our forests, where once all things were plentiful and every day was rich with blessing. We remember our villages, our fields, our songs, and our dances. Sometimes a great sadness comes over me. But then I look upon my son, little Sleeping Bear, little Abrahan, and I know. It is not the land, it is the people that must survive.

You told me once you'd like to come west. So far, I can recommend it. I will welcome you if you come. Were you serious? Or was it another of your lies, titmouse? If so, I forgive you. I forgive you everything.

~

The letter was signed with two words in Cherokee. Abe had no doubt it read Dark Water, which was, after all, her name, her only righteous name. He put the pages of her exodus down on his desk and looked upward at his wife, who regarded him with concern. She took up the pages to read them herself. While he waited for her to finish, Abe kissed the top of Gabe's head and set him on the floor. Judah and Raquel stood nearby watching everything the way children do, with open intensity, waiting without prejudice for whatever happens next. He rose from his desk and went to his wife. She finished reading and looked at him, a world of empathy in her eyes. He took her hand. "Come, wife," he said. "It's time I go home."

As they rode back to the house, cozy together up front with the children in back, Hart's ears perked in a way that made it feel as if all was right in the world. Hannah asked him, "Do you think in the end all will be well for Dark Water and her son? Will they prosper in the new land?"

Abe considered. He thought about his vision of America, a land of infinite opportunity that made mistakes but struggled to right them. Still, would anyone care enough about the Jacobs and the Dark Waters of the world to bring justice to their children? A part of him thought yes. A part of him thought no. At least, he decided, the Cherokee were now far enough away from the civilized world for anyone to care about their new land. Maybe they could even keep it.

"I don't know, Hannah," he said. "I don't know what could restore them after all they have lost. Time will tell. In the meantime, we have our own work to do."

On impulse, he brought Hart up to a quick trot, which jostled the children in the back. Raquel, Judah, and Gabe squealed and laughed until they were home.

In two months' time, Abe's birthday came as it always did. Although his wife and children celebrated their natal holidays, he'd never adopted the habit of celebrating his own, a habit he considered very American but also very pointless. He commanded his family ignore it. That year, however, Hannah insisted. "The children enjoy a little party," she told him, "and besides, this year I have something special I want to give you." He could not refuse. She was pregnant yet again and he knew by now not to oppose her when she carried a child. Contention never ended well at such times.

That day, which was the seventeenth of August, Hannah cooked a special meal of his favorite delicacies and baked a cake, smothering it in blackberries, cinnamon, and browned sugar. The children sang him tribute, presented him with homemade cards and gifts, and went to bed. Abe thought the celebration was over. He sat on the couch facing the fireplace. His wife had installed an arrangement of flowers and dried leaves inside the hearth in lieu of wood, as they had no need of an evening fire in that season. Its fragrance was a delight and inspired him to rambling thoughts of the past, of Hannah and Dark Water both, so that his chest filled with warmth. "Wife," he called out, "come sit by me and let me thank you for the day."

Hannah called out in response. "It's not over yet," she said, a lilt to her voice. "The best is yet to come!" When at last she came to him, she carried a large rectangular package wrapped in brown paper and twine. She handed it to him with a merry flourish, her eyebrows raised, her eyes large, her lips curled in a mischievous smile. He untied the twine, pulled the paper off, and caught his breath.

It was Lord Geoffrey's portrait of Marian and her family,

the smudged Jacob and doomed Lulu eternally behind them, all of it cleaned and stretched in a new gilt frame. "Oh my, Hannah," he muttered. He stroked the image of his first love in the same way he might a sacred object or the brow of his eldest child. He'd not looked at the portrait in at least a year. From time to time, he'd touched it as it lay scrolled up in a drawer but that was all he'd dared for fear of restoring feelings he'd worked hard to digest. Now he felt as if he viewed the painting for the first time. His eyes went moist. "How did you—? When did you—?" Hannah laughed.

"Oh, it was easy to fool you, husband," she said. "I put another canvas in the spot you were used to while I took this to Greensborough. It's such a big town nowadays. Without much trouble, I found an artisan who could do the job."

Abe remained flummoxed. "But why, my darling, why?"

She shrugged.

"In so many ways," she said, "we would not be here if she and hers had not gone before. Not you nor I nor the children. And although she is gone to the new territory, in so many additional ways this is where she truly belongs. Here. In the foothills. In Laurelton. Since she cannot be, she should at the very least reside above our mantel, as a tribute, maybe, or anyway, as a sign of the greatest respect. This way, neither our children nor our children's children will ever forget her." She took the portrait from him and lifted it to the place she'd so designated, resting it at a tilt against the wall. "Hmm," she said. "Yes, that's it." She returned to the couch to sit next to her husband. "It looks wonderful, doesn't it? What do you think?"

Abe gathered her close to his side and kissed her head. "I think you are very wise," he said. "There are both people and events, though well and gone, we forget at our peril." For a long time before bed, the two sat holding hands in the afterglow of the longed-for, the honored past.

AUTHOR'S NOTE

Many Americans feel an inherited shame over Native American issues, as well we might. But that guilt can color perceptions of native life. When I began research for *An Undisturbed Peace*, I was struck by the fact that although there is a wealth of reputable scholarship on the removal era, there is also an abundance of New Age fantasy surrounding the domestic and social life of Native Americans that is little more than wishful thinking.

It is the accurate portrayal of the everyday details and social habits of a people that brings a historical novel to life. This careful rendering allows the author to sleep soundly at night knowing she has not violated the honor of an ethnicity not her own, and during the research phase of *An Undisturbed Peace*, I found myself struggling to find a way to fulfill that requirement. My previous novels tracked the Southern Jewish experience throughout the twentieth century, so I understood something about the early Jewish immigrants who wandered the southeastern countryside in the nineteenth century with packs on their backs providing goods to settlers, slaves, and Native Americans alike. I knew that as roads improved, the status of these itinerant Jews progressed from foot to mounted peddler, and from wagon driver to shopkeeper in the newly minted towns. The protagonist of *An Undisturbed Peace*, Abe Sassaporta, through whose eyes the Cherokee tragedy is witnessed, was not difficult for me to imagine. Thanks to that prior research and the relationship between the Southern Jewish and African American communities I wrote about in those earlier novels, I felt reasonably comfortable in the fictional but historically accurate portrayal of African American slaves as well.

But when it came to the Cherokee, how was I to sift through the dross to find the gold? Texts by John Ehle and Vicki Rozema were particularly helpful in imagining the time line and process of the removal. But the most exciting moment of my research occurred when I discovered the work of Reverend Daniel Sabin Butrick and his editor, John Howard Payne, at the Museum of the Cherokee Indian in North Carolina. The six volumes of the Payne-Butrick Papers stand as the richest extant collection of information on nineteenth-century Cherokee culture. Compiled during the expulsion era, they are especially valuable to historians because many of the Cherokee's own records were lost during the forced removal.

Although Reverend Butrick romanticized the Cherokee as a lost tribe of Israel, a belief that taints a number of his reports, it is not difficult for a reader to look past that and discover a world of reliable knowledge. The volumes represent a grand testimony of the diet, clothes, gender roles, parenting practices, law system, politics, cosmology, theosophy, medicine, and rituals of the Cherokee Nation. Reverend Butrick traveled the Trail of Tears with the people he loved, and despite his sentimental flaws, I respect him for that tremendously.

The reverend's editor, John Howard Payne—who was a playwright, actor, and incidentally the author of the American standard "Home! Sweet Home!" as well as Washington Irving's onetime rival for the affections of Mary Shelley—originally became interested in the Cherokee as a subject for his new journal, one that would be decidedly "pure American" and "not European," and thus attract a foreign audience. Once Payne hooked up with Butrick, that research became his life's project.

Attempts to "civilize" the Cherokee began as a government effort to absorb Native Americans into the newly formed United States. It was enthusiastically taken up by certain Cherokee leaders, largely those of mixed blood, who stood helpless as their people drowned under a flood tide of white immigration. The leaders thought it might be a way to legitimize the status of the Cherokee as a nation with inviolate borders. Sometimes, the ploy worked—that is, until it no longer did.

The discovery of gold in the Georgia mountains under Cherokee control was the death knell of the once prosperous people. White Georgians were not going to let the Native Americans keep land that had so much potential for profit. General Andrew Jackson, whose life was heroically saved by a Cherokee warrior named Junaluska at the Battle of Horseshoe Bend during the War of 1812, turned against his former allies and, as president of the United States, worked tirelessly to divest them of their territory and cruelly transport them to what became Oklahoma. Junaluska famously said during the removal, "If I'd known then what General Jackson would do now, I'd have let him die."

An Undisturbed Peace seeks to explore these injustices and many others that the civilization movement inspired, the most striking among them being the adoption by Cherokee of chattel slavery so that they might be seen as equal to their white neighbors. The work of Dr. Fay Yarbrough, particularly her book *Race and the Cherokee Nation: Sovereignty in the Nineteenth Century*, informed me greatly on this issue and provided me with a pivotal event in the novel.

An equally disastrous effect of the civilization movement was the erosion of the role of women in Cherokee society. In the eighteenth century, early colonists were shocked to find that Cherokee women enjoyed an empowerment unheard of in Europe. Carolyn Johnston, professor of American studies at Eckerd College, writes in *Cherokee Women in Crisis: Trail of Tears, Civil War, and Allotment, 1838–1907*:

> Women had autonomy and sexual freedom, could obtain divorce easily, rarely experienced rape or domestic violence, worked as producers/farmers, owned their own homes and fields, possessed a cosmology that contains female supernatural figures, and had significant political and economic power. . . . Cherokee women's close association with nature, as mothers and producers, served as a basis of their power within the tribe, not as a basis of oppression. Their position as "the other" led to gender equivalence, not hierarchy.

However, as the civilization movement took hold, the position of Cherokee women weakened, especially in regard to their property and inheritance rights, along with all the attendant degradations of status and freedom the disenfranchised experience. As I reviewed the manuscript from this perspective, I structured certain elements to ensure that readers would see Dark Water as a woman empowered in every intimate sense. Never does she make a sexual choice that is not her own.

When I work on a historical novel, I go back and forth between imagining the actions and conflicts of my characters and learning more about the time and environment in which they live. There are always surprises and rewrites along the way, but this is part of what makes the work interesting. The two activities feed on each other—a research discovery inspires a plot thread, a character's dilemma demands a new investigation. There is never a day spent staring at a blank screen.

For example, my discovery of the "rubber fever" of 1827 to 1830 was serendipitous. I have entirely forgotten which tiny aspect of the novel inspired me to Google rubber to make sure it was in use during the time frame of *An Undisturbed Peace*, but once I became aware of that disastrous craze over an untried commodity, I realized I had hit metaphoric gold. The fragile properties of early rubber in conditions of extreme weather nicely reflect the white man's despoiling of the natural resources Native Americans cherished. It was a short step from there to fictionalize a financial crisis for the Sassaporta family by taking advantage of the spikes of brilliant success and wretched failure endured by Charles Goodyear before he eventually discovered the durable rubber we know today to fictionalize a financial crisis for the Sassaporta family.

Abe's journeys to drum up new markets after his family's ruinous experience in the rubber market enabled me to explore the Choctaw removal, which preceded that of the Cherokee. In the end, I found that inclusion very meaningful since, according to some sources, the first occurrence of the phrase "Trail of

Tears" or "a trail of tears and death" was during the Choctaw's ordeal. It also seemed important to me to stress that the Cherokee Nation was, while the largest, only one of five Native American nations that suffered the horrors of displacement.

The research process never ends. In a few weeks, I plan to travel back to North Carolina to check out details of Cherokee history I have discovered since finishing my novel. Perhaps I will use the information I gather in a new book, perhaps not. But as I gain an even deeper and richer understanding of these remarkable people, I find myself humbled and inspired.

—Mary Glickman, 2015

ACKNOWLEDGMENTS

A huge thank you goes to Peter Riva, my fabulous agent, for suggesting I write about the Trail of Tears. It sort of stunned me when he proposed the idea. I wasn't sure I saw myself as he did, as an author for whom the subject would prove unusually fertile, but once I began learning about this shameful era of American history, I realized he had sent me off in a direction that would awaken my literary passions and reflect my deepest felt thematic concerns. His support of this novel from its inception to its completion has been stellar.

I must also, of course, thank my two editors: Peternelle van Arsdale, whose remarkable structural intelligence reformed aspects of the novel's vision, and Tina Pohlman, whose tenacious genius pulled material from me that I would never have mined on my own. Peternelle and Tina, you leave me breathless. I understand that such productive and intense partnerships between editors and authors today are rare. You make me feel blessed.

As for the production and promotion of this text, I must once again thank the usual suspects from Open Road Integrated Media for their expertise in shepherding my novel across all

ACKNOWLEDGMENTS

media. I am deeply indebted to the undeniable genius of Jane
Friedman, the shining wisdom of Tina Pohlman, the knife-sharp
shrewdness of Rachel Chou, the sundry and glittering talents of
Nicole Passage, Rachelle Mandik, Catherine Foulkrod, Andrea
Worthington, Mauricio Díaz, Jesse Hayes, Amanda Shaffer,
Joan Giurdanella, Nadea Mina, Laura De Silva, and my own
Rachel Krupitsky. Thank you all. Your energy and commitment
astound. Brava!

Lastly, with all my heart I thank my husband, Stephen K.
Glickman, whose patience and industry are always invaluable.
He has schlepped me to Cherokee, North Carolina, and Oklahoma City without complaint, listened to my ideas and discov-
eries with the most supportive excitement and enthusiasm, and
untiringly lent his own brilliance to help shape my story.

ABOUT THE AUTHOR

Born on the South Shore of Boston, Massachusetts, Mary Glickman studied at the Université de Lyon and Boston University. While she was raised in a strict Irish-Polish Catholic family, from an early age Glickman felt an affinity toward Judaism and converted to the faith in her late twenties. She now lives in Seabrook Island, South Carolina, with her husband, Stephen. Glickman is the author of *Home in the Morning*; *One More River*, a National Jewish Book Award Finalist in Fiction; and *Marching to Zion*. *An Undisturbed Peace* is her fourth novel.

MARY GLICKMAN

FROM OPEN ROAD MEDIA

OPEN ROAD

INTEGRATED MEDIA

OPEN ROAD

INTEGRATED MEDIA